Love's Eternal Breath

Eagle Harbor Book 4

Naomi Rawlings

Love's Eternal Breath: © Naomi Mason 2017

Cover Design: © Clarissa Yeo 2016

Cover Photographs: Shutterstock.com

Editors: Melissa Jagears; Roseanna M. White

Formatting: Polgarus Studio

To my readers, especially those among you who are sick and suffering. May you embrace each new day as a gift from God, and may you have the courage and fortitude to serve Him regardless of the trials you face.

Chapter One

"I told you not to come back."

Lindy Marsden looked into Jenny O'Byrne's brown eyes and attempted to scowl as fiercely as the irate woman in front of her—if Jenny could even be called a woman. Given her youthful face and unblemished skin, Jenny couldn't be more than sixteen or seventeen.

"I brought you bread and flour, even some sourdough starter from the bakery so you can make your own bread." Lindy would have made the words louder, her voice firmer, had she the breath to do so. But after walking two miles uphill to reach the cabin, her lungs were wound tighter than a jack-in-the-box and nearly ready to burst. She sucked in a small breath. The burning sensation would abate. Eventually. If she rested long enough.

She hoped.

She set the sack with the dough and flour on the rickety table, then straightened and held out the loaf of bread to Jenny, drawing in another small breath before she spoke. "Don't be upset with me."

Even with the door open, the cabin was so dim it should've been impossible to see Jenny's anger. But the woman's fiery eyes burned through the shadows nonetheless. "What part of 'don't come back

1

again' is that difficult for you to understand?"

The part that entails leaving children to starve in the woods. But if she ever hoped to return, she dare not speak the words. She made a show of glancing around the windowless cabin instead.

The squat little building was only about fifteen feet wide and fifteen feet long. Nestled into a grove of pine trees, she would have missed it entirely two weeks ago when she'd been searching for the hidden meadow where she'd played with her sister when they were girls. The sound of a child crying that day had caused her to look more closely at the thatch of trees.

Lindy glanced at the corner of the shack where a pile of freshly picked thimble berries lay on an old apron. Outside of those and the rabbit that had been strung up outside, there wasn't any other food.

"So you don't need the bread?" Maybe if Jenny admitted her predicament aloud, she'd find some sense and welcome help. And maybe the harbor would freeze in August. "I don't see any more food than I did last week. Or perhaps you found a job?"

Jenny crossed her arms over her boney chest. "I told you before. I don't need a job, I don't need your help, and I certainly don't need your charity. What I need is for you to leave us alone."

Jenny spun on her heel, though where she planned to storm to inside the tiny cabin, Lindy didn't know. There was barely room to sleep the four O'Byrne children on the floor. The cabin's only amenity was a potbelly stove, one so old it was starting to rust. The building was probably used as a trapping cabin in the winter, and as soon as the weather turned cold, some backwoodsman would find the O'Byrnes and kick them out.

"Caught another rabbit, Jenny. It's hanging outside." Jack O'Byrne stomped into the cabin and blinked, likely letting his eyes adjust to the dimness. He paused when his gaze landed on Lindy, and then he smiled. "Miss Lindy, you're back!"

He didn't quite run to her and offer a hug, not like the two younger ones had done last week, but the look on his face was still worth the two-mile hike from Eagle Harbor.

"I brought bread." She raised the sack that Jenny didn't want, then nodded toward the second sack on the table. "And ingredients to make more once it's gone."

"Did you hear that, Jenny? We can have bread now." He took the sack from her hand and patted his stomach, the grin on his face only growing wider. "Don't suppose you brought jam? Or maybe some butter?"

"Jack O'Byrne!" Jenny spun around. "How dare you? You know what Pa would say."

"He's not here, is he? And unlike you, not all of us enjoy eating broth with nothing but leeks and fiddlehead ferns for three meals a day."

Jenny planted her hands on hips so slender they nearly disappeared in the folds of her faded gown. "We have thimbleberries too."

"Right. Can't forget those. They go so well with the handful of leeks and ferns in our water." Jack turned back to Lindy, his brow furrowed. "What about salt? Can you bring salt next week? Reckon the broth would taste better with some salt."

"She most certainly cannot, because she's not coming back next week, or ever again." Jenny stomped her foot on the floor. Except her foot didn't quite stop at the floor. It went clear through the old board, causing the wood to splinter and crack. Jenny huffed and jabbed a finger at her brother. "Look what you've done. And don't think this isn't your fault. If you would mind me like Pa said, none of this would have happened."

Jack rolled his eyes. "Sure, Jenny. My fault."

"What's Jenny yelling about?" Alice poked her head into the

cabin. "Did you tell her about the rabbit that got away?" The girl blinked much as her brother had as she stepped inside. "Oh, Miss Lindy is here!"

She ran across the cabin and threw her little body against Lindy's legs.

"Alice, don't tell me you left Toby outside again." Jenny flew toward the door, shouting something about the young girl needing to do a better job of watching her brother as she raced outside.

Alice only clung tighter to Lindy's legs.

"There, there." Lindy patted the top of the child's dark head. "If I were you, I'd have trouble watching Toby too. Boys like to run around so much it's hard to keep track of them."

Alice turned her watery eyes up toward Lindy, her lip protruding in a darling little pout. "He doesn't listen."

What toddler did? Especially to a sister only a couple years older than him? "I'm sure you do your best."

"If only that were good enough for Jenny." Jack took the bread out of the sack, set it on the table, and removed the knife from the sheath on his belt before cutting himself a slice.

Jack and Jenny's dark hair and eyes might have labeled them siblings, but the two couldn't act more differently. Jenny was always contentious and stomping about, while Jack was calm and comfortable, his eyes dancing and his lips inching up into a smile of one sort or another. If the boy attended school, he'd probably be everyone's first choice to play with at recess—including the girls'.

"Do you have time to play?" Alice tugged her toward a ragdoll lying on the pile of blankets in the corner.

"Of course." She couldn't think of a better way to spend her afternoon, plus sitting would give her lungs more chance to rest before she returned home. "What's your doll's name?"

"It's Molly." Alice plopped onto the blanket and picked up the doll. "One day Jenny will make me another dolly so Molly has a friend, but she's too busy now."

"She's always too busy." Jack spoke around a mouth filled with bread.

Stomping sounded on the path outside, then Jenny rushed back into the cabin, a toddler clamped to her slender hip.

"He was trying to eat a rock. How many times have I told you to keep him away from rocks, Alice!" Jenny screeched, her voice so shrill Lindy half expected the beams above them to give way and the roof to crash down on their heads.

"She's five." Jack dropped his knife back into its sheath. "You couldn't keep me out of trouble when I was little, and you were six years older than me."

"Don't you sass me, Jack Andrew. Things are different now than they were when Ma was alive."

Lindy looked between the brother and sister, then sighed. Was Jenny always this agitated, or was it worse because she was here? She truly did want to play with Alice, talk to Jack for a while, and give her lungs more of a rest. But maybe she should do as Jenny said and leave.

"I'll sass you if I wanna sass you." Jack glowered at his sister. "You ain't Ma."

"If you think for one moment that—"

"I need to start home," Lindy shouted over Jenny. "Want to be back before dark." And she'd spend the entire walk home praying Jenny would calm down and start thinking reasonably.

"Don't go." Alice jumped up from the blanket and hugged her arm, but at least Jack and Jenny had stopped arguing. "You said you were going to play with Molly and me."

"Can't she stay for dinner, Jenny? We've got two rabbits plus bread. There should be enough for her." Jack gestured toward the door where the rabbits hung outside.

Under normal circumstances, that would have been perfect. If she rested until after dinner, she'd be able to get down the hill without a breathing attack—not something she could guarantee if she left now.

"I've got dinner waiting for me in town." It was a lie, but she'd tell it again rather than ask the children to share their tiny portions of meat with her. Her pa had been able to eat a whole rabbit by himself when he was alive.

Jack shoved a thatch of dark hair off his forehead and turned to her. "At least promise you'll be back next week."

Lindy opened her mouth to answer, but Jenny was quicker.

"No. So say goodbye now and be done with it." Jenny picked up a rusted knife hanging on a peg and tromped outside with Toby still on her hip.

Jack scowled after his sister before picking up another slice of bread and turning back to her. "Can we walk with you for a while? Must be boring going all that way by yourself."

"I want to go for a walk!" Alice tugged on her skirt.

Lindy rested her hand on the girl's head. "As long as it's all right with your sister."

"Better not to ask." Jack grabbed another piece of bread off the table. "She'll say no to anything fun."

"Come on." Alice tugged on her hand, and she followed the girl outside, where the shaded path seemed overly bright after standing in the cabin.

"Where are you going?" Jenny sat on a stump skinning one of the rabbits. Toby kneeled on the ground a few feet away, playing with animals that had been whittled from wood.

"We're walking to the meadow with Lindy. We're allowed to go that far, remember?" Jack turned his back on his older sister and stuffed half a piece of bread in his mouth as he tromped down the rocky path ahead of them.

"Don't go into the meadow!" Jenny called.

"We used to be able to play in the meadow." Alice repositioned her sweaty little fingers around Lindy's hand and pulled her down the hill.

She let the girl set the pace, even though her lungs were burning once more. She could always stop and rest on the other side of the meadow before continuing home by herself.

"But Jenny won't let us play there no more, cuz somebody might see." Alice looked up at her with her pouty lip poking out again.

"Nobody's gonna see nothing." Jack held a sapling branch out of the way. "Jenny's just being obstinate."

Yes, obstinate was a good word for Jenny, but why couldn't the O'Byrne children be seen by anyone? And why was Jenny so adamant she not return?

She didn't need to be a Pinkerton agent to know O'Byrne wasn't their real last name. That much had been apparent only a few minutes after she'd stumbled upon Alice crying over her skinned knee two weeks ago and heard the Cornish accent in the girl's words. Plus half the Cornish that came to America were named either Jack or Jenny.

But if the Irish-sounding O'Byrne wasn't their surname, what was? Why did their heritage need to be hidden? And perhaps the most pressing question of all, where was the father they talked about?

If people in Eagle Harbor knew how the O'Byrnes were living, they'd help. Women in town could make meals, and she'd guarantee Elijah and Victoria Cummings would open their home to the children.

But she could only imagine what would happen if she returned next week with Elijah and Victoria. Jenny would still refuse help, then as soon as they were gone, Jenny would pack up her siblings and their few belongings and leave without a word to anyone. Lindy sighed. At least with how things were now, she could help a little.

But could she help enough?

"Here we are." Jack slung his hands on his hips and surveyed the meadow as keenly as a fifty-year-old backwoodsman. "Wish we could go with you. I'd be bored hiking all the way to town by myself."

"Actually, I find the walks rather pleasant." It was the tightening in her lungs and the short breaths that she minded. Oh, to be young again and race through these trees, to draw in a lungful of clean air and laugh without being short on wind. She closed her eyes and tilted her face up toward the sky, drawing in a long breath as the warm rays of late summer touched her skin.

"You're going to come back, aren't you?" Alice pulled on her dress.

"Please come back, Miss Lindy." Jack scuffed a bare toe into the dirt beneath him. "Jenny, well, she don't know what she's saying all the way. She thinks we can handle everything on our own, but it's not wrong to want some salt, is it?"

Her throat grew as tight as her lungs. She'd been living in her own dilapidated shack with little food not all that long ago. "It's not wrong, Jack. I promise it's not. I'm honored to help you."

And she was. People had helped her leave that shack in Chicago behind. It only seemed right that, as long as she was able, she aid others in need.

She might have little to look forward to in her own life, but Jack O'Byrne wanted jam, butter, and salt. She'd buy those things and bring them back next week, even if doing so meant she ended up eating leek broth for a week herself.

And she'd do the same thing the week after that, and the one after that, and after that. Until their father came back and the children were better cared for.

She sucked a small breath into her tight lungs.

Now if only her health would last until Mr. O'Byrne returned.

Chapter Two

Why couldn't her lungs be stronger?

Lindy plucked a box of salt off the shelf of the mercantile and surveyed the sacks of flour on the shelf below. If Jenny had made bread every day, then the flour she'd taken to the O'Byrnes last week would be about gone. But with rutabagas, potatoes, carrots, butter, jam, and a ragdoll at home waiting to be taken to the cabin, plus the salt in her hand, her lungs would be struggling for breath before she got halfway to the cabin, and that was on a good day.

Her breaths were already short today, her lungs tight against the air she tried to draw in, never mind she hadn't done more than walk from her room above the bakery to the mercantile. If her lungs gave her the same trouble tomorrow, she'd be lucky to get to the O'Byrnes' without collapsing.

She pursed her lips and fiddled with the rolled top on the smallest package of flour. She should buy it. What did it matter if it took her half a day to walk to the cabin? There were four people up there who needed food, and her lungs were going to protest no matter what she carried.

Why me, God? Maybe Aileen should have found the O'Byrnes, or Victoria. They could walk to the cabin without trouble.

But for some reason, God had given this task to her. Besides, it wouldn't last forever, just until the O'Byrnes' father returned.

And how long would that be? It hadn't sounded like Jenny and Jack expected him soon.

"Lindy, I'm so glad I caught you."

Lindy left the flour in its place and turned to find the town seamstress coming down the aisle, the basket on her arm already laden with foodstuffs.

"I'm sorry I missed you when you dropped off the mending this morning. I'd promised to take the girls for a walk."

"It was fun." The blond girl clinging to Jessalyn Dowrick's skirt gave a firm nod of her head, then stuck her thumb in her mouth and sucked.

Lindy grinned down at the youngest of Jessalyn's three girls. What was her name? Claire? Or was it Megan? Maybe Olivia? Since they all had their mother's blond hair and blue eyes, it was impossible to keep them straight. "I'm glad you had fun."

The thumb came out. "Mama says we can go again tomorrow." Then the thumb went right back between her rosy lips.

"I have more mending, if you're able to take it. Do you think you could have three shirts finished by tomorrow?" Jessalyn smiled apologetically and tucked a wayward strand of hair behind her ear. "If you don't mind the rush, that is."

Mind the rush? She wasn't going to complain about work that would give her money to buy things for the O'Byrnes. "I should be able to finish three shirts tonight, yes."

"Excuse me. I need to get to the flour."

Lindy turned to find three sailors standing behind her and stepped to the other side of the aisle. "I'm sorry for blocking your way."

"No worries, miss." The sailors each hefted a fifty pound sack over their shoulders and carried them toward the counter at the back of the mercantile.

"You're an absolute angel, Lindy." Jessalyn rested a hand on her shoulder. "I don't know what I'd do without your help."

"Mama, I want candy." A towheaded little girl that looked to be about Alice's age came up and tugged on Jessalyn's skirt.

Jessalyn didn't even glance at her daughter. "Can you walk back to the shop with me? Just let me pay for my things. Oh, and this." She plucked the salt from Lindy's hand. "Consider it a bonus for getting the clothes you dropped off this morning done in only two days' time."

"Mama!"

"Not now, Claire." Jessalyn still didn't look at her daughter. "Remember how you're working on not interrupting Mama while she's talking?"

"I want candy!" The smile left the girl's face, and her sweet little features contorted with temper. "The pink ones at the top." She jabbed a finger toward the top shelf along the side of the mercantile, where Mr. Foley apparently kept the extra stores of candy that weren't displayed by the counter.

"That may be, but that still doesn't excuse your behavior."

Claire stomped off, her hands clenched into fists and her jaw set.

Jessalyn blew out a breath. "I'm sorry. She's been going through a spell lately, and I've been so busy with the shop that I haven't done a good job of addressing it." Her shoulders sagged. "I try to keep reminding myself that they'll be grown and I'll miss all this one day."

Yes, one day the girls would be grown, and who knew where they'd be or what they'd be doing. She'd had dreams of her own when she'd been a little older than Claire, her list of things that were supposed to happen.

One day, I'll be a teacher like my mother, grandmother, great-grandmother.

One day, I'll have a husband to love me.

11

One day, I'll have children.

Instead that list had changed into *One day, I'll have a job and rent my own room, and if I'm lucky, my lungs might last long enough that I'll live to watch someone else's children grow up.*

Jessalyn snatched a jar of beets off the shelf. "It will only take a minute to pay for my things. Then we'll head back to my shop."

Lindy shoved away her dark thoughts, then grabbed the package of flour she'd fiddled with earlier.

Instead of thinking about all the things she would or wouldn't do in the future, she'd concentrate on one day at a time. Today was about the O'Byrnes, and tomorrow too, when she went to their cabin. After that, well…

God, please let their father return home soon. Please let my health last until I see those children cared for.

"Let me get that as well." Jessalyn took the flour from her hands and added it to her basket. "You deserve something extra for all the work you've done."

"No, I can…"

Without waiting to listen, Jessalyn spun on her heel and made a beeline toward the counter at the back of the mercantile.

"Ma!" Another towheaded girl, this one with a bandage covering her ear, ran up the aisle while pointing toward the side wall. "Claire's climbing the shelf!"

Lindy turned to see Claire standing on the second shelf from the top and straining toward the jar of pink candy.

"Claire, no!" She raced toward the child and stood on her tiptoes, arms extended to reach her, but she fell about three feet short. Pulling her skirt back, she tested her weight on the first shelf.

"Claire! What are you doing?" Jessalyn's panicked voice rose over the thudding of numerous footsteps rushing toward the shelf.

Lindy stepped onto the second shelf, which didn't wobble even slightly beneath her weight, but she still had one more shelf to climb if she was going to get the scamp.

"Do you have her?" a male voice asked from behind.

"Want me to do that?" said another man.

"I'll get her." Why leave the girl on the shelf a moment longer than necessary? She drew in a small breath against her protesting lungs, then stepped onto the third shelf. Finding a good grip on one of the higher shelves with her left hand, she reached for the child with her right.

"All right, Claire. Down you go." She hooked her arm around the girl's waist and pulled her from her perch.

Claire let out an ear-piercing scream and kicked. "I want my candy! I want my candy!"

"Claire, hush!" Jessalyn's sharp voice silenced the child, and Lindy looked down to find Jessalyn reaching for her daughter while a dozen or so shoppers formed a crowd around her.

Lindy leaned down to hand Claire over, but Claire arched her back and let out another wail, causing Lindy's foot to slip.

She pushed the girl toward her mother, but didn't have time to catch a shelf before careening downward. She shoved her hands out to brace for the worst of the fall.

Snap!

Thud.

"Ahhhhh!" She rolled onto her back and clutched her hand to her chest. Pain seared through her pinky and radiated up her arm.

"Quick, send for the doctor."

"I saw Dr. Harrington on the street just a few minutes ago."

"Lindy, oh, Lindy! I'm so sorry." Jessalyn knelt beside her, the other woman's voice full of panic.

Lindy glanced down at her hand, which was streaked with blood, but that wasn't nearly as appalling as the way her pinky was bent at a grotesque angle—a white spike of bone protruding from the wound.

She attempted to draw another breath, but her lungs refused. Not now! Oh, why must her lungs constantly fail her?

"Mama, what's wrong with her hand?"

"Get the girls away." Lindy barely recognized the sound of her wheezy, panicked voice.

"I'm not leaving, not when this is all my fault." Jessalyn's pale face stretched tight with worry.

"Lindy's right, dear." Mrs. Foley, the proprietress of the Foley-Smith General Store, knelt beside them and rested a hand on Jessalyn's arm. "You take the girls away, and I'll stay with Lindy here."

Jessalyn glanced between the two of them. "But..."

"Go." Lindy forced a strength that she didn't feel into the word.

"Mama!" A young voice cried, probably Jessalyn's smallest daughter.

"Ah, Mrs. Dowrick?" a man spoke. "One of your daughters just ran out of the store, crying."

Jessalyn stiffened at that, then shoved to her feet. "I'm sorry I can't stay, Lindy." And then she was gone.

Lindy turned her head to the side and let out a whimper.

"There, there." Mrs. Foley patted her shoulder. "Mr. Foley left for the doctor as soon as you fell. He'll be here any moment."

"No." She clutched her hand to her chest, causing another bout of pain to course up her arm. "No doctor."

The bell at the front of the store jingled, and she drew herself up against the shelf of canned goods.

"Is that Dr. Harrington? Let him through." Mrs. Foley made a shooing motion with her hands, and the crowd shuffled into a different position around her.

"Heard somebody needed a doctor."

Lindy's lungs grew even tighter. The voice coming from the doorway didn't belong to the young doctor in town, but to the older Dr. Greely. She'd never be able to forget that voice, nor would she forget the hundreds of dollars her father had paid Dr. Greely for medicine to heal her mother—medicine that never worked.

"No doctor," she said again, louder this time.

"Now, now, there's no reason to be afraid." Mrs. Foley patted her shoulder a second time, as though the simple action would help. "That finger needs to be tended."

Tears blurred her vision, and she struggled for a breath that her lungs refused to draw. "You're not listening to me. I said no doctor."

Dirty brown shoes appeared at her side, then Dr. Greely squatted beside her, his position itself a near miracle considering the large girth he carried about his midsection. He surveyed her hand for only a moment.

"No point setting that." His knees popped as he rose to his feet. "Needs to be amputated. You men there, carry her to my office."

"No!" She squealed as people shifted around her and two men from the group of onlookers stepped forward.

The bell on the door clamored wildly.

"I heard Lindy fell?" Victoria Cummings's voice echoed through the store. "Is it true? Is Lindy hurt?"

Footsteps scurried across the floor, only to stop when Victoria reached her side. "Lindy! Oh, my dear. Just w-wait a moment, and we'll g-get you some help."

A flurry of pearl earbobs and necklace blurred with the yellow silk of Victoria's elegant gown above Lindy's head. But the woman didn't think anything of kneeling on the floor in the place Mrs. Foley had just vacated, never mind how soiled her dress would get.

"Don't want help." At least not the type Dr. Greely would give. "Just want to go home." She winced as another bout of pain flashed up her arm and tried to suck in another pitifully small breath. "Make it stop hurting."

"I'll make it stop hurting soon enough," Dr. Greely boomed. "Now move aside, Mrs. Cummings, so these men can carry her to my office."

"Don't let him touch me." She met Victoria's gaze, or tried to. But things were starting to blur and her lungs still struggled for air. "He wants to cut it…" And then she started coughing, great noisy coughs that wracked her body and caused more pain to shoot from her pinky.

A hand stroked hair back from her face. "Calm down, Lindy. It will be all right."

But it wouldn't be all right. Because she couldn't get enough air into her lungs, and she couldn't stop coughing. And as much as she never wanted to see a doctor again, her finger really did need tending which meant she was going to have to let a doctor examine her, and she'd be lucky if she came out of it with only an amputated finger.

Tears swam before her eyes, blurring her vision even more than the pain.

"Has anyone sent for D-Dr. Harrington?" Victoria asked, though Lindy struggled to hear her voice through her coughing. "He's quite proficient at setting bones."

"It's folly trying to set something like that." Dr. Greely's filthy shoes appeared at her side once more. "Infection will set in and she'll end up losing her whole hand."

"No!" Lindy pressed her injured hand harder against her chest, covering it with her good one as more coughing shook her. Then her world went dark.

～.～.～.～

He walked in on chaos. Utter and complete chaos.

"That's where she fell." Mr. Foley pointed to a crowded side aisle where two people shouted at each other. "I knew we were in trouble when I heard her scream, but when I saw the bone sticking out of her finger, I went running for you. You healed up a break like that for Victoria Cummings's father, didn't you?"

Dr. Seth Harrington gave a quick nod. He had indeed set a compound fracture for Edward Donnelly earlier that spring, though that had been a break to the tibia rather than a phalanx.

Leaving Mr. Foley at the back of the crowd, he edged his way through the group of people that had closed in around an unconscious woman lying on the floor. Was she unconscious merely due to the pain in her finger, or had she hit her head when she'd fallen? Hopefully the first. A broken bone was much easier to heal than a head injury.

Dr. Greely and Victoria Cummings stood above her, shouting at each other. Another time, another place, and he would give half an ear to the argument while he worked, but not if the break was as bad as Mr. Foley claimed. As to Dr. Greely arriving first but arguing rather than getting a splint around the broken finger, well, the onlookers could draw their own conclusions about the other man's doctoring.

Opening his medical bag, Seth dropped to his knees beside the woman—Miss Lindy Marsden, if he was remembering correctly. He gently lifted a blood-covered hand from her chest, then winced when he saw what lay underneath. Mr. Foley hadn't been lying about the severe break that left the phalanx protruding from the wound and her fifth finger bent at a cruel angle.

He took her injured hand in his, but she didn't so much as whimper. Hopefully she'd stay unconscious for another minute or two.

Images flooded his mind, bloody limbs and stumps, men moaning in pain, blood soaking their uniforms until he didn't know whether the color was blue or gray, Union or Confederate. As a ten-year-old boy watching the injured who'd been brought to his family's farm after the Battle of Antietam, he'd been helpless to stop the suffering.

He blinked the memories away and focused on the finger before him, probing the break until he knew exactly how he needed to pull the bone—something he wasn't helpless to fix these days.

He took a flask from his pocket and gripped her hand firmly before he poured the whiskey onto her finger. He half expected her eyes to spring open and a scream to loose from her throat. Then he'd need to go through the hassle of either having men hold her or giving her something to dull the pain before he set her finger. But she merely whimpered and coughed, her eyes staying shut.

Good.

He probed the injury once more. The voices around him faded, as did the people surrounding them and the shelf behind her, until he saw nothing but Miss Marsden's smallest finger.

He sucked in a breath.

Then he yanked.

Miss Marsden's eyes sprang open and she loosed a scream similar to those he'd heard after Antietam. Good. At least she hadn't suffered a head injury.

She tried to pull her hand away, but he kept his grip firm. "Be still now, lest you bump your finger and I need to reset it."

"I said no doctors," she heaved through what had to be excruciating pain, but though her chest rose as if she gulped air, she only inhaled small breaths.

He reached into his bag for a bandage and the splint he'd brought when Mr. Foley had burst into his office and explained the injury. "Think of me as a peddler then, one good at setting bones."

She didn't even attempt a smile.

He wrapped the injury to keep it clean until he could stitch it, then he then lay the slim wooden splint against the underside of her pinky.

"C-can I do anything to help?"

He sensed Victoria's presence beside him, but he kept his gaze focused on Miss Marsden's finger as he tied thin strips of leather around the splint. "You'll find laudanum in the second pocket of my bag. She needs a few drops on her tongue."

"No, just bandage it and…" Miss Marsden started coughing, her hand shaking with the coughs.

Drat! He gripped the flat of her hand so tightly she might find bruises come morning. At least he'd gotten the splint on before she started coughing, but he didn't care for how much the coughs caused her hand to jerk.

As quickly as the coughing started, it stopped, leaving the lady unconscious once more. He frowned. Unconsciousness after a coughing spell? He'd need to take a closer look at her lungs once he got her to his office. The woman might have tuberculosis.

"I suppose we d-don't need the laudanum now?" Victoria asked.

"Best give it to her anyway. I don't want her waking up and jarring the set."

Victoria did as he instructed, dabbing the laudanum onto Miss Marsden's tongue as though she were an experienced nurse—one he was in desperate need of hiring.

He ran his gaze briefly down Miss Marsden, looking for anything that might be amiss before he moved her. She wasn't coughing anymore, but her breathing was far too rapid. Did he have any Dover's Powder in his bag?

No, he'd given the last of it to Mrs. Ranulfson this morning and needed to go back to his office for more, which was just as well, because he still needed to stitch her wound and then bandage her pinky to her fourth finger.

"Can you carry my bag?" he asked Victoria.

"Of course."

He stood and scooped Miss Marsden up in his arms, then stilled. Since when had the crowd become so quiet? Since when had Dr. Greely and Victoria stopped arguing? Since when had others come into the store so that the path to the door was completely filled with people?

Heat crept up the back of his neck as he glanced around the onlookers, every one of which seemed to be staring at him and Miss Marsden.

"Now just a minute." Dr. Greely stepped in front of him, his breath laced with liquor even though he wasn't necessarily drunk. Given the amount of spirits the man regularly consumed, his breath always reeked. "Where are you taking her?"

"To my office. I need to stitch her wound and give her something to ease her breathing."

"I arrived on site first, which means she's my patient, not yours. If you stitch her yourself rather than take her to my office, you'll get no payment for the work you've done."

When Seth had first started practicing in Eagle Harbor, he'd have laughed at the ridiculousness of Dr. Greely's claim. But now he knew all too well that Dr. Greely was serious, never mind that he'd argued rather than helped Miss Marsden.

"He wanted to amputate her p-p-pinky!" Victoria raised her chin and glared at Dr. Greely, her dark eyes flashing. "He said the break was too bad to fix and that infection would set in if you tried resetting the bone."

Was that what they'd been arguing about when he arrived?

"And it will!" Dr. Greely's flabby face turned red, his jowls jiggling with indignation. "I don't want to hear any wailing when I have to amputate her entire hand next week."

A hush fell over the crowd, expectant gazes blinking as people looked between the two of them. He could almost hear their thoughts.

Didn't Dr. Harrington fix a bad break for Victoria Cummings's father earlier this year?

Maybe, but Greely's been doctoring in Eagle Harbor ever since the town was founded.

Do you really trust the word of an outsider more than Dr. Greely's?

Might depend on how drunk Doc Greely is.

And on the debate would go. He'd grown entirely too familiar with the argument over the past two years.

"You won't need to amputate anything." He spoke loudly enough for the crowd to hear, then met Dr. Greely's bloodshot eyes. "As long as she keeps the wound clean, it won't become infected, just like Mrs. Cummings's father's leg never became infected after I set his compound fracture. Now if you'll excuse me, I have a patient to tend."

The other doctor planted himself more firmly in the middle of the aisle, his wide midsection making it impossible to move around him without jostling Miss Marsden.

Seth could bark at him to move or launch a string of insults. Indeed, part of him wanted to—a part his genteel Southern mother would be horrified to know existed. Instead he turned, walking to the back of the store and around the aisle before heading to the door. Victoria trailed behind him while Dr. Greely sputtered a string of insults about young know-nothing doctors stealing his patients.

He stepped out into the afternoon sun, still hot with the warmth of summer, and headed down the street. To his left, the harbor glistened in the afternoon sun, and a warm breeze wafted across Lake Superior lying to their north. Another day, he'd stop and take in the scene, so very different from the rolling fields he'd left behind in

Maryland and the salty air and tempestuous ocean off the coast of Boston. But today he quickened his pace, drawing Miss Marsden closer to his chest lest he jostle her more than necessary.

With her delicate face and golden lashes, she looked almost like one of the Bisque dolls from Germany sitting in his mother's cabinet—and felt as light as one.

"Miss Marsden lives with you, does she not?" He moved aside so a wagon laden with produce for the summer market could pass.

"She did, up until a few d-days ago. Lindy and Aileen Brogan are renting rooms above the bakery now." Victoria bustled along beside him, her silky skirt and pearl earbobs something he'd be much more apt to see in Boston than the rugged town of Eagle Harbor.

"How often does she eat?"

Victoria stumbled over her skirts, causing him to pause for a moment. When she looked up at him, her brow was furrowed and her eyes upset. "Elijah and I f-f-fed her very well while she was staying with is, if th-that's what you're asking."

Oh, drat. He'd become a doctor and not an orator for a reason. "I didn't mean to imply you did anything wrong, but she should weigh more."

Maybe she did have tuberculosis. It was known as the wasting disease for a reason.

Victoria resumed her walking, pulling her skirt up just a bit. "Rebekah said Lindy was sick right b-before she came here. I really don't know more than that, but if anything, she's filled out since she's been staying with us."

Ah, yes. Rebekah Cummings had mentioned something about him needing to examine one of her friends with a cough, and he'd seen Miss Marsden with her shiny gold hair around town, but she had always seemed to disappear whenever he'd called on Rebekah.

He headed up the log steps to his office and glanced down at the limp woman in his arms once more. If this was what she weighed after putting on a few pounds, he should have made more effort to see her before now. Tuberculosis could be spread, though not nearly as rampantly as diseases such as whooping cough and typhus. Still, if someone in Eagle Harbor had tuberculosis, he needed to know.

Chapter Three

"You c-can't keep her here. It simply isn't proper."

Pain, hot and searing, started in her finger and flashed up her arm like lightning. Lindy fluttered her eyelids open for a moment before clamping them shut against the light.

"You heard Dr. Greely. I need to make sure infection doesn't set in. It's imperative the wound stay clean."

Lindy drew in a breath—or tried to. If only her lungs would inhale. Instead it felt as if a weight rested upon her chest. She took another tiny breath, the struggle to put air in her lungs far greater than it should be.

"You can g-g-go check on her at the bakery. Elijah will get a wagon to t-take her, right Elijah? I'm sure she'll be more comfortable in her room."

"If it were just the wound, I'd let her leave. But the pain from the break will be greater than she can treat on her own, and her breathing is labored, which further complicates how to treat her pain, as laudanum can depress lung function. The earliest she could leave is tomorrow, and that's if I can figure out something for her pain while still getting her to breathe better."

Who was talking? Lindy recognized Victoria's voice, always laced with concern and compassion, but she couldn't place the male voice.

She attempted to open her eyes once more, but between the stabbing pain in her finger, the struggle to breathe, and the blinding light, her eyelids remained open for only a second.

"You need a wife, Seth. Then it wouldn't be improper for you to keep a female patient."

Now that was Elijah, but who was this Seth? She'd been in Eagle Harbor long enough to meet nearly everyone in town. She attempted to run through the people she knew, but her lungs were so starved for air and her finger so painful she couldn't hang onto a thought for more than a second or two.

"Thank you for reminding me of that." The man's voice again, Seth.

"Elijah! How could you say such a thing?" And Victoria.

Lindy shifted on her bed. Maybe if she sat up a little, it would be easier to breathe. But another wave of pain shot up her arm, and she groaned. What was wrong with her hand? She was used to fighting for breath, but not to the blinding pain in her finger.

Oh, wait. Her finger. The mercantile. Her fall. Was this what amputation felt like? She groaned. The pain from the surgery was nearly as bad as the break itself.

Footsteps thumped against the floor.

"Lindy, honey, are you awake?" Victoria's voice grew louder. "How are you f-feeling?"

"It hurts." She wheezed out the words and sucked another painfully small breath into her lungs.

"You're struggling to breathe again." It was Seth's voice this time. "Here, let's prop you up." The pillows behind her shifted, and she whimpered at the pain the movement caused in her hand. Then someone helped her sit—Victoria? Rather than look, she pressed her eyes closed even tighter lest the pain make her cry.

A hand landed on her forehead, long and large and not Victoria's.

She jolted her eyelids open to find herself staring into a set of somber grass green eyes.

She jerked away, crying out when a sharp bout of pain pierced her finger and flashed up her hand and arm. "No. No doctors."

"Calm yourself. You're struggling to breathe as it is." Dr. Harrington placed his hand on her forehead again.

She looked past him to Victoria and Elijah standing at the foot of the bed. "Take me home."

"Lindy, honey." Victoria came around to the side of the bed and took her uninjured hand. "Dr. Harrington is just trying to help."

She was entirely too familiar with the kind of help doctors gave. The scar on her leg began to throb. Which was ridiculous. An old wound couldn't be hurting more than her amputated finger, but she felt it all the same. "I don't want help; I want to leave."

She swung her legs over the side of the bed, but even that caused more pain in her finger. She cried out again, tears pricking her eyes.

A hand smoothed hair away from her face. Whether it was Victoria's or Dr. Harrington's, she couldn't tell.

"Do you remember what happened?" Victoria asked gently. "How you br-broke your finger?"

She couldn't think of anything besides the pain—and the fact she was at the mercy of a doctor yet again.

"Please," she whimpered, "I don't want to be here."

"Dr. Greely said your finger had to be amputated, but Dr. Harrington saved it while you were unconscious."

He had? She glanced down at her left hand. The bandage covering her last two fingers was so bulky she couldn't tell what was there and what wasn't. But it felt as though her pinky was still attached—very painfully attached.

They hadn't taken off her stockings, had they? She forced her gaze down to her feet. No, they were there, her scar completely covered despite her dress riding higher than was proper as she sat on the bed. The last thing she needed was to fend off questions about that. Or maybe if Dr. Harrington saw the scar, he'd want try a similar procedure on her leg.

Her stomach roiled with nausea, and she wrapped her good arm around her waist.

"You can't go anywhere at the moment. Even if you haven't jarred your finger with all your unnecessary movement, you can barely breathe. Let me get some more Dover's Powder." Dr. Harrington turned for the door. "No, no. That has opium, and I feel like the laudanum from earlier made your breathing worse."

"No medicine." It never made her better. Nothing a doctor did ever made her better—as her leg could attest.

"Stay with her while I check my cabinet for ipecac." Dr. Harrington stopped beside Elijah, who was stationed at the door to the small room, his mouth grim within his short, caramel-colored beard. "If I use a small dose, it should suppress the coughing without inducing vomiting. Or maybe I should try Fowler's Powder."

"No!" she wailed. "I said no medicine." But Dr. Harrington didn't even look at her. They never did. Whenever a doctor was near, it was as though she wasn't a person but a mouse or a bug on which they could perform experiments and try out new medicines. It didn't matter how sick she got or how much she protested. No one listened to her, not ever.

And Dr. Harrington was no exception. Instead of turning back and asking her what she wanted, he reached out and gripped Elijah's shoulder. "Don't let her go anywhere."

"I won't."

The throbbing in her leg increased. She looked away from the men. If ever she'd trust people to listen to her, it was Elijah and Victoria Cummings. But it seemed not even they would go against a doctor.

"Lindy, you n-need to calm down so you can breathe." Victoria smoothed hair away from her face. "Let's get you back into bed before you upset the bone Dr. Harrington just saved."

"I don't want to go back to bed. I want to go home. Why won't anyone listen to me?" She was nearly screaming now—and crying. And the pain, oh, she wasn't going to think about the pain.

Except she had to, because her stomach was still roiling as though she might retch from the throbbing and the thought of a doctor treating her again.

"I don't want a doctor. I'm done seeing doctors. I told Rebekah that before I left Chicago." She was blubbering now, probably incoherently, but she didn't care, just as long as she could convince Victoria to take her away before the doctor forced medicine into her.

"Don't you want something for the pain?" Victoria spoke again, her voice as gentle and sweet as a meadow.

"Lindy, if you want to go home, you need to calm down." Elijah left his post by the door and approached the bed, his swarthy mariner's face serious as he ran his eyes down her. "We can't take you anywhere like this."

"But if I calm down, you'll take me home?" She drew in a breath at that, even though it was tiny and shallow and didn't give her near enough air to slake the burning in her lungs. "The doctor said I couldn't leave until tomorrow."

"If you calm down, you can go." Dr. Harrington strode back inside the room, two glass bottles and a handkerchief in his hand.

"No medicine! I don't need medicine to calm down!"

"Of course you don't," he said as though he agreed. But he couldn't agree with her. No doctor ever did. "Here, I'll set the medicine on the table. It's not even near you."

She watched through bleary eyes as he did just that and approached the bed.

"It will be easier to relax if you lie back against the pillows. Can you do that for me?" He helped her move her legs back onto the bed while Victoria adjusted the pillows. "Is that better?"

She nodded, and he reached out to rest a hand on her forehead again.

Only when the white handkerchief covered her mouth and nose, and she inhaled a sickly-sweet scent, did she realize she'd been fooled.

⌐.⌐.⌐.⌐.⌐

Seth pulled the chloroform-soaked handkerchief away from Miss Marsden's face and sighed.

"I don't like you tricking her like that." Elijah crossed his muscular arms over his chest.

"Neither do I." Victoria whirled on him, her expensive dress and jewelry doing nothing to soften the displeasure on her face.

"I don't like it either." Seth's shoulders sagged. "But I'm not sure how else to go about treating her."

"Maybe you should do as she says and let her go home." Elijah rubbed the back of his neck, his skin tan and weathered from the time he spent on his fishing boat. "She's a grown woman. She should have a choice about it."

"A grown woman with a fear that's about as rational as a child being afraid of the dark." Still, he didn't like lying to her.

"I agree with Dr. Harrington." Victoria reached out and took her husband's hand, lacing her fingers with his own. What a picture they made, the elegant socialite with her pearls and silk, and the rough fisherman with his wind-burnished skin and clothes that smelled of the lake. "You d-d-didn't see how bad the break to her pinky was. Can you imagine what would have happened if my father refused to let anyone treat him after he broke his leg this spring?"

"He'd have died from gangrene before the month was out." Elijah's voice was gruff.

Seth turned back to Miss Marsden. He could help with the bone, but the breathing was another matter entirely. He took the ipecac syrup from the table and moved to the bed, then pulled out his stethoscope and listened to her breathing.

Wheezing sounded in her bronchial passages, and her chest heaved though she sucked in only small bits of air. But those were symptoms of asthma, not tuberculosis. Hopefully his initial assessment had been wrong and she had a manageable breathing disorder rather than a disease that would claim her life.

"I'm sorry about the things she said." Victoria came up beside him, the bottle of Fowler's Powder he'd left on the table in her hand. "I'm sure once she c-calms down and the pain subsides, she'll understand that you helped her."

Would she? He'd been accused of many things since he'd started practicing medicine. Carelessness, ineptness, inattention to detail, arriving too late, causing pain to worsen. But intentionally trying to hurt a patient? Not even Dr. Greely had accused him of that.

"I'm not even sure she realizes you saved her finger," Victoria tried again, her voice soft in the otherwise quiet room.

And why did he care so much what Miss Marsden said about him? He'd taken the Hippocratic Oath, and his job was to make his patient better—whether she liked it or not.

"I need to keep her until at least tomorrow, and I'll leave her sedated, providing I can do so in a way that doesn't further depress her breathing. If that means you two need to stay in my other sickroom to keep things proper, then you're welcome to do so."

"Yes, I'm starting to think she should stay longer too. I'll go home and pack a b-bag for the night. I should be back in under an hour." Victoria stepped away from the bed, then paused. "Unless you need my help right now?"

"No, no." Seth waved her off. "She'll be unconscious for at least an hour. You don't mind sitting with her for a few minutes, do you, Elijah? I want to look up a couple articles on asthma before I give her any more medicine."

"Not at all." Elijah pulled his wife to him and gave her a quick peck on the lips before letting her scurry out the door. "Though you might scrounge up something for me to read if I'm going to sit here long."

"I'll see what I can do." Seth rose from the side of Lindy's bed, but a faint discoloration on Miss Marsden's uninjured arm caught his eye. He gently took up her arm and undid the buttons along her wrist.

"What are you doing now?" Elijah came up beside him.

Seth had already glimpsed enough to know what he would find. He slid the sleeve up, thinking he could stop a few inches above her wrist, but that wasn't far enough. So he went farther still, to her elbow. But even then, another mark peeked from beneath the fabric of her shirt.

The sleeve was nearly to her shoulder by the time he finally stopped. He drew in a ragged breath, half in fury and half in disbelief, as he blinked at the mass of angry red scars, all thin lines made with a knife's blade.

He'd been wrong. He hadn't the faintest notion what he would find when he unbuttoned her sleeve.

"Perhaps this is why she's so afraid of doctors," his voice came out as a strangled rasp.

Elijah's swallow echoed through the room. "What is it?"

"She's been bled." His disbelief gave way to fury, coating his words like the thick syrup he'd just given Miss Marsden. He'd seen similar scars before, but never anywhere close to this many.

"I know you don't want her moved, but she might be more comfortable recovering in her own home rather than staying here."

Elijah's keen gray eyes took in every detail of Miss Marsden's arms. "It's not that I think you'd do this to her, but some doctor did."

"I'd not call the man a doctor. More like a charlatan. But you're right, under the circumstances she might fare better at home. Perhaps Victoria can tend to her rather than me?" Seth spoke through a tight throat. He wouldn't force his doctoring on this woman, not now that he knew why she objected so strongly to him. "At least until it's time for the stitches to come out."

Elijah slowly shook his head. "I almost wish I hadn't seen it."

He'd seen countless bodies during his years of doctoring, male and female, naked and clothed. But never before had looking at a person's body—any part of it—felt so invasive.

He slid the sleeve slowly back down, then glanced at her other arm. Was that one just as scarred? For the sake of all that was sane and right in the world, he hoped the skin on her other arm matched the porcelain complexion of her face and not the angry red welts he'd just seen. But since all the scars on her right arm were old and healed, he had no medical reason to look at the second.

He stepped away from the bed, his hands suddenly trembling, and turned to Elijah. "How soon can you have a wagon with straw prepared to take her to her to the bakery?"

Chapter Four

A stab of pain started in her pinky and shot up her arm. Lindy couldn't hold back her moan.

"Finally. I was worried ye'd not awaken."

At the sound of the Irish-laced voice, she opened her eyes. Aileen sat beside her bed, her red hair creating a frizzy halo about her freckled face.

Wait. Aileen? Her bed? She blinked at the friend she'd made while traveling from Chicago to Eagle Harbor, then pushed herself up against the pillows, wincing at the fresh jolt of pain in her finger.

"I'm home." If the rooms she and Aileen rented above the bakery could be called that. "How long have I been here?"

"Ach, since just after lunch, so eight hours maybe?"

She blinked away the blurriness from her eyes and looked around again. She didn't remember much beyond that she'd woken in Dr. Harrington's office and he'd wanted to keep her there. He'd listened when she said she wanted to go home? It was probably the first time in her life a doctor had taken her wishes into consideration.

"How're ye feelin'? I was startin' to get worried. The doc said ye should come out o' the stuff he gave ye a few hours ago. But ye just kept on sleepin'."

"The stuff he gave me?"

"Ach, to make ye sleep, he gave it to ye."

Hadn't she told him no medicine? Maybe he hadn't listened after all. Or maybe she hadn't said anything. The hazy memories slipped and slithered through her mind. She lay back against the pillow and drew in a breath.

Oh, that's right. He'd tricked her! He'd promised she could go home as soon as she'd relaxed, and then put a sweet smelling handkerchief over her mouth once she'd calmed.

But she had a bigger problem than Dr. Harrington's trickery at the moment. She glanced at the corner of her room, where two jars of jam and the ragdoll she'd made sat. How was she going to get them to the O'Byrnes tomorrow?

"Do ye need anythin'? Maybe some water?" Aileen stood, then twisted her hands in her skirt. "Sorry, but I amn't much for nursing. Victoria is supposed to be here."

"I'm fine, I just... yes, some water. And maybe something for the pain." Was there a medicine that wouldn't make her unconscious?

"Oh, I forgot there's broth down stairs. I'll bring ye some of that."

"No need." Victoria bustled through the door, a tray with toast, broth, and a steaming mug in her hands. "I've already got it, and I figured our p-patient would be wanting some willow bark tea by now."

Aileen pressed her lips together, then plopped back down on the chair beside the bed. "Told ye I amn't much for nursing."

"Nonsense. I'm sure you've been doing fine." Victoria set the tray on the small table that stood against the wall.

"Only because she was sleepin'."

Lindy yawned. Evidently she couldn't expect Aileen to tend her when she came down with her next lung ailment. Not that it would be fair to ask such a thing of her roommate anyway.

Victoria took the mug of tea from the tray, sat on the side of the bed, and held it to Lindy's mouth. "This should ease the pain."

"I can drink by myself." Lindy moved to take the mug, then gasped when another flash of pain traveled up her finger.

Victoria nudged the mug closer. "Don't be stubborn. Dr. Harrington wants you to rest that hand."

Lindy blinked away the burning in her eyes and reached for the mug with her other hand. If she couldn't hold a mug with her right hand, then how long before she could sew? She didn't have enough money saved to pay for her share of these rooms without working.

She took a sip of the bitter tea. Oh, why had she gone and broken her finger?

"Here now." Victoria set the tea back on the table and poured some medicine into a spoon, then held it to her lips. "It might not taste the b-best, but Dr. Harrington says it will help your breathing."

She turned her head away. "I don't want any."

"But your lungs."

"Are fine." It might be a little hard to draw breath, but she wasn't feverish and coughing so hard she couldn't breathe, wasn't in such a bad state she'd be confined to her bed for weeks. The O'Byrnes, on the other hand, were all but confined to their cabin with nothing to eat. How long until she could visit?

~.~.~.~.~

"Where is she?" Elijah paced across the kitchen until he reached the sink, turned, then paced back the other direction. "She should have been home before now."

"Something may have gone wrong with Lindy." Ma picked up the kettle from the stove and poured hot water over the leaves in the tea pot. "I wouldn't worry."

Not worry? At this time of night, The Pretty Penny would be filled with drunkards, and she needed to walk right past the brothel to get to their house.

He glanced out the window above the sink, but no lantern flickered in the yard. "I don't want her walking by herself this late. I'm going to get her."

"How do you think she feels when she sits here with Ma while you're out in the dark during a storm?" Isaac dunked a cookie in his coffee and shoved a bite in his mouth.

If only the sugar would sweeten his younger brother's disposition.

Why must his brother turn their every conversation into an argument about his volunteer life-saving team? Couldn't the man see sailors didn't deserve to drown just because their ship wrecked coming into port? "Victoria understands why I rescue shipwrecked sailors, even if you don't."

"I understand better than you," Isaac spoke in a voice more bitter than over-steeped tea. "I was the one who watched Pa die in those waves, remember?"

Elijah rubbed the back of his neck. "You could have—"

"Stop bickering, boys." Ma set the kettle back on the stove with a thunk. "Elijah, if you're so worried about Victoria, then walk back to town and look for her. It's better than wearing out the floorboards. And Isaac, isn't it about time for you to head home for the night? Unless you wanted to stay here?" Ma's voice rose on the slightest hint of hope. "No one's sleeping in the loft these days."

"Going home," Isaac answered without so much as a glance at Ma. He tossed the remainder of the cookie in his mouth, then drained his coffee with one long gulp.

"Let's go." Elijah grabbed two of the lanterns hanging on the wall and lit them. He and Isaac would be lucky if they made it to North Street without throwing punches, but at least they wouldn't be fighting in front of Ma. "I'll wait outside." He left one lantern on the table for his brother and tromped outside with the other.

The sound of the lake greeted him, waves washing against rocks in the blackness. If the swells were always this subdued, then there'd be no need for a life-saving team and no endless feud between him and Isaac. But the giant lake to their north could turn angry and brutal within minutes.

The door closed behind him, and Isaac's footfalls resonated against the porch floorboards.

"Honestly, Elijah, you've been going out into storms since Pa died. Why can't you turn over your life-saving team to someone else?" Isaac strode across the yard, his pace brisk as they entered the twisting wooded path that would eventually take them to the outskirts of town. "You trained your men. You established a team to save shipwrecked people. Now that you're married, you should stay home with your wife during storms."

Elijah scrubbed a hand over his face and sighed. Evidently the night air wasn't cooling off his brother any. "You need to come to terms with what I do. Everyone else has."

"No, you need to come to terms with how you recklessly risk your life."

He opened his mouth, but he couldn't deny Isaac's words. Though he wasn't an official United States life-saver, he and his crew well knew their motto: *You have to go out. You don't have to come back.*

He glanced up at the sky. *Father, how long do I have to be at odds with my brother?*

There'd been a time when they'd understood everything about each other. When they ran through these trees and played in the woods, when they'd gone angling on the river and fishing with Pa in his boat. Why had Pa's death driven such a wedge between them?

Maybe he should try to see things from Isaac's perspective. Maybe if he'd been in the lighthouse tower with his siblings three years ago and watched Pa's boat trying to make harbor, then...

No. He wouldn't have stood there and watched. He would have taken a dingy and gone to rescue him.

Maybe he would have died trying, but he at least would have *tried*. Why couldn't Isaac understand? And how did Isaac live with himself knowing he'd watched their father die without raising a finger save him?

But he couldn't blame Isaac, not really, because as Isaac so often reminded him, he hadn't been there to see what happened. Besides, casting blame at Isaac's feet would only widen the rift between them—if that were possible. Because at the moment the gulf felt so large Isaac may well have been standing in Canada on the opposite shore of Lake Superior.

A twig snapped beneath his foot. "You're my only brother. I don't want to fight with you anymore."

"Then stop going on rescues." Isaac's words were terse against the night songs of toads and crickets.

"Won't you at least admit I do good?"

Isaac's jaw stiffened under the orange glow of the lantern.

"Victoria would be dead if I didn't go out on those rescues."

"Enough!" Isaac roared into the darkness, the noise bouncing off the trees before an eerie silence descended.

Elijah stared at the dark path ahead. How could he live with himself if he sat home during a storm when he had the ability to stop others from knowing the pain and grief his family experienced when Pa drowned?

"Do you hear that?" Isaac whispered, his eyes instantly alert.

Elijah listened for a moment, then shook his head.

"It came from this direction." Isaac walked forward, his footsteps soundless on the worn dirt trail.

Elijah heard it then, a faint whimper.

"Victoria?" He scanned the woods for her lantern but found only darkness.

"E-Elijah. Is th-th-th-that you?"

He strode forward, holding his lantern high while Isaac followed. "Where are you, sweetling?"

She stepped into the path, where the beam of light revealed half her hair had been pulled down to hang in tangles around her shoulders.

He raced forward and wrapped his arms around her, his heart pounding like waves against the rocks during a storm. "What are you doing out here?"

She clung to him, her breath catching on little sobs while her body trembled. "I-I-I-I-I heard t-t-t-talking and then someone yell, and since I d-d-d-d-didn't know who it was, I h-hid."

Hid? Since when did his wife hide on the property they owned?

"What's wrong?" He bent to set his lantern on the ground, then smoothed the hair back from her face. Was that a bruise around her eye or a shadow caused by the light below? "Did someone do something to you?"

She pressed in closer. "Not really."

His muscles tensed around his wife. "What do you mean? Are you hurt?"

"Just sc-sc-scared." She kept her head burrowed against his shoulder.

"Tell me who it was, and Isaac and I will take care of him."

"That's right," Isaac agreed. They might disagree on everything else under the sun, but never on protecting their womenfolk.

"I d-d-don't know. A miner. He was drunk. I h-h-hit him over the head with my lantern when the sheriff r-refused to help."

He rubbed her back with long, soothing strokes. "Your lantern?" That explained why she'd been walking in the dark. "I'm glad you're safe."

"What do you mean the sheriff refused to help?" Isaac shifted his lantern so the beam shone more fully on Victoria's face.

She half turned in his arms so she could see Isaac, then sniffled and wiped her eyes. "Sh-sheriff J-J-J-Jenkins was there, sitting on the p-porch of The Pretty Penny with D-D-Doc Greely, watching the whole thing. I called out to him, but he just waved and s-smiled, t-t-t—"

"Too drunk to do his job," Isaac finished.

Elijah clenched his jaw so hard his teeth ached.

"The m-miner was drunk too. I think he thought I was a... a... one of the women that worked inside. I tried t-telling him I was walking home. He might not even remember what he was doing, but his h-hands..." She closed her eyes and shivered. "That's when I hit him over the head with the lantern."

Elijah tucked her tight against his chest, her head nestled perfectly in the crook of his neck. They'd talk more about where the knave's hands had been when they were alone. "Then what did the sheriff do?"

"Still n-n-nothing. Just sat there smiling and drinking with D-D-D-Doc Greely."

He rubbed his wife's arm, up and down, to calm her trembling. "Looks like I'm having a talk with the sheriff come morning."

Isaac snorted. "Yeah, and if you're really lucky, the good ol' sheriff might be sober enough to remember it."

"He'll remember, all right." Elijah would make sure of it, and not just for Victoria's sake, but for the sake of all the women in Eagle Harbor.

Chapter Five

"There's three letters waiting for you, Dr. Harrington." Mr. Foley turned from the mail shelf behind the counter at the mercantile and handed Seth the envelopes. "Arrived on the Sinclair steamer yesterday."

"Thank you." He scanned the first envelope and frowned. It came from Washington D.C. but wasn't in the handwriting he expected. The second envelope was from his brother in Maryland, which was fairly usual. But his mouth turned dry as he saw the insignia on the third envelope and the handwriting that had become all too familiar since he'd lost his position with the Marine Hospital Service four years ago.

"Is that the letter you've been asking after?" Mr. Foley leaned on the counter to peer at the letters.

"It is." Seth slipped the first two letters into his pocket and picked up his medical bag.

Mr. Foley pointed at the fancy wax seal on the third envelope. "What's the Office of the Surgeon General?"

"The Surgeon General is the doctor in charge of the Marine Hospital Service. You might think of him as the most important doctor in the country." Or at least the most powerful one. "Now if you'll excuse me, I best be on my way."

He headed for the door, but rather than turn down North Street toward the lighthouse where his next patient awaited, he ducked around the side of the mercantile.

The answer would be different this time. It had to be different. Surely his work this spring was enough to see him reinstated to his former position in Boston.

He loosened the flap and slid the stationary out, the thick, creamy paper bearing the insignia of the Surgeon General just as the envelope did.

Dr. Harrington,

We regret to inform you that we are unable to accept your application at this time.

Sincerely,
Richard Hamilton
Surgeon General of the United States

That was it? No mention of the case notes he'd sent detailing Edward Donnelly's broken tibia that spring or the splint he'd created to make sure the bone healed straight? That had to be of interest to the Marine Hospital Service. Seamen suffered leg fractures all the time, and they often got infected. Those mariners usually ended up as amputees or dead before they reached the next port. Surely a splint like his could be used on naval and merchant ships.

Had Hamilton even looked at his notes? Seth crinkled the letter in his hand. Yes, he'd made a mistake at the Boston hospital, but that had been four years ago. Surely his recent success with orthopaedics made up for one missed diagnosis.

Except for Hamilton to know of his progress, he'd have to read his letters. Seth dropped the crumpled paper into the top of his bag

and took the next letter out of his pocket. But as he did so, the letter
from his brother slipped to the ground. He left it there as he looked
once more at the return address on the letter in his hand—a
Washington D.C. address but no name. He ran his finger under the
flap and unfolded the note.

> *Seth,*
>
> *I wanted to let you know I found your case study of the
> broken tibia fascinating. You said there was no infection and
> you used a splint you designed yourself? Can you send a
> diagram of the splint? I just lost a patient due to a compound
> fracture of the tibia that became infected while the man was
> at sea. Perhaps if the leg would have been bathed in antiseptic
> and splinted to allow more air circulation to the open wound,
> no infection would have set in.*
>
> *As for your persistent letters to Hamilton, I suggest you give
> the notion of returning a rest. Hamilton's determined not to
> hire you back, no matter how many of us want it, and you
> know why.*

Seth leaned back against the wall. Did he? Was it because of the
mistake he'd made in Boston or the fact that the Surgeon General
was now married to the woman Seth would have been calling wife?
That is, if he'd not been fired for his misdiagnosis that had, in effect,
ended both his career and his engagement.

It didn't matter. It was over and done and he couldn't change any
of it.

Except it did matter. Because if Harriet was the reason he was being
denied a position and not his medical skills, then he'd... he'd...

What? Go to Washington D.C. and try to talk to her? What good
would that do him?

He sighed and glanced back down at the remainder of the letter in his hand.

I'd like to stay informed of your progress, especially if you treat any more compound fractures. I'd appreciate any further information you can send along with that diagram.

Rand Jameson's signature scrawled over the bottom of the page, the letters large and loopy, even friendly looking, if that were possible.

But what good did having a friend in Washington D. C. do when Hamilton refused to rehire him?

He refolded the letter and put it back in the envelope, then grabbed the letter that had fallen to the ground and stuck them both in his bag. He'd read the one from his brother after he visited the Oaktons. It wasn't as though Theo ever said anything new. Every letter over the past fourteen years boiled down to the same question: *When are you going to stop this doctoring nonsense of yours and return home?*

And every response he penned contained the same answer: *I'm not.*

He pushed himself away from the building and headed toward the lighthouse, passing the ragtag little clapboard and log buildings that lined the road. Loggers, miners, and sailors filled these buildings, moving in and out of the town in accordance with their jobs. And if the town wasn't rough enough because of the inhabitants, the miles of rugged wilderness surrounding it made it fiercer yet.

With Lake Superior lying just to the north, the town got hammered with thirty feet of snow in the winter, and buffeted by wind and storms off the lake come summer. His mother wouldn't last a single winter here, nor would either of his former fiancées.

Seth passed the Front Street intersection and continued up the rocky incline toward the lighthouse. The building perched on the bluffs between the calm waters of the harbor glistening and the white-capped waves of Lake Superior. The lighthouse tower itself wasn't nearly as high as those on the Maryland coast, but it probably didn't need to be given the way the rocky outcropping it had been built on was twice the height of the tower.

Seth knocked on the lighthouse door, and it swung open almost instantly to reveal Victoria Cummings. He should have guessed she'd be here. She might not be a trained nurse, but he wasn't going to complain that she kept her eye on his patients.

Though she didn't seem to be enjoying her unpaid position very much at the moment. Frizzy little strands of hair poked out from her updo, her shirtwaist was twisted so the buttons listed to the side before disappearing into her skirt, and was that chocolate on her sleeve?

"Oh, there you are. Good." She peeked around him. "Where's Mac?"

"Is he supposed to be with me?" He looked out over the yard and path leading to the lighthouse. Still empty.

"He went looking for you about a quarter hour ago."

Probably about the time he'd been hiding behind the store. "I assume Mrs. Oakton isn't faring well?"

"She says it hurts when the baby moves."

His blood thrummed. It should be impossible for Tressa Oakton to have anything more go wrong with her pregnancy. "Has she been out of bed?"

"Not that I'm aware of."

He entered the lighthouse and was nearly through the kitchen before Victoria spoke again. "Before you go up to see Tressa, have you looked in on Lindy today?"

His heart gave a little thump at the mention of Miss Marsden's name. "Why? Is something wrong with her finger? Her breathing?"

He'd not seen her since treating her finger and sending her home four days ago, but then, it wasn't as though she'd welcome him if he tried calling.

Victoria's shoulders rose and fell. "I don't know. She wasn't at the bakery when I stopped by this morning, and Aileen said something about Lindy being gone for most of the day."

"I'll pay her a visit this evening. I should check her stitches, though I doubt it's time for them to come out yet." Hopefully she wouldn't be so put out at the sight of him that she refused treatment. He had saved her finger, after all. Surely the woman would be able to recognize that, despite the scars on her arm.

He headed down the hallway toward the tower stairs that would take him not just to the lamp above but to the second floor of the house.

Victoria trailed behind him, stopping in the parlor first. Her gentle voice carried through the lighthouse as she gave the Oakton children instructions to behave. The iron railing on the circular staircase felt cool beneath his hands, while the stairs shook and echoed inside the brick tower.

"Dr. Harrington." In her room, Tressa Oakton lay on a bed of creamy white, a hue that matched her too-pale skin. Indeed, her auburn hair and light brown eyes were the only bit of color around her. "I told him not to send for you. He calls you for every little thing." She closed her eyes and swallowed as though the strain of talking wore her out.

"Victoria said the babe is hurting you?"

"Feels like she's punching me when she moves. And don't tell me it's normal for a babe to kick. This is different. The pain's on the inside, like it's bruising my innards."

"Do you mind if I feel?"

She shook her head slowly, as though doing so any quicker would require too much energy.

He gently pulled back the covers, exposing her nightgown and bare feet before he rested his hands on her abdomen. The hard spine of the baby's back ran just beneath her skin into his hand, and farther up, near her ribs, he could make out the round form of the child's head. "It's still breech, but there's plenty of time for the baby to turn yet."

"Then what's wrong?"

This was precisely why he should be working for the Marine Hospital Service, not practicing medicine in Eagle Harbor. He understood only the basics of caring for a pregnant woman, while all of the MHS facilities had obstetricians who would likely know what was wrong with Tressa.

He pressed the sides of her abdomen and once again felt the hard bones of the babe. "It appears as though you don't have much amniotic fluid."

"What's that?" Victoria came into the room.

"A baby should be surrounded by fluid within its mother's uterus. I can't feel much fluid, but an obstetrician might be better able to tell. A midwife might suffice as well."

"Will the baby be all right?" Tressa opened her eyes, now moist with tears.

He opened his mouth to respond, then closed it. If only he knew what to say, how to treat her. If she could be treated, or if the babe was doomed even now. "It might have to come out early. I'm afraid I don't know anything more."

"It's too soon!" Victoria pressed a hand to her mouth.

"Not if Tressa's health is at risk." He hated himself as he said the words, but what choice was there? Tressa wasn't due for another seven weeks, but she seemed to grow sicker each day, and he didn't have the slightest idea why.

He rubbed a hand over his hair. If the Surgeon General would rehire him, then he'd be able to spend his time doctoring people he could actually help and referring patients like Tressa to specialists. Instead he was here in Eagle Harbor, having already failed at his first two jobs as a doctor, and about to fail at this one as well.

Tressa moved a hand protectively over her belly. "I want the babe. I don't want you to try to make it come early."

What mother would say differently? Sometimes during difficult pregnancies, one had to choose between mother and child. But when would Tressa reach the point where it was unsafe for the babe to stay inside her any longer? Would he recognize when the time came? Was she there now?

Frustration welled inside him. Yet more things he didn't know. He'd sworn after the Battle of Antietam, when he'd watched countless men suffer and die, that he'd not let this happen, that he'd never again be helpless in the face of someone's need. Yet standing here beside Tressa's bed, he may as well still be that ten-year-old boy at the door of the surgeon's tent.

"You want the babe to come early?" A masculine voice echoed behind him.

He looked over his shoulder to find Tressa's husband, Mac, standing in the doorway, his towering form nearly reaching the trim at the top of the door.

"I know the idea isn't pleasant, but it might be the only way to ensure your wife's health."

Tressa placed her second hand on top of the first on her abdomen. "I'm fine."

But she wasn't. "Besides the babe hurting you when it moves, has anything else changed? Can you stand up without feeling lightheaded? Walk a few steps?"

She closed her eyes again and gave her head a slight shake. "Everything spins and my vision starts to go black."

"I won't even let her get up to use the chamber pot." Mac rested a hand on the top of his wife's head, his fingers intertwining with her mussed strands of hair.

Two tiny red splashes of color appeared on Tressa's face before dissipating back into her ghostlike complexion. "This whole ordeal is humiliating. Who knew pregnancy could make you so ill?"

A healthy pregnancy didn't, but they were long past the point of pretending anything about this pregnancy was healthy.

"Let me take your blood pressure." Seth sat down at the side of the bed and took the sphygmograph out of his bag, strapping the wooden frame to the inside of Tressa's forearm and positioning the small weight over her radial artery. The weight immediately began moving up and down, measuring the amount of pressure needed to stop blood flow in the artery. He took out his pocket watch and kept an eye on the second hand while simultaneously watching the series of levers that connected to the weight move. The levers eventually attached to a pencil at the top of the apparatus, which then recorded a graph of Tressa's blood flow.

"It's low," he said, taking the straps off her arm and studying the graph. "Much lower than is normal."

"But you don't have any way to fix it." Tressa tucked her arm back under the covers and blinked her eyes tiredly.

They'd been over this before, too many times to count. "Not until the babe is born."

"Will that cure everything? I won't still be this sick afterwards, will I?"

"Likely not, you're hardly the first woman to fall ill due to pregnancy." He at least knew that much, even if he had no answers as to why this pregnancy had been so difficult. "Have you been eating?"

"I try."

He looked to Mac.

"Eggs, bread, not much else." The man rubbed the back of his thick neck and gave his head a shake. "She couldn't even stand the taste of the thimbleberries I brought her."

He'd never have guessed she'd gotten the eggs and bread inside her given how emaciated she was everywhere but her swollen belly, and even that didn't look large enough to be holding a babe due in less than two months. "I'm going to send word to Central to see if a midwife can visit you. I spent last night looking at more medical texts, but I can't find anything describing your condition. I'm sorry, Tressa. I wish…"

What? That he could snap his fingers and make whatever troubled her disappear? That he could be like Christ and heal someone by simply touching her hand? "…That I could be of more help."

She swallowed thickly. "Thank you for coming."

If only he felt worthy of her thanks. He packed up his blood pressure machine and closed his bag. "If anything changes, send Mac for me straightaway. I know you don't want the babe to come before it's time, but if things get worse, we might have to force the matter."

Tressa pressed her eyelids together, but a tear rolled down her cheek nonetheless.

He shifted from foot to foot. If only he could promise things would be all right in the end. Instead, he turned and headed down the hallway, before his own eyes grew damp.

"Dr. Harrington."

A soft thud sounded, and he turned to see Mac headed toward him, the door to his bedroom closed.

"You said the babe might need to come early? Will that mean… for the babe, that is… will it…?" Mac's tawny colored eyes sought his, pleading for the smallest bit of hope.

He couldn't give it. "It won't live. Not if it comes this soon."

The big man pressed his eyes shut, the hope fading into lines of anguish on his face. "Will Tressa live if the babe stays inside her much longer?"

Most days, he loved being a doctor, loved saving people, loved helping people like Lindy keep their pinky fingers and Victoria's father keep his leg. Loved seeing a patient overcome flu or pneumonia or whooping cough.

But then there were times like this, when he wished he could lie, if for no other reason than to shield people from the pain the truth would cause.

"I don't know," he spoke softly. And he didn't.

Chapter Six

Lindy sucked in a painful gasp of air as she approached the bakery. She'd known visiting the O'Byrnes would take most of the day, and she'd known she'd be wheezing and starved for breath by the time she returned home. But she hadn't expected her finger to ache this much, nor had she expected the trace of blood seeping through her bandage.

Just a little farther, then she'd be able to lie down and sip some willow bark tea. Except she wouldn't have any energy to make willow bark tea, and Aileen was at a beautification society meeting tonight and wouldn't be home to make it for her.

She pulled a small breath into lungs that convulsed against the air, then rounded the front of the closed bakery and headed along the side of the building toward the back door that led to the kitchen.

But visiting the O'Byrnes had been worth her shortness of breath and aching finger. When she hadn't arrived earlier this week, Jack assumed she wasn't coming back. The boy's face had lit with excitement when he'd seen her, as had Toby's and Alice's. Jenny, on the other hand, had stomped about as though—

"Miss Marsden." Dr. Harrington pushed himself off the wall where he'd been standing near the back door to the bakery.

She stopped, her chest heaving with exertion and her breaths coming in and out with high-pitched wheezes. What was he doing here? She didn't have the strength to fend off a doctor tonight, especially not one that had tricked her the last time she'd seen him.

He came toward her. Any other time she might wonder whether the lines creasing his face were anger or concern, but she simply didn't have the energy. "Victoria said you weren't here when she stopped by earlier to check for infection."

"It's not infected." Just painful. And bleeding. She moved her hand behind her back to shield it from his view, then winced at the jostling.

A wince he noticed, if the way his eyebrows drew down was any indication. "Do you mind if I take a look? I'd like to check the stitches as well."

"Yes, I mind." She pressed her hand farther behind her back, which only caused her to gasp with the fresh stab of pain. "Victoria's been by to check my finger once already this week. I don't see any reason for you to look at it too. Now if you'll excuse me, I have business to attend inside."

Like collapsing on her bed. She tried to move around him, but he stepped with her, blocking her path to the door.

"I don't doubt Victoria's care of you, but I can only ascertain so much from her reports."

Reports? "What do you...? No, never mind. I don't want to know." She took a step back from him. Last time they'd been this close, he'd given her chloroform to force her into doing what he wanted.

"Victoria reported your progress to me," he answered, evidently not the least bit interested in listening to her when she said she didn't want to know.

Doctors. What was a person to do with them besides run as far away as possible and hide? Or lock oneself in their room. Except this doctor had actually helped her. She did owe him thanks for saving her finger—even if he'd tricked her as soon as he was done.

And she also owed him money. She blinked. Of course that's why he was here. How could she have forgotten? This concern about her finger was probably just an attempt to give her the bill. Though he'd waited longer than most doctors to get paid. Dr. Lathersop would have given her the bill for her finger before she'd left his office.

"You don't think I'd leave a patient with a compound fracture to herself after I set the bone, do you?" He frowned at her.

She had, and had assumed Victoria was just being, well, Victoria. Always trying to help. Always looking for someone to mother.

But rather than producing a bill, Dr. Harrington's frown only deepened, his eyes narrowing as they ran up and down her in that methodical, clinical way he had.

She took another step back.

"You're growing paler by the minute. What am I doing standing here talking your ear off? Come inside and rest." He gestured to the door as though he owned the building.

She gritted her teeth, half against the man's stubbornness and half against the pain in her finger. "I will as soon as you leave."

"Then we're at an impasse, because I'm not leaving until I examine your finger." He widened his stance, still keeping her from the door unless she darted around him.

Did she have the breath to do so? Then she could lock him out of the bakery and be done with him—at least until morning. "There's no need to examine anything. I'm fine."

"You're wheezing." The lines of concern creasing his face were almost convincing enough to make her believe he cared about more than the money she owed him.

Almost. "I said I'm fine."

"And now you're being insulting. I'm a doctor. I can tell when

54

someone's fine, and you, Miss Marsden, are far from fine." Those lines were turning from concern to frustration. Good. Maybe if he got half as frustrated as she felt, he'd stomp off and leave without her needing to beat him to the door.

"I don't need you to look at my finger." Never mind that it was bleeding. "Or listen to my lungs."

"I'd be remiss in my work if I failed to make sure your wound is healing."

She looked up into his eyes, a grass green shade that resembled none of the calm, serene aspects of grass given the stubborn set to his jaw and determined furrow in his brow. Had she been wrong about him? He'd yet to shove a bill at her and seemed bent on looking at her finger, even though she'd said nothing about paying him.

She drew in a breath through lungs that were still far tighter than she'd like, but at least they were loosening some while she stood here. Still, she needed to go inside and lie down. Something told her he'd stay here half the night arguing until he got his way, but she was too spent to argue for another minute.

Which gave her precisely one option.

She drew in another breath, filling her lungs with as much air as she could, and made a beeline for the door. Inserting the key, she twisted the knob, rushed inside, and slammed the door behind her.

Or rather, she would have slammed the door, had a brown shoe not wedged itself in the opening.

"Dr. Harrington." She swung the door open and found herself standing entirely too close to the imposing man. Whatever concern she'd glimpsed earlier was entirely gone now, leaving her with a seething doctor instead. "You fail to understand. I don't need—"

"They're high and fast."

"What?"

"Your breaths. Sometimes people with lung ailments have deep, murky breaths, but yours are high and fast. I think its asthma."

"You scoundrel!"

She shoved his chest with her good hand. If he would just step back from the door, she could close and lock it. But before she could pull her hand away from him, he caught it and held it against his shirt.

"Did you just call me a scoundrel for listening to you breathe?" Some of his frustration disappeared, and a small smile twitched at the corner of his mouth.

She scowled. "It's not funny."

"Funny? No. But perhaps a bit amusing. In ten years of practicing medicine, I've never been called a scoundrel for listening to a person's inhalations."

Oh, he was a double scoundrel for turning this into some joke. She yanked on her hand again, but he still didn't release it.

"Are you coughing at all? Is it deep? Do you ever expel phlegm when you cough? Blood?"

"Let me go!"

"Answer my questions."

"Not until you let me go."

His green eyes twinkled as though he was almost ready to start laughing, the knave. "Again we find ourselves at an impasse, because I don't trust you to answer my questions once I release you."

"And I don't trust you to…" She clamped her lips shut, her chest suddenly tight for a reason that had nothing to do with breathing and everything to do with memories best left buried in the dust of Chicago.

Dr. Harrington must have sensed a change in her, because his grip turned almost tender. Then he glanced down at her hand and the ribbon of skin around her wrist where her sleeve had slid back slightly.

No. She yanked her hand away and shoved it behind her back. He hadn't seen a scar, had he? She swallowed, the sound so loud in her ears it may as well echo off the walls of the bakery kitchen.

He must not have seen, because he didn't say anything, and people who saw always asked. There really wasn't an answer she could give beyond *I hate doctors.*

The old wound in her leg began to throb, and she swallowed again before taking a step back from him.

"Miss Marsden…" He drew in a breath, then let out more air in that single breath than she could expel with ten of her own. "I truly need to look at your finger. If you knew more about me, then you'd understand how seriously I take my doctoring, and, well…" He shifted on his feet, his eyes issuing a plea that matched his words. "Please. Five minutes is all I need."

As though she'd never heard promises from doctors before.

The memory rose up to choke her, the cloying scent of her bedroom at her aunt's house in Chicago, the men who'd invaded her room to hold her down for the procedure, the bowl set out for her blood, and the beans. Those wretched, cursed beans.

But she wasn't in Chicago now. She was in Eagle Harbor, with a doctor who had helped her, even if he'd tricked her immediately after. And why hadn't he mentioned the bill yet?

She met Dr. Harrington's eyes. "Why did you give me that chloroform after I told you no more medicine?"

"Is that why you're being so stubborn?" Some of the rigidity left his body, and he sighed. "I didn't want to be deceitful, Miss Marsden. In fact, that's something I detest in other doctors. But you were in hysterics, and I was concerned you would upset the bone I'd just set. Either that or go into a breathing fit I couldn't stop. It probably wasn't the best choice, but I'm still not sure how else I could have calmed you."

She shouldn't believe him. How many times had doctors lied to her before? And yet as he stood there, with concern once again etched across his face and his eyes warm with sincerity, she couldn't quite harden her heart to him.

But that still didn't mean she trusted him to look at her finger. What happened if she objected to how he wanted to treat her? Would he use chloroform again and claim it had been in her best interest when she woke up?

"Why don't you take a seat here?" He gestured toward one of the wooden chairs at the table shoved up against the wall. "This shouldn't take long."

She crossed her arms over her chest, planting her feet on the floor so firmly he'd have to drag her to the chair if he wanted her to sit in it. "I won't pay you for this visit. You're the one insisting on it, remember? Not me."

There. That would get him to leave. Why hadn't she thought of this plan sooner?

Except it didn't work, because the next words out of her mouth were, "It's a deal. Now sit so we can get this done."

⸎.⸎.⸎.⸎.⸎

He'd shocked her. Seth could tell by the way her eyes grew large and her body stiffened, the way the arms she was crossing over her chest grew tighter around her.

"Well? Have a seat." He gestured to the chair once more. "I'd like to get home in time for supper, if you don't mind."

"W-w-wait. Those aren't... aren't my only terms."

Why was she being so stubborn? Because of the chloroform. Because of the scars. Because she probably had a whole host of other unpleasant memories to go along with those scars. He drew in a breath. She had her reasons, valid ones, even if they were making his job overly difficult.

Still, did she understand how frustrating it was for him to stand here, pleading with her to let him help when he actually could… well, help? He might be helpless when it came to treating Tressa Oakton, but he could certainly handle a compound fracture to a phalange.

Yet here he was begging her to let him do his job, something that had never happened in Boston. He was of half a mind to walk away and let her deal with the finger on her own. She almost deserved for it to heal crooked.

Almost. But not entirely. He rubbed the back of his neck and scowled. Drat, but he was too compassionate by half. "It's not very sporting of you to change the terms of the deal, especially when you're the one who set them."

"I never agreed to a deal, and I don't care whether it's sporting or not. It's my hand. I'm the one with a say over what happens to it, not you." She still hadn't sat in the chair, and now she hid her bandaged hand behind her back, as though that would somehow fix whatever she'd done to her pinky.

"True, but you also strike me as an intelligent woman." At least when she wasn't being stubborn. "I'm sure you realize that if you had been successful in denying me access to your hand earlier this week, you'd either be missing a pinky or have gangrene by now."

She pressed her lips together, her weight shifting from one foot to the other as she glanced from him to the chair and back again.

He'd give her about thirty seconds to agree, and then he was going home. He'd delayed his supper long enough. She could tend the finger on her own if she wanted, or even go to Dr. Greely.

Probably the first time ever he'd happily lose a patient to the man.

"No knives if you look at my finger. No bleeding. I don't care if bleeding helps the bone heal faster. I don't want you to do it."

That's what she was so worried about? The muscle along his jaw pulsed. "I don't bleed my patients."

"Ever?"

"Have you heard of Dr. Pierre Louis? He's a French physician whose studies on bloodletting for pneumonia prove that patients take longer to recover when they're bled."

"They do?" She blinked at him.

"Yes."

She stood there for a moment, head cocked to the side as her nervousness seeped away. "All right, you can look at my finger. But no medicine."

"Ah, I'd like to use one of the things I brought, but it's not medicine. Have you ever heard of carbolic acid?"

"No." She made a slashing motion with her hand. "I certainly don't want any acid."

He stifled a wince. Perhaps he shouldn't have named the antiseptic he favored. It did sound rather frightening if one didn't know what it was. "There's a doctor in England, a baron, actually. His name is Sir Joseph Lister, and he's done numerous studies proving that washing wounds with certain chemical solutions keep infection from setting in. Carbolic acid is one such solution."

Her gaze moved to the medical bag at his feet. "Will it hurt?"

"If the wound is still open, it will sting when it touches blood, but no worse than whiskey or any other antiseptic. Now will you take your seat, Miss Marsden? Please." He gestured to the chair for the third time.

She lifted her chin and marched to it as though she were an imprisoned soldier facing the gallows.

He drew in a breath, long and deep. She was terrified of his profession, not him personally. Though why he felt better reminding himself of that, he didn't know.

"I need to see your hand." He spoke softly, hoping the calmness in his voice would soothe her.

She winced at the slight jostling as she lowered it to the table from where it had been clutched against her chest.

His gaze immediately travelled to the small red stain spreading through the bandage. "You reopened the wound. Why didn't you say anything?"

She clamped her mouth shut and looked away while he gently unwound the bandage.

It wasn't as bad as he'd first guessed, but somehow one of the stitches had pulled free. He dabbed away the blood with a handkerchief. "What did you do to it?"

"Nothing, I just... had some things to carry today. Too much for one hand."

He pressed his eyes shut and rubbed his forehead. Maybe he should have sent her to Dr. Greely. "Miss Marsden, I thought you knew not to use this finger while it was healing."

"I didn't use it."

He raised an eyebrow.

"I used the rest of my hand," she mumbled and looked away.

Maybe she wasn't as intelligent as he'd thought. It was one thing to be afraid of doctors, but quite another to behave in a way that would cause more injury to herself—especially if she wanted to see less of doctors. "It can't bear any weight. I don't know where you were earlier or why you were carrying something, but such slight movements now shouldn't be causing you pain. If your pinky hadn't been splinted and wrapped to your other finger, you would have rebroken it."

"So it's not rebroken?" A faint note of hope echoed through her voice.

"I don't know." There was no infection, but that was all he could determine with a visual examination. "Is the wound the only part that's hurting, or is your bone aching too?"

"My bone," she whispered.

"Did your finger hurt this badly when you woke up this morning?"

She squeezed her eyes shut, and a small whimper escaped.

"Did it?"

She shook her head.

"So it started after you carried something?"

"Yes."

"I'm going to remove the splint. Normally this wouldn't hurt, but in your situation…"

He gripped her wrist solidly with his left hand so she couldn't pull it away, then removed the splint and used his fingers to probe the bone. She gasped and, as he'd anticipated, tried to jerk her hand back. Why had she decided to carry something with this hand today? What had made her think she was healed enough to do so? It had been four days since the break, surely the bone still pained her even when it wasn't carrying weight.

Oh, why couldn't he be like Christ, healing people with a mere touch, no pain, no weeks of healing, no further trouble from the injury or illness. He held her hand in place and finished his tactile examination, ignoring her whimpers—or at least trying to.

But the moisture welling in her large hazel eyes didn't make it easy. Nor did the trembling in her delicate jaw.

"Did I rebreak it?" A tear rolled down her cheek.

He released her hand. "No, but you've overtaxed your injury. I can cut out the torn stitch and put another in, clean your skin, and put the splint back on your finger, but the one thing I can't do is keep your finger still and free of weight. You have to see to that part yourself, and if you want to keep your fifth finger, I strongly suggest you keep it immobilized and unstressed. Do you understand?"

"I'm sorry. I should have thought more before I started using my finger again."

He straightened from his hunched position. Half the women he treated would have swooned by now, but she stayed still, her back straight as she sat on the chair. Her face contorted into a mask of pain though she didn't voice a single complaint about it.

How foolish of him. Of course she'd be used to the pain. He glanced at her arm, well covered with its sleeve buttoned to the base of her hand. A person couldn't be bled that many times without learning to cope with a certain amount of pain.

And he was about to cause her more. He reached for the bottle of carbolic acid. If ever he'd been tempted to not clean a wound, it was now. But he couldn't risk infection. "This is going to sting, but as I said earlier, I need to cleanse the wound to keep infection from setting in."

"And I shouldn't move my finger even though that acid stuff hurts?"

"I'm sorry." And he truly was. "You don't want to upset the new bone growth, and your finger is vulnerable with the splint off."

She clenched her jaw, looked away, then pressed her eyes shut and drew in a short, asthmatic breath. "Do it."

Taking her hand in his once more, he swabbed the antiseptic onto her finger.

She hissed sharply, and a tear slipped between her tightly clamped eyelids.

"I know." He blew on her finger to lessen the burning, then reached for his scissors to snip away the torn stitch, which wasn't as easy as usual given the shaking in her hand. Her breathing had grown short again too. Did nervousness aggravate her asthma?

"I'm going to need to put another stitch in. Last time you were unconscious, but this time—"

"Just get it over with." She looked away again, hissing a half minute later when he pulled the needle and thread through her skin.

"There, the worst of it is done." As long as she didn't reinjure it again.

She blinked away a few more tears and stared down at her hand. "You said I didn't rebreak the bone, but is my finger going to be crooked after it heals?"

Crooked? What did she take him for, a charlatan? "No. When a bone is set correctly, no one can tell it has been broken."

"I knew someone in Chicago who walked with a limp. She said it happened as a child when she'd broken her leg and that the limp couldn't be helped."

He ran his gaze over her finger, the skin slightly puckered red where the remaining stitches poked through the healing wound. "The woman was likely mistaken and the physician who set the break did so incorrectly. A doctor familiar with orthopaedics probably could have prevented the limp. Once a bone grows incorrectly though, nothing can be done to straighten it."

"Orthopaedics." She rolled the word softly over her tongue.

"The study of bones, yes."

"And you said my bone is growing correctly even though it hurts?"

"Yes." He looked up into her eyes, round and soft. She really was quite lovely, in a delicate kind of way. If she hadn't just argued with him for twenty minutes about treating her finger, if she weren't terrified of doctors, if she didn't have two dozen scars on her arm to justify her fear, maybe...

No. He'd been down that path too many times before. He'd do better to hire a nurse than look for a wife. His past nurses had all stuck around for at least a couple years, which was more than he could say of the women he'd pursued.

"I... I haven't gotten a bill."

"You said you wouldn't pay one." He dabbed more carbolic acid onto her wound to clean it before putting a fresh bandage on.

She sucked in a fast, shallow breath when the yellow liquid met her cut. "That was for tonight. I'm talking about when I broke my finger."

"Don't worry about it."

"But you helped me. It's only fair that I pay you. For everything but the chloroform you tricked me about."

He pressed his lips together to keep from smiling and nestled her finger gently back into the splint. "I said it was fine, but I want to make you some willow bark tea before I go. You won't mind if I get some from my medical bag?"

She scowled. "As long as you truly give me the willow bark and not something else."

She wasn't going to let him forget that anytime soon, was she? This time, the side of his lips inched up into a half smile while he bandaged her fourth and fifth fingers together. Then he straightened and headed toward the kettle on the stove. "I'll only give you willow bark tea tonight, I promise."

She rolled her eyes. "As though the promise of a doctor means anything."

He laughed. "Maybe not the promise of all doctors, but a few of us know what we're about."

She held out her hand in front of her, twisting it at the wrist a bit. "When will you be back to check my finger again?"

"I'll need to remove most of the stitches in about three days' time." He moved to the sink and pumped water into the kettle.

"Are you sure you don't want money? You're right, I'm certainly not fond of doctors, but I'd be a fool to deny that you've helped me. And, well, thank you."

He stilled, his hand with the kettle hovering above the stove. What had that admission cost her? He looked over his shoulder at the slender young woman hunched in her chair, her shoulders slumped with weariness and eyelids drooped with both exhaustion and pain. But rather than complain about any of those things, she thanked him.

Oh yes, another time, another place, without whatever had happened to put those scars on her arm, she'd have been a woman worth pursuing.

Chapter Seven

"What in tarnation is that?" Elijah stopped, one foot on the bank's step and another on the dusty road, and blinked as Doc Harrington lugged a long wooden contraption down the road.

"It's a leg splint." The doc paused and drew in a breath, his chest heaving, and it was little wonder why, considering the size of the thing he was carrying.

"A leg splint."

The doc dabbed at his brow with his handkerchief. "What else could it be?"

What else, indeed. "Never would have guessed."

"Really?" Dr. Harrington frowned at him. "It's for a femur fracture, not a tibia or fibula fracture. See, this part here straps over the pelvis, and then the wood stretches down the length of the leg, of course. But the pulley on the end is for traction, so I can straighten the bone to see that it sets properly. Don't you remember this? I used it on Victoria's father when he broke both his femur and his tibia in the shipwreck."

"Ah, I was a little out of it that night, if you recall."

The doc merely blinked at him, then looked back down at the splint and wiped some dust from one of the straps.

"Did someone break their leg? Do you need me to help you carry it?" Elijah glanced at the sun over the water. He didn't have much time to see Ranulfson before he had to report to the saw mill, but as much as he didn't want to put off his meeting another day, if someone had broken their leg, then—

"No, no." Seth waved him off. "No one broke their leg, at least not recently, which is why I have to mail this to Washington D.C."

"You're going to mail that?" He nearly sounded like a girl with the way his voice squeaked. Who mailed a four-foot-long wooden contraption with a pulley at the end?

"To a doctor at the Marine Hospital Service, yes."

"Will the post even take it?"

The doc scowled. "They'd better. I sent diagrams last week, but letters are easy to ignore. An actual splint, on the other hand, would have to get the Surgeon General's attention, don't you agree?"

Surgeon who? But it hardly mattered. It's not like he understood half the medical stuff Seth Harrington talked about. Nobody in town did, not even Doc Greely—which wasn't really saying much.

Dr. Harrington stood there looking at him, eyebrows raised as though he expected an answer about a surgeon person living in a big fancy city.

"Ah, well... yes. Um, definitely? Maybe."

Dr. Harrington scowled again.

"So do you want help carrying it to the mercantile?" He still didn't really have time, but he couldn't withdraw his offer without being rude. Plus it just might be worth lugging the thing through town to see the look on Mr. Foley's face when the doctor walked in the door and said he needed to mail it.

"No, no. I can handle it. It's not heavy so much as awkward, and I'm sure you're busy."

"Well, ah... good luck." He turned and headed up the stairs to the bank, letting the door bang closed behind him before the doc could change his mind. If Ranulfson wasn't in a meeting, then he still had enough time to see the bank owner before heading to the sawmill.

Indeed, a minute later he found himself walking into the fancy office with upholstered chairs, a soft rug, and framed certificates hanging on the walls. Not that hanging certificates on a wall had ever made much sense to him, but maybe he'd see things differently if he owned a bank rather than a fishing boat.

"Elijah, what can I do for you today?" Ernest Ranulfson set his pen down and leaned back in his chair.

Elijah closed the office door behind him. "The town needs to do something about Sheriff Jenkins."

Ranulfson raised an eyebrow. "Do we now? And what would you have us do?"

"Find a new sheriff. The one we have is acting more like a sot than a lawman." As chairman of the town council, Ernest Ranulfson was in the best position to make sure the sheriff did his job.

"While I might agree that Sheriff Jenkins is no longer as good at performing his duties as he once was, he's an elected official. The council can't simply remove him because we're getting complaints. People need to vote him out of office."

Elijah braced himself on the front of the desk. "That should be easy enough. Who wants a sheriff that smiles and waves while a woman is being assaulted?"

Ranulfson straightened, his clean-shaven face growing as dark as storm clouds over Lake Superior. "Someone assaulted a woman while Jenkins watched?"

"Victoria was coming home after dark a week ago, when a man confronted her in front of The Pretty Penny. She says he was drunk and didn't realize who she was, that she tried explaining she wasn't part of what went on inside the brothel, but she also said our good old sheriff was sitting on the front porch, watching. She called to him for help, but evidently he was too drunk to realize what was happening."

The color that had crept across the banker's face drained away. "Is she all right?"

Elijah stared at the shiny finish on the wooden desk beneath his hands. "She is, but only because she hit the lout over the head with her lantern. Said she left him lying unconscious in the street. Evidently Dr. Greely, who was also on the porch with Jenkins, was too drunk to get up and help him."

A hint of color returned to the man's stark features. "I had no idea. Why did you take so long to come to me?"

Did the man think he could amble into the bank whenever he pleased? He was only here today because he'd stopped fishing early, giving himself a half hour before he had to report to the sawmill. "I tried taking the situation to Jenkins first. Three times."

"Let me guess, he didn't remember what you were saying and claimed you were making the story up." Ranulfson rubbed his forehead.

"I take it I'm not the only one to have this trouble?"

"This is the first time I've heard of him refusing to defend a woman, but there have been other complaints."

"What about?"

"Money." Ranulfson withdrew a paper from the top drawer of his desk and handed him a list of a half dozen names. "A few people in Eagle Harbor claim they've been robbed, but since the amount is always under five dollars and there doesn't seem to be any repeat robberies, the sheriff refuses to do much."

Elijah glanced at the names, then handed the list back. "Except the robberies are repeating, just not with the same person."

"Correct."

"A little money here and there almost sounds like a kid."

"Or an adult who doesn't want to arouse suspicion. Since our sheriff refuses to pursue the incidents, there's not much I can do." Ranulfson returned the paper to his drawer.

"So what *can* we do?" Elijah crossed his legs and leaned against the desk.

"Unless you plan to run against him in November, nothing."

"You want me to be town sheriff?" How would he do that? "Not only would I have to give up fishing, I'd have to stay in town to keep tabs on all the drunk sailors during storms rather than go out on my rescues, and I wouldn't have evenings to spend with Victoria either."

"Yes, well that seems to be the problem." Ranulfson picked a pencil up off his desk and fiddled with it. "The sheriff's hours aren't exactly appealing, and he hasn't had a raise since he's taken the job."

"But Jenkins is the only sheriff our town's ever had." And he'd used to be a good one, before he spent more time drinking than he did enforcing the law. "So that means he makes…?"

"A dollar a day."

Elijah cringed. How did the man feed himself on that kind of pay, let alone have money to go to The Pretty Penny? "You need to raise his salary."

"And what do we use to pay him? There's no room in the budget to increase the sheriff's salary, at least not without raising taxes."

"So that leaves us…?"

"With Harold Jenkins still serving as our town sheriff."

"You can't leave him in that position, not when women are being assaulted. Victoria got away, but what if the next woman doesn't? Or what if the next attacker is more than a friendly drunk?"

Ranulfson drew in a breath and let it out on a long sigh. "Should I leave him in that position? No. But I don't have a choice. If you want things to change, perhaps you should tell a few more people what happened to your wife."

His mouth grew dry. Though Victoria had been more frightened than harmed, there was no reason to spread the news that some strange man had hung on her and tried to force her inside the brothel. "That wouldn't solve anything."

"Maybe if enough people feel the sheriff isn't doing his job, we can implement a slight tax increase to raise the sheriff's salary and then find a different man for the position. But until the town finds a way to increase its revenue…" Ranulfson raised his hands in a helpless gesture. "We're stuck with the sheriff we have."

"Thanks for your time," Elijah muttered before he headed to the door. All the hassle he'd gone through to see Ranulfson, and what were his choices in the end? Tell everyone about his wife's attack or deal with a sheriff who'd let it happen again, perhaps with even worse consequences the next time.

~.~.~.~.~

"Lindy, I'm so sorry about your finger. I made Claire scrub the floor as punishment, and that girl isn't getting any candy until Christmas." Jessalyn tucked her teeth between her lips, her angelically blue eyes moist. "She felt really bad about what happened. We all did. I should have been paying better attention to her."

"Don't be too hard on yourselves. I didn't mind everything my ma said when I was little either." Lindy set the stack of clothing she'd mended on a table already heaped with clothes in the cluttered seamstress's shop. "I only wish I could stitch faster with my finger."

"I'm amazed you can stitch at all." Jessalyn pulled a pair of rough woolen trousers off the top of the stack and examined the stitching. "This looks excellent."

Lindy wiggled her bandaged finger—at least as much as the splint would allow. "It takes longer than normal, but it's not as though I hold the needle with my little finger, and I don't have anything else to do."

Unless she counted taking food to the O'Byrnes, but she couldn't afford to do that if she wasn't mending.

Jessalyn folded the trousers and set them back atop the pile, then peered at Lindy's finger. "Dr. Harrington expects you to make a full recovery? I'm glad he was able to set the bone. I can't imagine what would have happened if Dr. Greely..." She pressed a hand to her mouth, her face pale. "Oh dear. Some things are best left unsaid, aren't they?"

Lindy tamped down an urge to shudder. "A full recovery, yes."

"How much was his bill? I insist on paying every penny."

"No." The woman might have more work than she knew what to do with, but she was also raising three daughters on her own. They couldn't have much extra money.

"It's only right. If my daughter wouldn't have misbehaved, there'd be no need to pay Dr. Harrington." Jessalyn stepped over a bag of buttons on the floor and around a pile of scrap fabric as she headed to the shelf in the corner where a money box sat—along with lace, more buttons, more fabric, and several piles of odds and ends Lindy couldn't begin to categorize. "Here. I'll pay you for the mending you just returned too."

"You can give me money for the mending." She'd never be able to accuse Jessalyn of not paying her promptly. "But Dr. Harrington refuses to give me a bill, so I don't need your money for that. Truly."

"He hasn't given you a bill, even after a week's time?" Jessalyn tilted her head to the side. "That's interesting."

Lindy dug the toe of her shoe into a crack in the floor. "It's not like that. He feels sorry for me—I think."

"Well, he's a good man, that's for sure. And there aren't many of them in Copper Country. Aren't many of them anywhere, actually."

"I'm sure he's a fine man." After his visit to check on her finger, how could she say anything else? Well, except for him being a doctor. And him tricking her with chloroform.

73

"Are you sure there's not another reason he's treating you for free?" Jessalyn raised an eyebrow. "Like maybe he wants to put a ring on one of your fingers instead of a bandage?"

How ridiculous. Seth Harrington couldn't possibly have designs on her, not when he knew how terrified she was of him. "You misunderstand. I'm not in the market for a husband."

Jessalyn closed the money box with a metallic thunk. "Well, that makes two of us—and probably the only two in the whole of Copper Country."

It did? Was there some reason Jessalyn didn't want to remarry? With three girls to care for, it seemed the easiest solution to her troubles, and she'd just admitted Dr. Harrington was a good man. Maybe the two of them could...

"Can you take more mending this afternoon?" Jessalyn waved a hand absently around the cluttered space that served as her seamstress shop. "The work just keeps coming. Last night I had five Cousin Jacks drop mending off, and Mrs. Ranulfson ordered another dress just a few minutes before you came—plus she's wondering where the mending she dropped off last week is. Now if only I could find where I put it. I did do it, didn't I?" She glanced around the room, her forehead furrowed.

"Send me with however much you need finished." At least she didn't have to worry about losing her job, even if she couldn't sew as much as usual.

Jessalyn picked her way back across the shop and handed her a crisp five dollar bill. "This is for the mending, but if Dr. Harrington changes his mind about the bill, you bring it straight to me, yes?" Jessalyn gave her a stern glare.

Lindy smiled. "I'm not your daughter, Jessalyn. That look won't work on me."

Jessalyn's shoulders rose and fell on a sigh. "Perhaps not, but it's not right for you to pay for the harm my daughter caused. Promise you'll bring me the bill if Dr. Harrington gives you one."

"All right. I promise."

"Good." Jessalyn glanced around the shop. "Since that's settled, it's time for you to learn how to work the sewing machine."

"The sewing machine? I'm happy to keep mending by hand." She didn't have a choice if she wanted to work when she was sick, and though she'd been healthy since moving to Eagle Harbor a few weeks ago, another sickness was coming—they always did.

"The machine is much quicker, and with that finger slowing you down, now is the perfect time."

There was no way she'd be able to come to the shop and work when she was feverish and coughing and struggling for each breath she took. Right now Jessalyn gave her mending whenever she stopped by, but if she learned to sew on the machine, would that change? Would Jessalyn not want to keep her employed when she was sick? "I'd rather not, if it's all the same."

"Oh, don't be foolish." Jessalyn waved her hand, as though an action that simple could make Lindy's lung ailment disappear. "Sewing on a machine is a useful skill to have. One day you might even own a machine of your own."

And there she was, back at her list of things she might do one day.

One day, I'll be a teacher like my mother, grandmother, great-grandmother, and so on.

One day, I'll have a husband to hold me close and whisper words of love in my ear.

One day, I'll have some children of my own.

One day, I'll have a sewing machine.

Except she wasn't going to live long enough to see all those things done. Her mother had only lasted seven years with her lung ailment, and Lindy had already used up four sickly years of her own. Seeing that the O'Byrnes were provided for until their father returned was a better dream to have. At least that one had a chance of being fulfilled.

"Come on." Jessalyn stepped back around the sack of buttons sitting in the middle of the floor and headed toward the monstrous looking machine. "The girls are playing upstairs, and this will only take a minute."

The girls were here? She'd neither seen nor heard them this entire time. "Are you sure you don't need to check on the children first?"

Jessalyn looked up at the ceiling. "Now that I think of it, they're being awful quiet."

"Honestly, Jessalyn, I have no idea how you manage a seamstress shop plus three girls on your own." Even if the shop was so disorganized she needed a map to walk from one side to the other.

Jessalyn's jaw turned hard, her shoulders rigid. "Yes, well, there are some things a man doesn't explain when he stands before the altar. Like how that 'till death do us part' bit really only means 'till I get bored with my wife and think I can earn a bigger fortune out west'."

Lindy winced. That was why Jessalyn didn't have a husband? She'd assumed the woman was a widow, though she'd not exactly asked about it. "I'm sorry."

"Why?" Jessalyn's voice was sharp, her normally sweet disposition gone like steam disappearing above a boiling pot. "It's not as though you had anything to do with Thomas leaving."

Jessalyn yanked some fabric off the shelf near the sewing machine, then huffed. "You're right. I need to go check on the girls, but you can look at the machine while I'm gone. Maybe try putting a seam in some of this scrap fabric. Just pump the treadle underneath to make the needle go."

Jessalyn marched toward the stairs in the back corner of the shop, nearly tripping over a pile of fabric scraps on the way.

Lindy glanced at the door leading outside. She should probably go if she didn't want to learn how to work the machine. But Jessalyn hadn't given her any more sewing yet, and she couldn't walk away without work for this evening.

Maybe she could find a project to busy herself with while she waited, a simple tear to mend in a shanty boy's shirt or the like. But where did she find an easy sewing job amid the piles of disorganized clothes?

She sighed and picked her way across the shop toward the sewing machine—because she had nothing better to do, not because she was curious.

A rose-colored dress hung on a hanger from the ceiling. She reached out and fingered the silky fabric trimmed with lace. Had Jessalyn made this on the machine? It was prettier than any of the premade dresses sold in the mercantile.

Maybe if she survived the next bout of her lung illness and was able to save enough money hand-stitching garments for Jessalyn, she'd purchase a machine for herself. She took the skirt of the dress in her hand and raised the soft fabric to her cheek. With a machine like this, she could make new pants for Jack O'Byrne in a few hours' time.

A crash sounded upstairs, followed by a thumping and then a trampling of feet on the stairs as a flurry of girls descended. Jessalyn tromped down the stairs behind the girls, flyaway strands of hair sticking out from what had been a neat bun when she'd left a few minutes ago. "Do you mind taking a walk with us while we finish our conversation? Olivia has another earache, and we need to visit Dr. Harrington."

Dr. Harrington? The man may have helped her finger, but she wasn't going to voluntarily meet with him. "Actually, my finger's rather sore, so I'd better go home and rest it. Maybe you could give me the clothes from the Cousin Jacks and I can start them tonight?"

"No, no. I remember now that I didn't do the work for Mrs. Ranulfson last week." Jessalyn turned around in her shop once, then twice. "If only I can find where I... oh yes, here." She headed to the back wall and came away with a stack of fancy garments.

"Thank you." Lindy took them while Jessalyn corralled the two younger girls out the door, their giggles as light and fluffy as the handful of clouds floating overhead, while the oldest one followed with her head tilted to the side and a hand pressed to her right ear.

"Don't get too far ahead," Jessalyn called, though that seemed to only convince the two little ones to race past the shop's windows.

"I'll be back with these tomorrow morning." Lindy lifted the stack of clothing in her arms while Jessalyn held the door open for her.

"Thank you so much." Jessalyn offered her a quick smile, then grabbed Olivia's free hand and hastened down the street after her other girls.

Lindy blew out a breath as she headed in the opposite direction. She had no doctor's bills and more work, which meant she'd have money to take supplies to the O'Byrnes soon. Now if her lung illness would just hold off until their father returned...

Chapter Eight

"What's wrong with him?" Lindy dropped the sack of supplies on the cabin's rickety table and headed straight to the blanket along the wall on which little Toby lay.

"I don't know." Jenny knelt beside him, her face lined with worry as she lay a cloth over the boy's brow. "He was fine yesterday, but he started with the fever during the night."

The little boy mumbled something before shaking the rag off his head and rolling over, only to roll back the other direction a moment later.

"Calm down, Toby. I'm just trying to help." Jenny spoke smoothly, her tone so gentle it seemed impossible this was the same woman from Lindy's other visits.

"Does he have a rash, or is his face red from the fever?" She didn't need to be a doctor to know the signs of scarlet fever—or what that would portend for the entire family.

Jenny bit her lip, her dark hair hanging in tangled strands around her face. "I don't know."

"Have you given him some water?"

Moisture appeared in the other woman's wide brown eyes, but she blinked it away and nodded to the cup at the end of the pallet. "I keep trying to get him to drink, but he refuses."

She glanced around the cabin. "There must be some miasmas nearby."

Jenny swiped a tangled strand of hair away from her face. "Is that what's making him sick? A miasma?"

"It's what makes everybody sick." If she'd heard it once, she'd heard it a thousand times. She was coughing, feverish, and bedridden because there was a miasma in the air, or maybe because she had weak lungs and was more susceptible to miasmas than most people. "Was he playing outside yesterday? There must be some foul air close by. Once Jack and Alice get back, you'll probably want to keep them inside lest they get it too."

Jenny worried her bottom lip again. "Then how will Jack snare rabbits and squirrels?"

"I don't know, but he won't be able to snare rabbits if he's sick either." Lindy ran her eyes over little Toby, his dark lashes fluttering restlessly against his flushed face. "I can stay here for a few hours if that will help you."

"Yes, I haven't had a chance to get lunch on, and Alice and Jack will be hungry when they get back."

Lindy looked over her shoulder at the half loaf of bread sitting on the table. "I see the bread has been helpful."

Jenny handed the cool rag to her, then ducked her head. "Maybe I was a little harsh on you for trying to help. Thank you for the food, and for staying today."

A lump rose in Lindy's throat, and she looked away lest her own eyes grow moist. "I lived in a shack not much different from this in Chicago. Others helped me when I was in need, it only seems right to help you in return."

She stayed for several hours, until the crickets began their evening song and the forest grew dim with the waning sunlight. She bathed Toby's forehead and tried getting him to drink, but he only grew worse, his skin so hot it burned to the touch and his face so red she was no longer certain whether the color was due to a simple fever or scarlet fever.

"There's a doctor in Eagle Harbor." Lindy spoke softly so as not to awaken Toby from where he slept fitfully in her arms. "He treated my finger when I broke it, and I'm sure he'd—"

"No." The knife Jenny was using to cut carrots hit the table with a forceful *thwack.* "No one can know where we live."

"I don't like the look of him." Jack set a bowl on the table. "If Ma were alive, she'd—"

"But Ma's not alive, is she? Pa wouldn't want a doctor here, and you know it."

"Miss Lindy?" Alice crept toward the blanket where she sat. "Is Toby going to die like Ma?"

Lindy pressed her eyes shut for a moment. If only she could speak the words the girl wanted to hear. "I don't know."

"I don't want him to die." The girl's little jaw trembled. "I love him."

"And he shouldn't be expected to die." Jack set a pile of spoons on the table with a clatter. "Not when there's a doctor that might help."

Jenny sliced the last of the carrots and turned to look at Toby, her jaw set in a rigid line.

"He's getting worse. I wouldn't lie about that." Lindy propped the child's head up with her arm, held the cup of water to his lips, and tried to coax some liquid down his throat. But he still refused to swallow, letting the water dribble down his face to dampen his shirt instead.

"What if I carry him to Eagle Harbor?" Jack swiped a tear from his cheek. "Then Toby can still get help, and the doc won't know where we live."

"Dr. Harrington is a good doctor." Lindy stilled. What had she just said? She'd never expected to hear those words out of her mouth, but Seth Harrington wasn't like most doctors. If anyone could help, it was him.

Jenny crossed her arms over herself in a lonely hug. "We don't have the money."

"What about that bit Pa left us in case…?"

Jenny gave Jack a sharp look.

"He treated my finger for free," Lindy spoke into the quiet cabin, even though I offered to pay. I'm sure if I explained, he'd—"

"I told you before, we don't need charity."

"He might be dying, Jenny, and that's all you can say? *We don't need charity.*" Jack mimicked his sister in a high-pitched voice, though his words carried a cruel edge. "You're willing to let him die because he'd be charity?"

"I agree with Jack." Lindy tucked a blanket around Toby and shifted him to the floor before standing. "Your brother needs help, and if you won't let us carry him to town, then I'll bring Dr. Harrington back whether you want me to or not."

Jenny looked between her and Jack, her bottom lip caught between her teeth once more, then she threw up her hands and scowled. "Fine. Take him. But only on the condition that Jack doesn't leave the woods. I don't want him going into town, do you understand?"

Jack rolled his eyes. "Yes, Jenny, I know. You don't want anyone to see me."

Lindy frowned. "But how will you know how Toby fares?"

"Think up a meeting place on your way to town and give Jack a report tomorrow." Jenny jabbed a finger at her. "And don't you dare think you can bring someone back to the cabin, not ever."

~.~.~.~.~

The pounding woke him. Blinking, Seth rolled out of bed, pulled on his dressing gown, and headed into the kitchen.

The banging sounded again, louder and faster this time.

"I'm coming." He lit the lantern on the hutch, then hastened the last few steps to the back door, and swung it open.

"You're not going to bleed him if I let you help, are you?" Lindy Marsden heaved a wheezy, labored breath, her eyes pleading in the darkness. "You told me you didn't bleed your patients."

Of all the people who might need his help, he'd never expected a late night visit from the woman who despised his profession. Yet she stood before him now with a child in her arms, her hair falling down from her updo to hang in wild tresses about her shoulders, and her chest heaving with exertion.

He reached out and slid his arms beneath the boy, then lifted him from her arms. The heat from the child's burning skin radiated into his body. "I won't bleed him. Now what's wrong?"

"He has a fever."

As though that wasn't obvious. "When did it start?" He turned and headed into the kitchen, leaving Miss Marsden to follow.

"Last night, according to his sister. But it's been getting worse all day, and then on the way here, he started shaking. He was lying in my arms, and he just started shaking."

Did that mean he had a seizure? Hopefully not, but the temperature of the boy's skin made that the most likely scenario. "You've been caring for him since earlier today?"

"Yes."

The boy chose that moment to start convulsing, his eyelids fluttering while his arms and legs jerked. Seth gathered the child closer to his chest and held him until the seizure subsided, his own heart thumping in time with the spasmodic jerking.

He gestured to the wooden wash tub sitting beside the sink. "He needs a cold bath."

"A cold bath?"

He didn't have time for questions, not if he wanted to prevent another seizure. "Can you drag that tub out and start filling it?"

"Of course." Despite her wheezing lungs and shallow breaths, she flew into motion, scraping the tub across the floor and frantically pumping water from the sink into a bucket before emptying the bucket into the tub. "Do I need to boil some water, or is it all supposed to be cold?"

The boy started shaking again.

"There isn't time to boil any." Most places, water direct from the pump was sufficient to bring down a fever, but water in the cold, copper-laden stretch of Michigan called Copper Country came out of the ground so frigid it could cause hypothermia if someone was immersed too long. Normally, he'd heat a little to make the cold bath more comfortable, but that was if he treated a patient *before* they were having fever-induced seizures.

When the seizure passed, Seth lay the child on the floor and removed his shirt. His skin was red and flushed, but his chest and face didn't have the rash that went along with scarlet fever—yet. Still, the child's skin was so warm, heat from his little body pulsed through the air.

"Is he going to be all right?" Miss Marsden's voice was high, her breaths still too shallow for his liking. "Don't tell me he…?"

"Just keep filling the bath," he barked a little rougher than intended.

Her gaze half on the boy, she sloshed another pail of water into the tub a bit too quickly, causing the water to splash up and soak his dressing gown and her shirtwaist and skirt.

"I'm so sorry," she pressed a hand to her mouth, a horrified look on her face.

The icy cold of the water chilled his skin, and he shivered.

"Just keep filling the tub." He peeked over the edge. "Another two buckets should do it. Then I have some women's clothes in the small sick room if you'd like to change."

He divested the boy of his short pants and picked him back up before easing him into the tub.

When his skin touched the water, the child's eyes sprang open and he loosed a scream.

"There now." Seth forced a calmness to his voice that lay at odds with the rapid thumping of his heart. "We've got to cool you down a bit."

The boy didn't talk, just started sobbing. Seth's dressing gown got only wetter as the child scrambled to get out of the water.

"I'm sorry son, but you've got to go in farther." He inched the boy deeper into the tub but still not all the way to the bottom.

Miss Marsden returned from the sink, looking about ready to cry herself as she poured another bucket into the tub. "Is he going to be all right?"

"The water woke him. That's a good sign."

She sniffled and turned back to fill the pail once more.

"Heat a couple kettles of water next." He raised his voice to be heard over the boy's crying. "The longer I can keep him in the bath, the better, but the water shouldn't be this cold for long."

She nodded and dumped the last pail of cold water into the tub. When he tried easing the boy farther into the frigid water, he screamed again and cried even harder. But if his body temperature was going to drop, then his chest needed to be submerged.

Seth held him in place, even as Miss Marsden filled the kettle for the stove and opened the firebox to lay kindling. With a fire only now flickering to life, it would be a quarter hour or more before the water was hot enough to do any good.

"Jenny," the boy sobbed, his cries finally calming enough to be understandable. "I want Jenny."

Seth looked to Miss Marsden. "Who is Jenny?"

"His older sister. She takes care of him."

"Where is she?"

"She can't come right now." Miss Marsden set a bigger log on the fire.

"Did you send word? Surely she'll come if she knows her brother—"

She blanched and turned toward the stove, blowing on the little flame to coax the fire higher. "She knows and refused to bring him, so I did."

He looked between the boy and her. "How do you—?"

"Is he cool enough now? How long does he need to stay in there?"

The child had gone from wailing to shivering, his eyes now closed though he wasn't incoherent like he'd been before. "Do you know where the large sickroom is?" He nodded toward the doorway that led from the kitchen into the parlor where his patients waited when they came during normal hours. "I've got some blankets in the chest in the corner. Bring me two of those."

He lifted the boy from the tub as she left the room and dried him with a towel, never mind his dressing gown got even wetter in the process. The child's skin was still warm, but not searing hot like before.

When Miss Marsden returned with the blankets, he removed his dressing gown and hung it by the fire. It wouldn't do to get the blankets wet while carrying the boy to bed. He should change into trousers and a shirt anyway if he was going to be treating a patient all night. "What's his name?"

"Toby." Miss Marsden bent to check the fire once more.

"Toby," he repeated as he stroked a finger over the small, flushed cheek. "Keep heating the water. I'll give him several more baths before the night is done to make sure he doesn't start seizing again."

"Seizing? Is that what you call his convulsions?"

"The medical name is seizure, yes. They can happen for multiple reasons, one being that a person's body gets too hot."

"So cooling them down will stop the seizures?" Her gaze moved from the tub to the boy and back again.

"When they're caused by a high body temperature, a cold bath can be effective, yes."

She nodded, then tilted her head to the side as though almost frightened to speak her next words. "Thank you for helping, especially in the middle of the night like this."

Had she expected he wouldn't? He sighed. Maybe he didn't want the answer to that. "You're welcome. I'll lay him in the same room where you were after you broke your finger, and I'll give him another bath in about an hour."

She gave no indication that she heard him, instead busying herself with blowing on the fire again.

He left the kitchen and headed into the dark parlor before entering the small sickroom. The boy had fallen soundly back to sleep, not uncommon after having seizures. Moving around the room in the darkness, he laid the boy on the bed, then slid his hands through the folds of the blankets to feel the boy's chest. Still hot, but not dangerously so.

A knocking sound resonated through the room, and he stilled.

Not another one. Please, God, not another one.

His heartbeat, only just calming from the race to get the boy cooled down, ratcheted back up. Maybe the boy did have scarlet fever but wasn't showing the rash yet. Another child with the same symptoms could only mean one thing.

He hastened through the parlor and into the kitchen, only to stop short at the sight of the town banker standing inside the door and staring at Miss Marsden. Her hair was now completely fallen around her shoulders, and her shirtwaist untucked from her skirt, both of which were still half soaked.

Oh no. No. No. No. No. No.

He stepped forward and spoke in the most professional voice he could manage. "Mr. Ranulfson, is there something I can help you with?"

The banker's eyes moved to him, and he narrowed his gaze, accusation practically leaping across the room.

Despite the fire, the room felt suddenly cool, which was of course due to his standing there in nothing but his wet nightshirt.

"We can explain…"

"My patient was having fever induced seizures and…" He and Miss Marsden spoke at the same time.

"No need." Mr. Ranulfson held up his hand. "I've seen quite enough." He spun on his heel, and the door slammed behind him.

"Did he say what he wanted?" Seth looked at Miss Marsden, his heart now pounding with a fear that had nothing to do with Toby's welfare.

She stared down at herself, as though only then stopping to take in her disheveled appearance. "Something about cough syrup for his wife."

Of course, getting dressed and heading out into the night was probably easier than listening to Betty Ranulfson complain about her cough until morning.

Miss Marsden crossed her arms over her middle. "You don't think he'll…?"

Ernest Ranulfson? The man married to the biggest gossip in town? Yes, he did think. In fact, he'd bet his medical practice on it.

Chapter Nine

"Lindy, are you awake?"

Lindy fluttered her eyes open, then rolled over and groaned. What was Victoria doing in her room? Hadn't she moved out of the Cummingses?

The bed moved with the weight of someone sitting beside her. "Are you all right?"

"I'd be better if you let me sleep," she mumbled into her pillow.

"We heard about what happened last night." Aileen's Irish voice floated through the room.

"Too tired," she muttered, then pressed her eyes closed again.

Wait. Last night. Toby. The fever. She sat up in bed and threw off the covers, planting her feet on the wooden floor warm from the fire in the bakery kitchen beneath her room.

How long had she slept? Never mind. She needed to get to Dr. Harrington's. He'd sent her home as soon as Mr. Ranulfson had left last night, saying he'd stay up and deal with Toby since it wasn't proper to have her in the office. She hadn't wanted to leave Toby's side, but she couldn't exactly take the boy home only for him to have more seizures.

She stepped to the wall where her clothing hung on pegs and quickly exchanged her nightgown for her shift.

"Tell me he didn't…" Aileen reached out and grabbed her arm before she could finish dressing.

Lindy glanced down at the scars starting above her wrist and climbing all the way to her shoulder. "They're nothing you haven't seen before."

She and Aileen had been sharing a room ever since they'd left Chicago, and scars such as those on her arm weren't easily hidden. The one on her leg, however, was another story.

"W-what are those?" Victoria whispered from where she sat on the bed, looking entirely too lovely in her pearls and blue silk dress.

Lindy pulled her arm away from Aileen. "My aunt took a liking to a doctor who insisted bleeding me would cure my lungs."

"Is that why you hate d-d-doctors so much?" Victoria asked. "I thought it was simply—"

"I don't see any bruises," Aileen ran her gaze down Lindy with enough scrutiny she just might be able to see through her shift to the scar on her leg.

Lindy pulled her dress over her head and plunged her arms into the long sleeves that she wore even in the dead of summer. "Why would I have bruises?"

"If a man is too forceful with a woman…" Aileen's face flushed. "I always had bruises afterwards, is all."

"After…?" She swallowed. Why were they talking about what had happened to Aileen in Chicago? Aileen had nothing to fear in Eagle Harbor. And she didn't have time for this conversation, not with Toby waiting.

"Oh, Aileen." Victoria scurried around the side of the bed and wrapped Aileen in a hug.

Aileen stiffened, but that only convinced Victoria to tighten her embrace.

Thankfully Victoria was here to handle Aileen's worries. Lindy bent to lace her boots. She'd make time to talk with Aileen later today, after she got back from Dr. Harrington's. Surely Aileen would understand why she had to run out once Aileen learned about Toby's seizures.

"I'll see you later." She straightened and headed for the door.

"Lindy, wait." Victoria released Aileen from her hug and scampered after her. "We n-need to know what happened."

"What happened? In Chicago? Hasn't Aileen told you?" And if not, why was Victoria asking her when Aileen stood not three feet away? "I'm sorry, but I don't have time to talk this morning. Maybe after lunch?"

Depending on how Toby was, of course. *Oh, dear God, let the boy be improving, not growing sicker.*

Dr. Harrington would have come for her if Toby got worse, wouldn't he?

She darted down the stairs and into the bakery kitchen. Ellie stood at the counter mixing batter. Her face so flushed from the heat of the kitchen that her freckles disappeared.

She waved at Ellie as she headed for the back door. "Good morning."

A hand gripped her arm so abruptly she swung around, only to find herself face to face with Victoria.

"Would you stay still for a moment and talk to us!" The color was rising on Victoria's face too, but something told her it wasn't due to the warmth from the oven. "We want to know what happened between you and Seth Harrington last night."

"Me and Seth Harrington?" She looked between Victoria and Aileen, both of whom had apparently trailed her down the stairs, Victoria in her fancy silk and Aileen in a shirtwaist and skirt as worn and threadbare as Lindy's. "That's why you're here?"

"He didn't force her." Aileen pointed to her arms. "It's as I said upstairs. There would be bruises if he had."

The mixing spoon in Ellie's hand clattered to the counter. "So the rumors are true? You and the doctor were together?"

"What are you talking about? What rumors?" She looked around the room, but all three of her friends stared back at her as though expecting a beanstalk to sprout from her head, or her face to turn blue and fall off, or some other bizarre calamity to befall her right then and there. "Dr. Harrington helped me treat a child last night. That's all."

Victoria crossed her arms over her chest. "Not according to Mr. Ranulfson."

She took a step back. It couldn't be true. Yes, Mr. Ranulfson had seen them together, but a simple conversation would clear up any confusion about why she'd been with the doctor last night.

Unless the rumor was already around town.

But how many people could a person gossip with in the space of a few hours?

"Well…" Ellie bent to retrieve her mixing spoon. "Tell us what happened."

A lump started in her chest and rose into her throat, so large and hard she could barely speak around it. "The doctor and I weren't together like that. Toby was seizing because of his fever. If Mr. Ranulfson said anything different, it's because he stormed off without asking us what was going on."

"Who's Toby?"

"What's a seizure?"

Lindy threw up her hands. "I don't have time for this. If you want answers, come to Dr. Harrington's with me."

Aileen's eyes widened. "Ye're goin' back there after what happened?"

"Nothing happened that should keep me away from a sick boy."

"There's a sick boy?" Of course that was the thing Victoria latched onto.

"Who else do you think Toby is?" Lindy turned for the door, escaping into the alley before anyone could stop her.

"Were you in your n-nightclothes?" Victoria followed behind her.

"Of course not."

"That's not the story I heard from one of the men who came to the bakery this mornin'." Aileen rushed to keep up with her as they rounded the side of the building and started down Center Street.

"We had to cool Toby down, and some water splashed on me and made me look bedraggled." She rushed around a slow-moving wagon laden with hay and skirted a trio of sailors headed toward the bakery, never mind the growing tightness in her lungs at the quick pace she kept. "I think my shirtwaist came untucked, but I wasn't in my dressing gown or nightclothes."

"That's n-not the story I heard either." Victoria walked ahead of them, her steps somehow dignified and elegant despite her quick pace. "Tell me Dr. Harrington was dressed. Tell me that part is false too."

She tamped down the dread welling in her stomach. At the moment she needed to get to Toby and see how he was, not dwell on any of this. Besides, Dr. Harrington had probably already set the story straight. If Toby was well, maybe the doctor had even gone to visit Mr. Ranulfson to further explain things. "We weren't thinking about how we were dressed. We were just trying to cool Toby down."

"I don't think anyone cares what ye were tryin' to do, leastways not with Mr. Ranulfson tellin' such a different tale. I heard tell of what happened three times over already, and none of those rumors match what ye say."

The dread swirled in her stomach again. This was just a simple matter of setting the record straight, wasn't it? She hadn't done anything wrong, and neither had Dr. Harrington. "Are… are you sure everybody knows?"

"It's all right, dear." Victoria patted her arm. "We'll find a way through it."

She looked down at her shoes, her footsteps faltering on the dusty road. "This is bad, isn't it?"

"It d-d-depends whether or not you can correct the rumor."

It wasn't fair. She'd done nothing wrong, nor had she done anything to encourage such a rumor. "And if I can't stop it? The rumor, that is?"

Victoria patted her arm again. "You might end up needing to m-marry the doctor, at least if you want to remain respectable in the eyes of the town."

"No." She jerked away from Victoria, her body turning instantly stiff.

"Don't say no so quickly." Victoria reached up to toy with the strand of pearls around her neck. "Seth Harrington is a good man, and it might be the only way to keep this from hurting you both."

"I stand with Lindy." Aileen raised her chin defiantly, as though she were the one refusing an unwanted marriage. "She shouldn't marry him if she doesn't want to."

"And I don't. He's a doctor." What more explanation did she need?

"You might not have a choice unless you're willing to m-move, which would still leave Dr. Harrington with a damaged reputation." Victoria ran her fingers nervously along her pearls once more, then drew in a breath and pasted on an overly bright smile. "Let's just hope things can be cleared up."

Aileen rolled her eyes. "Sure, and while we're at it, we can hope..."

Victoria elbowed Aileen in the stomach.

"Ugh!" Aileen scowled at Victoria before looking back to Lindy. "Um, I meant, I hope things can be cleared up too."

The scar on Lindy's leg began to ache, and she could almost feel the cool slice of the surgeon's tools against her skin. Yes, Dr. Harrington had helped her finger and Toby's seizures, but that didn't mean she wanted to spend a minute more than necessary with a doctor, let alone marry one.

~.~.~.~.~

"As I said before, Mrs. Ranulfson, Miss Marsden was here because of the boy, not for the reason your husband imagined." Seth put his fingers to his temple and massaged where his head was beginning to throb.

The middle-aged woman poked her head into the door of the sickroom where Toby was sleeping, as though needing to verify that Toby truly did exist and was ill. Then she turned back to him with a humph. "You don't seem the type of man who needs a lecture in propriety, doctor. But let me inform you of something—there's nothing proper about having an unmarried woman in your kitchen after dark, especially not when both of you are in your nightclothes."

"Miss Marsden wasn't in her nightclothes." If he'd said it once, he'd said it a thousand times that morning, but no one seemed to believe him. "And as I said, it was an emergency."

Mrs. Ranulfson looked over her shoulder toward the room where Toby lay, the ostrich feather in her hat swaying precariously. "It doesn't look like an emergency."

"It was last night."

She humphed again. "What's wrong with the boy?"

"I believe he has a throat infection, which can cause a high fever."

"You believe?" Her eyes narrowed. "So you don't know for certain."

He sighed. Once, just once, he wanted to talk to someone in this town that didn't question his doctoring. "I'm certain he has a throat infection, yes, and it's likely the cause of his fever, but I'm watching for…"

Signs of scarlet fever. But he couldn't say that, not to Mrs. Ranulfson. The woman would have half the town quarantined before lunch. "…To make sure the infection doesn't worsen."

"Where did you say he came from again?" She looked over her shoulder once more, as though she might find the answer written on the door to Toby's room. "He certainly doesn't look familiar."

It was a good question, one he'd not gotten an answer to last night because Mr. Ranulfson had arrived. "Miss Marsden knows him."

The door to his office burst open, banging against the wall with a thud. "Oh, Betty, you're already here. Good."

Mrs. Kainer, the boardinghouse owner, came straight toward them, her eyes sparkling. "When is the wedding? Today? Tomorrow? I can make my mashed potatoes for the dinner. They won the award at the Thimbleberry Festival this year, you know. I figured they could have a little reception at the beach. It's so nice out yet, and the weather is sure to turn soon. We should have one last party before winter, don't you think?"

"Trudy, what has gotten into you?" Mrs. Ranulfson turned to her friend, her face grim. "Weddings such as this don't deserve a celebration."

"Oh, don't be so prissy. Lindy and the doctor here will make a fine match. I see no reason not to celebrate. Even if they did get a little ahead of themselves in the romance department, eh?" The widow sent him a not-so-secret wink and nudged him with her elbow.

"There wasn't any getting ahead of ourselves," he gritted. Maybe he should climb atop the roof and shout the truth from the pinnacle—not that it would do much good with these two, but maybe the rest of the town would listen. "I was treating a sick boy."

"Excuse me?" A knock sounded on the door Mrs. Kainer hadn't bothered to close behind her, and in stepped the very last person he should be seeing this morning, followed by Victoria Cummings and Aileen Brogan.

"Lindy! There you are, dear." Mrs. Kainer rushed forward, thoughts of wedding bells and fancy dresses shining in her eyes.

"Hi, Mrs. Kainer, Mrs. Ranulfson." She smiled tightly, then sidestepped around Mrs. Kainer and headed straight toward him, her face lined with concern. "How's Toby?"

"Better." He nearly reached out and laid his hand on her shoulder, a gesture that calmed loved ones who were concerned for a patient. But he wouldn't, not given the accusations of last night and the parlor full of women staring at them. "He still has his fever, but the seizures have stopped."

"I want to check on him." Miss Marsden started for the door to Toby's sickroom.

"Now just a minute, dear." Mrs. Kainer's hand shot out to grip Lindy's elbow before she took more than a step. "We need to talk about the wedding."

Miss Marsden stilled, her face losing every last bit of color. "What wedding?"

"The one between you and Dr. Harrington, of course."

Her hands clenched into fists at her side. "There's not going to be a wedding."

Seth cleared his throat. "Because we didn't do anything inappropriate."

Mrs. Ranulfson whirled on him. "Are you saying it's appropriate to have a woman in your home after midnight while the two of you are dressed in your nightclothes?"

"I keep telling everyone." Seth crossed his arms and spoke in the commanding voice he used when treating stubborn patients. "Miss Marsden wasn't in her nightclothes."

"But you were?" One of Mrs. Kainer's gray eyebrows winged up.

Seth drew in a long breath and let it out as slowly as he could, but even that didn't help calm the blood that was racing through his veins.

He glanced at Miss Marsden. He was going to have to try harder to establish the truth, because if the look on her face was any indication, there wouldn't be a wedding between them if he were the last man in Copper Country.

Which shouldn't bother him in the least. He'd been down this road before, and if he couldn't keep a woman who professed interest in him from marrying another, then how could he marry a woman who didn't even want to be in the same room?

Chapter Ten

"What do you mean he's gone?"

Lindy wiped a strand of hair clinging to her cheek away from her sticky skin and tucked it behind her ear. "Exactly what I said. His sister came and took him home yesterday."

"Yesterday?" Dr. Harrington set his medical bag on the floor of the bakery's kitchen with a thunk and crossed his arms over his chest. "He only left my office the day before that."

Lindy bent back over the sink full of dishes and scrubbed a cake pan, the water bathing her hands with its warmth. "Yes, and you said he was getting better, that his fever had broken and he was on the mend."

He ran a hand through his hair and started pacing, jerky, frustrated steps. The bakery kitchen ran the entire length of the shop, but one might think it the size of a closet given the way Dr. Harrington covered the floor with his long-legged stride. "How could you let him go?"

"If you two are going to shout, do you mind going into the alley?" Ellie bustled through the open doorway that led from the storefront into the kitchen. "You're disturbing the customers."

"No, no. Let them argue." Aileen followed behind her, an empty cookie platter in her hands. "As soon as word gets out, half the town might decide they need a dozen cookies so they can eavesdrop on these two."

Ellie shrugged. "Hadn't thought of it that way."

Lindy scrubbed the cake pan even harder, never mind that it had already been cleaned thrice over by now. The tension between her and Dr. Harrington had been awkward the first few times she'd visited Toby, but it had fallen away over the course of the week. They'd done nothing together except save a boy.

Now if only they could convince the rest of the town. Unfortunately, Mrs. Ranulfson seemed to be doing a much better job convincing people of her story.

Aileen set the platter in the sink. "Mrs. Kainer and Mrs. Foley are eating their muffins at the table in the corner just now, rather than takin' them home like usual."

Lindy withdrew her hands from the water and shook the suds clinging to her skin off before turning and glaring at the doctor. When his pacing brought him near her again, she whispered, "This is your fault."

"My fault? For wanting to check on a patient?" He didn't even try to keep his voice down. "Yes, well, I suppose it is my fault. How dare I make sure the child gets better?"

"He's not my son. When his sister came to take him home, I asked her to let him stay. I promise I did. But she refused." Just like every other time she asked anything of Jenny, the woman's only response had been a stubborn *no*. "You did say he was well enough to go home. So what reason did I have to keep him?"

"Did you consider…? Oh, never mind." He threw up his hands. "Tell me where they live and I'll go visit him myself. You said it was in the hills outside of town?"

Her throat turned suddenly dry. *And don't you be bringing anyone to this place or I'll take the young'uns and leave, I swear it,* Jenny's voice echoed through her mind.

She shook her head, but the doctor didn't seem to notice.

"How far is it? Is there time for me to go today and be back before dark?"

And here he was insisting he treat a patient even though he'd been told no. Did all doctors have to be so demanding and brutish? Why had she taken Toby to him in the first place?

Because he saved Toby's life.

Because he saved your finger.

She couldn't compare him to the doctors who had treated her in Chicago—at least not yet. But just because he'd done a good job doctoring so far didn't mean she could trust him completely.

"Miss Marsden, I asked if I had time to travel there and return before dark." He stopped pacing in front of her, his green eyes boring into hers as though he might find a map to the O'Byrnes' if he stared at her hard enough.

"I don't know."

His eyes flashed with a dangerous glint. "You said you'd been there."

She took a step back from him. "I can't tell you where they live."

Silence descended, the tension as thick as the slices of bread Ellie cut each morning. Even the storefront seemed quiet. Because it was empty, or because everyone out there was eavesdropping? A quick glance around the kitchen told her both Ellie and Aileen had left without her realizing it. She started to peek through the doorway that led to the shop, but stopped. She didn't want to know how many people were out there.

"Miss Marsden, perhaps you don't understand the seriousness of the situation." He took a step closer, then another, covering the space she'd put between them and bringing him near enough she could reach up and touch the muscle pulsing in his jaw. "I think Toby will be fine, or I wouldn't have released him to your care. But there's a slight chance the boy could develop scarlet fever."

A chill traveled up her spine.

"Do you understand how devastating scarlet fever can be? How quickly it can pass from one person to another? How high the mortality rate is with a disease such as that?"

"I understand, yes." Though probably not as well as he did. She clasped her hands tightly together at her waist. Perhaps she couldn't fault him for wanting to check on the boy, but neither could she give him directions to the O'Byrnes'. "There're a lot of things about Toby's life that I would change if I could, but I was barely able to get Jenny's permission to bring him to you in the first place. The treatment you already gave will have to be enough."

"But it's not," he gritted the words through a clenched jaw, his hands fisted so tightly at his sides that his knuckles were white.

She took a step back, bumping into the sink as she did so. She'd only seen a doctor this mad once before, when she'd tried refusing to let him put leeches down her throat in Chicago. He'd won, of course. Doctors always got their way.

She put a hand to her throat, where she could almost feel the soreness, and blinked against the hot pin pricks at the backs of her eyes. "Please don't go looking for him. You don't understand the trouble you'll cause."

"Don't look at me like that, Miss Marsden." He took a step back and relaxed his hands, though they still looked stiff at his sides. "It's not as though I'm going to flog you for arguing with me."

"Or bleed me?" Uh-oh. Why had she asked such thing? Surely he'd have questions for her now. More of them. As though he hadn't already asked enough.

But he only sighed, a long, deep exhale that held five times the air she could fit into her own lungs. "No, I won't bleed you either."

He rubbed two fingers back and forth along his forehead as though trying to ward off a headache. "If you won't tell me where

Toby lives, will you at least tell me why I can't pay a house call?"

"I'm sorry, but I can't say."

"Of course you can't." He turned without a word, his shoulders slumped as he picked up his medical bag and headed for the door to the alley.

It closed behind him, not with a loud bang, but with a soft click, which almost seemed worse. She'd disappointed him somehow, but what could she have done differently? She might not like Jenny's decisions for Toby, but she was in no position to make choices for the boy herself.

She stood there a moment, in the middle of the hot kitchen, staring at the door. Oh, what did it matter if she'd disappointed him? He was a doctor, of all people. A doctor!

She needed to put him from her mind and be done with him. Never mind the soft way he'd looked at her after restitching her finger last week, or the way he hadn't complained when she'd brought Toby to him in the dead of night, or the concerned look in his eyes as he'd explained the seriousness of scarlet fever a few moments ago.

Nope, she wasn't going to think about any of that. She was going upstairs and finishing her mending instead.

Chapter Eleven

Seth paced back and forth in the parlor of his office. His empty office. No one had come to him for medicine since he and Miss Marsden had been seen together in the middle of the night six days earlier.

Six long, interminable days.

Was the town really being that petty? He claimed he'd done nothing wrong. Miss Marsden claimed she'd done nothing wrong. They'd had a sick child in the other room to prove why they'd been together. Surely there had to be people who refused to believe the worst.

The church bell rang, calling people to Sunday services. Last week he'd been treating sailors with the flu during church. The week before that, a mother and boy had come with a cut that had become infected. And before that, well, it seemed like someone in town always needed treatment on Sunday morning.

But he wasn't likely to get any patients this morning, and where better to bring his problems before God than in the Lord's house? If anyone could make the rumors go away, it was the same Being that had power to heal the sick and lame.

The church bell rang again. He straightened his tie and fiddled with his suit jacket. *Dear God, please fill my spirit with peace—Your peace. Help me to enjoy the time I can spend in Your house today.*

He drew in a deep breath, filling both his lungs and his spirit with a sense of calm. Then he opened the door and left his office. The sun above was bright, though the wind off the harbor held the crispness of fall.

"Excuse me." He stepped out of the way of a woman with three children in tow, then again moved aside as a wagon passed. The white clapboard church sat opposite the harbor on Front Street, just like his office, its doors spread open to welcome any and all.

Perhaps the sermon today would give him some insight about how to proceed with Miss Marsden, because denying the rumors and telling people the truth certainly wasn't working. He climbed the steps to the church and strode inside.

It started with a glance. Mrs. Kainer looked over her shoulder and saw him standing near the back, then she turned and whispered something to Mrs. Ranulfson beside her, who whispered something to Mr. Ranulfson. Soon the whole church was whispering and turning and looking back and forth between him and Miss Marsden, who was seated at the front of the church with the Cummingses and Miss Brogan.

Miss Marsden glanced back at him, and her face went pale. She turned back to face the pulpit, her back as stiff as the pew she was sitting on.

He swallowed and looked away. Why hadn't he realized she'd be here?

Likely because he hadn't been to church since she'd arrived in town several weeks ago.

He clenched his teeth together and stretched his fingers only to ball them into fists at his side. He should ignore the whispers, stride to the front of the church, and sit in the same spot he always did when attending services—beside Elijah Cummings and Mac Oakton. Except Miss Marsden was seated in the same row.

He tromped to the empty pew at the very back of the church and plunked himself down. Who was preaching today? Isaac Cummings? Ernest Ranulfson? Dwight Fletcher? Was it too much to hope the sermon was going to be about gossip—and that Mr. Ranulfson wouldn't be the person delivering it?

Two dockworkers walked inside and glanced his way, but rather than sit with him, they crossed to the pew on the other side of the aisle, causing an older man to stand so they could scoot into the middle.

Because they didn't want to sit by him? Surely the rumors weren't so bad even the dockworkers would avoid him.

A moment later Ruby Spritzer entered the building with her nine children in tow. Seth slid over in the pew. With the church nearly filled, surely they'd sit by him. Besides, he'd treated the family for countless ailments free of charge during the two years he'd been in town.

Ruby glanced at him, then looked away. Shoulders stiff, she walked two pews up and whispered something to the couple seated there. Shuffling ensued as the couple moved to the pew across the aisle so the Spritzers could file into the now-empty row.

Ellie, who worked at the bakery with Aileen, looked over her shoulder and mouthed, "I'm sorry." But her mother must have seen, because Ellie jerked and then stiffened, turning forward a second later.

Seth raked a hand through his hair. Did Mrs. Spritzer truly think him so terrible he couldn't sit by her eldest daughter? Her eldest, *single* daughter?

He wasn't doing this. Absolutely not. Seth shoved himself off the pew and stalked out of the building, a walk on the beach by himself suddenly more appealing than sitting through a church service. Crossing Front Street, he trudged into the sand that lined the harbor on the other side of the road. Tiny granules filtered into his shoes, but he didn't stop to pull off his loafers and stockings, he just put his head down and kept walking.

"Seth, wait."

He slowed at the sound of Elijah's voice, but didn't stop walking.

Singing sounded in the distance, the twangy piano ringing out with the unharmonious sound of a congregation that turned Amazing Grace into a barely recognizable tune.

"You're going to miss church," his friend wheezed as he reached his side.

"So are you."

"Yes, but Isaac's preaching today. Do you have any idea what it's like to be preached at by your brother?"

Seth's lips tipped up into a small smile. He could only imagine what it would be like to sit under his own brother's preaching. "I suppose you're allowed to play hooky with me then."

They walked in silence, his head down while Elijah surveyed the harbor and lake. Maybe if they both pretended not to know why Elijah tracked him down, they could enjoy the gentle lap of the waves against the sand and the soft call of the gulls above. He drew in a breath of air tinged with the scent of Lake Superior and cast his gaze over the rocky outcropping that marked the mouth of the harbor.

The town had lovely scenery, a natural wildness that called to him, but he couldn't stay in a town simply because of where it was set. Hardly anyone in Eagle Harbor wanted his doctoring at the moment, and the few people who did—like Tressa Oakton—were beyond his ability to treat. If only he could go back to the Marine Hospital Service. He'd work at any of their facilities; it didn't have to be the Boston hospital.

How long would it take to hear soon about the splint he'd sent? He'd yet to receive a response regarding the diagrams he'd sent Rand

Jamison several weeks ago, so he'd have to be patient.

Maybe it was foolish of him to have sent the splint at all. As Rand had implied in his letter, the Surgeon General wouldn't rehire him— if for no other reason than he'd once been engaged to Harriet. Never mind he'd been the best bonesetter at the hospital in Boston, and that was before he'd invented his new splint.

If only he'd been as good at detecting whooping cough as he was at setting bones.

He raised his face to the sky as an eagle lighted from a nearby pine and swooped toward the harbor. Maybe he should leave Eagle Harbor and go home to Maryland. That would be akin to admitting he was a failure in his family's eyes, but wasn't he?

And that reminded him, he'd never read the most recent letter from Theo, just tucked it in his medical bag before he'd gone to visit Tressa Oakton.

"Funny how Lindy's not skipping church, even though you are." Elijah looked over his shoulder and jutted his chin toward the white clapboard building with its small steeple.

Seth looked behind him as well. They were far enough away now that the strains of music no longer reached them. "You don't believe I was anything less than gentlemanly with her, do you?"

"No, but it doesn't look good." Elijah repositioned his hat brim low on his forehead. "And in a town the size of Eagle Harbor, with Betty Ranulfson being the first to hear about what her husband saw, well…"

Seth kicked at a stick in the sand. "Maybe I should just leave town."

"Don't leave. This town needs you."

His laugh came off a little too sharp. "I'm not sure many people agree."

"If they haven't figured it out already, they're starting to."

"Then why haven't I seen anyone in my office all week?"

Elijah stared out at the open lake beyond the harbor, his face tilted toward the crisp autumn wind as though he stood on a boat surveying the horizon for perilous weather. "It's like I told you when Lindy broke her finger, all this would have been averted if you had a wife."

Seth stopped walking. "You're telling me to find a wife? Do you remember what happened when I tried courting your sister?"

And he wasn't about to bring up his previous two failed engagements. He should be married three times over by now, and here he was being scolded for lack of a wife.

"I'm sorry about what Rebekah did." Elijah rubbed at the dark gold stubble along his jaw. "Had I known Sinclair would come back for her, I'd have warned the both of you against pursuing anything."

"I don't want to talk about it." Now if only he could stop thinking of Rebekah's long auburn hair and flashing green eyes. Being married to her would've been a bit like trying to tame the lake to their north, impossible to accomplish and yet impossible to resist trying.

Were she and Gilbert Sinclair happy? He wished her the best, he really did. But he also wished she would have told him of her feelings for the shipping heir before they'd started courting.

He started walking again, his pace brisk lest Elijah try to bring up marriage again. He was Seth Harrington, son of Preston and Martha Harrington and heir with his brother to an estate worth half a million dollars. He should have been able to marry any young woman he chose.

A hand landed on his shoulder, and he halted before turning to face Elijah.

"I don't think you heard me the first time." Elijah squeezed his shoulder. "I'm sorry about Rebekah, Seth. I really am. And I know Rebekah's sorry for hurting you. She never intended that."

No, she hadn't. She'd felt bad when she'd left him for Gilbert, something he couldn't say about the two former fiancées who'd left him. He swallowed and looked down, staring at the tiny grains of yellow sand below him. "Has she written? Is she happy in Chicago with Sinclair?"

Now it was Elijah's turn to stay silent.

"Tell me she's happy." His throat felt suddenly thick. "Tell me I didn't give her up only for her to hate her life."

Elijah drew in a breath and removed his hand, staring out over the jagged rocks that made Eagle Harbor such a dangerous port to enter if a pilot missed the channel. "You didn't. She's always been adventurous, but in the letter we got last week, I don't think she's ever come across as so content before. She's going with Gilbert on his next business trip, and you know how Rebekah is with sailing. Can't keep her away from the water."

The thickness in Seth's throat loosened, and he nodded. He only hoped Harriet and Penelope were as happy with their husbands.

Or rather, he *should* hope that. Just because they'd jilted him didn't mean he wished them a life of discontent. But how would his life be different today if either woman had married him? Would he be happy? As content as Rebekah was with Gilbert? As Elijah with Victoria, or Mac with Tressa?

"So are you going to marry Lindy?"

He choked. "Is that what you've been attempting to say? You want me to marry Miss Marsden?"

"It's the quickest way to get people back to your office. Show the townsfolk you'll stand by your honor and protect women if needed."

"I doubt she'd have me, even if I asked. You've seen how terrified she is of doctors." He turned to survey the rocks with Elijah—it was easier than meeting his eyes.

"I believe you when you say nothing happened, but others have questions. Marrying her not only makes the situation acceptable, but

having a wife will prevent something like this from happening again."
Elijah started walking again, though Seth didn't know where to.
They'd already passed the town pier, empty of ships today, and had
almost reached the place where sand gave way to the boulders that
guarded the harbor.

"Come on." Elijah stepped onto the first rock, then climbed the
next.

Seth stood on the sand and raised an eyebrow. "What are you
doing?"

Elijah turned back and frowned, as though only then realizing he
hadn't followed. "Why are you standing there?"

"I have a certain affinity for my neck, and I like it how it is now—
which is not broken."

Elijah motioned for him to start climbing. "You've been here two
years. If you haven't climbed the boulders by the lighthouse yet, you
just might deserve to get run out of town for being a chicken liver,
never mind what you did or didn't do with Lindy."

Seth ran his eyes over the rocks. They weren't so high here, but
they quickly grew taller until they formed both the hill where the
lighthouse sat and the sloping breaker for the waves thirty feet below.

Perhaps keeping his feet firmly on the sand was worth being called
a chicken liver.

Elijah stepped onto the next boulder, a large flat one that hardly
required any balancing. "I've been climbing these things since I was
in short pants. They're not going to reach up and kill you."

"No, but a fall might." He stepped onto the first rock, the surface
rough and craggy enough not to be slick, so he joined Elijah on the
next one. "Is Miss Marsden's reputation going to be ruined if I don't
marry her?"

But he already knew the answer. It didn't matter whether he was
in Sharpsburg or Washington, Boston or Eagle Harbor. Proper

society had its rules, and they didn't bend even in a place as rough and wild as this.

"It won't just be Lindy who's hurt if you don't marry." Elijah surveyed the pile of boulders. "It will take a while to build your practice back up."

"Don't tell me people will go to Greely because of this." Surely the townsfolk had more sense than that.

Elijah remained silent, his gaze still roving the boulders as though deciding where to go next.

"He uses leeches, for goodness' sake. Leeches!" He kicked at the boulder to his left, then winced when the impact reverberated up his leg.

"I see your position. Really, I do." Elijah's shoulders rose and fell on a sigh. "But the other side makes sense too. Women won't trust their children with a man who compromises an innocent like Lindy and then refuses to stand by her."

"But I didn't do anything wrong!" He thrust his hands out, only to let them fall helplessly back by his sides.

"Everyone thinks you did." Elijah climbed onto the next boulder, then another and another.

He had no choice but to follow if he wanted to continue the conversation. He found a foothold and climbed up the next rock, then stepped easily onto the one beside it.

"Did you know one of Ruby Spritzer's girls fell and cut herself this week?" Elijah called back to him. "They went to Dr. Greely for the stitches."

And now she wouldn't let her children sit by him in church. His chest hurt. Yes, he'd been caught in an improper situation with a single lady, and Ruby had her oldest daughter's reputation to protect. But did Ruby truly think he'd behave in a way that would harm Ellie?

And why wouldn't she? He might not have done anything

inappropriate with Miss Marsden, but the Ranulfsons believed he had, and Mrs. Ranulfson had convinced the entire town of her story before he'd been able to set things straight. So how was he to overcome a lie everybody believed?

Maybe he should ask Lindy to marry him if for no other reason than propriety. Then he'd not bear any responsibility when she told him no. Because there was no doubt in his mind she'd refuse him. Never mind that he'd saved her finger and little Toby.

"I don't understand it," he called to Elijah, who was two boulders ahead. "I was only trying to help a sick boy."

"I don't understand everything that's happened in my life either." Elijah stopped and waited while he scrambled across the rocks.

"Why would God allow this?" he panted as he caught up. "I know He could make the problem between Miss Marsden and I disappear. Or have seen to it that Ranulfson arrived a few minutes later, when Miss Marsden would have been in the sick room with Toby and I would have been alone in the kitchen."

"Hopefully dressed."

He rolled his eyes. "I was headed to my room to change when Ranulfson came in. Not that anyone seems to care."

"My brethren, count it all joy when ye fall into divers temptations; Knowing this, that the trying of your faith worketh patience. But let patience have her perfect work, that ye may be perfect and entire, wanting nothing."

He blinked. "How do you do that?"

Elijah shrugged. "You didn't grow up here, so I suppose you never heard the stories about how my pa would make us memorize Bible verses at the dinner table each night."

Seth shook his head. "Nope, never heard that, but if Isaac has as much of the Bible memorized as you, I know why he preaches at the church."

Elijah turned to look out over the wide expanse of lake before them. The white-tipped waves, rolling blue seas, and endless sky above almost made up for the bite in the wind. "Maybe I should try sermonizing one of these Sundays. See how Isaac likes being preached at by his brother."

"Or you can just track people down on the beach and make them listen to your private sermons," he muttered.

Elijah thumped him on the back and grinned. "Don't just listen, take the verses to heart. We both know you did nothing wrong, and we both know God could have stopped this rumor from spreading, or from even starting in the first place, but He didn't. Maybe He's trying to teach you to have patience, or to have joy when things aren't going your way."

He was supposed to be joyful? Seth scratched the back of his head. About what? Losing his patients to Dr. Greely? Was he supposed to be joyful about misdiagnosing a case of whooping cough and losing his job in Boston too? Or about getting fired from his position as a mine doctor in Central when he'd refused to amputate a man's arm and tried setting the bone instead?

"There's something else you should do before deciding anything about Lindy." Elijah turned to him, his serene gray eyes serious against the sparkling blue backdrop of the waves. "Pray."

Pray. It was a simple thing, really. Almost too simple to solve a problem that felt so impossible. "What would you advise I pray for?"

Elijah hopped onto the next boulder before calling back over his shoulder. "Pray for wisdom to know whether she's the wife God has for you. Could be this is the woman the Lord intended all along, and this is just His way of bringing you together."

The woman the Lord intended. He'd been praying for that very thing for years. But if this was God leading him and Miss Marsden together, God sure had a strange way of going about it.

114

"Could be that you're the exact man she needs. I don't think she's terrified of you as much as your doctoring." Elijah waited on the next rock. "Could be that God wants you to heal both her soul and her body."

Seth joined his friend on yet another boulder and then shook his head. He wasn't a preacher, and he wasn't even that good of a doctor—at least not according to the Surgeon General. So how was he supposed to heal the soul and body of a woman who barely spoke to him?

But Elijah wasn't really asking that he solve all Miss Marden's problems with a snap of his fingers. He was asking for something far simpler, something he should have gotten on his knees and done the second Mr. Ranulfson left his kitchen last week.

"All right, I'll pray." Even though Miss Marsden would say no if God led him to propose.

And yet, there was some part of him that hoped she'd say yes. Some fragile, ridiculous, overly hopeful part.

He'd already had three women refuse him. Only a fool would he invite yet another woman to share his heart.

Chapter Twelve

He'd expected to pray for a week, maybe two. Considering his last three attempts to take a wife, he needed to be certain of what God wanted for him and Miss Marsden. But as soon as he'd knelt in prayer yesterday afternoon, he'd simply known what he needed to do.

Maybe God wants you to heal both her soul and her body.

What if Elijah was right? What if God had orchestrated the debacle last week to bring him and Miss Marsden together?

But first he had to convince her to marry him—and convince himself that marrying her wouldn't turn into a bigger disaster than his three failed courtships. He drew in a breath and knocked on the bakery's back door.

"Come in," Aileen's Irish accent drifted through the door.

A wall of heat hit him when he stepped inside.

Aileen glanced over her shoulder as she removed pies from the oven. "What are ye after today, doctor?"

"Why didn't you come through the front?" Ellie poured batter into a tin for the muffins that looked to be next in line for baking.

"I'm not here to purchase anything." Though the pies smelled awfully good. "I'm here to call on Miss Marsden."

"You're here for… Oh." A blob of Ellie's batter missed the muffin tin and landed with a plop on the counter. She set the bowl down and brushed her hands on her stained apron, a wide grin spreading across her face. "I'll go get her."

She scampered upstairs. Did she know what he intended? It wasn't as though he'd hung a sign about his neck that read *I'm about to propose to Miss Marsden.*

"Are ye sure ye don't want to buy somethin'?" Aileen tilted her head to the side. "Like some cookies? Might be nice to share some with yer lass."

"Um..." Aileen was right. What was he thinking, coming to propose to a woman without cookies? Or flowers. Or baubles. Or anything at all. He hadn't even started his new role as husband, and he was already failing to pay enough attention to his wife.

Except she wasn't going to be his wife, because she wasn't going to say yes. He rubbed his damp palms on his waistcoat and shifted from one foot to the other.

"So is that a yes on the cookies?" The corner of Aileen's mouth quirked up into a half smile.

"Ah..." Perhaps he should leave and come back after he'd picked some flowers and gone by the mercantile to see if they had a necklace Miss Marsden might like.

"Dr. Harrington?" Footsteps sounded on the stairway, and a moment later Miss Marsden appeared in the opening, her blond hair pulled up in a loose bun with wispy tendrils hanging beside her face. "Did you need something?"

She didn't look nervous, not like she had the night he'd come to check her finger. Nor did she look upset like she had when he'd come to visit Toby and found the boy gone. Maybe the proposal wouldn't go too poorly then.

He stepped to the bottom of the stairs where she stood with Ellie and extended his elbow. "Might you accompany me on a walk along the beach?"

"Accompany…? Oh…"

"Of course she will." Ellie pushed her forward.

"Here's some cookies lest ye get hungry along the way." Aileen handed him a paper sack and winked at Ellie, all while Lindy stood with her forehead wrinkled in befuddlement.

Did she really have no idea what this walk would entail? The others seemed to have guessed. Perhaps he did have a sign about his neck, one visible to all but him and Lindy.

"Thank you for the cookies." He offered Aileen a slight bow and then extended his arm to Lindy once more. "Shall we?"

This time she slipped her hand against his arm. "I can't be gone too long. I have mending to finish."

"We can return whenever you'd like." Not that he planned to be gone overly long. He knew from experience it only took a handful of minutes for a woman to break a betrothal. Turning one down altogether should be even faster.

He led her out the kitchen door and around the side of the bakery to the road. Silence hung over them as Lindy walked beside him, her arm tucked into his while they headed down Center Street toward the beach.

Her breathing seemed clear and strong this evening. He opened his mouth to comment, but last time, she'd gotten mad at him for paying attention to her lungs. She wouldn't get upset over such little things if they wed, would she?

The curtain in the boardinghouse across the road fluttered, and he sighed. Really, he shouldn't concern himself if Mrs. Kainer peeked out the window at him, nor if she ran straight over to Betty Ranulfson's and told the banker's wife she'd just seen him and Miss Marsden together. The entire town was talking about them already. At least there was nothing untoward about a walk.

They paused at the intersection of Front Street and Center Street, waiting for a wagon to pass before they crossed the road and stepped onto the sand while the silence lingered between them.

"Have you seen Toby since he went home?" Perhaps if they found something to talk about, his proposal wouldn't seem so abrupt.

"Yes, on Saturday."

"And?"

She twisted her lips together as though displeased.

"Was he worse? Do I need to visit him?"

"No, no. You were right about him getting better, and there wasn't any sign of a scarlet rash."

Thank goodness. "So what was that look for when I mentioned Toby?"

A small wrinkle appeared between her eyebrows. "There are other things about his situation that need to be changed."

He'd guessed as much when he'd arrived at the bakery last week to find the boy gone. "How so?"

She shook her head. "I can't say. I'm sorry, but I promised."

Was that promise a good thing? When he'd wanted to check on Toby, it certainly hadn't seemed so.

A gust of cool wind ruffled his hair, and he looked out over the water, where gray clouds gathered on the horizon. "It looks like a storm's coming."

He might be doing some doctoring tonight. Whenever a ship wrecked along the rocks lining the harbor, Elijah Cummings would bring the rescued sailors to his office to be examined.

Lindy wrapped her shawl tighter about her shoulders. "It's September already, so about time for the weather to turn. That was one nice thing about living in Chicago. Some people complained about the wind, but I don't know why. It's not as windy there as here, and winter comes two months later."

They continued along the sand, silence falling between them yet again. She had to know why he'd invited her to walk, and yet she didn't act nervous. Wouldn't a woman be nervous if she knew she was about to receive an offer of marriage?

He huffed. He needed to stop stewing and ask his question. If he didn't do so soon, she'd be ready to return to the bakery before he said his piece. "Miss Marsden, I've a need to speak frankly with you."

She drew in a breath, though not as deep and free as her breaths had been a few minutes ago.

"Go on then." She gave a little nod, but no smile tilted the edges of her lips.

"Since Ernest Ranulfson found us together last week, things have erupted into a bit of a scandal. I don't know if you're aware, but I've only had two patients all week. I know we were only caring for Toby, but it seems people think the worst about what happened between us, and the best way to fix that might be for—"

"I can't marry you."

"—you and I ..." A sinking sensation started in his chest and crashed into his stomach.

Curse his ridiculous, overly hopeful heart. Why was he disappointed? He'd known all along what she would say. Wasn't even sure he wanted her to say yes. "Because I'm a doctor?"

"Because I'm dying."

He blinked. Or maybe he hadn't known what she would say.

He ran his eyes over her thin frame and height that made her slightly taller than most women. Her creamy skin had a healthy hue, and her silky blond hair looked soft enough he nearly reached out to touch one of the strands hanging beside her face. The delicate features made her seem more suited to a gilt-trimmed salon in Washington D.C. or Boston rather than a windswept beach on Lake Superior's wild coast.

During his decade as a doctor, he'd seen dying people numerous times. The woman before him might be too thin, but she definitely wasn't dying. "Why do you say such a thing?"

"I have a cough."

"While I agree that you have asthma, which can cause coughing, nothing I observe about you indicates you're dying."

She stiffened and turned forward, her jaw set. "You may have fixed my finger, Dr. Harrington, and you may have given me medicine for my breathing, but you don't know everything about my health."

"All right, let's say you're right and save ourselves the argument." At least until after they were wed—hopefully. "How long do you think you'll live? One year? Two? Five? Are you going to balk at spending the last year of your life with a man that can make your passing comfortable, and perhaps make you better?"

Was he really trying to rationalize their marriage by turning her death into an escape? He pinched the bridge of his nose. How far he had fallen from his days as a young man when he could have his pick of any woman in town.

"Surely you want to choose a wife for yourself. Surely you want a woman who feels more kindly about your profession." She didn't meet his eyes, only picked at her shawl. "Surely you want a woman that you love and who loves you in return."

He'd given up on getting what he wanted—concerning both his doctoring and women. "I want a respectable medical practice, which I currently find in jeopardy."

She loosed a shaky sigh, a slight wheeze escaping with the breath. "There must be another way."

"I can't come up with one, unless I'm willing to give up treating women and children." He forced himself to unclench his teeth. She hadn't spent years in training to become a doctor or dedicated a decade to healing people. She couldn't know how frustrating it was to have

Ruby Spritzer and others refuse to visit him because of one mistake.

Or how frustrating it was to lose an esteemed position with the Marine Hospital Service over a single misdiagnosis.

Or lose his position as a mine doctor for saving a man's arm rather than cutting it off.

"Is it truly that bad?" She stopped walking and turned to face him, her bottom lip tucked between her teeth as she searched his face. "Are you losing that many patients because of the rumor?"

"You shouldn't act so surprised. I could be living anywhere—Sharpsburg, Boston, Washington—and if word spread that I'd compromised a woman while doctoring, then no other women would come to me, nor would they bring their children."

Her bottom lip turned white beneath the teeth biting it. She was considering his proposal. Despite her hatred of doctors and insistence she was dying, she was contemplating saying yes.

Not because she wants anything to do with you or marriage, you dolt, but because she feels responsible for you losing patients. It was an honorable sacrifice on her part. If only he didn't feel an ache in his heart that should have long ago turned hard.

Maybe he should tell her about his family. About the estate worth half a million dollars that he and his brother had inherited. Maybe she'd say yes if she knew she'd be provided for.

And maybe the money would only complicate things. It certainly had with both Harriet and Penelope.

Lindy slid her hand off his arm and took a step away from him, then wrapped her arms tightly around herself. "If I say yes—and I'm not promising I will—would you agree not to doctor me? My lungs are what they are, and I don't want any treatment for them."

"Asthmatic is what they are, as evidenced by how your breaths have shortened and your lungs have started to wheeze the longer we've been on our walk."

"This is exactly what I mean." Her lips pressed into a firm line. "I understand your doctoring isn't all bad and that you help others. I'll consider marriage so you can doctor people, but I don't want you treating me."

Her request wasn't remotely reasonable. "I'd have to at least try to help you, especially if what you claim about dying is true."

"No. You'll promise not to doctor me, or I won't even consider the wedding." Her hand fisted in her shawl, a worn, thin piece of fabric that he'd replace the moment she became his wife—if she became his wife.

"You can't expect me to sit in your room and watch you die without attempting to help you."

Fear flashed across her serene, hazel eyes, but she blinked it away. When she met his gaze again, her eyes were as hard as the rocks by the lighthouse. "I know what kind of help doctors give for lung ailments, and if it doesn't kill you faster, it makes you wish you were already dead."

She spun on her heels then, hastening over the sand without so much as a glance in his direction.

"Lindy, you're wheezing. You really shouldn't run when your lungs are..." But she was already out of earshot, her chest probably heaving and her lungs struggling to draw shallow breaths.

And she didn't care. Or rather, she cared more about escaping him than getting oxygen into her body.

He blew out a breath and ran his fingers through his hair. He should have been more careful. He'd seen the scars on her arm, could conjure them up in his mind if he pressed his eyes closed for a few moments. How was he going to heal both her body and soul if he trampled her feelings and opinions?

But then, she wasn't going to let him heal her body, and he'd just proven he didn't have either the compassion or the patience to help her soul.

God, why? He looked up at the sky, quickly growing gray with the impending storm. But the only answer he got was the howl of wind over the water. He hunched his shoulders against the wind and turned back toward his office. His empty, lonely office with nary a single patient.

⸱⸱⸱⸱⸱

He'd asked her to marry him. Lindy wrapped her arms around her chest and blinked away the tears as she raced through the streets of Eagle Harbor. She pulled up short as a wagon barreled down the road, the team of horses trotting at the behest of the driver.

"Excuse me." A miner bumped her shoulder.

She stepped to the side, threading her way through the passersby. For once, the streets seemed nearly as crowded, the air nearly as thick as Chicago.

She edged her way toward the outside of town. She needed to get away, somewhere open and free where she could calm down and think. Going back to the bakery where Aileen and Ellie would be waiting simply wouldn't do. But there was a place in the woods she'd gone to a long time ago with her family. It wasn't as far as the meadow by the O'Byrnes. A fifteen minute walk at most.

She probably shouldn't be going anywhere, not given the way her lungs burned, but how else would she find privacy?

She followed the dirt path up to the cemetery that sat on the hill outside of town, then headed into the trees, hastening down a narrow deer path that twisted through the foliage.

Had Seth Harrington really asked her to marry him?

That had been on her "One Day" list.

One day, I'll have a husband to hold me close.

One day, I'll have a man who loves me.

One day, I'll have children.

She'd never expected to receive a proposal, at least not since she'd contracted the same lung ailment as her mother. Her lung illness and endless doctors' bills had long ago scared off any potential suitor.

Except sickness didn't scare doctors, and there wouldn't be any medical bills if her husband was a doctor.

A doctor. Oh, what was she thinking? Why was she considering pledging the rest of her life—however short it might be—to a doctor?

Because she'd have warm, strong arms wrapped around her when she went to sleep at night.

Because she'd never again lie alone in a cold, dank hovel while she coughed up her lungs.

Because she'd be loved.

But was he offering love? He hadn't said anything to that end. And how could he offer to love her when she despised… well, she couldn't say she despised him, per se. But his profession, yes.

Though thus far his treatments had made sense. Thus far he'd helped both her and Toby. In fact, she hadn't heard a single bad thing about his doctoring from anyone in Eagle Harbor. But she didn't know everything about him or his medicine. What if he thought co-irritation could heal her lungs?

The wound in her leg began to throb, and she shuddered as she broke through the trees and into the little clearing near the stream where her family had picnicked during the summer. If only the spot could give her the peace she needed, if only the rushing water could tell her what to do about Seth Harrington.

But she knew what to do. Had already done it, in fact.

So why was her heart so heavy? Why did she want nothing more than to plop down on one of the boulders and cry?

A drop of water landed on her head, thick and fat and cold. Then another followed, and another. She looked up at the sky, dark with clouds.

How could she have forgotten the storm? She'd noticed it coming on the beach, but it had slipped her mind as she'd headed out of town. That was probably why the streets had been so busy. Everyone was trying to take cover before the rain.

Everyone but her.

Even covered by the dense forest, the strong wind tugged at wisps of her hair and howled through the trees.

More raindrops fell, growing steadily faster and stronger. She'd never make it back to town before the worst of the storm broke, especially not with how her lungs struggled for breath.

But there was a cave around here, one she and Betsy had discovered when playing hide and seek. She walked along the stream, searching for a pile of boulders beside a rocky incline. It was here somewhere, just a little higher on the hill.

The rain beat harder on her head, quickly soaking her shawl and dress with its chill. Why hadn't she paid better attention?

She spotted the outcropping of rock and the dark craggy shape of the cave and barreled through a line of shrubs toward the shelter. A cough bubbled up from her chest, wracking her body as she huddled inside the shallow hole carved in the rock.

A shiver traveled up her frame next, then another cough followed. If only she'd arrived a few minutes earlier. Surely she wouldn't feel so cold if her clothes were dry. Surely then she'd be able to stop shaking.

She closed her eyes. Maybe if she thought of warm summer days, she wouldn't feel so chilled. But all she saw against the blackness of her eyelids was Seth standing on the beach, asking her to marry him.

A tear slid down her cheek, then another, and another. She didn't know how long she stayed in the cave, waiting for the storm to pass, crying for the hopes and dreams that had died when she'd first fallen ill in Chicago. Then she started to cough, not simple, little coughs, but large, wracking ones.

She burrowed as far as she could inside the cave, pressing her back to the cold stone behind her. There must be a miasma in the storm to make her cough so. Did this mean she'd get a fever again? She'd only been in Eagle Harbor a month. Was it foolish to hope for three or four months of health before she fell ill again?

Probably, just like it was foolish to hope for a husband. And even more foolish to marry a doctor.

Chapter Thirteen

"Th-thanks for coming out to get us."

Though Gerald Farnum sat crammed onto the bench of the surfboat beside him, Elijah could barely hear the sailor through the howling wind of the storm.

A wave crashed into the rocks off the starboard side of the small boat, spraying his crew plus the two sailors they'd just rescued with icy droplets of Lake Superior water.

"Break to port, men. Break to port," Elijah shouted, digging his oar into the water. They needed to get away from the boulders lining the shore before the violent sea drove them into the rocks.

Rain slashed down from the sky, driving hard little pellets into the angry lake as they fought the pounding waves and inched farther into the open water. They crested the top of a wave before dropping down into the trough.

Elijah plunged his oar into the sea once more, his muscles burning as he worked in tandem with the five other surfmen on his crew to propel the boat back into the safety of the harbor.

He glanced over his shoulder at the brown, craggy boulders they'd just left. He'd rescued sailors from ships that had been stuck on boulders before, but never a person who'd literally been standing on a rock. This was the first time he'd had to get his surfboat so close to the dangerous shoreline.

"Did you hear me, Elijah?" Gerald called. "I said thanks. Don't know how much longer Roger and I could have held on."

"I heard you." Elijah blinked away the rain droplets that had somehow found their way beneath his hat brim to cling to his eyelashes, then scowled at the bearded sailor who couldn't be much younger than him. Surely the man didn't expect him to smile and say *you're welcome*, not when a foolish bet had led them to take a dinghy out just before the storm. When the team they had been racing made it back to town without any sight of Gerald and Roger, the sailors at least had the sense to get him and the other rescuers.

His crew had found the men huddled on one of the large boulders about a quarter mile east of the lighthouse. A wave had caught their rowboat and dashed it into the rocks, and only a few pieces of wood still floated in the water by the time Elijah and the others reached the men.

"Is that how you're going to be, Elijah? You going to ignore me?"

"Probably what you deserve after a stunt like that," Floyd answered from where he sat rowing on the starboard side of the bench the three of them shared.

Up until a few months ago, Mac Oakton had occupied Floyd's seat. But when the lighthouse service told Mac he wasn't allowed to go on rescues anymore, Floyd had stepped in to fill the void, and it wasn't an easy one to fill. The rowers at the back of the boat had the most control over steering the little vessel, and also needed to put the most force behind their rowing.

"I can't rightly answer for Elijah," Emmet, one of the surfmen on the middle bench, called over the storm. "But risking my neck to come out here and rescue you two louts because of a bet doesn't make me feel like talking to you."

"He's right," Roger called from where he sat beside Emmet, his clothes soaked and quickly dampening the wool blanket wrapped around him. "It was a stupid bet."

Gerald shifted on the bench, his own woolen blanket brushing against Elijah. "Aw, now you wouldn't be saying that if we'd won."

"Instead you almost died." Elijah thrust his oar into the water as they passed the lighthouse and steered the nose of the boat toward the harbor. He glanced at the rock he and Seth Harrington had sat on just yesterday, now only visible between troughs of waves while the cresting water pounded at the rocks high above the shoreline.

Once they passed the rocky point, the waves turned instantly calmer, and the boat glided quickly over the swells toward the patch of beach near Dr. Harrington's office. A moment later, sand crunched beneath the hull, and Ian and Steven, the newest surfman on the crew, hopped out of the boat and began heaving it farther onto the beach.

"Everyone to Dr. Harrington's office." Elijah set his oar in the boat and stretched his shoulders before climbing over the gunwale. Rain still pelted them, though the oilskins he and his crew wore had kept them fairly dry. The blankets around Gerald and Roger, however, were soaked.

"Come on, up you go." Elijah took Gerald by the arm and helped him over the side of the boat, then started him toward the squat log cabin on the other side of Front Street. Ahead of them, Roger listed to the side, then stumbled before being caught by Emmet.

"He hit his head awful hard when the boat wrecked." Gerald jutted his chin toward Roger. "Probably a good thing you're making him go to the doc's."

It was the precise reason he made everyone stop by Dr. Harrington's after a rescue. Out on the sea, he was too busy rescuing others to pay attention to each little bump, bruise, and thump everyone got. "We'll have the doc look you over too, Gerald."

"Aw, there's nothing wrong with me. I don't need to—"

A squeal sounded before he could take another step forward, and a tall figure dressed in yellow careened out the door of the doctor's office and barreled toward him.

"You're back!" Victoria threw herself into his arms so hard he nearly stumbled. "I'm so glad you're safe."

He wrapped his arms around her and held her tight, drawing in the sweet scent of his wife as he buried his face in her hair. This, right here, was the best part of returning from a rescue. "I'm back, yes, and you're getting your fancy dress wet. Let's get out of the rain."

He released her, but she stayed exactly where she was, her arms wound tight about him and her wide brown eyes meeting his. "Is the story t-true? Did you really have to go out because of a b-b-bet?"

He reached behind him to loosen her arms, then turned her toward the office. "Let's just say this doesn't rank high on my list of most rewarding rescues."

A story like this was sure to be all over town already. He could only imagine what Isaac would say when his brother found out he'd risked his life because some fools had decided to race their boats against a storm.

Victoria climbed the porch steps and entered the familiar parlor of Dr. Harrington's office. "Even if the r-reason for the rescue was dumb, I'm still glad you went. What would have become of them if you hadn't?"

And that was one of the many reasons he loved his wife. She always had a way of seeing people's needs, even when everyone else wanted to bash some numskulls' heads together.

He grabbed her cloak from the peg on the wall. It would keep her dry enough on the way home. "Let's go."

She frowned up at him. "The doctor hasn't looked you over yet."

"No need. It wasn't that difficult of a rescue—just a frustrating one."

She didn't need to know how close to the rocks they'd had to row to rescue Gerald and Roger. That hadn't been easy, even if there had only been two sailors to save and neither needed to be coaxed into the surfboat.

"Don't you w-want to wait until it stops raining? I'll make you a cup of tea while you sit by the fire. You have to be c-cold."

Yes, yes, and yes. He was cold and he'd probably have himself a good case of the shakes later. But if he had a choice between curling up in his own bed with his wife or lying on one of the doc's uncomfortable mattresses, well, there really wasn't much choice. "We'll do all that when we get home."

She crossed her arms over her chest and scowled. "I thought you had a r-rule about no one leaving Dr. Harrington's after a rescue until they'd been examined."

He had that rule more to protect other people than himself. "I'm fine. Let's get out of here before the doc sees me."

He tugged her toward the door, but she planted her feet firmly on the floor, her eyes flashing with stubbornness. "Oh no, you don't. You need to be examined. And I'd rather wait until it's done raining to walk back home, thank you very much."

Unfortunately Dr. Harrington chose that moment to step into the parlor. "Yes, Elijah, I agree with your wife. Let's have a look at you. I can already see you need some dry clothes."

He bit back a groan. "Is this some sort of payback for making you climb out on the rocks yesterday?"

"No." Dr. Harrington took him by the arm and led him toward the small room on the opposite side of the parlor. "That's what the needle inside the sickroom is for."

Elijah rolled his eyes. "I'm not a chicken liver. It's going to take more than a poke to scare me off."

He got himself poked five or six times over, the doc seeming to use a bit more force than normal when pricking his fingers and toes to make sure they hadn't gone numb. Then the doc listened to his heart and lungs. All in all, the exam only took a few minutes before he was declared healthy enough to leave, but they still had to wait another hour before the rain let up enough to head home.

"I'll walk as far as The Penny with you." Floyd followed him and Victoria out of the office and onto the street. "Have me a little drink before I go home."

"Sure." He'd come to expect that of his surfman. Without a family to return home to, the man usually spent the hours after a rescue with a pint or two of beer.

"I'll come too."

Elijah paused for a moment, scowling as Ian Fletcher caught up to them, auburn hair flopping over the smooth skin of the lad's face. "What would your ma and pa say about that?"

Ian's cheeks turned red. "Don't see what that's got to do with anything. If I'm old enough to go out on rescues, then I'm old enough to have a drink afterward."

Elijah scratched at the stubble on his jaw. He didn't like it, but Ian really was less of a boy and more of a man these days. How old was he, anyway? Twenty? Twenty-one? Probably old enough to be settling down with a wife and not worrying about water rescues anymore.

"Come along, Elijah." Victoria tugged on his arm. "It might not be raining, but it's c-colder now than it was before the storm."

They started down Front Street, the four of them picking the driest path through the muddy road. The lighthouse burned ahead of them, casting its beam out into the mass of open water still churning in the storm's wake. The cold fall wind whipped across the lake, bringing thoughts of winter and the snowstorms that would buffet Eagle Harbor soon enough. They turned onto North Street and headed toward the edge of town.

"Of all the rescues we've gone on, that has to go down as one of the craziest." Floyd shook his head.

"Or one of the stupidest," Ian muttered.

"Maybe so." Victoria clung to Elijah's arm for balance as she stepped around a puddle. "But those men would be dead without your h-help."

"They almost deserve it." Ian stepped in the puddle Victoria had missed, causing mud to splatter his trousers.

"I suppose you've never done anything stupid, Ian Fletcher." Victoria raised an eyebrow. "Like going to a brothel when you should be headed home."

The boy turned red again. "That isn't the same as…"

"Stop! I said no!"

At the sound of a woman's voice, Elijah tensed and whipped his head around to survey the buildings.

"That s-sounded like Lindy," Victoria whispered.

"It came from over there." Ian pointed, then strode to the little break between the telegraph office and the seamstress shop.

Elijah dropped his arm from around Victoria's shoulder. "Stay here with Floyd."

"Who says I'm staying?" Floyd called.

But Elijah was already jogging after Ian. A squeal sounded as he rounded the corner of the telegraph office. Ian was holding a sailor by the collar. His fist connected with the man's jaw, and a *thwack* echoed off the buildings as, then another and another.

Lindy Marsden huddled against the wall, her face damp and her wet hair hanging in matted tangles down her back and shoulders.

"Lindy, are you all right? What happened?" Elijah strode toward her.

Rather than answer, she doubled over, pressed a hand to her mouth, and loosed a cough so hard that it could probably be heard a mile away at his cabin.

"Lindy?" He stopped beside her and reached out to… what? How was he supposed to help someone having a coughing fit?

"Oh, Lindy!" Victoria raced past him, only stopping when she reached her friend's side.

He scowled at his wife. What was so hard about staying where he'd told her? What if there'd been a group of men with Lindy and not just one for Ian to easily take in hand?

He glanced over his shoulder toward where he'd left Floyd, only to find him and Ian propping the nearly unconscious sailor up beneath their shoulders.

"Reckon the sheriff's at The Penny," Floyd said. "Can you bring Miss Marsden along when she stops her coughing?"

"Sure will." Though given the way Lindy was still doubled over, her body shaking with each cough, they might be paying a visit to the sheriff later rather than sooner.

Victoria wrapped an arm around her friend's shoulder. "Try to breathe through it, Lindy. Try to c-calm down. Can you draw your breaths more slowly? Maybe that will help."

Lindy gasped in a high, wheezy breath.

"That's it. Nice and slow." Victoria rubbed a hand up and down Lindy's back. "Why are you so w-w-wet? Did you get caught in the storm?"

Wet? Elijah ran his gaze down Lindy once more. Yes, her hair was wet, but he was a dunce for not noticing how damp her clothes were. He took his oilskin off and draped it around her shoulders. It nearly swallowed her thin frame, but it would have to do until they could get her some drier clothes.

"Caught in the storm, yes." Lindy sucked in a shallow breath.

He didn't need years of medical school to know the sound would soon lead to more coughing. "Are you well enough to visit the sheriff? Or do we need to get you to the doc?"

"The sheriff." Her words were so wheezy, she almost sounded like she whistled. "He needs to know."

"Oh, Lindy." Victoria drew her friend into a hug. "Tell me we g-g-got here before he hurt you."

"You did." Another cough shook her, but this bout ended quicker than the last. "But we can't let this happen to someone else."

It was a bit too late for that, considering what had happened to Victoria several weeks ago. This time, however, with the man caught and Floyd and Ian going to the sheriff only minutes after the assault happened, Sheriff Jenkins wouldn't be able to turn a blind eye.

At least that's what he hoped as he propped Lindy beneath his shoulder and they headed down North Street to The Pretty Penny.

"There she is now." Ian called as they approached the porch of the saloon and brothel, where Sheriff Jenkins sat in his usual chair beside Doc Greely. "You can see for yourself what he did."

"Is that Miss Marsden you're talking about?" Sheriff Jenkins squinted his bloodshot eyes in their direction. "I thought you said a lady had been assaulted."

"He did say that." Elijah tromped up the porch, his boots pounding on the wooden planks as he strode to the overweight lawman. "If you'd stop drinking long enough to do your job, you'd realize you're putting the ladies in this town at risk when you fail to protect them."

"Ladies?" Sheriff Jenkins spit at the road. "I don't see no lady. If she's willing to pay calls on Doc Harrington, who says she shouldn't be willing to spend some time with Fred here?"

Lindy's face turned white, while Victoria's gasp carried clear up to the porch. Even Ian and Floyd glanced at each other over the drunkard's head.

Elijah curled his hand into a fist. Jenkins just might deserve to be punched, lawman or not. Except that meant he'd be the one spending the night in jail, and there was another person far more deserving of the cell. "You'd best watch what you say, Sheriff."

"What he said is right." Lindy's attacker shouted, no matter that he was still restrained by Floyd and Ian. "I've sampled everything at The Penny. What's wrong with looking for someone new? I'm willing to pay an' all." He looked over at Lindy, a broad, goofy grin spreading over his face as he winked. "Don't worry, darlin'. There's plenty of others who will pay ya too. Been a while since Reed's gotten a new girl in."

"I'm not that kind of woman." Lindy's wheezy protest ended with a cough.

"That's not what I heard." Sheriff Jenkins propped his boots up on the porch railing and tilted back in his chair.

"Now just a minute," Elijah growled, his hands still clenched into fists. The man got closer to being knocked out with each word he spoke. "That was a misunderstanding. You owe the lady an apology."

But the sheriff was either too drunk or too arrogant to heed the warning. Instead he settled his hands atop his protruding belly and kept right on talking. "I understand a woman's got to earn a living, but I don't much care for women who act one way in church on Sunday and another at night. Did Fred here strike you?"

Lindy shook her head. "No, but he tried—"

"Don't know why you want me to thwart a man who just wants the same thing you're giving to Doc Harrington. Ian and Floyd, let Fred go."

Victoria started for the porch, her eyes flashing hazel fire. "How dare you!"

Her words were nearly drown out by the harsh fit of coughing that overtook Lindy. Elijah glanced at Ian and Floyd, who exchanged their own mortified looks with each other before quietly releasing Lindy's assailant.

He'd had enough. Lawman or not, Sheriff Jenkins deserved one thing and one thing only. Elijah pulled back his fist and swung.

Chapter Fourteen

"Dr. Harrington?"

At the sound of the Irish-laced voice, Seth looked up from the medical text he'd been studying.

"Hello? Are ye here?"

"I'm coming." He scooted his chair back from the desk and stood, then nearly tripped over a stack of books on the floor as he picked his way to the door of the small storage room he'd converted into an office and supply room. At least his bedroom was clean, even if there was no hope of ever keeping his medical supplies and texts from overtaking the old closet. He moved quickly past his bed, dashing into the kitchen, and from there into the parlor, only to look down and discover he'd left his neck cloth undone. After last night's excitement with the shipwrecked sailors, he assumed he'd have a quiet morning studying—just like every morning since the incident with Miss Marsden—and had dressed for comfort.

Should he tie it now, or would that only draw more attention to his state of disarray?

"What can I help you. . .?" His words trailed off when Miss Brogan turned to face him, her face so pale her freckles disappeared. "What's wrong?"

"Lindy got stuck out in the storm last night, and she's coughin' somethin' fierce."

Lindy had gotten caught in the storm? How? After running away from him on the beach, she'd had plenty of time to get home before the rain started.

"Well, are ye coming?"

"Yes, yes, just let me get my bag."

It took only a matter of minutes to reach the bakery, never mind how many people he nearly trampled in his haste or Aileen's calls for him to go slower. When he burst through the back door, Ellie didn't even look surprised, just pointed a finger toward the ceiling.

"She's up there with Victoria."

As though Lindy wanted to confirm Ellie's words, a faint cough sounded from above. The coughing grew louder as he climbed the stairs and headed down the hallway toward the door the vicious hacking sounds emanated from.

"That's the one." Aileen appeared at the top of the stairs, her cheeks flushed and chest heaving. "Just go in."

He opened the door to find Victoria propping Miss Marsden up while she had a coughing spell so fierce it caused not just her body to shake, but the bed as well. Her long blond hair fell in tangled strands around her shoulders, while her flushed face and bright eyes warned of a fever.

"Breathe, Lindy." Victoria bent her head near Lindy's ear, though her voice could barely be heard over the coughing. "You need to breathe."

Lindy wheezed in a breath, so short and tight it couldn't possibly give her the oxygen she needed for the new bout of coughs that shook her body.

Seth swallowed and ran his eyes down the woman he'd asked to be his wife the day before. Was this what she'd been talking about when she'd said she was dying?

Because lung infections such as this certainly could claim a person's life.

~.~.~.~.~

Burning. Her lungs were burning. Lindy tried to suck in a little breath, but her chest convulsed with another fit of coughing. How much longer could she go on like this? Maybe she'd pass out soon from lack of air, then she'd not be able to feel the fire in her lungs.

"That's it now, draw in a breath, slow and steady."

She raised her head and blinked at the blurry image of Dr. Harrington's face. He must have replaced Victoria at her bedside at some point, but she'd been too busy coughing to notice exactly when or how long he'd been there.

An image of him standing on the beach filled her mind, the storm clouds looming on the horizon.

I can't marry you. She'd spoken the words before he'd even had a chance to ask the question.

Because I'm a doctor?

Because I'm dying.

Was that why he was here now? Did he know what had happened? Would he marry her even though she might be dying?

"Slow and steady, Miss Marsden. You can manage it."

There was never anything slow and steady about her breathing, but especially not when she had one of her ailments. She tried to suck air in anyway and got three tiny breaths before she started coughing again.

"Miss Marsden, can you look at me? I need to give you some medicine."

"Don't want..." Another cough shook her body.

"I'm not asking, I'm insisting. Your lips and fingertips are turning blue, which means you need more oxygen in your body. The only way to do that is by getting you to breathe better. Now open your..."

The coughing started again, which was just as well, because it prevented her from taking his medicine. Didn't he remember her refusing treatment on the beach? That she'd stormed off when he insisted on doctoring her if they got married?

Her bout of coughing ended too quickly this time. The second her lungs stopped convulsing, he was there, shoving a spoonful of medicine into her mouth before she could even ask what it was.

"Very good. And this one too."

She turned her head away. "I don't…"

Somehow he got the spoon into her mouth again, filling her tongue with a bitter liquid. She swallowed the medicine and blinked up at him. "Are you here to marry me?"

He stilled, the medicine bottle and spoon still in his hand. "Do you want me to marry you?"

Did she? She leaned farther back against her pillow and closed her eyes, turning her face away from him. Why had he proposed earlier? And right before her ailment claimed her, at that? It made everything so much more complicated.

"I can't promise not to treat you. In fact, at the moment, I rather insist on treating you, whether we're married or not."

If he was going to be this stubborn, then it made little difference whether they wed.

But the sheriff publicly proclaiming he wouldn't protect her made a big difference in whether she should wed. Without the sheriff's protection, more men like Fred were sure to approach.

Lindy's face heated with something more than fever. As much as she might want to provide for herself, staying here as sick as she was would only make her a burden to Aileen and Victoria. Plus marriage would stop the rumors spreading around town, both the one about her and the doctor and the one about her means of earning money.

If she had a choice, she'd… she'd…

Oh, she couldn't even think clearly enough to know what she'd do. But it hardly mattered. She'd lost control of her choices long ago—or at least control of the ones she wanted to make.

"No bleeding," she rasped as she slid from her sitting position down beneath the covers. "Not ever."

He shook his head as though the notion were ridiculous, as though her arms weren't full of scars where other doctors had bled her. "I already told you, I don't bleed my patients."

"And no co-irritation."

His brow furrowed, and he gave her a puzzled look, discernible even through her hazy vision. She braced herself for the questions that were sure to follow. What other doctor had used co-irritation on her? Where had he done it? For how long? The scar on her leg began to throb despite the burning in her lungs.

But rather than ask questions, he simply said, "No co-irritation. I promise that as well."

She drew in a breath, short and raspy, but at least it didn't lead to another round of coughing. What reason did she have to refuse him now? "All right. Send for the justice of the peace."

~.~.~.~.~

"Well, well, well, if this isn't a sight for sore eyes."

From his position on the small pallet in the corner, Elijah rubbed his eyes and blinked at the barred door of his jail cell.

"I see the rumor is true." Isaac leaned against the cell door, his legs crossed at the ankles, and his auburn hair mussed as though he'd rolled out of bed without bothering to comb it.

"Stow it." Elijah propped himself on his elbows.

Mirth danced in Isaac's eyes, and a small grin tipped the corners of his lips, like when they'd been boys and Isaac had just beaten him and Mac at a game of hide and seek. A pang stabbed Elijah's chest, and not because of the cramped position he'd lain in after finally falling asleep. How long since he'd seen Isaac smile like this? It was almost worth getting locked in a jail cell for.

Almost. Elijah winced as he pushed to his feet and stretched his aching shoulders. If there were a decent size bed, then maybe.

"Did you really punch the sheriff, or is that just scuttlebutt?" Isaac still hadn't wiped the doltish grin off his face. If anything, it got larger.

"Lindy was assaulted, and the sheriff not only refused to do anything about it, but said she deserved it given her new line of work. What was I supposed to do?"

"He said that?" The smile dropped from Isaac's face and he rubbed a hand over his jaw. "Still shouldn't have punched him. Where did you think you'd end up after that kind of stunt?"

Elijah crossed his arms over his chest and glared. "You'd have done the same thing, and you know it."

"Yes, but I wasn't there, which gives me the right to taunt you." The teasing glint was back in his brother's eyes, another smile creeping across his face. "Just imagine what Pa would say if he saw you in a jail cell."

"Reckon that would depend on whether he knew how I got here." Elijah scratched behind his ear. "So why are you here? Don't tell me you came to laugh without getting me out." Elijah moved to the bars and craned his neck in an attempt to see down the corridor to where the sheriff's office was. "Where's Jenkins with the key?"

"I'm not sure Jenkins has the key anymore, seeing how Ian Fletcher's pa is on the town council. Evidently Ian had quite the story to tell after he got home last night. And you already complained to Ranulfson about how the sheriff responded to Victoria a few weeks ago. They should both be here shortly."

"Does that mean Jenkins isn't the sheriff any longer?"

"That's my guess, but as to who will replace him..." Isaac shrugged.

"It should be you."

"What?" Isaac took a step back.

"I mean it. I'll ask Ranulfson who the council will appoint until the election in November, but even if they don't appoint you, you should still run."

Isaac smirked, and not in a way that resembled his earlier grin. "I'm sorry. For a moment there, it sounded like you thought the town toymaker should turn lawman."

"You're only the town toymaker because you're stubborn. It's hardly the job Pa raised you to do."

"Yes, well, spending my days making toys seems a whole lot more appealing than fishing. I don't die if a storm comes up. But you intentionally go out into those storms, even if it means nearly killing yourself to rescue half-drunk men from a stupid wager."

Elijah winced. He should have realized Isaac would hear that rumor too. "That still doesn't change anything. You're a good seaman, and probably an even better boat builder. I don't know why you hole yourself up in the shed making toys, but if you're that insistent on never stepping into a boat again, at least do something useful and be the town lawman."

Isaac lunged toward the cell door, gripping the bars with white knuckles. "I don't hole myself up, and I'm certainly making better money than you, and that's with you working at the sawmill every day after you get back from fishing."

Truly? How much did Isaac's little toy endeavor make him? Never mind. He'd only get frustrated if he knew, or rather, more frustrated than he already was. "If your toy making does that well, then you're the perfect candidate for town sheriff, because the position pays beans."

Isaac took a step back from the bars and surveyed the line of three identical jail cells.

Did he realize how much he looked like Pa as he stood there? Elijah had a darker version of their ma's blond hair, a sure sign of her German heritage, whereas Isaac was tall and a bit lanky, but with shoulders too broad to be considered thin. He had their pa's coloring and build, all right. The difference was, if Pa would have had the chance to replace a lazy sheriff, he'd not have even stopped to think, he'd just have done it.

God may have modeled one of them after their pa and another after their ma, but He'd mixed up their personalities, giving Elijah their pa's character and making Isaac like their more timid mother.

"What makes you think I want to be the town sheriff?" Isaac finally asked.

Elijah blew out a breath. "Nothing makes me think you'd *want* to do it, but you'd do a fair job. Sometimes it's not about what you want to do so much as what you should do."

Isaac's face grew dark, all semblance of his earlier smile gone. "Why does my brother, who regularly does something he knows he shouldn't—like take a rowboat out into a storm—get to lecture me on what I should do?"

"It's not that I *want* to be out there, it's that I *should* be out there." Elijah's shout echoed through the jail. How many times did he have to explain before Isaac understood?

"Find another man, brother, I'm not him." Isaac's quiet words reverberated through the cell with as much intensity as Elijah's shouted ones, and his brother's shoulders slumped with their familiar cloak of sadness.

Elijah hooked a thumb in his pocket. If his shoulders were constantly slumped from trying to carry the weight of half the town, then Isaac's were slumped beneath an endless weight of grief for their pa.

A few minutes ago Isaac had come into the jail smiling and happy to see him—even if he was being a bit smug about it. For a moment, it was almost as though they were brothers first and enemies second.

And that had lasted for how long? Five minutes?

God, why? Why does everything I try to do or say to him end up in an argument? How much longer will this go on? I'm ready for peace, not war.

The sound of an opening door brought his head up, and voices came from the direction of the sheriff's office. A moment later Mr. Ranulfson and Mr. Fletcher appeared in the corridor, the jail keys dangling from Mr. Fletcher's hand.

"Elijah, we're both very sorry." Mr. Fletcher inserted the key in the cell door.

Elijah glanced at Isaac. He was sorry too, but for a reason that had nothing to do with the town's drunken sheriff and everything to do with the loss of a brother who'd once been his friend.

"Obviously we can't let Jenkins's actions last night go unpunished," Ranulfson's voice echoed through the jail. "We've just come from an emergency town council meeting. How do you feel about being the sheriff for the next seven weeks, until the election in November?"

There were a million reasons why he shouldn't. The first one being Isaac was better suited for the job. But before he could open his mouth to speak, Isaac spun on his heel and stormed off.

Elijah gripped the bar of the open cell door. He could find a way to be sheriff for a few weeks if he had to, but he was far more interested in finding the brother he'd lost when their pa died.

Chapter Fifteen

He had a wife.

Sitting in the chair beside her narrow bed, Seth let his gaze rove over the woman sleeping in his small sickroom. Her chest labored with each breath she drew, a wheezy, rattling sound that made him involuntarily clench the stethoscope in his hand and nearly lean over to listen to her lungs again.

But he knew what he'd find, what hadn't changed since he'd first held the stethoscope to her lungs that morning—fluid and constricted airways.

Was this what she'd faced in Chicago? The illness that had plagued her mother and the reason Lindy was convinced she was dying?

He muffled a yawn with his hand. He'd do everything in his power to keep her from dying. He'd already gotten her to stop coughing. The atropine and small, carefully measured doses of ipecac had helped that, and her lips and fingers were no longer tinged with blue.

But there was only so much he could do for the infection in her lungs. If he could wash them in carbolic acid like he did open wounds, maybe that would kill the infection. But alas, how was he to get carbolic acid into her lungs, and how was he to know whether doing so would harm another part of her?

She coughed slightly and turned her head to the side, rustling the covers. He fingered his stethoscope once more, but he'd done all he could for now—including marrying her.

What would his family say if they knew? At thirty-two years of age, he had two broken engagements, one failed courtship, and countless other years of looking for a wife who might aid his medical practice. Here God had given him one in the span of two weeks' time.

He raised his eyes to the ceiling and blew out a breath. *Thank you, Father, for my wife.*

What kind of things lay in store for them? Something better than if he would have married the daughter of the Surgeon General? Something better than if he would have married Penny and stayed in Maryland managing the Harrington family estate? Something better than if he would have married Rebekah and had her help him with his practice?

"There you are." Victoria appeared in the doorway. "I didn't realize you had come back in here."

"Sorry." He muffled another yawn. "I should have told you where I was going."

"Does she n-need anything more? What can I do?"

"Thank you for all your help today, but you can go home to your husband. I'm sure he's missing you." Indeed, Victoria had been a blessing in helping to move Lindy to his office, witnessing their wedding, and playing the role of volunteer nurse for him yet again. But the windows showed dusk falling over the town, and Victoria had stayed with Lindy all night yesterday.

"Elijah knows I enjoy helping." Victoria shrugged, something she likely wouldn't have done six months ago, when she'd been living amidst the finery paid for by her father's shipping business. "He'll understand."

Lindy coughed and turned fitfully in her sleep, then loosed another longer, deeper cough.

He stood and pressed a hand to her forehead. Still feverish. He let his hand linger overly long against her skin, then smoothed a bit of hair back from her face. Would she object to a kiss? Just a simple one on the forehead?

He leaned down for the briefest of instants and touched his lips to her burning skin. It was nothing like the first kiss he'd thought he'd be sharing with his wife one day. Her eyelids didn't even flutter.

"Perhaps I will get going," Victoria's voice filled the room.

Victoria. Heat burned up the back of his neck. What was he doing kissing Lindy in front of an audience? It wasn't even dark yet, and already his brain was turning into a pile of mush.

He looked at Victoria despite his hot ears and neck. "What do you know of Lindy's mother? About how she died?"

Victoria shook her head. "I remember her g-getting sick a year or two before my family moved to Milwaukee. To hear others talk, Mrs. Marsden got progressively sicker after we left, and then when Mr. Marsden p-passed, she and Lindy moved down to Chicago, where she eventually died."

He'd already pieced that much information together. "Do you know what she died of? Were her lung infections the same as Lindy's?"

"I think I've heard Dr. Greely mention tuberculosis, perhaps, but I d-don't know for certain."

He ran his gaze back over his wife. A connection between a mother's and daughter's illness would lean toward tuberculosis or some other type of contractible disease, but nothing about Lindy's condition indicated she'd been infected with the slow-acting, deadly bacteria. "She doesn't have that."

Victoria looked at Lindy and frowned. "I trust your word over Dr. Greely's."

"You said her father died." He scrubbed a hand over his face. "How? Was it the same thing?"

Victoria shifted. "I thought you'd already know."

"No, there wasn't time to discuss much." All they'd talked about yesterday was his proposal and whether he'd doctor her after they wed. Perhaps if she wouldn't have stormed off, he could have asked about her parents, her siblings… Did she have any? Yet another thing he didn't know.

"It might b-be best if you talk to Elijah about it." Victoria smoothed a wrinkle from the folded quilt at the end of Lindy's bed. "He was here, not me."

"Can you give me the gist of it? It might be a week or better before I can leave the office and talk to him."

"I suppose Lindy's in no condition to tell you." Her hands stilled on the quilt, and she sighed. "Reginald Marsden was a dockworker, and it was spring. The harbor had just opened. I imagine you know the hours d-d-dockworkers keep that time of year."

Indeed. The ships were stacked up three thick trying to load all the copper from the winter and get supplies to the mines inland. He'd come to Eagle Harbor during the spring. His first patient had been a man who'd broken his arm when he slipped while carrying two crates. "How did he die?"

"Elijah says it was the end of the day, and Mr. Marsden had been working twelve hours or so already, but Byron Sinclair insisted the ship be unloaded that night so he could leave the next morning. Mr. Marsden was climbing a stack of crates to get to the top of another stack in the cargo hold and fell, pulling the crates down on top of him. He b-broke his neck instantly."

Seth's chest tightened, and he looked down at his wife, reaching out to coil a tendril of hair about his finger. He'd never have guessed she'd lost her father in such a tragic way.

Victoria ran her hands over the top of the quilt again, though there were no wrinkles to be smoothed this time. "Her ma had been sick for some time already, which left the family with no money after they bought her medicine. And there aren't a whole lot of j-jobs for a woman in Eagle Harbor, at least not of the respectable sort. Lindy's younger sister ran off to work in a b-brothel up in Central."

"She did?" That answered whether she had siblings.

"Yes, her name was Betsy. I heard she left Central this spring and went out west, but it's been years since I've seen her, even if she was only living a few miles away. After Mr. Marsden died, Elijah asked Lindy to m-marry him."

Seth nearly choked. Elijah had proposed? To the same woman now lying in his sickbed and married to him? "Clearly Elijah changed his mind."

"No. Lindy t-turned him down. I guess she said something about him needing to find a woman he loved one day, and that the woman wasn't her." Color rose on Victoria's cheeks, and she gripped the log post at the end of Lindy's bed.

Ah, yes, he could see the story unfold now. Elijah wasn't the type of person to stand by and watch someone struggle or be mistreated. It was the same reason he'd formed a volunteer life-saving team. He couldn't stand by and let sailors drown during storms without trying to help. And what better way to help a woman in a difficult situation than by marrying her and pulling her burdens onto his shoulders?

"I'm glad they never married, for all our sakes," he spoke against the raspy sound of his wife's breathing.

It was the right thing to say, but was he truly glad that he'd married Lindy?

Yes, of course he was. He was doing exactly what God desired of him.

So why had Lindy turned down Elijah's offer of marriage but not his? She must see some hope for their future together, must think they could grow to love each other in a way she and Elijah couldn't have.

"I hope the story doesn't disturb you too much. Elijah's father paid for Lindy and her mother to move to Chicago, but after they were there, I believe Lindy received help from Gilbert Sinclair too." Victoria offered him a tired smile and pushed a wayward strand of hair behind her ear. "That's about all I know. If you have more questions, you should ask Elijah."

"Lindy and I will have time to learn more about each other as she recovers." Would she be more willing to answer his questions now that she was Mrs. Seth Harrington?

Victoria bit the side of her lip, her fingers tracing a pattern on the log post while she looked at Lindy. "D-do you think she'll recover?"

He couldn't blame Victoria for the question. Indeed, at the moment, with her pale face, raspy breaths, and rattling lungs, Lindy looked nothing like the healthy woman whose finger he'd set several weeks ago.

"I can't make any promises about her recovery." But how he wished he could. How he wished someone in this town had a dose of medicine that would see her better come morning. Or that he had the power to lay his hands on her and heal as Christ had.

Lindy coughed, and Victoria's brow furrowed. "Are you sure there's nothing more I can do for her?"

He rubbed a hand over his face, his eyelids drooping. "Thank you for your offer, but there's nothing more to be done besides sit here and watch." And pray that his wife had the strength to fight off the pneumonia invading her weak lungs.

"Perhaps you should lie down for a bit and I c-can sit with her. It might be a long night for you."

A long night, yes. And just like their first kiss a few minutes ago, tonight would be nothing like the wedding night he'd dreamed of. "I don't want to leave her."

Victoria pressed her lips together, a slight sheen covering her eyes.

"I'm happy you married her, doctor. She needs someone to care for her, to love her. You're the p-perfect fit."

This from the woman whose eyes lit up whenever her husband came into a room. Who had no reservation about kissing her husband goodbye or whispering secrets in his ear while surrounded by a roomful of people. "You only say that because you're besotted. Did you know your husband is the one who told me to propose to Lindy? You think that just because you're happily married, everyone should be."

She smiled as brightly as she did when seeing Elijah safe after a ship rescue. "Well, yes. Marriage is a wonderful institution—when you're sharing it with the right person, that is."

"I hope one day we have what you and Elijah share."

He spoke more to himself than Victoria, but she answered anyway. "I'm sure it will come with time. As I said, she needs someone to l-love her."

According to Elijah, she also needed someone that could heal her body and soul. But was he the right person? Because at the moment, he didn't know what more to do for her body, and he hadn't the faintest notion how to help her soul.

⁓.⁓.⁓.⁓.⁓

"No, I don't think you need to stop by." A woman's muffled voice spoke. "I was just there, and Tressa seemed fine."

Lindy opened her eyes and stared around the small log room that had become all too familiar during the past three days.

"I find it hard to believe she's suddenly healthy." The doctor's voice rumbled through the wall—another thing that was becoming overly familiar. "But since Lindy's still sick, I may wait another day or two until I pay a visit."

"You should t-talk to Mac first."

Victoria. That was the voice she heard. Lindy pressed her eyes closed again and focused on her breathing. A draw of air in, a push of air out. Her lungs still felt as though a giant weight rested atop them, but the weight wasn't as heavy as it had been when she'd first come to Dr. Harrington's office.

When she'd married him.

Oh goodness, had she really done that? What had she been thinking?

But she already knew. She'd been sick and scared. Staying at the bakery would have meant being a burden to Aileen, Ellie, and Victoria, and so she'd leapt at the first solution that had come along—without considering what a burden she'd be to her husband.

Or that she didn't want to be a doctor's wife.

"Tell Lindy I'm sorry I missed her, but I hardly want to wake her just to visit. I'll stop by tomorrow." Victoria's voice resonated through the thin wall of the sickroom again.

Lindy drew in another breath. That's why Victoria had stopped by? To see her? She nearly called out to her friend, but then her husband would learn she was awake.

"Sounds good," he answered. "If you see Mrs. Kainer, will you tell her the medicine came in? Oh, and send Mrs. Spritzer here too if you can. It's odd. I thought I'd be swamped once word spread that I married Lindy. Instead, things are just as slow as before."

Victoria's voice sounded again, but her word were too muffled to make out. Then the thud of the door closing echoed through the room, followed by the tapping of shoes on the floor.

Lindy drew in another rattling breath and sank farther beneath the covers. He couldn't hear her breathing through the wall, couldn't discern that she was awake, could he?

Oh, this was never supposed to happen. Unlike her mother, she refused to drain the coffers of friends and family in some vain hope she'd grow better rather than worse.

Which was why she never should have gotten married. Her doctor husband would probably deplete his savings trying to rescue her from the inevitable.

To everything there is a season, and a time to every purpose under the heaven: A time to be born, and a time to die.

She'd memorized those verses in Ecclesiastes while her mother was still alive. Ma had always focused on the time to laugh and time to dance, but Lindy had memorized the entire passage. A time to be born and a time to die came long before any laughing and dancing.

Which meant she needed to be mending—she'd couldn't let the cost of her medicine pauper her new husband. And mending was the best way to earn her keep.

She raised herself up on the bed, jostling the pillows behind her until she was in a sitting position, then reached for the shirtwaist, needle, and thread she'd left on the table. Hopefully Jessalyn would give her more mending after she returned these things. But considering it would take her a week to do the work she usually finished in a day, she might well find herself out of a job. She shoved the needle through the fabric.

The door to her room opened, and in walked the man she'd unwittingly married, his blond hair a bit ruffled, his frame tall and narrow, and his green eyes filled with concern.

Why had God given her such a handsome husband? It wasn't as though she deserved any husband at all, let alone one good looking enough she'd be tempted to kiss him—if she could breathe, that was.

"I didn't realize you were awake." He approached the bed and held out his hand to touch her forehead. "Your breathing is improving, though you still have a fever. I told you to ring the bell when you woke. Do you not remember?"

She glanced at the bell on the table near where her mending had been. "I could hear you talking through the wall. You were busy."

155

Never mind that whenever he came into the room, her breathing grew shallower, her stomach tightened, and her tongue turned as heavy as a copper ingot. Surely he would think those signs of ill health, wouldn't he?

He stood there while her stomach tangled itself into knots, watching her with those somber green eyes as though he expected her to… to…

What? Given the way he kept his eyes trained on her, he had to expect something.

"I've done some reading on your illness." He took a step nearer, then sat on the edge of the bed, which brought him entirely too close.

There was a chair by the bedside table. Surely he could have used that.

"I made arrangements for a treatment I think might help. Let me bring you a bowl of broth. You'll need your strength for this. Then I want to—"

"No."

"We talked about this before we married." His brow furrowed, and he repositioned himself on the bed, evidently in no hurry get up. "You said it was all right for me to treat your pneumonia and asthma."

"Is that what I have? Pneumonia? The doctor in Chicago thought it was tuberculosis but could never explain why it went away after several weeks." Would he notice if she moved away from him? She shifted toward the wall, just the slightest bit. Perhaps he'd think she was stretching, or getting comfortable, or—

He reached out and captured her hand, then scooted himself closer. "Lindy…"

How could he do that? Say her name with such emotion? It was as though a hundred different thoughts were caught up in the five letters of her name, and the thoughts didn't even go together.

Sadness, pleading, hope, and about ninety-seven other emotions she couldn't quite name.

With her hand still caught in his, he used his free hand to slide the loose fabric of her nightgown back, exposing her scars. "Was he the doctor who did this? The one who said you had tuberculosis?"

She needed a shirtwaist. One that buttoned all the way down to the base of her hand. She shifted to tug her arm away, but he rested his fingers on a scar, the longest and fiercest looking of the bunch. Her skin warmed beneath his touch, and the breath she'd been holding came out in shaky little bursts.

He slowly trailed his fingers down the line of the scar, and the warmth that had started with his touch crept into her chest and face. He might be a doctor, but his hold was nothing like the cruel grip her arm had been locked in the day she'd gotten that scar.

"Do you know if this man went to medical school?" His jaw turned firm, and a hard edge crept into his voice. "Because no true doctor would do this to treat tuberculosis, or pneumonia, or asthma, or any other lung ailment."

That was ridiculous. All doctors bled their patients, except maybe her husband.

"Tell me about him. Maybe if I understand what he was thinking, it will help."

Heat pricked the backs of her eyes. She didn't want to talk, not about the scars on her arm or the one on her leg, not about any of it. But he kept his hand in place, the touch somehow firm enough she couldn't easily pull away but gentle enough to soothe.

"You weren't supposed to see them." She stifled a small cough.

"I've been treating you for three days. Of course I saw them."

Had he seen the one on her leg too? *Please, God, anything but that one.*

"Truth be told, I first discovered them when I treated your broken finger. You were unconscious, and I wanted to make sure you hadn't sustained further injuries when you fell."

She did jerk her arm away then, and he let it go. "You had no right."

"I didn't mean to invade. But now that you're my wife, I want—"

"I'm so sorry."

"Sorry?" He stilled. "What are you sorry for?"

Her throat grew tight, but she forced the words out anyway. "I'd nearly been attacked the night before we married, you see."

"Yes, Elijah told me. You should know he's been made the town's temporary sheriff, so you needn't worry about such things happening again."

She blinked at him. "He has?"

"Yes. Evidently your assault wasn't the first instance of Sheriff Jenkins neglecting his duties."

"Oh, well…" She shifted uncomfortably. "I assumed I'd be unprotected if I didn't marry. And then I was so sick, and I didn't know what to do. I couldn't stay in the bakery and be a burden on the others, and you'd offered to marry me the night before, so when I saw you there helping me, I just…"

She blinked away the tears. "Please forgive me. I'm not sure what I was thinking. Maybe it was that I'd die and you wouldn't have to care for me very long, but now I seem to be getting better, which means you're stuck with me, which will probably ruin—"

"Enough!" His voice cut through the room with the power of an ax splitting a log. Then silence descended, so large and awkward that a couple more ax swings might have been better than the eerie quiet.

Her husband looked at her, his body tense, his jaw working back and forth. But that wasn't the bad part, oh no. His eyes were the part she didn't know what to do with, because they weren't tense or angry or determined like the rest of him. They were… hurt.

Which didn't make sense. Surely he understood how much of a burden she'd be as his wife.

A pounding sounded on the outside door, then a creak as it swung open. "Hello? Dr. Harrington, are you in there? Billy fell and I need some of that acid stuff you put on cuts so it don't get infected."

"Excuse me, Lindy. I'll be back in a few minutes." He stood from the bed and strode out of the room, closing the door behind him with a solid thud.

She turned her head to the side and loosed the cough she'd been holding in. She couldn't blame him for escaping her. After all, who would enjoy being married to a wheezy burden of a wife?

Except that wasn't what the look in his eyes had told her a few moments ago. Oh no. That look had carried a much more dangerous meaning—one that would only lead to heartache.

~.~.~.~.~

Seth's feet were leaden as he headed back into Lindy's room, a bowl of broth in his hands. He had a wife, something he'd been praying God would give him for as long as he could remember. True, their wedding night had been spent with her lying delirious in bed, and him keeping vigil with a stethoscope and bottle of atropine. But he'd known he wasn't marrying the healthiest woman and could handle such things.

What he couldn't handle, however, was the first thing she said when she could finally talk without coughing.

What had driven her to apologize for marrying him?

He paused outside the door to her room. Their marriage hadn't been a mistake. He'd felt so certain when he'd prayed about proposing, even more certain when he'd stood beside her bed and exchanged vows. He wasn't wrong for wedding her, even if she was convinced otherwise.

He opened the door and stepped inside as a deep bout of coughing claimed his wife. Though she'd only been awake for a quarter hour, her eyelids drooped with fatigue, but neither the tiredness nor coughing stopped her from mending. Even when her cough had been worse, she'd been determined to mend as much as possible.

A series of small coughs ended her spell, and she looked down as he approached the bed, moving the needle in and out of the fabric the moment her hands stopped shaking.

He stared at the bowl in his hands. What did one say to a wife who thought herself more a burden than... well, a wife?

"I brought you broth." Which probably didn't make her feel like any less of a burden. "I want you to know, I'm not sorry I married you. I think it's what God wanted for the two of us, even if I can't entirely explain why."

She still didn't look up at him, staying so quiet he could hear the faint wheezing in her lungs without using his stethoscope.

"Just as Christ didn't think of the people he healed in the Bible as burdens, I don't think of any sick person that way either." He set the bowl on the table and sat on the side of her bed once more.

She loosed a cough and shifted away from him.

She wouldn't always be so skittish, would she? Surely she'd feel comfortable once they became more familiar with each other.

"I don't know anything about this quack of a doctor who treated you in Chicago, but you should know why I'm a doctor."

She kept her head down, her needle working in and out as she stitched the seam of a shirt. Did she not want to hear his story? Medicine was such an important part of his life. Shouldn't she care what drove him to practice it?

But that would probably involve caring about him as a person first.

Still, she was his wife. What better time to learn about each other than now? "I grew up outside Sharpsburg, Maryland. Have you heard of it?"

Her brow furrowed, and she shook her head, her gaze still riveted to her mending.

"A battle was fought there during the War Between the States. The injured from the Confederate army were brought to our farm, and the doctors set up a hospital of sorts. At least it's what they'd call a hospital on the battlefield, though it was nothing like the hospitals I worked at in Baltimore and Boston."

The memories rose up, fresh in his mind even though they were over two decades old. His nostrils filled with the scent of blood and sweat, his ears with groans of the injured and dying. "I was only ten, and there were so many wounded there, laid out on our family's lawn, not all of them even in tents. They say now that Antietam was the bloodiest battle of the war."

He drew in a breath. If only he could expel the memories from his mind as easily as he expelled the air from his lungs. "We supported the Union, not the Confederacy. But when those men were lying there, having legs and arms amputated with little to no anesthetic, dying beneath one of the countless tents, it didn't matter whether their uniform was blue or gray. It mattered that they were sick and injured—and that I didn't have the ability to do more than hold cold rags to their foreheads.

"That's the most helpless I've ever felt in my life." His voice cracked, and he swallowed the tightness clogging his throat. "I decided I was going to become a doctor that day. The next time someone sick or injured came to our house, I wanted to help them, maybe even heal them, like Christ did in the Bible."

He glanced up to find Lindy's hazel eyes were open and soft, not bright with fever or shuttered as they had been so many of the times he'd tried talking to her before.

Did she have something to say? She had such strong opinions about doctoring and medicine, surely the story affected her in some way.

He waited for a moment, but she didn't speak. No, of course she didn't. She barely told him any of her thoughts. That had been true before she'd gotten sick, and she didn't seem in a hurry to change it now that they were wed.

"I wish I could be like Christ, speak a few words and make someone recover in an instant." He stared down at his hands, hands that had been trained to heal at one of the top medical schools in the country.

Hands that had failed to heal people too many times. "But God hasn't given me that ability, so I help when I can and leave the rest for Him."

Lindy ducked her head to stare at her mending, but her fingers didn't move.

He shifted awkwardly on the bed, then glanced at the table where he'd set her broth. "You'd better eat."

"As soon as I finish this." She took up her needle again.

He laid a hand over hers before she started sewing. "You'll eat it now. I made arrangements for this evening, and I need you strong."

Her hands fisted in the shirt she held. "I told you, I don't want—"

"It's a steam bath. There's no medicine or scalpels or other medical instruments. It's just sitting in a room with a stove and steam. I'm wondering if it will help break your fever, and the moisture in the air might aid your lungs. I can't say for certain, but I don't see harm in trying."

"Oh." She loosed a small cough. "I've never taken a steam bath before."

"This one is called a sauna. One of the Finnish families in town has one we can use."

"I just sit there and breathe wet air?" She bit down on her bottom lip.

A lip he hoped to kiss one day, after her health was better. After their relationship was better. "And you'll sweat a great deal."

She looked down for a moment, then back up at him. "I know I'm not your easiest patient, but well, thank you for not giving up on me. For trying to find something that will help."

Thank you. He pushed himself up from the bed and swallowed thickly.

This wasn't the marriage he'd dreamed of. This wasn't love or even trust.

But *thank you* was at least a place to start.

Chapter Sixteen

Another week with only two patients. Seth glanced at the door to the small sickroom where Lindy slept. Marrying her was supposed to bring the townsfolk back to his doorstep, yet he had less work now than the first week he'd set up practice in Eagle Harbor.

He rubbed a hand over his face. Were the Ranulfsons that bent on ruining him? The couple might be gossipy, but sabotaging a man's business was a different matter entirely.

He huffed out another breath, then pulled out his pocket watch and glanced at it. Six thirty. The bank would be closed by now, and Lindy had already eaten supper. Maybe he should pay the Ranulfsons a visit. If nothing else, he could set the record straight about what happened the night Mr. Ranulfson found Lindy in his office.

He cracked open Lindy's door and peeked in on her. She slept soundly, her golden hair spread like a giant fan across her pillow. Her fever had abated yesterday, and her cough lessened more every day. But she was still pale and tired, and her lungs weren't fully clear when he listened with his stethoscope. He moved to the bedside table and jotted a quick note letting her know he was going to the Ranulfsons. He shouldn't be gone long, but it was the first time he'd be leaving her alone since their wedding.

He took a step closer to the bed, then reached out his hand and touched her forehead. "God, heal my wife. Give me wisdom to know how to treat her, give her body the strength it needs to be well. And once you've healed her, Lord, bless our marriage. Help me to…"

What were the words he needed? "Understand her. Love her. Help me to love her in a way that makes her return my love. I want us to have a true marriage. The kind that Elijah and Victoria have. The kind that… that I've prayed for since medical school. I feel like I'm stumbling. Help me to find my way again, and to love my wife in the manner she deserves to be loved."

He drew in a breath, and his spirit filled with a sense of peace. *Trust in the Lord with all thine heart.* It was a simple Bible verse, one he'd learned years ago in Sunday school, yet the truth it proclaimed was more profound than most people realized.

He needed to do a better job of trusting. What had Elijah said on the beach? Something about how the trying of his faith would result in patience. He'd prayed over whether to marry Lindy, and regardless of her reasons for marrying him, he needed to trust this was God's will.

But as for him not having any patients? Something told him that had less to do with God and more to do with two gossiping townsfolk.

He placed a kiss on his wife's forehead, then turned and headed for the door.

⌐.⌐.⌐.⌐.⌐

"Dr. Harrington?"

The Ranulfsons' front door swung open to reveal Mrs. Ranulfson rather than the housemaid he'd been expecting. "Do come in. We were about to have some pie in the parlor."

He stepped inside the Victorian home. While it wasn't as large or finely appointed as the Sinclair and Donnelly mansions that towered a story above every other building in Eagle Harbor, it wasn't made of log or clapboard like most homes either. "Thank you, but I don't think this visit warrants pie. I would, however, like to speak to both you and your husband. Alone."

The younger of the Ranulfsons' sons, who was stuck in that awkward stage between boy and man, peeked around the corner of a doorway, then headed down the hall that led deeper into the house, likely to find his father.

"Why don't you step into the parlor? Erik will go get Ernest." Mrs. Ranulfson led him into the room to his right. Appointed in dark wood with plush, colorful rugs, it was almost like walking into one of the sitting rooms of his childhood home near Sharpsburg.

"Please, have a seat." Mrs. Ranulfson gestured to one of the dark wooden chairs with red upholstery, then clasped her hands together as she took a seat on the sofa across from him. "What's this about?"

"I'd prefer to wait for Mr. Ranulfson."

"Of course." Mrs. Ranulfson gave him a curt nod, but her voice wobbled as she spoke.

Mr. Ranulfson appeared a moment later and sat beside his wife. He almost looked small without his suit coat on, and certainly less intimidating than when he was seated behind his large desk at the bank.

Seth tried to sit still, he truly did. But his knees bobbed up and down of their own volition. He clasped his hands together and leaned forward, resting his elbows on his twitching legs. "I'll keep this brief. I never did anything untoward with Miss Marsden—Lindy—my wife. Back before she was my wife, I mean."

He stopped and drew in a breath before he made a bigger muck of the words tumbling out of his mouth.

The Ranulfsons just blinked at him. Because he wasn't making any sense? Or were they waiting for more gossip to spread around town?

"That night you found us in my kitchen, I was working to save a boy's life." Seth jumped up from the chair and paced in front of the fire. Though why they had a fire going, he didn't know. The room suddenly seemed too hot despite the dipping autumn temperature outside. "Toby was having seizures due to a high fever, and Lindy and I had just finished cooling him down with a bath."

"Is this the reason for your visit?" Mr. Ranulfson shifted beside his wife and cleared his throat. "I admit it didn't look good when I stepped inside your kitchen that night, but once you explained about the boy, it was rather clear what you were doing."

"But it was still inappropriate to have an unwed woman of Miss Marsden's age there at that time of night." Mrs. Ranulfson gave a sharp nod of her head, but without her usual hat and the ostrich feathers that always bobbed in agreement, the gesture didn't seem nearly as definitive as normal. "I know this is a backwoods town, but it's still important we maintain a level of propriety, especially considering some of the men we have coming through here. Whether you intended anything improper or not, the situation that night certainly looked improper."

"But it wasn't improper, and if you two would have kept your mouths shut about what you had seen, if you would have asked questions instead of spreading rumors, then…"

Then what? He wouldn't be married to Lindy, and for some foolish reason, he wanted the marriage, even if she didn't.

"Then I'd have patients," he finished. That's why he had come here tonight, to revive his medical practice, not get distracted by his wife. "But even though I've set things right in the eyes of the town by marrying a woman I never compromised, I still don't have any patients, and my practice kept me almost too busy to sleep a month ago."

"Of course you don't have patients." Mrs. Ranulfson sniffed. "Nobody wants to catch what your wife has."

"What my wife has?" He stilled and turned to the woman, letting the fire blaze at his back. "But she's not contagious."

"Are you certain?" Mrs. Ranulfson blinked at him. "I thought sure it was unsafe to visit your office."

"She has asthma, which is a lung condition one is born with, not something a person can catch. Pneumonia is an infection that develops usually because some other condition in the lungs make them prone to infection. In my wife's case, her asthma and the storm she got caught in were enough to cause pneumonia. Sometimes you can spread the conditions that lead to pneumonia, such as a cough or cold, but it's difficult to spread pneumonia itself. After all, not every person with a cough gets pneumonia." He met Mrs. Ranulfson's gaze. She was even now trying to stifle a cough.

"Oh, well, that's…" She furrowed her brow and looked to her husband.

"Helpful." Mr. Ranulfson's eyes had glazed with boredom. "Thank you for the explanation."

"So does that mean it's safe to visit your office?" Mrs. Ranulfson had more of a confused look on her face than a bored one. "I certainly need more cough syrup. The stuff Dr. Greely gives is worthless."

"You went to Dr. Greely for cough syrup?" The words came out a little harsher than he intended.

Mrs. Ranulfson just blinked again, that confused glint still in her eyes. "Yes, I thought I told you. I'd heard your wife would make me sick if I got too close. You know, like how people with smallpox have to go into quarantine."

He barely stifled his groan. How could Mrs. Ranulfson know so much about propriety and be so ignorant about common diseases? "Pneumonia and smallpox are hardly comparable conditions. Perhaps if Lindy had diphtheria or typhus, I could understand your hesitancy to visit my office, but certainly not over asthma and pneumonia."

Not even over tuberculosis, really. While that disease could definitely be spread, it was usually done so among family members or people who lived in close, crowded conditions.

He sighed and turned back to the Ranulfsons. "Since the two of you did such a good job of informing the town that Lindy was in my office late at night, I'd appreciate it if you'd do an equally good job of informing the town that my wife can't spread her illness, and I'm more than happy to see patients again."

The couple looked at each other, then Mr. Ranulfson cleared his throat again. "That's just the issue, Dr. Harrington. We didn't do a whole lot of talking about what happened with you and your wife the last time."

Seth raised an eyebrow.

"I mean, maybe at first." Mr. Ranulfson squirmed the way a schoolboy might when caught putting a frog on a neighboring girl's desk. "But once we realized there truly was a boy you'd saved, well, we didn't keep talking on about the impropriety. A child's life is more important than propriety. Even Betty understands that, right Betty?"

"I won't say the situation in your office that night was proper." Mrs. Ranulfson's hands fluttered up to fiddle with the lace collar at her neck. "But I didn't keep harping about it. Usually rumors die if people stop talking about them, but for some reason, this one didn't."

Were they telling the truth? It was rather difficult to imagine Mrs. Ranulfson refusing to harp about anything, ever. And if they were being honest, why had the rumor about him and Lindy spread?

Seth shook his head. He wasn't here to rehash the past; he just wanted his patients back. "Perhaps you could stop by my office tomorrow morning for that cough syrup? And maybe you could go to the bakery and mercantile tomorrow and mention you purchased some medicine from me without catching what my wife has?"

Mrs. Ranulfson nodded again, and he could almost imagine the ostrich feathers on one of her hats waving determinedly as she told her story at the mercantile tomorrow. "And Trudy been complaining of headaches. Perhaps I'll encourage her to go to your office for some headache powder."

Seth couldn't stop the smile from curving his lips. He'd have a line of patients by the end of the day, no doubt.

Chapter Seventeen

Lindy's eyes fluttered open to find morning sunlight streaming into her room. She drew in a breath, deep and free, and pushed the air back out of her lungs again. The steam baths were working. She'd tried her first one a week ago, had taken another about four days ago, and another again last night. Not only had her fever fled and most of her coughing abated, but her lungs seemed clearer than they had been before she'd fallen ill.

Would the baths truly be able to cure her? Between that and the ipecac and atropine Seth insisted she still take, she truly was improving.

Perhaps she'd dress and go for a short walk today. She'd certainly been lying in this sickroom long enough. She swung her legs over the side of the bed and drew in another breath before stretching her arms wide.

She stood and looked around the room for the dress she'd worn last night when walking to and from the sauna, but it wasn't hanging on the peg by the door, and her shoes weren't on the floor either.

Aileen must have brought her things from the bakery to Seth, so where were her clothes being stored? Seth had been bringing her a dress, shoes, comb, and anything else she'd asked for this past week and a half.

She sank down onto the bed and glanced around the room once more—the room that was meant for sick patients, not for a wife. Were her things in his room? And if so, would he expect her to share that room as soon as she was well?

I want us to have a true marriage, Lord, a real relationship. The words from the prayer she'd overheard earlier that week came back to her. Yes, her husband wanted a marriage in full. If she'd had any question before, his prayer had answered that. He didn't seem to care that she'd married him half by accident. He was determined to love her anyway.

It didn't make any sense. She'd done nothing to attract his attention, nothing worthy of having him as a husband. She'd told him she'd only burden him, for goodness's sake.

One day, I'll be a teacher like my mother, grandmother, great-grandmother, and so on.

One day, I'll have a husband to hold me close and whisper words of love in my ear.

One day, I'll have some children of my own.

And maybe even, *One day, I'll have a sewing machine.*

She'd never dreamed she'd marry a man she didn't love, but who was determined to love her anyway.

Telltale footsteps sounded in the parlor, growing louder as they approached her door.

She pressed a hand to her throat. Perhaps she wasn't quite ready to dress and take a walk, not today, not until she'd figured out what to do about her husband.

She swung her legs back onto bed and pulled the covers up to her chin.

It wasn't deceitful to lie there when Seth came in. It couldn't be. She'd been lying in bed for a week and a half. Why should today be any different?

Because I'm getting better and not telling the man who's spent hours caring and praying for me, dolt!

But what if he expected her to act like his wife as soon as she was better?

She drew in a breath through lungs that had suddenly become tight.

The door creaked open and more footsteps sounded on the plank flooring. She stared at the bed positioned against the opposite wall until his legs came into view. If she didn't pretend to be sleeping, then maybe she wasn't deceiving her husband.

"I brought you some porridge for breakfast." He set the tray with tea and a bowl on the bedside table. "Though if you feel up to eggs, I can scramble some. We should work on increasing your diet. Protein, fresh fruits, and vegetables can be especially helpful when a person is recovering from an illness."

Eggs did sound rather good, but she'd caused him enough trouble as it was. She wasn't about to waste the food he'd already made too. "Perhaps for lunch."

"For lunch then." His voice turned tender, and a small smile tilted the corners of his lips.

The simplest things made him smile, like saying she'd eat eggs, have a steam bath, or take the ipecac and atropine.

"Do you need help sitting up?"

She didn't, but he'd already stepped to the bed and started moving the pillows behind her. She scooted herself up, causing his hand to brush against her back. She stilled for a moment, her lungs growing tight once again. Did he feel the warmth of her skin when he'd touched her nightgown? Evidently not since his hand brushed her back twice more as he helped with the pillows.

Then he rested a hand on her shoulder, and her lungs suddenly forgot how to work. She looked up at him, but he merely guided her back against the seat he'd made, then settled his hand on her forehead.

Had he touched her this much when she'd been ill? If so, it certainly hadn't caused her heart to race or a tingling sensation to spread through her body then.

"Still no fever. Excellent." He smiled even larger this time, then handed her the bowl of porridge. She glanced down at it, her gaze skimming her nightgown until it disappeared beneath the quilt at her waist. She needed to get some different clothes. It was hardly proper for her to sit here wearing nothing but her nightdress.

"Aren't you going to eat?" Once again, he ignored the wooden chair at the side of her bed and sat on the mattress. Why did he keep the chair there if he was never going to sit in it? She forced herself to look down at her porridge rather than shift away from him. She couldn't exactly play shy with a man who prayed to God about how to love her better.

Unless the man intended to move her into his room before she was ready.

And if she was never ready?

Oh, she hadn't thought things through nearly enough before agreeing to marry him. Maybe if she hadn't been so sick, she could have convinced him to have a marriage in name only.

She kept her gaze on the porridge so she didn't have to look at him, then dipped her spoon in and took a bite. The sweet taste of sugar mixed with the grainy taste of oats filled her taste buds with subtle, yet perfect flavor. What had he put in it?

"Do you like to walk in the woods?" he asked as she took another bite of porridge. And another. And another.

"Why?" She spoke around a mouthful of food.

"You seem to be improving, and the weather has turned warm of a sudden. If it holds for a few more days, I was thinking we might take a stroll. You grew up here, so you must know of a picnic spot or two I've yet to discover."

A picnic? He couldn't know about the ones her family had taken when she'd been a girl. She inhaled, and it almost seemed as though she was filling her lungs with the crisp air of autumn outside rather than the warm, still air of her sickroom.

He chuckled. "I'll take that as a yes."

Her gaze collided with his, her spoon clattering against the nearly empty bowl as she stared up into soft green eyes filled with hope. For them. As a couple.

"Don't look at me like that." She tightened her grip on her bowl.

"Like what?"

"You know, all soft and… friendly-like."

"Friendly-like?" His smile only widened. "We're married, Lindy. I'm allowed to look at you friendly-like."

First he prayed for her, now he sat here and pretended they had the kind of marriage where they went on picnics and discussed the weather. The kind of marriage where he prayed to love her better— as though she'd be alive long enough to bother.

It had to stop. "Not when I'm dying."

"What's happened?" He reached forward and laid his hand on her forehead again, a frown marring the face that had been so happy a half minute earlier. "I left my stethoscope in the supply room. Let me get it."

"I don't mean I'm dying today." She pulled his hand from her forehead. "But the infection will come back. It always does."

Had she really hoped before breakfast that she might get better? That the saunas and medicine would cure her of the illness that had claimed her mother? Maybe it was good Seth had offered to take her on a picnic and given her that silly, besotted look. Otherwise she might not have realized how futile her dream was.

"Then we'll treat the pneumonia and asthma again, the same way we did this time. How long was your mother usually ill for? A week? Two?" Determination saturated his voice, and he leaned forward to stroke a strand of hair away from her face.

She looked away, but he kept his hand on her, spreading out his fingers to stroke the hair on the side of her head while the faint scent of sunshine and bergamot twined around her. Why did he always seem to be touching her? And in a manner that would make her look like a shrew if she pushed him away?

"A couple weeks at the beginning," she muttered. "But at the end, her coughing bouts would last for months."

"And what about your lung infections when you were in Chicago? How long did it take one to leave then?"

"A month. Sometimes longer."

"And the worst of this was over in a week?" His hand stilled in her hair, and another smile crept across his face. "That's improvement, Lindy. I'll have to write Rand and see if he knows of any other treatment possibilities. If he usually treats bronchitis with atropine, I wonder what would happen if..."

Seth kept talking, but his words blurred together.

He was assuming she'd stay better, but she wouldn't. How many times had she hoped for the best with her mother? Whenever Doc Greely would come with a new medicine, she'd wonder if maybe that would be the time Ma stayed well. Even after Pa died and they moved to Chicago, she hoped one of the doctors Aunt Edith hired could treat Ma. But Ma only got worse.

A knock sounded at the front door, and Seth stopped muttering about doctor friends and letters to Washington D.C. "That might be a patient. Excuse me."

He bolted for the door, nearly knocking over the chair by the bed in the process. He grabbed the wobbling back an instant before it careened toward the floor and righted it. "Sorry about that."

And then he was gone, rushing away without even making sure the door latched behind him.

She frowned. Was he in that much of a hurry to leave her side, the man who had just been stroking her hair? But no, that didn't make sense. It must be the patient he wanted to see so badly. Given how seriously he took his doctoring, he was probably in that much of a hurry to see everyone who needed him. Though she didn't really know for certain, because only a few people had stopped by the entire time she'd been here.

That was a bit unusual, wasn't it? He might not have had patients after Mr. Ranulfson found them together, but getting married was supposed to fix that. If people had been avoiding Seth for the week and a half before they wed, shouldn't he be doubly busy now?

The door to her room burst open, and a brown-headed form raced toward her bed.

"Miss Lindy, are you all right?" Jack stopped beside her, his chest heaving as though he'd run the entire way from his cabin. "I didn't know you were sick or I'd have come sooner, I promise."

"Jack." She reached over from her position on the bed to give him a sideways hug.

He gripped her so tightly he nearly pinched the skin off her side. "I went to the bakery looking for you, but the lady there said you married the man who helped Toby."

"That would be me." Seth entered the room and offered the boy a lopsided smile. "I'm Dr. Harrington, and this is my lovely wife, Mrs. Lindy Harrington."

"You're the one who treated Toby?" Jack's eyes grew wide as he stepped away from her side and moved toward Seth.

"I am."

"I don't have no money to pay you, but if you need chores done,

I can probably sneak into town for a day or two a week."

"Thank you for your offer, young man, but that's quite all right." Seth reached out as though about to pat Jack on the head, then paused for a moment and rested a hand on the boy's shoulder instead. "I was happy to help with Toby. He's doing better, I assume?"

Jack's head bobbed up and down. "It's like he never got sick. Even Jenny's happy about it, and don't nothin' make her happy anymore."

"Jenny, is it?"

"Yes sir." Jack gave another firm nod, his eyes latched on his new hero. "She's looking out for us until Pa gets back."

"And Jenny is your...?"

Lindy glared at her husband. She'd told him to leave the O'Byrnes alone, but here he was wheedling information out of someone half his age.

If he saw her look, he ignored it, which allowed Jack to barrel on.

"She's my big sister. Well, she's more part sister than whole sister. She don't share the same Pa as me and Alice and Toby, but she stayed around to help Pa with us after Ma died."

"Mmmmm." Seth nodded so gravely one would think he'd just received news of an enemy ambush and not information about a boy's parentage. "That must keep her quite busy."

Jack grimaced and tucked a hand in his pocket. "Not sure if busy's the word for it, sir."

"Well, if you're ever in need of a doctor again, I can always pay a house call."

Jack stilled then, as though finally realizing how much he'd shared, and took a step away from Seth. "Um... I don't think Jenny'd like that much. She's awful particular about who she lets visit."

"I see." Seth raised his gaze to meet Lindy's then, his eyes promising questions for later. "I have a patient to call on today, so I'll leave you two to chat." He turned for the door, then paused and looked back at her. "I'm sorry, Lindy, I should have asked. Do you feel comfortable with me leaving? If not, I can arrange for Victoria or Aileen to sit with you while I call on Tressa."

Warmth started in the vicinity of her chest and spread through her. Again. Which was utterly ridiculous. What was it about this man that turned her insides to mush? He was merely being polite by asking what she wanted. It wasn't as though he actually cared.

Except that was the problem. He did seem to care. Far more than he should considering her health and how little they knew each other. "I'll manage just fine, but thank you for asking."

Chapter Eighteen

"I wondered why you hadn't come to visit." Jack sat on the side of Lindy's bed, his eyes glued to her face as though he expected her to stop breathing and turn blue any second.

"Another week, and I should be well enough to walk to your cabin." There was no sense worrying the boy further, not when he had so many concerns of his own. "Now does Jenny know you're here today?"

The boy's cheeks turned pink.

"I see." She could hardly blame him for running off though, especially if they needed food. Had they found enough to eat while she'd been sick? "I had some food set aside for you at the bakery, but I'm not sure where it got moved when I fell ill."

"That's not why I came." Jack twisted his lips together and looked down at the quilt for a moment. "All right, maybe it's some of why I came. We could use a few carrots and potatoes if you have any, but I also wondered about you. You didn't come back when you said and…" He swallowed thickly.

She reached out and took his hand, his small fingers already calloused from work. "I'm fine, Jack. See?" She waved her hand to encompass herself. "But I do need to get out of bed if we're going to send you home with supplies tonight."

Jack bit the side of his lip. "Are you allowed to get up?"

Was she? Seth hadn't told her to stay abed, and she'd left the office three times over the past week when they'd walked to and from the sauna. "As long as I don't overdo things." Or so she hoped. "The trouble is, I'm not sure where most of my things are. I was pretty sick when Dr. Harrington brought me here."

"Were you sick when you married him too?"

Heat rose in her cheeks. "Yes."

"Is that why you got married? So he would make you better?"

"Something like that." She stood and started for the door, the wooden floor cool against her bare feet. "Let's see if we can find that food. And if I take my mending to Jessalyn, I'll have money to purchase some jam and flour before you head home."

He followed her into the parlor and through the doorway that led to the kitchen. Seth likely would have stored the potatoes and rutabaga she'd set aside somewhere in here, but she'd check his room first. Hopefully she'd find her dress hanging on a peg and not need to do much rummaging through his things. She walked toward the room off the kitchen, the one she assumed was Seth's bedroom, though she'd never been inside it.

"Miss Lindy?"

Something in Jack's tone made her pause and turn back. "What is it?"

"I just, well…" He scrunched his shoulders up and shifted from foot to foot. "Thought you should know Jenny's decided not to wait around for Pa no more. Ma has a sister back in Cornwall, see, and—"

"Cornwall? Your surname led me to believe you were Irish." At first. Jenny's Cornish accent had told her the truth after only a few minutes of conversation.

The boy's face flushed. "O'Byrne's not our real name."

She tried to keep her face impassive, her voice even lest she frighten him away from answering. "Oh? What is your real name, then?"

His brow furrowed. "I don't rightly know. Before we came here, we spent time down by Rockland, and we went by Walsh there. Then before that it was Spence. Oh, and I think we were Wards for a while too. Don't really remember what we were before that."

A sinking sensation filled her stomach. There were reasons for a man to change his family's name so many times—but none of them could be good.

She was supposed to help the O'Byrnes until their father returned, and then everything was going to be better. But what if things only grew worse when Mr. O'Byrne came back? Had she been hoping for the wrong thing?

"So you have an aunt in Cornwall, yes?" Maybe she needed to be saving money to buy passage for the children rather than spending the extra on clothes and dolls. "And Jenny wants to earn enough to pay for passage back there?"

Jack clutched the sleeve of her nightgown. "It's a bad idea, Miss Lindy. You've gotta talk her out of it. Nothing good will come of her job."

"Why is it a bad…?" She frowned. "Jenny has a job?"

Jack shifted again, and this time the redness in his cheeks spread down his neck. "She's, um, going into Central a couple nights a week. So she can… work."

Work at night in a mining town? It could only mean one thing. "Tell me she's not become a soiled dove."

The hardness in Jack's jaw answered her question without him uttering a word.

She gripped Jack's shoulders, her fingers digging into his shirt as she bent to meet his eyes. "No. You can't let her."

He pulled away. "She won't listen to me. That's why you need to talk to her."

"You're mistaken if you think I can convince her of anything. Each time I visit, she threatens to move without telling me where you're going." But there had to be a way to help Jenny see her mistake. As soon as she was well enough to make the walk, she'd visit the cabin.

~.~.~.~.~

"What do you mean I can't see Tressa?" Seth's terse words bounced off the boulders lining the shore near the lighthouse. "I've been treating her since the beginning of her pregnancy."

"That was before you had a wife that might get mine sick." Mac crossed his large arms over his chest, his towering frame filling the doorway so Seth had no chance of peeking around him.

Not that a view of the lighthouse kitchen would be of much help if Tressa was in bed like she was supposed to be. "Lindy won't get Tressa sick, and neither will I. Where did you come up with such a thing?"

Probably the same place the Ranulfsons had. He should have realized sooner why Mac hadn't called him to the lighthouse the entire time he'd been tending Lindy.

"Lindy's got a cough, doesn't she?" Mac's face remained impassive, his eyes not offering even the tiniest bit of remorse. "Seems that's a good enough reason to keep the both of you away from Tressa."

Seth raked a hand through his hair and shook his head. "The cough is from pneumonia and asthma. Asthma is a genetic lung condition, which means it can't be spread, and pneumonia is very difficult to spread. Come now." He took a step closer to Mac. "If I thought seeing Tressa would put her at risk, I wouldn't be here. But it's not as though I've just treated a case of scarlet fever. Lindy can't share her lung infection that easily."

The large lightkeeper didn't budge an inch from his position in the doorway. "That's not what Ruby Spritzer said. Have you heard a couple of her young'uns are sick? Ruby swears Ellie brought the cough home after being around Lindy."

The Spritzers were sick? He gripped the handle of his medical bag tighter. "Why wasn't I called?"

"Reckon they probably called Doc Greely, considering."

"Considering what? Lindy's not contagious!" Seth's words echoed over the rocks, though they'd hardly do the seagull circling above much good. "Tell me you're not letting Greely tend Tressa. I know you've got more sense than that."

Mac dropped his arms to his side. "No, not Greely. The midwife from Central is coming down tomorrow. It'll be her third visit."

"Oh. I didn't realize…" What more was there to say? He should be happy Tressa was getting the help she needed. Except he hadn't expected to be excluded from Tressa's care once the midwife came.

"You set up that first visit with the midwife, remember? But I heard you were a little busy getting married the day she came down."

"Among other things," he muttered as a vision of Lindy lying on the bed above the bakery came back to him, her hair in tangles and her chest heaving as she struggled to breathe between bouts of coughing. He'd forgotten all about the midwife's scheduled visit.

"Are things going well with Tressa then?" He looked back up at Mac. "Surely you can tell me what the midwife's said."

The man's shoulders drooped, the first sign he was a human discussing the woman he loved rather than a stone gargoyle defending a castle. "The midwife says about the same as you. There's not much fluid inside Tressa, and I guess a babe is supposed to have that. It's still breech, too, even though the midwife tried turning it."

"She wasn't able to turn the baby?" No, no, no. That was one of the biggest reasons he'd sent for the midwife.

"I never expected turning a babe would hurt that much, and the midwife didn't even get it in the right position." Mac's voice grew hoarse, his face pale.

"I've heard of it being uncomfortable, but not usually painful." Still, better to turn the child now and endure the pain rather than have Tressa deliver a breech baby—if she could. Breech deliveries didn't always end well.

"She says it's because there's no fluid. Hurts more when the babe moves, I guess."

Seth glanced up at the second story window that marked Tressa and Mac's room. "If you change your mind and decide to let me see her before the baby's born, please send word."

Mac eyed him and swallowed. "You're a good man, doc. I know you are. And maybe Lindy can't give Tressa her cough like you say, but if it were your wife, would you risk it?"

Seth took a step back and sighed, his medical bag suddenly as heavy as one of the boulders rimming the lawn. "I would, because I know Lindy's not contagious. But I can understand your position. You love your wife and don't want to take chances with her health. It's admirable, really." Or it would be if he hadn't been the one excluded from seeing his patient. "I'm assuming this is why Victoria told me I didn't need to stop by last week? Why she told me to talk to you?"

Mac looked over his shoulder into the kitchen. "She's inside now tending to the children."

"I'll let you get back to your family then." He turned and headed down the rocky path that led toward town without waiting for a response, not that there was anything more either of them could say.

First, he'd lost his job at the Marine Hospital Service, then at the Central Mine, though leaving there was more of a mutual decision. But doctoring in Eagle Harbor had been different. Sure, he'd been slow to gain patients, being the new doctor in town. But it hadn't taken long for people to realize he was better at treating ailments than Dr. Greely. Anyone who didn't want to be bled with leeches or spend money on useless cough syrup came to him.

Or at least they had until that night with Lindy.

The night the Ranulfsons claimed they hadn't gossiped about.

Seth kicked at a rock. How had the rumor started then? And even more, how was he going to set it straight? Neither marrying Lindy nor visiting the Ranulfsons had done any good. And now there seemed to be another rumor that Lindy would make anyone he treated ill.

Seth paused when he reached the intersection of Front Street and North Street, where the path to the lighthouse ended. Where did he go next? Should he pay a visit to the Spritzers and see if any of the children were sick? Even if they were ill, they would likely send him away.

If Eagle Harbor was this set against him, maybe he truly should go elsewhere to doctor. But where? If one rumor was enough to destroy his practice in Eagle Harbor, then what prevented another rumor from doing the same once he'd established himself in a different town?

Maybe he should go home and be the businessman his family wanted. Surely Lindy would rather be the wife of a businessman than a doctor. But moving would leave Eagle Harbor under Dr. Greely's care. Seth cringed at the thought. The man would injure more people than he helped.

But perhaps that wasn't his problem. He couldn't force people to come to him for help, and he could hardly stay in Eagle Harbor with all of one patient to treat—if Lindy even counted as a patient now that they were married.

But then, she didn't want his doctoring either.

Chapter Nineteen

"Do you mind waiting here? Olivia has another earache, and I'd hate for her to get your cough on top of it."

Lindy furrowed her brow but handed the mending over to Jessalyn. "Sure, I'll wait."

The door closed behind the petite woman, but that didn't stop Jack from peeking into the seamstress's shop window. "She don't seem very nice. Maybe you should try working for someone else."

Except Jessalyn usually was nice. With her bright smile, sunny hair, and cheerful eyes, the woman might even be too nice, if such a thing were possible.

Lindy stared at the closed door to the shop. It was strange. Jessalyn had met her at the door, but hadn't let her step foot inside. She still had a cough, yes, but not so severe she worried about giving it to others.

Jessalyn appeared a moment later with a five dollar bill in her hand. "Here you go."

Lindy reached for the bill. "Do you have more mending?"

"More?" Jessalyn looked over her shoulder into the shop. "Well, maybe a piece or two, but business has slowed recently."

"It looks like you got piles of clothes in there, miss." Jack pressed his face against the window, cupping his hands around his eyes to give him a better view.

187

Lindy couldn't resist her own brief glance inside as well, which revealed a shop just as cluttered as it had been the last time she stopped by. Even if business had slowed, it would take Jessalyn half a year to work her way through the mounds of clothes inside.

"I'll take whatever you can give me."

"You will?" Jessalyn blinked as though baffled by the request. "Now that you're married to the doctor, I figured…"

"You figured wrong." As though it was any of Jessalyn's business whether she continued to work after she was married. "I'll wait here while you get the clothes."

The door closed again, but even if Jessalyn only decided to give her one garment, nothing said she couldn't return tomorrow. Then maybe she could talk Jessalyn into giving her more work for the next night.

Yes, that's exactly what she'd do. It wasn't as though she had much choice if she wanted to help the O'Byrnes purchase passage across the Atlantic and pay Seth for her medicine.

~.~.~.~.~

The telltale cough echoed down the steps of the mercantile before Seth had even climbed onto the porch. Why was his wife out shopping? Had she needed something in the hour he'd left to check on Tressa and the Spritzers? He hurried up the set of steps and reached for the wooden handle on the door.

"She's going to contaminate the town, I tell you."

He paused at the sound of Dr. Greely's voice rising above the coughing fit, then pushed into the store. Lindy was hunched over beside a shelf, coughs racking her body to the point that her hair was slipping from its bun. A wide-eyed Jack stood to her side, his face pale as he attempted to rub her back.

Dr. Greely stood near the door with several townsfolk clustered about. The lout didn't have his medical bag open, nor was he trying to stop the cough. Instead he pointed his finger at Lindy.

"It's tuberculosis, I tell you." The portly doctor's gaze met his. "And Dr. Harrington's been hiding it from us."

"She doesn't have tuberculosis." He barely spared the other man a glance as he strode toward his wife and rested a hand on her shoulder. "Slow deep breaths, sweetheart. Try to hold the air in your lungs for a few seconds."

She looked up at him, the green and brown of her eyes burning bright as the asthmatic cough wracked her lungs, but she held off her next bout of coughing for a few seconds.

"There you go." He stroked a strand of hair behind her ear. "I've got some atropine in my bag. Let's see if that helps."

He glanced up at the Foleys, both of whom had come around the counter at the back of the store but were keeping their distance from Lindy. "Do you have a cup of water?"

"Of course." Mr. Foley scrambled into his back room and returned a moment later with a mug.

"Thank you." He opened his medical bag and shook some of the atropine powder into the water, then stirred it with his finger and waited for Lindy's newest round of coughing to abate before handing the glass to her. "Sip slowly."

She wheezed in a breath as she drank, her inhalation sounding as though a whistle lodged in her lungs. But she did as ordered, sipping and slowing her breathing.

He stroked the back of her neck, soft with the hair that had fallen during her asthmatic fit. "That's it. Relax now."

"Is she gonna be all right?" Jack's knuckles had turned white around Lindy's hand.

"She is now, yes."

Mrs. Foley edged closer, her hands clutched together in front of her ample stomach. "I didn't know it was possible to stop a cough that fast."

He turned to the motherly woman with gray-streaked hair. "Not all coughs, but sometimes asthmatic ones can be calmed quickly. If she had tuberculosis as Dr. Greely here thinks, nothing I could do would help."

"He helps my cough too." Mrs. Ranulfson came to stand beside Mrs. Foley, the ostrich feathers in her hat bobbing with the movement. "Dr. Greely's syrup never does anything for it, and it costs twice as much."

He stroked the back of Lindy's neck again. Because he needed to listen to her inhalations and exhalations, of course. Not because he was looking for an excuse to touch her in the middle of the mercantile. "That's because you have asthma, Mrs. Ranulfson, though not as severe as Lindy. I stopped giving you opiate cough syrup long ago and started giving you a syrup with atropine, this same powder I just gave Lindy."

The woman merely blinked at him. "Oh. I… I have asthma?"

"A slight bit of it, yes. It seems to bother you certain times of the year more than others."

Mrs. Ranulfson looked at his medical bag, then back up at him. "I didn't know."

"Now see here." Dr. Greely jabbed a finger at him, though he still seemed too frightened of Lindy's asthma to approach. "I've been doctoring since before you were born, and I know a tubercular cough when I hear one. That woman has tuberculosis."

"I do not," Lindy rasped on a wheezy breath. "You only say that because of all the years you sold useless cough syrup to my mother. I'm sick because my lungs are weak and easily susceptible to miasmas. But it doesn't mean I'll make you sick by coming into the mercantile."

Miasmas? Seth dropped his hand from her back. That's why she thought she was sick? Clearly he needed to give his wife a little lesson about germs—which actually existed, unlike miasmas.

"But what if that doctor's wrong and she is contagious?" one of the sailors standing with Dr. Greely asked. "If one of us catches it, we could give it to the whole crew when we leave tomorrow. I don't think she should be about town until her cough goes away."

Seth glanced at Lindy, the color slowly returning to her face. He didn't think his wife should be about town either, but for a different reason than the sailor's.

"No one objected to me being out before I got sick, and I still had my cough then." Lindy raised her hands and then let them fall listlessly at her sides. "I'll always have my cough."

"Then maybe you should go back to Chicago. We don't want you contaminating the whole town." One of the dockworkers with Dr. Greely took a step closer to Lindy. "I got me a wife and babe at home, and I don't need neither of them getting sick."

"Miss Lindy's not going to get anybody sick," Jack pronounced.

Dr. Greely shifted his large girth to stand the front of the group. "There'd be more people for you to treat in Chicago, Harrington. A town the size of Eagle Harbor doesn't need two doctors. You should consider moving there with your new wife."

Seth stilled. Was that what this was about? Dr. Greely getting him to leave? His lack of patients suddenly made sense. The Ranulfsons had likely been telling the truth regarding not spreading rumors about him and Lindy. But if Dr. Greely had been looking for a way to take patients, the incident with Lindy had provided the perfect opportunity.

As had Lindy's lung ailment.

And her breathing attack today in public.

"No, the town doesn't need two doctors, just one who knows

what he's doing," he gritted. They were fighting words. Uttered to a doctor his own age, they would have led to a brawl in the mercantile, and he wouldn't have minded defending himself.

But Dr. Greely was too overweight and wheezy himself to do much more than sputter while his face turned red. "Which is why you need to leave before you lead anyone else astray with your misdiagnoses."

Seth held back his sigh. Did he truly know what he was doing? Enough he could defend it? Not according to the Marine Hospital Service. Still, when compared to Dr. Greely, there was no question who could better serve the town.

"I don't think any of the Cummingses are sick, are they?" Mrs. Ranulfson's ostrich feathers swayed as she jutted her chin toward Dr. Greely. "Seems like if Mrs. Harrington could give people her cough, then the whole Cummings family would be ill by now."

"And Aileen at the bakery." Mrs. Foley settled a hand on her pudgy hip. "I was just there this morning, and she's not sick."

"And Aileen's been with me since I left Chicago." Lindy leveled a look at Dr. Greely. "That's plenty of time for her to catch my cough."

"But Ellie has a cough," Dr. Greely snapped.

"She does?" Lindy blinked, questions written across her face.

Seth raised a shoulder and let it fall. "I just heard of it this morning, but I wasn't able to see her."

"And you won't because she's my patient." Dr. Greely thumped his chest.

That, at least, was true. Seth had stopped at the Spritzers house after leaving the Oaktons, but only to be turned away.

Mr. Foley repositioned the spectacles on his nose. "Even if the Spritzers are sick, how can you know Lindy was the cause and not something else?"

"I know she's the cause because I say she's the cause." Dr. Greely puffed out his chest, though the effect was a bit lost considering the girth around his waist. "I've been a doctor for almost fifty years, I know how these things work."

"I don't know nothin' about doctorin'." Jack released Lindy's hand and crossed his arms over his chest. "But I know that Doc Harrington here saved my brother's life. So if he says Miss Lindy's cough won't make me sick, I'm gonna listen to him before I listen to you."

"Now see here..." the doctor bellowed.

But his words were lost in the chaos that erupted through the rest of the mercantile. Mrs. Ranulfson and the Foleys proclaimed they agreed with Jack, while the crowd that spent their nights at The Pretty Penny with Dr. Greely shouted their objections.

Dr. Greely stayed for a few more minutes, his face turning so red Seth feared the man might suffer an apoplectic fit. Then he stormed from the store, taking the sailors with him, and leaving utter silence in their wake.

Seth rubbed his forehead. Today's battle might be finished, but the war brewing between him and the other doctor didn't seem like it would end until one of them left town.

⌐.⌐.⌐.⌐.⌐

The scene at the mercantile might have been a disaster, but at least they'd not had any problem getting Jack the food Lindy had left at the bakery—or they wouldn't if he could convince Jack to let go of his wife's hand.

Jack stood there now, in the alley behind the bakery, gripping Lindy as though she were drowning and he held the life ring. "Are you sure you'll be all right if I leave?"

Lindy smiled down at Jack, and Seth swallowed. It seemed inane to be jealous of a twelve-year-old, but how long before he'd be the one holding Lindy's hand and causing her to smile? Whenever he touched his wife, she stiffened and pulled away.

Except for in the mercantile a half hour ago, but he couldn't actually wish more breathing fits on her, even if it was a good excuse to touch her.

"I'll take good care of her." Seth took a step closer to the pair. "In fact, she's headed home for a nap."

The boy looked back and forth between them, placing his weight on one foot and then the other before his gaze settled on Lindy again. "Are you tired, Miss Lindy?"

She was. He could tell by the way her eyelids struggled to stay open, even while she talked to Jack. And her breathing was growing more labored, something he hoped was due to her asthma, but could well be caused by the remnants of her pneumonia.

"A little, yes." Her words were slow with fatigue.

"I'd better go, but don't you worry, Miss Lindy. I'll be back next week." Jack slung the knapsack that had been sitting on the ground beside him up over his shoulder, then stilled. "They're not going to make you leave town before then, are they?"

Seth cleared his throat. "No, and don't let what happened in the mercantile bother you. It was more about me than Mrs. Harrington's cough."

Lindy's eyes met his. "And your lack of patients?"

"So it seems."

"But Miss Lindy can't get anybody sick, like you said back at the store, right?"

Seth ran his eyes down his wife, from the top of her golden head down to the worn shoes peeking out from beneath her faded dress. Would she let him replace them? Or would she argue about that like she had over the majority of things he'd tried doing for her?

"Only herself." He looked at Jack as he spoke. Maybe Lindy

would be more apt to listen if she didn't think he was giving her orders. "If she doesn't get enough rest, her pneumonia can come back."

"Don't worry about visiting next week." Lindy patted the boy's shoulder. "By then I'll be well enough to visit you."

Or maybe she wasn't going to listen no matter how he imparted the information. "We'll have to see about that." Seth moved his gaze to Jack. "It seems you live back in the woods quite a way."

Jack nodded. "About two miles, near as I can figure it."

Two miles? Surely Lindy didn't expect to be hiking two miles in another week. He'd not brook argument over that. And would she still refuse to let him accompany her because of Jack's sister? If that was the case, she wouldn't be visiting the O'Byrnes until spring—if ever.

"Plan to come here, Jack. We'll have some supplies waiting for you." Seth jutted his chin toward the knapsack slung over the boy's shoulder.

Lindy stiffened beside him, her lips pressed together as though she had a lecture planned the moment Jack moved out of earshot.

Which was fine, because he had one for her about what she could and couldn't do while recovering from a life-risking bout of pneumonia.

"All right, I'll come here. Might even bring Alice with me, if Jenny allows it. Goodbye." Jack waved and then started off, his long strides only drawing attention to the inches of skin around his ankles where his trousers had grown too short.

Seth raised a hand in farewell while Lindy smiled beside him. But the moment the boy rounded the corner, she let out a wheezy breath and sagged against the wall of the bakery.

"I'm ready for that nap."

"You should have never left your bed this morning." He extended an arm. "Come, let's get you home where you can rest. Or do you need to sit for a few minutes first?"

She reached for his arm. "I'm not sorry I left."

He raised his eyes to the heavens as he led her around the corner of the building. If God was only going to give him one patient to treat, why did it have to be the most headstrong woman in the state of Michigan?

"How else could I have gotten those supplies for Jack?"

"You could have asked me before I left to visit the Oaktons." They might be new to marriage, but wanting her to ask a question or two surely wasn't expecting too much.

"I didn't know what you would say."

"Truly? A rail-thin boy with clothes two sizes too small comes to the office, and you thought I'd refuse him food?" He clenched his jaw as they turned onto Center Street. "You must think you married a tyrant."

"No, not a tyrant. I'm sorry. It's just…" She sighed, her eyelashes fluttering. "Here, maybe this will help."

She reached into her pocket and pulled out her fist, which was clenched tightly around something he couldn't see.

He held out his palm only to feel the weight of a few coins and the brush of paper against it. "You're giving me money?" He stopped walking and stared down at the dollar and change in his hand.

"For the medicine I've been using. I'm sure this doesn't cover all of it, but I've got more mending to do." She raised the basket on her arm with two folded shirts.

"Is that where you got the funds to buy supplies for Jack? All that mending you've been doing?" The words came out harsher than intended, echoing over the sound of crunching gravel and passersby's chatter.

"Why are you angry?" She sucked in a short, shallow breath. "Of course that's where the money came from. Where else would I have gotten it?"

"I don't know. Perhaps the cigar box on my dresser where I keep extra money."

"I'd never steal from you." She shook her head. "We might be husband and wife, but I told you I didn't want to be a burden. I fully intend to pay my own way through our marriage. You don't need to worry about me taking your money."

"Pay your own way?" He couldn't help the shout. Nor could he help it when Mrs. Kainer, who'd been sweeping the boarding house steps across the street, stopped and looked up at him. Nor could he help the way the cluster of children playing kick the can all turned toward him.

He gritted his teeth and tugged his wife closer. Or maybe it was more of a jerk then a tug, but either way, they now stood close enough so as not to be overheard. "Not *my* money, Lindy. *Our* money. I want you to take it, as much as you need and whenever you want. Had you asked about food for the O'Byrnes this morning, I'd have given you funds before I left. Here." He held out his hand to give the money back. "Take it. Use it to buy…" He waved his hand. "Ribbons or lace or whatever it is women spend money on."

But she didn't hold out her hand, and her chin lifted in a defiant pose. "Medicine is expensive. How many times must I tell you I don't want to be a burden?"

"You're not!" The second the words were out, he clamped his jaw, but it was already too late. Everyone on the street had turned to stare at them again, even the children.

He shoved the money in his pocket. Taking her hand in his, he placed it back on his arm before leading her down the street. "We'll continue this discussion later."

Lindy walked along beside him, her steps tense and jerky, and her breathing faster than it should be given their slow pace. "I lived with a sick woman for a decade before she died. If I want to pay you back for some of the trouble I put you through, you should let me."

They turned from Center Street onto Front Street, and the log walls of his office two blocks down came into view. "That's not how marriages work. There's no tally sheet where we keep track of who spent the most money or who owes who. There's just... love. We both make sacrifices for one another, and we let love cover the petty grievances between us."

"But I don't love you."

The words fell like boulders from her mouth, shaking the ground beneath him until everything seemed unstable. He shouldn't be surprised. There'd been no talk of love when he'd proposed, nor on the day they'd married. So why did it feel as though she'd just taken the scalpel from his medical bag and sliced through his heart?

He forced his feet forward, walking by rote rather than stopping to cause another scene.

"I'm sorry." Lindy squeezed his arm. It was probably supposed to be a comforting gesture, but it only caused the vice around his heart to twist tighter. "I shouldn't have said that."

But she had, and they weren't words a man could easily scrub from his mind. "I didn't become a doctor for the money. I became a doctor because of Antietam. Because I wanted to help people."

"But you still need money. How can you not? You've barely had any patients since you married me." She looked down, her gaze riveted to her feet, though her steps grew tighter and faster as they approached his office. "I bet you had plenty of patients before I came along. You don't need to lie and pretend I have nothing to do with it, and you'd be nothing but stubborn to refuse the money I earn from sewing."

"I had plenty of patients before Dr. Greely started spreading false rumors. If he could have scared my patients away by spreading a story about a rabid cat, he'd have done so. You gave him a convenient rumor, nothing more."

She stopped abruptly and looked up at him, her eyes searching his face.

For what? Reassurance that she hadn't ruined his medical practice? Not love, though. Heaven forbid she'd want to find that in his gaze.

He pressed his eyes shut and drew in a deep breath. *God, what do I do? How do I reach this woman you gave me?*

"Yoo-hoo. Seth, darling, is that you?"

His eyes sprang open at the sound of the Southern voice. Lindy attempted to peer over his shoulder, probably trying to figure out who called to him in such a manner, but it could only be one person. A person who wasn't supposed to be in Eagle Harbor.

"Seth, dear?" she called again.

He turned to see his mother leaving a cluster of people gathered on his porch and climbing down the steps.

"Mother," he croaked.

She paraded toward him, the rich rose hue of her dress a blaze of color amid the dusty street and log buildings. Then another woman broke away from the group and hastened to catch up to his mother.

A hard ball of copper lodged in his stomach. Mother couldn't have—

"Seth! Good, we did come to the right spot." She stopped in front of him, her face wreathed in smiles. "The man at the shipping office sent us this direction, but when no one answered the door, I started to worry."

"Ah, yes, you found me." He stepped forward to give his mother a peck on the cheek. "Though I must say I'm surprised by your visit."

A rustling sounded beside his mother, and he let his gaze fall to the woman his mother had dragged all the way from Sharpsburg to Eagle Harbor. "And yours, Penelope."

He should take her hand and kiss it. It would be the gentlemanly thing to do, and indeed, he could feel his mother and Penelope watching, their gazes heavy with expectation.

"This is your mother?" Lindy stifled a cough.

Mother glanced at Lindy standing beside him and raised an eyebrow, but Penelope bustled right up to her. "Hello, I'm Penelope Griggs."

He'd forgotten how beautiful she was. With her dark hair and fine cheekbones and jaw, she'd never been difficult to look at. But the smile she gave Lindy, large and infectious, transformed her entire face from being pleasing to unforgettably lovely.

"Lindy…" The smile plastered on Penelope's face made his tongue heavy and sluggish. "Penelope was my neighbor growing up."

"I'm also his fiancée." Penelope brightened her smile, which shouldn't have been possible given how wide her lips were already spread.

Lindy sucked a raspy breath, bringing her telltale asthmatic whistle to life. "Your fiancée?"

"My *former* fiancée." He reached down to grip Lindy's hand. "Mother, Penny, I'd like you to meet my wife, Lindy Harrington."

"Your wife!" his mother screeched. She drew a fan out of her reticule and swished it violently at her face. "You can't be married. That's why I brought Penny here!"

Chapter Twenty

"What do you mean that woman used to be your fiancée?" Lindy whispered.

Her husband didn't even look at her as he closed the door to the larger sickroom, shutting in the entire entourage his mother had brought to Eagle Harbor.

Evidently people like Penelope and Seth's mother didn't travel alone or with a friend. Oh no, they brought ladies' maids and children and nannies. Half of them needed to nap after the long journey, evidently. And the servants were rambling about how they'd unpack everyone's trunks just as soon as they knew where they were staying.

What were she and Seth going to do with so many people? Surely a group that traveled all the way from Maryland wouldn't turn around and head home tomorrow—even if their reason for coming had been ruined.

Seth headed across the parlor and into the sickroom she'd been using without answering her question.

She followed behind him and shut the door. "Well?"

He yanked the quilt off her bed. "There's no such thing as a miasma."

"What?"

"Miasmas." He folded the quilt with brisk movements. "They don't exist. It's an antiquated theory of medicine that assumes disease travels by foul air rather than by germs."

She blinked at him. For someone who was so bent on learning all her secrets, he certainly wasn't in a hurry to volunteer information about himself.

"Did you not hear my question? I don't want to talk about germs." Not that she knew what they were.

"Well, I'd like to, especially before you go telling people about miasmas in the mercantile again. Do you remember when I told you about Joseph Lister's studies in England? That's why I bathed your finger in carbolic acid when I treated it. It kills the germs, which are tiny microorganisms that spread all manner of disease, from gangrene to cholera to tuberculosis." He set the quilt on the opposite bed with such force that his folds nearly came undone.

"Can we talk about the people in the room next door and not these micronisms, or whatever they're called? Particularly the woman who used to be your fiancée?"

He stalked back across the room to her bed and yanked off a sheet. "Fine, but no more mention of miasmas with others. I can give you several journal articles to help explain my position, but the germs theory of disease is far more likely than the miasma theory."

She threw up her hands. "I don't care about germs, I care about that Penelope woman. You obviously have a past with her, yet for all your insistence that we talk and get to know each other better, you never once mentioned her."

He tucked the first sheet under his arm and pulled off the one surrounding the mattress. "She was my fiancée before I went to medical school and she decided she didn't want to marry a doctor."

She sucked in a breath, long and slow. He'd been engaged to such a lovely woman, and one who clearly had money. He must have been devastated when she jilted him. "So why did she want to marry you now? You're clearly still a doctor."

"Why indeed?" He paused, the sheets now wadded into a ball in his arms. "Here, hold these. I need to get my medical bag."

"What does…"

He plopped the bed linens into her arms and slipped into the parlor.

Your medical bag have to do with anything?

He returned a moment later, his black bag in one hand and two envelopes in the other.

"This is the letter I got at the mercantile today." He waved an envelope with elegant, looping handwriting around. "The one Mr. Foley gave me when you bought that flour for Jack? It's from Mother and probably explains she's coming with Penelope. This one I got a month ago, but I was late for calling on Tressa, so I put it in my bag, where I forgot about it."

He stuck his finger beneath the flap and tore the paper, only to slide a second envelope out of the first along with a piece of stationary.

He scanned the note, then shook his head. "Penny's husband died several months ago, and seeing how our family lands border each other, Theo—my brother—wondered… well…" He blew out a breath and looked at her. "He wanted me to marry Penny and join the family lands. Said everyone would benefit, et cetera. Must be why Penny is willing to marry a doctor now."

His brother had asked him to marry Penelope before they'd been caught together in his kitchen? Lindy's lungs started to burn, and she sank down onto the bed, the sheets still wadded in her arms. What would Seth have done if he'd read that letter when it first arrived?

He opened the second envelope that had been concealed inside the original. Rose water wafted into the air as he unfolded the stationary.

He took a moment to glance at the note, then crumpled it in his hand. "Or maybe not so willing. She wanted me to take over the brickworks in Sharpsburg that her late husband left her."

"But your lands would still have merged if you'd married her?"

"Of course. It's always about the land." He sank down onto the bed beside her. "If I would have known…"

What? Would he not have married her? But he let the words trail off without any interest in finishing them. The burning in her lungs increased, which didn't make any sense. She didn't want him to be saddled with her.

Seth narrowed his eyes, then ran his gaze down her in that clinical way of his. "I'm sorry, Lindy. Here I am so worried about me I forgot about your asthma. You need to lie down. It's too soon to give you more atropine, but we can try some ipecac and see if that calms your lungs. Let me take those sheets from you."

He reached for the armful of linens, but rather than hand them over, she clutched them to her chest.

"How can I lie down when you just stripped my bed?" As soon as she said it, she knew the answer. Because it wasn't her bed, not really, and it wasn't her room either. And now that they had guests staying in the large sickroom, this room needed to stay open in case he got a patient.

She sucked a breath into lungs that felt as though someone had taken a match to them.

Seth leaned close, the faint scent of bergamot twining around her. "Lindy, I know most people start off with courting, then betrothal, then marriage. We seem to be going about things backward, but I still intend for us to have a real marriage. Now that you're well, I want to woo you, and court you, and love you. But we'll have to do it while living under the same roof." He offered her a lopsided smile. "I'm hoping that makes the process go faster."

"Faster?" she squeaked. "How much faster?" She stared into Seth's eyes, only inches from hers. Then her gaze dipped to his mouth. The slightest movement from either one of them, and their lips would touch. Did she want them to?

No. She needed to keep her distance so that he didn't... she didn't... Oh, the reasons where there somewhere. She just couldn't remember them when he sat so close.

He shifted back and cleared his throat. "Furthermore, sharing the same room will help convince Mother and Penelope our marriage is a love match."

"Why does that matter?" She fisted her hands in the sheets still clasped against her chest. Good thing these were soiled and not fresh, or they'd be wrinkled before they got on the bed.

"I don't want them to try pushing for an annulment."

Was an annulment possible? And if so, why had she not thought of it sooner? "D-do you want an annulment? Do you want to marry Penelope?"

He scowled and took the sheets from her, never mind that left her with nowhere to dig her nails. "No. I do not want to be married to a woman who says she'll be true one week but finds herself a new fiancé the next."

She swallowed and sucked in another wheezy breath. Could he truly be happy to have married her instead?

Oh, who was she kidding? He'd obviously rather have a healthy wife who didn't hate doctors. She couldn't be that big of an improvement over a jilting ex-fiancée.

⁓.⁓.⁓.⁓.⁓

"This is missing something, though I can't say what." Mrs. Harrington spooned soup into her mouth and dabbed her lips together. "Had I known you didn't have a cook, I would have hired one for the trip, or perhaps brought Gemma. Her cooking's come along quite nicely since your last visit."

Seth looked at his mother, seated across from him at his small but serviceable kitchen table, then glanced at Penelope on his left and Lindy on his right. "I don't know who Gemma is, Mother."

"You don't remember Margaret's daughter, Gemma?" Mother took a slice of bread from the plate in the center of the table and buttered it. "I hired her to work in the kitchen now that she's old enough for service."

"Sometimes you forget how long ago I left Maryland." He shifted and narrowed his gaze on Penelope. "I think both of you have."

Penelope looked down at her plate, where she'd broken her piece of bread into tiny, bite-size portions she'd yet to put in her mouth.

A noise sounded from the parlor, and he glanced at the doorway only to remember his mother had insisted on closing it while the four of them ate. The others would eat afterwards—because it would evidently be the end of civil society if they sat down with Penelope's children or the maids.

"You need a dining room." Mother looked around the kitchen. With its log walls, small stove, and simple sink, it was only about a third of the size of the polished kitchen at the Harrington family home in Maryland. "Isn't there a better house in town you can buy?"

There was. The Donnelly mansion was for sale to help cover Victoria's father's debts. He'd have to be sure she didn't find out about it.

"I know you're trying to be good to us by putting us in that large room you have, but we'll need to move to a hotel." Mother lifted her spoon to her mouth but paused before the utensil reached her lips. "Women such as myself and Penelope should not be sleeping in the same room with children and maids."

Lindy's spoon clanged against her soup bowl, and when she

looked up at him, he could easily read the thoughts in her eyes. *My family all slept in the same room.*

"There isn't a hotel, Mother."

She stopped chewing. "There's not?"

"No, though the town needs one."

"We should talk to Gilbert Sinclair when he visits again." Lindy fiddled with the spoon in her soup. "Maybe he could buy the old Donnelly mansion and turn that into a hotel."

"The Donnelly mansion?" His mother's voice turned suddenly sweet. "Is that in town? Is it for sale?"

He pressed his fingers to the bridge of his nose.

"Well, is there a mansion for sale or not, Seth?"

"The size of my practice doesn't warrant purchasing such a large house. The two sickrooms I have are more than sufficient." Especially given his sudden lack of patients.

Another noise sounded from the parlor, followed by the sound of a child's wail. "No, no, no. She stole it from me. I had it first."

A muted adult voice followed, then, "I want my momma. I want my momma!"

Penelope shifted in her chair. "You'll have to excuse Phillip Jr. He's not quite been himself since his father's passing." She reached for one of her tiny pieces of bread and put it in her mouth.

Lindy looked at Penelope. "Aren't you going to find out what's the matter?"

"Heavens, girl." Mother set her glass on the table with a thump. "What do you think the nanny is for?"

"Sorry." Lindy slouched in her chair—something that his mother was sure to notice.

Seth took his own bite of bread, though it tasted like sand.

More voices rose from behind the parlor door, but neither his mother nor Penelope paid them any mind. Maybe this was part of the reason he'd left Maryland. He'd yet to be introduced to the servants or Penelope's two children, as though they weren't worthy of his attention. And now he was simply supposed to ignore them. Did Mother and Penelope realize how pretentious that was?

But had he met Lindy in Maryland, his mother wouldn't have deemed her important enough for introductions either. He reached beneath the table and took his wife's hand, then tilted the corner of his mouth into a smile. She pressed her lips together to hide her own smile.

"So Lindy, how long have you known Seth?" Penelope took a sip of her water.

"About two months." The answer fell from her mouth easily. And why wouldn't it? It wasn't as though they'd discussed answering questions about their relationship with anything other than the truth.

The spoon in Mother's hand paused on its way to her mouth. "If you've only known my son two months, how long ago did you marry?"

Lindy glanced at him, but what could they say?

He squeezed her hand before answering in her stead. "A week and a half ago."

Penelope stood up, causing her chair to scrape against the plank flooring. "Did you not receive my letter?"

"I got Theo's letter but never opened it until you arrived. I'd gotten called away to a patient and forgot about it."

"But if you would have read the letter..." Penelope's jaw trembled as she looked between him and Lindy. "I sent the letter with Theo's because I didn't know if you'd open one from me. I assumed once Theo explained that—"

"That you'd dangle your late husband's brickworks in front of me, and I'd decide I didn't want to be a doctor anymore?" He pushed his own chair back and tossed his napkin on the table.

Penelope sucked a breath in through her nose, her jaw so hard it might have been chiseled from stone.

"I'm sure there are plenty of men willing to marry you for the brickworks."

"But the land!" His mother wailed.

"Yes, I doubt ten thousand acres of land will hurt your attempt to find a husband either, Penny."

"Ten thousand acres?" Though Lindy's words were soft, they echoed through the kitchen as loudly as though she'd shouted them across the harbor. "How much money do all of you have?"

"An impertinent question, but plenty more than you." Mother's eyes turned to glare at him across the table. "Why did you marry her? She clearly didn't have anything to bring to your marriage, not like Penny did."

He reached out and twined Lindy's fingers with his, this time placing their hands on the table for all to see. "Because I wanted to be her husband. Now I refuse to hear more about it."

"You certainly won't." Penelope pivoted on her heel and stormed out of the room, slamming the door behind her and rattling the dishes on the table.

Mother stayed at the table, her jaw trembling with indignation. "I can't believe you married a woman after Penelope sent that letter."

"The woman's name is Lindy," Seth gritted. "And if you intend to stay in my house while you're here, then you'll treat her with respect."

"Why didn't you think about your family before you made such a rash decision? Do you know how helpful it would have been to own land that borders Antietam Creek? But of course you don't care about what your family wants, just about your doctoring."

"I don't care about what my family wants?" He dropped Lindy's hand and rose from the table, his voice thunderously loud. "How conveniently you forget I was willing to marry Penny and set up a medical practice in Sharpsburg so you could have that land. She was the one who didn't want to marry a doctor, and she still doesn't. She wanted me to take over her late husband's brickworks. She only cares about the land because she can use it to get what she wants, which was evidently me, for some reason, but only if I gave up my work."

"Access to the creek would've meant—"

"Then buy the land from her."

"Do you pay attention to nothing?" Mother slammed her hand on the table, causing the dishes to rattle again. "Her land has to stay in the family. It's been in her family for over a hundred years and will go to her children. If you would have married her and produced an heir—"

"You should have arranged for Theo to marry her instead of me."

"He's fifteen years older than her!"

"Worse matches have been made under the banner of an advantageous union."

Mother huffed again and stood, her large bosom heaving against the constraints of her elaborate silk dress as she turned and stormed from the room.

The second the door slammed behind her, he slumped into his chair and rested his head in his hands. Three years since he'd seen his mother and this was how their first meal together went. But what could he have done differently? His family had been there on the day of Antietam. They'd seen the injured and dying soldiers and knew he'd sworn to become a doctor because of it.

Yet ever since his father's death, they claimed they'd only be happy if he gave up his doctoring. Was this how Elijah felt always arguing with Isaac about the life-saving team? How did Elijah tolerate it?

He didn't know how long he sat there, his palms pressed against his eyes, trying to erase the disaster of a meal from his mind. Trying, but not succeeding.

A dish clattered on the table. Then another. He raised his head to find Lindy stacking the bowls and plates.

"I'm sorry." He rubbed at his bleary eyes. "You keep apologizing for your illness, but I'm the one who should be apologizing—for the family you inherited when you married me."

She reached across the table for Penelope's plate. "At least I don't have to wonder if you regret your decision to marry me and not Penelope."

"You never needed to wonder about that."

She nodded as she collected the silverware.

"What are you doing?"

"The dishes. Forgive me, but I don't think your mother or Penelope will volunteer to wash them—or volunteer their servants, for that matter."

Seth rested his head back in his hands. Who was going to cook the next meal? Throwing the soup together while Lindy napped had been hassle enough.

Maybe he did need to buy the Donnelly mansion, if for no other reason than to have somewhere to stash his mother, Penelope, and their entourage. But what were the chances of arranging a sale before nightfall?

Chapter Twenty-One

"This is where I've hung your things."

Lindy stood near the bed while Seth opened one side of the wardrobe. Sure enough, her spare shirtwaist and skirt hung there, taking up only a few inches of space in the line of clothes that otherwise belonged to him.

"I commissioned Isaac Cummings to build a dresser that matches mine." Seth moved to the polished chest of drawers in the corner. "But ah, I didn't realize... that is, I hadn't paid attention to how many things were brought over from the bakery, and well... I'm afraid it's not very full. Yet. I've already spoken to Mr. Foley about getting some fabric to make you new dresses."

She nodded, but he must not have seen, because he left the dresser and came toward her, reaching out to take her hand. She stared down at their entwined fingers. Her hand felt damp and clammy against his warm skin, and she fought the urge to pull it away.

If only they were a normal husband and wife and she could enjoy her husband's touch.

"I want you to ask if you've need of anything. I have every intention of providing for you as my wife."

She drew in a small, shaky breath, which didn't make much sense considering she'd breathed fine the entire time Seth had shown her around his room. But then, he'd been on one side of the room or the other while she'd stood in the middle. Now he stood beside her with the bed they would share only a foot away.

Her chest grew tighter still, and the room seemed to shrink. She looked at the bed again, the one that had been large and comfortable during her nap, but suddenly seemed tiny.

"Lindy?" He stroked a thumb over the back of her hand, still gripped tightly in his. "You'll come to me if you need something, yes? I want you to promise."

She forced her gaze back on her husband. What had he said? Something about coming to him if she needed clothes? "You... you have money to buy me things. Or rather, your family does."

"I don't reap the bulk of the estate profits the way Theo does, but I get a cut of everything he makes from the mill and the farm. Everything my father left the two of us."

"But you don't need to earn a living as a doctor. Your family has enough money that you don't need to work at all." It made so much sense now. The clothes that always seemed like something a Chicago lawyer would wear rather than a country doctor. The medical treatment he'd given both her and Toby for free.

"There will always be work in the sense that the estate and lands need to be managed if they're going to stay profitable, but I don't need to work a trade such as doctoring, no."

"So when you say you have enough money to pay for my medicine..."

He released her hand and tilted her chin up, then bent at the shoulders so their eyes were only a few inches apart. "I have enough to pay for your medicine, Lindy. I have enough to take you to a specialist in Boston, if you'd like. Or one in Washington if you'd rather go there. I have enough for whatever you need, for as long as you need it."

She sank down onto the bed. "I see why you were angry about me trying to hand you a dollar and eighty cents. You have more money than you could ever use."

His lips twisted. "I could use it all, I assure you. Fancy carriages, expensive suits, trips to Europe, gambling bills. I've seen it done more than once."

"But to live as you are now?" She worried her hands in the folds of her skirt—a worn, fading skirt he could afford to replace without so much as a blink. "Will the money run out?"

He sat beside her on the bed. "No."

She didn't know whether to shout or sob. A weight atop her chest lifted, almost as though her asthma was suddenly gone. "You're too good to me."

"No, Lindy. God is the one who's too good. And after the things you've gone through…" He reached out and touched her arm. Her sleeves hid the scars, but he seemed to have them memorized, or at least the biggest one, because his fingers traced it perfectly beneath the fabric. "If God can use me to help you, then I'm honored to do so."

There'd been doctors' bills to pay for as long as she could remember. Even before she'd gotten sick herself, there'd been ones for her mother. Now that burden was gone, like a heavy fog that lifted in only a few minutes' time. Was her husband right? Was God being good to her? But then, why was she sick at all if God was so good? She'd read the New Testament. She knew the stories of Christ healing the sick and lame. God had the power to make her well, so why did her prayers always fall on deaf ears?

"What's going on inside that head of yours?"

She shook her head, then wiped at the corner of her eyes and sniffled. He'd just told her he had money to pay for an infinite amount of medical expenses. She'd not ruin the moment by claiming God had forgotten her.

"Come now, don't cry." He cupped her cheek, turning her face toward him and giving her that lopsided smile that caused her heart to race, even when she wasn't having a breathing attack. "Most women are happy to know their husband can provide for them, not upset about it."

"It's not that, but I'm sorry for earlier. I didn't mean for what I said to be cruel, but it was, and… and you don't deserve that. Not from your mother, not from Penelope, and least of all from me."

His brow drew down. "What did you say earlier? Having you at the dinner table was like breathing spring air after a snowstorm. You were wonderful."

She twisted her hands in her skirt. "Not at dinner. Before. On the street."

He shook his head ever so slightly, the skin between his eyebrows still creased in a frown.

"About not loving you."

He grew still for a moment, then, "If it's true, why apologize?"

Given the glib way he asked it, the way his shoulders rose on a careless shrug before relaxing, it was supposed to be a rhetorical question. But for the past five years, she'd told herself she would die young, told herself that she had no chance of having a husband.

Would she recognize love if she found it? "Maybe I'm afraid to find out whether it's true or not."

"What does that mean?"

"Never mind." She looked away from him, but he only scooted closer on the bed, his chest pressing against her arm.

"You're afraid to find out if you love me?"

"I don't know you well enough to love you." Surely it was impossible to fall in love in so short of time.

"But you could love me." His breath fanned her ear, hot and sweet. "If you got to know me better."

215

"I… I d-don't know." She felt them then, the force of his expectations slamming into her, weighing her down. If her chest had turned light before, it grew doubly heavy now, as though she were having five breathing attacks at once. She gripped the quilt beneath her hand.

His fingers immediately dislodged hers, then held them loosely, as if attempting to relax them. Did the man have to be so perceptive?

Probably, considering he was a doctor who found symptoms people didn't even know they had.

"You're afraid." His voice vibrated with frustration. "Lindy, I won't force you to do wifely things until you're ready. I want to share this room with you, yes, but I figured the rest would come in time."

She pressed her eyes shut. She'd been right about not deserving him earlier. No one deserved a man this good. He offered to care for her when she would bring him nothing but medical bills, yet didn't demand she fulfill her marital duties in exchange. If all the men in the world were a quarter as good as Seth Harrington, then perhaps—

"Lindy?" His thumb rubbed the top of her hand. "Is that what you're afraid of? The marriage bed?"

She opened her eyes and swallowed the thickness lodged in her throat. "It's not just the bed, it's all of it. What if we end up loving each other and then I die? Where does that leave you? Do you know how hard it was to watch my mother pass? Even if we want to love each other, it will only lead to heartache in the end."

His hand turned lax over hers, his shoulders slumped like earlier when his mother berated him for not marrying Penelope. "What about all the years before she died? Your mother wasn't sick your whole life, was she?"

"She always had a cough, but no, not sick in the way you mean."

"So would you rather you never knew your mother? That you grew up in an orphanage somewhere instead of spending your childhood with her?"

Her hand trembled against the quilt, then her jaw quivered, and hot pricks of moisture gathered in her eyes. "I don't know."

"And now I've made you cry. Come here." An arm wrapped around her shoulder, then another slipped beneath her knees. A moment later she was sitting on Seth's lap, dampening his shirt with her tears.

Would she rather not have known her mother? Maybe, if it meant not watching her cough worsen while her body grew weaker and weaker, not watching her father hand over every last cent he earned to Dr. Greely. But in order to erase those memories, she'd also need to erase the picnics in the summer and Christmases gathered around the fire. The gentle sound of her mother singing her to sleep, the smile on her mother's face when they picked wildflowers together each spring.

"It'll be all right." Seth stroked the hair back from her face.

She didn't know how long she sat there, with the heat of his body radiating into hers and his hand rubbing little circles against her back. Long enough for her eyelids to droop with heaviness. Long enough to forget why it would be a bad idea to rest her head on his shoulder.

"I always wanted this, you know." She wiped the dampness from her cheeks with the flat of her palm, then settled her head back on his shoulder.

"What?" His chest rose and fell in even, rhythmic movements.

"A husband to hold me." She let her eyes drift closed, turning her head so her face nestled in the warm place between his neck and shoulder. "It was one of the things on my list."

His breathing hitched, just for a moment, the smallest pause in the steady movement of his chest. "What list?"

She yawned against his neck and kept her eyes closed, her words coming slowly. "The list every little girl has. Husband, children, house, sewing machine…"

"All those things are on your list?"

"Were..." she mumbled as she yawned again, "...before I got sick."

He kept talking, his voice soft and low. Something about putting a few things back on her list, about God giving her something or other. She should probably be listening better, but did he have to talk so fast? Especially when she'd rather him be quiet so she could focus on the rise and fall of his chest. Up and down, up and down, it went, until her world faded into sleep.

~.~.~.~.~

"Why you draggin' me ta jail?"

Elijah could barely make out the sailor's slurred words as he half dragged, half led the handcuffed man down North Street.

"I ain't done nothin' wrong."

Elijah tightened his hold on the man's arm as they started up the steps to his office. "Shattering the mirror above the bar because the barkeep didn't serve you fast enough isn't exactly nothing wrong."

"Aw, come on. You know how long we been at sea for? I needed me a drink."

"Looks like you already had about a dozen." Elijah flung open the door to his office to find... candles?

"Elijah." Victoria sprang up from behind his desk. At least he assumed it was Victoria, since the voice sounded like hers, but he couldn't make out much more than a shadow.

"What happened to the lamps? Didn't I leave them lit?" If anyone besides his wife had decided to bathe his office in candlelight, well, they were going to find themselves in a cell next to a drunkard for the night.

"Oh, I'm s-so s-s-s-sorry. I d-d-didn't realize you'd n-need them!" His wife's voice again, then a scrambling sound before she lit one of the numerous lamps situated about his office.

"Hey, that there food smells good." The sailor slurred. "Can I have some?"

"The only thing you're going to have is some time in a cell." Elijah guided the man toward the corridor. "Just a minute," he called over his shoulder to his wife.

"This ain't fair. I ain't done nothin' to deserve being locked up while you eat all that food."

Elijah shoved him into a cell and locked the door. "We'll see how you're doing tomorrow, after you sober up a bit."

Key in hand, he turned and headed back to his office, closing the door that separated the jail behind him.

"I-I-I'm sorry." Victoria stood with her hands clasped nervously together.

Was that prime rib on his desk behind her? And mashed potatoes? Looked like she had some rutabaga too, and a creamy soup of some kind. The meal looked fit for one of the fancy society dinners she'd grown up with.

"I-if I'd known you'd b-b-be bringing someone back to the jail, I w-w-would h-have…" Her voice trailed off, and she looked at him with round eyes moist with tears.

He moved toward her. "There's nothing to apologize for. I just wasn't expecting this, is all. It smells delicious." He wrapped her in a hug, settling her head into the crook of his neck.

"So you c-can eat with me?" Her breath fanned warm against his skin. "You d-don't have to go back and deal with others?"

He could wait a half hour or so before checking on things down at The Pretty Penny. The oaf he'd just put in a cell had been the only person causing trouble at The Rusty Wagon.

"You're worth making time for." He bent and brushed a kiss on her cheek, then another along her jaw, before finally settling his mouth over hers.

She sighed into the kiss, her arms reaching up to fiddle with the hair at the nape of his neck. Did she realize how often she did that when they kissed? That it was one of his favorite things about kissing her? Well, besides the taste of her lips, and the way she melted against him if he kissed her long enough. The perfect way she fit into his arms, and the sweet little sounds she made in the back of her throat.

"Elijah…" She pulled back from him.

He stifled his groan. Really, what man wanted to eat when he could be kissing his wife instead? Even if his wife had brought him a feast.

"The food's getting cold, and since you didn't have time to come home—again—I brought dinner to you."

"I've missed having dinner with you too, love." They'd barely had two seconds to spend together since he'd taken the sheriff job. He tugged at one of the escaped strands of hair hanging by her cheek. "And this doesn't look like an ordinary dinner. I don't know how you managed this spread, but thank you."

She offered him a small smile and tilted her head to the side. "Anything for my husband." Her brow furrowed. "Do you think we can put out the lamp now? This is the kind of meal one eats with candlelight."

It was also the kind of meal where a man took his wife to bed after they finished eating, except that hadn't happened once since he'd taken the role of sheriff. Not exactly helpful for a couple trying to have a child. "Sure, you can put it—"

The door banged open, and Isaac tromped inside, dragging a sailor behind him. "Heard there was a bit of carousing down at The Penny, so I decided to stop by. Found this buffoon, and tied another up with some rope. He's waiting for you to bring him in."

Elijah sighed. The sailors from the ship that had docked at dusk weren't wasting any time celebrating landfall.

He reached for Victoria's hand and squeezed it. "I'm sorry, sweetling. We'll have to do this some other time."

Isaac looked at Elijah's desk and skimmed his gaze over the food spread out before them. "Never mind. You stay and eat. I'll go get the other one."

He would? Elijah took a step back. When was the last time his brother had offered to do something kind for him? "Are you sure?"

Victoria whacked him in the stomach. "Of course he's sure, now sit down and have a meal with me."

Isaac opened the door to the jail, grabbed the ring of keys off the hook on the wall, and disappeared into the long corridor.

"Come, sit." Victoria led him around the desk to where she'd set a plate for him, then she took the seat around the corner. "Do you want to say grace?"

He grasped is wife's hand, but the sound of keys rattling in the cell door gave him pause. A moment later, Isaac stepped back into the office and closed the door that separated the jail from the rest of the building.

"Thank you, Isaac." Victoria beamed at him.

Isaac glanced at the feast that was surely making his mouth water, then he moved his gaze between them. "You're welcome. I know sheriffing has put a bit of a strain on you, and, well, I want to help."

Huh. Elijah sat back in his chair. Looked like his brother truly did have an interest in helping for once.

"Enjoy your meal." Isaac tromped out into the night.

The moment they were alone, Elijah reached for the lamp to extinguish it, then he grabbed his wife and pulled her into his lap. If they only had a little time to spend together, it seemed a waste to have her in one seat and him in another.

Chapter Twenty-Two

"I told you I would help."

Lindy looked over her shoulder at Seth, then plunged her hands back into the sudsy water and continued scrubbing the pan they'd roasted the lamb in for dinner. "I don't mind. Besides, your mother wanted to visit with you."

"You could have come into the parlor and visited with the rest of us." Hands landed on her shoulder, big and warm.

She stiffened for a moment before her muscles relaxed. "No thank you."

He chuckled at that. "Dearest wife, you're not using kitchen chores as an excuse to avoid my mother, are you?" He moved his hands from her shoulders and wrapped them around her waist.

Another frisson of warmth traveled through her, and she blinked. What had she been about to say? Oh yes, his mother.

"Of course I'm hiding. She never stops nattering." The woman had been there three days, and ten seconds seemed to be all the longer she could keep her mouth shut. How had Seth managed to be in the same house as that women for years while growing up?

His arms left her waist, and the room took on a cold feel. Never mind that it had seemed plenty warm before her husband came in. He reached for a towel and one of the plates drying by the sink. "Let me help you put these away, then there's somewhere I want to take you."

"Take me? For a sauna?" They'd snuck out to one last night. He usually didn't have her go two days in a row.

"No, something better." He stacked the plates he dried on the table while she scrubbed an angry stain from the pan.

"A medical call?"

His chuckle filled the room again, rich and deep. "I said *better* than a sauna, not worse, love."

Love. She sucked in a little breath. Did he realize how easily he called her that? As though the word slipped from his mouth without thought?

"If not a medical call, then what?" Her voice trembled as she spoke.

"I'll be back in just a minute with what we'll need."

He set the plates in the hutch and left while she drained the water from the sink and reached for the towel to dry her arms. What could he be planning, and in the dark no less? If it were still light out, she'd assume they'd head to the beach and watch the sunset, or maybe even walk up the path to one of the lookouts in the hills that surrounded the town.

"Any guesses?" Seth returned with one blanket draped over his shoulders and another bundled beneath his arm.

"Ah…" She shook her head.

He lifted his arm, spreading the blanket to show there was room for her beneath the heavy quilt.

She went to him, and soon the warmth from both the blanket and her husband's body surround her.

"Now?" He raised an eyebrow at her.

"I'm guessing you want to go outside?" Though why they were sharing a blanket rather than wearing their own coats, she didn't know.

"We're going to look at stars."

"Stars?"

"Don't tell me you don't like gazing at them." He guided her to the door, his arm draped around her shoulder. "They're so clear this time of year, with the air crisp and cool."

Longing welled inside her, so thick she could barely draw breath. She'd never dreamed, she'd have a man want to stargaze with her, or marry her, or even wrap his arm around her shoulder and walk with her. Yet here she was, with all the things she'd never dared hope for walking beside her in the form of her husband.

She might not know what her future held or how long she'd stay healthy, but what was the harm in taking an hour or so to spend time with her husband?

⌐.⌐.⌐.⌐.⌐

Thump. Thump. Thump.

Lindy blinked her eyes open only to find darkness surrounding her.

Thump. Thump. Thump.

The warmth at her back shifted away, rustling the covers. Then Seth's voice, low and groggy with sleep, "Stay here. I'll get it."

Thump. Thump. Thump.

She blinked once more as the sound became familiar. Someone was knocking at the door. Again.

Patients were always coming in the middle of the night now, sometimes even more than one a night. Ever since Seth had confronted Dr. Greely in the mercantile five days ago, people had been trickling in. Even if no one came during the day, someone came at night, when Dr. Greely was sure to be slumped over the bar at The Pretty Penny. Of course, that didn't stop Seth's mother or Penelope from complaining about his lack of patients.

The mattress dipped, and more rustling sounded as Seth got out of bed and dressed in the darkness.

The door to the bedroom opened and closed, then a faint trace of lamplight shown beneath the crack. Muted voices followed.

She rolled over and grabbed his pillow, hugging it to her chest, but it didn't make up for the warmth that had left the bed with her husband.

Footsteps thudded, and a moment later the door opened to reveal her husband's shadow beneath the lantern light. She shifted to better see him.

"Are you still awake, sweetheart? I'm sorry. I just need something from the supply room, then I won't bother you anymore."

"What's wrong?" she croaked, her voice thick with sleep.

He sighed. "Sam Tublins broke his arm this evening, but his father proclaimed he didn't need a physician—until Sam kept the house up half the night with his crying."

"You can fix it, right?"

She couldn't see his smile in the shadows, but she could almost feel his familiar, lopsided grin.

"Of course. Now go to sleep. You need your rest."

He headed toward the supply room tucked off the corner of the bedroom, though "supply disaster" was a better name for the room. It was nothing short of a miracle the man could find anything in the crammed space.

He emerged a few moments later, a shadowy object—probably a splint—in his hand.

"How much longer will you be?" Again, though she couldn't make out his face, she could feel his response. A scowl this time, rather than a grin.

"You should be sleeping."

She yawned and burrowed into her pillow. "Can't sleep without you."

Silence filled the room, and not the soft, relaxed kind that hinted of sleep. She jolted awake and blinked. What had she just said?

Of course she could sleep without Seth by her side. They'd only been sharing a bed for five nights, and she still wasn't all that comfortable with the notion.

"It's… it's too cold, is all." Her voice shook, because of the cold. Yes, the cold. The nights were growing cooler, and they hadn't lit a fire in the stove tonight. Surely that was why she'd been unable to fall back asleep.

"I've a patient waiting, Lindy," he finally answered, and this time she couldn't begin to guess the expression on his face. "It will be a half hour or better before I finish." But he didn't tell her to go back to sleep again. Instead, he headed to the door and slipped out.

He'd heard that last part about it being cold, hadn't he? Surely he didn't think she missed him beside her.

But he hadn't exactly offered to build a fire, either.

Oh, why had she said anything about not being able to sleep? She needed to bite her tongue when she was tired. She was always saying the most ridiculous things to him, like the other night when she'd told him she'd once dreamed of having a husband and sewing machine.

Voices drifted from the kitchen, including the sound of a child's, though she couldn't make out the words.

She stared into the darkness for a few more minutes, then rose and slipped on her dressing gown, shivering because it truly was chilly. She cracked open the door, and the dim shadows of the kitchen came into view.

Sure enough, a child sat at the table, his arm outstretched as Seth settled a splint around it. A mug rested on the table by his mother, likely willow bark tea to ease the boy's pain.

Lindy scanned her husband's hunched form as he bent over the child's arm and spoke in soothing tones. Her cheeks warmed despite the cold.

Maybe she was lying to herself about why she couldn't sleep without him. Because how could she keep from loving a man who was always putting others above himself?

It wouldn't hurt to love him just a little. He couldn't love her, no. He'd only be devastated as she grew sicker and sicker. But as for her loving him, what was the harm in that?

Chapter Twenty-Three

"Two years in Eagle Harbor, and I've never been up this path before." Seth looked around him at the blaze of red, orange, and yellow. "It's beautiful."

"It's a chore to snowshoe in the winter, nothing but mud in the spring, passably pretty in the summer if you can endure the bugs. But this time of year..." Lindy tilted her face up toward a ray of sunlight filtering through the canopy of colored leaves above. "This time of year it's more than beautiful. It's magnificent."

"But I want to go this way!" Phillip Jr.'s shout echoed up the path from behind them.

Seth scratched his head. Did the boy ever tire of causing ruckuses?

But even with Phillip and the others along, his wife's idea to take a walk was turning out splendidly, especially considering they'd walked ahead of the others and were now out of view, even if they weren't entirely out of earshot. "We'll have to come more often, just the two of us. I want to see if it's as you say each season."

Lindy scrunched her nose, the gesture so endearing he nearly leaned forward to kiss the tip of it. "You can come by yourself in the spring. With no snow or leaves on the trees, the view's not worth seeing, and you have to slog through three inches of mud the whole way up the hill."

He stepped to the side of the trail and tugged her with him, looking over his shoulder to make sure the others had yet to catch up.

"The view will be lovely any time of year… as long as you're with me." He used his free hand to tuck a strand of hair behind her ear, just so she could be sure what view he was talking about.

Color rose on her cheeks, but rather than smile and tease in response, she glanced away.

What was she thinking? And why did she never tell him? Maybe she was remembering how they'd gone stargazing two nights this week. Or last night, when she'd said she couldn't fall asleep without him. She hadn't, either. But the moment he'd crawled back into bed, she snuggled up beside him and fell asleep with her head on his chest.

Her hands and toes had been frigid though. Perhaps she'd been telling the truth about being too cold to sleep, and he should have built her a fire.

Perhaps. But standing here today, with the early afternoon sun trickling through the bright leaves and the scent of Lake Superior on the breeze, he couldn't be sorry for the lack of fire. Not when he wanted nothing more than to sweep her into the woods and hold her while she snuggled against him all over again.

There were about ten hours left before bedtime, nine if he pled weariness and coaxed her to retire early. Would she catch on if he didn't build a fire again tonight? Even so, how was he going to wait nine more hours before holding her?

"Seth?" She looked up into his eyes, her own a beautiful, vibrant hazel that rivaled the color of the leaves beginning to change.

"Yes?"

"What are we doing at the side of the trail?" She whispered the words, her breath brushing his lips with each gentle exhale.

"We're…"

Kissing. Was it too soon? Would he scare her if he tried?

But considering her admission last night and the way she was staring at his lips right now...

He pulled her nearer, then closed his eyes and lowered his mouth. Her hands came to rest on his upper arms, and she met his kiss tentatively, uncertainly, as though she'd never been kissed before. And she probably hadn't.

"I see them!" Racing little footsteps sounded on the path behind them.

He released Lindy at the same moment she took a step away.

Phillip Jr. rounded the bend a second later.

"How much farther?" Mother's shrill voice carried up the hillside, then she came around the bend as well.

Seth took Lindy's hand in his and leaned toward her ear. "We'll finish that later."

The color in her cheeks deepened.

"Well?" Mother snapped. "I asked how far it was."

"N-not a quarter mile," Lindy called back to her. "The view is worth the hike, I promise."

"Can we do this again tomorrow?" Phillip Jr. didn't even pause as he ran past them. "This is fun."

"Not so fast, Jr." His nanny rounded the bend behind Mother, then raced to catch up.

"I thought you said this was a short walk." Mother glowered at Lindy as she tromped toward them.

Lindy blinked. "It's not even a mile to the bluffs."

Which was plenty far for his wife to walk. He'd expected she'd need the ipecac and atropine he'd brought before now, but she wasn't breathing hard.

Or rather, she hadn't been until their kiss. What did it say about his doctoring if he wanted to haul her into the woods and kiss her until she needed a full dose of atropine?

"I asked my son to take me on a promenade, not an expedition into uncharted wilderness." Mother readjusted the perch of her wide, frilly hat, tilting it back from her eyes.

Lindy muttered something under her breath, but he squeezed her hand before she spoke loud enough for Mother to hear.

"Looks like Phillip's ahead of us now." He settled Lindy's hand on his arm and started up the trail. "Let's see where he leads us."

"There better not be too much farther for him to lead." Mother stepped over a rut, causing her hat to slide right back down on her forehead. She humphed and traipsed forward with the fortitude of a general leading his troops into battle.

There wasn't much farther to walk at all. One more bend in the path and they were standing in a small clearing that sat atop some bluffs. The hill fell away below them, and they stared out at the basin where Eagle Harbor lay nestled into the woods. The calm waters of the harbor shimmered beside it, and Lake Superior sprawled beyond, an endless expanse of blue that contrasted with the blazing orange and red of the leaves sloping down the hillside.

"You were right." He tugged Lindy to his side and pressed his lips against her ear. "Magnificent."

The patches of color returned to her cheeks, and though the shade of red might not be as bright as the leaves at their back, it was just as lovely. "The view of the water, you mean."

He chuckled, low and deep. "No, something else entirely—"

"It's too cold to stay up here long." Mother pulled her flimsy lace shawl tighter about her shoulders.

Why own a shawl wind could whip through in the first place? Half the ladies in Sharpsburg and Washington seemed to have them, but that was one thing he'd never seen this far north.

Then again, if Lindy asked for one, he'd probably buy her five of various colors and patterns.

"Do you want to have the picnic or head back, Mrs. Harrington?" one of the lady's maids asked.

"Picnic, picnic, I want a picnic." Philip Jr. jumped up and down.

"Careful, Jr." Penelope clamped a hand to the top of her head to keep her hat from blowing off in the breeze. "Don't get too close to the edge."

His nanny reached out and pulled him farther away from the bluffs, even though the boy hadn't been anywhere near the ledge.

"Can we eat fast?" Penelope's daughter Emmaline looked at the blanket the maids were spreading. "I'm c-cold."

"It's chillier here than in Maryland, isn't it?" Penelope rested a hand on her daughter's shoulder.

"I like it here." Philip Jr. plopped on the blanket. "Do we have to go home?"

Penny turned to glare at him. "Yes, we do."

"When?" Emmaline sat down on the blanket and pulled her own lace shawl tighter around her. "We're not staying through the winter, are we?"

"Gracious no." Mother stepped to the blanket. "We leave in three days' time."

"You do?" Seth looked at his mother. "This is the first you've said so." Not that he was complaining. He'd help them pack tonight if they could find a ship leaving port sooner.

"I hope you enjoyed your visit." Lindy smiled sweetly.

So sweetly, in fact, that a hint of nausea twined through his stomach.

"Hardly." Mother sniffed. "I don't know why it took the justice of the peace nearly a week to tell me an annulment was out of the question."

Seth stilled, his hand turning stiff at Lindy's side. "What did you say?"

"You asked about an annulment?" Lindy blurted at the same time as him.

Mother tilted her nose and glowered at Lindy. "You didn't think I'd let you stay married to my son if I could help it, did you?"

The color that had flushed Lindy's face earlier drained away.

"You had no business going to the justice of the peace." Seth kept Lindy tucked closely against his side, but he couldn't quite keep his grip gentle.

"What… what did the man say?" Lindy's whisper could barely be heard above the breeze.

"It hardly matters considering my petition was denied. And you…" She turned to Seth. "I've prayed every day for years that you would return home and take up your proper place with the family. But if you insist upon doctoring, I don't know why you can't go back to the hospital in Boston. At least that was a worthy place to work, unlike this town."

"You worked at a hospital in Boston?" Lindy looked up at him.

"For five years after I finished medical school."

"Surely you miss the city. And the people." Mother absently tugged at her shawl. "I've only seen a handful of patients stop by since we've been here. Why do you stay with so few people to treat?"

Lindy swallowed. "I'm afraid that's my fault."

Seth used his free hand, the one that wasn't pinning her against him, to reach over and tilt her chin until their eyes met. "It's not."

"It is." If her eyes had been vibrant earlier, they were two hard crystals of ice now. "Just because you're too kind to admit it doesn't make it any less true. You lost your patients because you married me."

"And now they're coming back. It will be all right."

"If you don't have patients, Seth, then move back to Sharpsburg. Even if you have to bring her with you." Mother stepped around where Phillip Jr. was devouring a slice of cheese and waved a hand absently at Lindy. "Theo could use your help managing the properties. Or if you're that averse to working with your brother, perhaps Penny will sell you the brickworks. And maybe the justice of the peace in Sharpsburg will grant you an annulment." Her face lit with a smile. "Yes, why didn't I think of that? He's known the family for years. We can give him several months' supply of hay and—"

"I don't want to bribe anyone for an annulment, Mother." Seth clenched his teeth so hard his jaw ached. "I'm glad I married Lindy. Why won't you believe me when I say so?"

And truly, if she were determined to spout her mind about Lindy, must she do it in front of her? Lindy had enough to deal with already.

He looked over at Lindy, expecting her head to be down, her eyelids fluttering wildly in an attempt to keep tears back.

Anger blazed in her eyes instead. "What is wrong with you?" She took a step toward Mother, bringing them toe to toe, and taking her away from his side. "Why can't you leave him in peace? Your son is a grown man capable of making his own choices."

She reached for the hem of her sleeve and undid a button. "The people of Eagle Harbor need his doctoring." Another button. "You might not see him with patients all day long, yet he's been up every night since you've arrived tending people while you snore."

Penelope rose from where she'd been seated beside Emmaline and came toward them. "Mrs. Harrington was only trying to say—"

"Mrs. Harrington was only trying to belittle her son for making a choice she disapproves of, which she's done non-stop since she arrived. Seth might be polite enough not to sass his mother, but I'm not. In fact, I'm decidedly impolite."

"Well, I never." Mother's hand moved to her throat. "Of all the rude, impertinent—"

"You want impertinent? I haven't even started with impertinent!

Your son needs to be a doctor, because he helps people instead of doing things like this." Lindy released the final button on her sleeve and thrust her arm out.

Mother stood speechless—for once—her mouth agape as she stared at the patchwork of scars on Lindy's arm.

Penny moved a hand to cover her own mouth, her face turning a sickly shade of white. "Oh dear."

"Maybe you should take a moment amidst all your mutterings about needing Seth to leave town and make bricks and marry the woman you choose, and ask the people he's helped what they think he should do. Or better yet, maybe you should just ask him. Because though you can't seem to hold your tongue for anything, I've never once heard you ask what he wants and why."

His mouth was probably as wide open as his mother's. Had Lindy just defended him? And not just him, but his doctoring—that thing she claimed to hate so fiercely.

He swallowed back the thickness in his throat and tugged Lindy's sleeve. "Put your arm away now, sweetheart. They understand."

"Do they?" She didn't take her eyes off Mother. "You're trying to keep Seth away from what he's good at, and people will die because of it. Or be bled, time after time after time. Or they'll have their legs cut open and beans stuffed inside in an attempt to draw their lung ailment down into a bigger infection elsewhere."

He sucked in a breath, but the air turned to jagged glass in his lungs. His gaze drifted down to the skirt hiding her legs.

He should have figured there was more than just bloodletting, especially given her response when he'd first set her finger. But co-irritation? How could he have missed that? He scrubbed a hand over his face, nausea twisting through his stomach once more. She'd even mentioned co-irritation before they wed, but she'd been too ill to question further. How long had it taken for the doctor to decide that didn't work? Hopefully a few days, but if it was the same doctor that had given her arms all those scars…

"So before you start nattering again about how Seth should do a hundred things other than doctor, understand that I'm one of the people he's saved, and I want him to keep practicing medicine for the next fifty years. Now if you'll excuse me, I assume you can follow the trail back to town without me." Lindy turned and stalked off, leaving the rest of them in a cluster on the hill.

"What… what happened to her arms?" Penelope whispered.

"A doctor bled her." Seth watched his wife tromp into the woods. "Numerous times. Trying to get rid of her asthma, which he misdiagnosed as tuberculosis."

"And the beans in her leg?" Penelope raised a hand to her throat. "Was that the same thing?"

"I presume so."

Penelope looked at the path in the woods where Lindy disappeared. "And you're going to let her walk back to town alone?"

"Please do," Mother muttered. "Perhaps some wolves will find her, and then you can marry—"

"I've had enough." He made a slashing motion with his hand. "Lindy is right. I don't know what makes you think you can come into my house and ridicule my wife, my town, and my profession, but no more. Either you curb your tongue or leave. Tonight. I can make arrangements for you to sail to Houghton this evening, and from there you can take a train to Chicago. Or you can walk. Or grow wings and attempt to fly like a bird, for all I care. But you will be gone, do you hear me?"

"Seth, darling, I'm just looking out for you." Mother fished a handkerchief out of her handbag—never mind that bringing a handbag on a hike made about as much sense as bringing a lace shawl—and dabbed at the tears spilling down her cheeks.

"That woman, she's bewitched you." Mother flung her hand in the direction Lindy had stomped, then twisted her handkerchief. "Surely no man can be content married to someone so sickly. Penny here is healthy. And what was that bit about her causing you to lose your patients? I just want you to be happy, and I know you'd be happier in Sharpsburg with Penny than you are here."

"If you wanted to see me happy, you'd be asking how you could help with my clinic here in Eagle Harbor, not telling me where I should doctor. But then, you don't really want to see me happy, you want to see yourself happy. And because you can't seem to grasp that my version of happiness looks different than yours, you've spent the past week making everyone else miserable.

"You're out of line, and have been since you got here. If you expect to sleep another night under my roof, then you owe both Lindy and me an apology. Don't bother visiting again until you can accept that my choices are different from yours." He turned and stalked away, much as Lindy had, then hastened into the trees to find his wife.

Chapter Twenty-Four

Seth found his wife halfway down the hill, sitting on a log beside the path, nearly hidden by a bend in the trail. Even if he hadn't been looking for her blue skirt amid the colorful leaves, he could have followed the sound of her sniffling.

She wiped the tears from her face as he approached. "Your mother probably hates me, but I couldn't spend another minute listing to her belittle you."

He sat beside her and took her hand in his, weaving their fingers together. "She disliked you before that, simply because you're not Penny."

She blinked at him with swollen, red-rimmed eyes. "I suppose you're right."

"You defended me." He gave her hand tight squeeze and offered her a lopsided smile. "It seems you're not as fearful of my doctoring as you once were."

Her jaw trembled in response, and her eyes welled with fresh tears.

He dropped her hand and wrapped his arm around her shoulder, pulling her against him on the damp log. "Thank you for standing up for me."

"I should have left it to you." Her voice quivered. "I probably caused more problems than I solved."

"No, you got Penny thinking." And him. His gaze fell to where her boots disappeared beneath her skirt. Which leg had her doctor put beans in?

"Tell me more about this doctor in Chicago. The co-irritation." He tried not to grit the words. Tried to unclench his teeth and speak calmly. "I assume there's a scar on your leg. May I see it?"

She set her jaw and pulled her skirt up to her knee, then rolled her stocking down to reveal a semi-circle nearly the size of his fist. Angry red skin puckered and dipped over the area as though the doctor hadn't even bothered to use stitches once he'd finally stopped the co-irritation.

Seth swallowed back the bile rising in his throat and crouched beside her. He could tell simply by looking that the co-irritation hadn't been a short ordeal. "How long?"

"Five months."

He rested his head against her knees. Now it was his turn to fight back the tears, his turn to hang his head in shame over what another man had done in the name of medicine. "I'm sorry, Lindy. So very sorry."

"It's not your fault. Didn't you listen to anything I told your mother?" Her voice was firm, determined even.

He pulled the stocking back up, running his hands along his wife's leg, but not with the normal tenderness a man would use to touch his wife. "Tell me. I want to know the whole story, from beginning to end."

"You know most of it." She dropped her skirt so only her boots peeked out from beneath the hem, then smoothed a hand over the wrinkles. "Aunt Edith and Uncle Henry have money—not as much as your family, but enough to pay servants, buy fancy clothes, keep a carriage and horses. After Pa died, we went to Chicago for help. Dr. Greely had sold us so many medicines to make Ma well that we couldn't even afford the passage, so Elijah's pa gave us the money. We were only supposed to stay with Aunt Edith a short time, just long enough to find jobs and get our own apartment to rent. But when Aunt Edith saw how sick Ma was, she insisted we stay until Ma got better."

He pushed himself back onto the log beside her. "But that never happened."

"No, so when I started coming down with similar symptoms before Ma died, Aunt Edith demanded I see Ma's doctor right away. Dr. Trebair wasn't so bad, but after Ma passed, Aunt Edith insisted she'd found a better doctor, one that would help me rather than let me die like Dr. Trebair did with Ma."

"He was the one who bled you."

"Yes."

His hands tightened into fists. "Couldn't you refuse to see him?"

"I tried, but I think Aunt Edith felt guilty, like Ma's death and Betsy's choice to become a soiled dove were her fault. She'd known Ma was sick for several years but had never come to visit. I can still hear her voice in my head. 'No, Lindy, you're seeing Dr. Lathersop today. I'm not about to let what happened to your mother happen to you.'" Her voice took on a sing-song tenor as she mimicked her aunt.

Had there been more than blood-letting and co-irritation? He was almost afraid to ask, yet he had to know. "What treatments did Dr. Lathersop attempt?"

"He started with the bloodletting, but it only made me weaker and made my lung ailment—which both Dr. Trebair and Dr. Lathersop said was tuberculosis—linger or worsen. After six months of bloodletting twice a week, he insisted the infection was so bad we needed to irritate another part of my body. He said if my body was sicker somewhere else, then the infection from my lungs would get drawn down to the other infection, and my lungs could heal, or something along those lines."

Lindy stared at the ground, keeping her voice flat and emotionless as she spoke, which was somehow worse than if she would have been crying or raging. "He cut my leg open and put beans in the wound. He wouldn't let it heal, not even when it festered and swelled. He'd pull the beans out for a day or two, let it start to heal, and then put new back in to keep the infection going."

"You were confined to bed the entire time, then."

"For five months, yes. I finally pulled the beans out and told them I had enough, that it wasn't making my lungs better, but that I was going to get gangrene if he kept it up."

"You would have, eventually." After five months, it was a near miracle she hadn't.

"Dr. Lathersop said the illness was going into my head, that only an insane person would refuse treatment, and I needed to be put in an asylum."

Seth gritted his teeth. He had half a mind to sail to Chicago and track down this so-called doctor. "You're not insane, Lindy. You realize that, correct?"

Her jaw worked back and forth. "I was close. Not because of the illness, but because of Dr. Lathersop and Aunt Edith."

"Don't tell me your aunt had you admitted." He took her hand and squeezed it.

"I sneaked away first. I pulled the beans out of my leg after he left one day, doused the wound in some whisky I stole from Uncle Albert's cabinet, and bandaged it. Then waited until the day before Dr. Lathersop was to visit again and sneaked out the window. A few months after Mother and I had been in Chicago, Gilbert Sinclair came to visit us at Aunt Edith's. He'd felt bad about how his father treated us after Pa's death, and even though Elijah's pa was the one who paid for us to go to Chicago, Gilbert offered me money once we were there. I didn't take it then, but when I found myself on the street, limping because of my leg and with nowhere to go, I made my way to his office by the harbor. He gave me enough to rent an apartment while my leg healed, but I wouldn't let him call a doctor."

"Of course not." He could still hear her in his sickroom pleading with Victoria after she'd broken her finger. *I don't want help. Please, I want to go home.*

Lindy shifted beside him. "I grew well enough to take jobs at a slaughterhouse and stockyard. But every few months I'd get sick again."

"And lose your job."

She traced a stain on the lap of her skirt, still keeping her head down. "People were talking by then, about how I was always coughing, about how I had tuberculosis. And no one wanted to catch it."

"Lindy…"

She still didn't look up at him, so he gathered her into his arms and pulled her onto his lap. "I know you told me not to apologize, but I'm still sorry for everything you endured in the name of medicine."

"No." She looked up then, her lips only inches away from his. "I thought all doctors were the same at first, but I see the difference between you and Dr. Lathersop."

Her breath mingled with his as she spoke, and the scent of sunshine and soap from her skin rose to twine with the bergamot he'd dabbed on his neck that morning.

He rested his forehead against hers, the gesture somehow more intimate than the way she'd snuggled up to him last night. "I wish I would have been with you in Chicago, that I could go back in time and tend you there. You wouldn't have a single scar."

She cupped his cheek with her hand. "I wish that too, more than you know."

He lowered his lips to her mouth. One brush, then two, before he drew her closer. She kissed him back, her lips tangy from the salt of tears she hadn't quite managed to wipe from her face. Her hands inched up his arms to his shoulders, where they rested, delicate and light and unsure, before they finally relaxed against him. It was everything he'd ever hoped kissing his wife might be. Was she finally starting to see the brightness in their future? It was almost too much to hope for.

~.~.~.~.~

She could barely think, barely breathe, barely do anything but feel. The way Seth's hands stayed firmly at her waist, then inched up her back to toy with the hair at the nape of her neck. The way his arms wrapped around her, holding her close. The way his mouth covered her own, all warm and gentle as he kissed her over and over.

Had she wanted to snuggle with him last night? She should have attempted kissing him instead. Or maybe snuggling and kissing together. She'd have to try that tonight. Except that would involve ending this kiss and going home first, and she was perfectly content to stay right here, on this damp, rotting log with him forever.

But he broke away a few seconds later, his chest heaving, his breath hitting her cheek in rushed little bursts, as though he were the one about to have an asthma attack.

She smiled at him. "Can we do that again?"

He chuckled, low and deep. "We most certainly can, over and over." Then he wrapped his arms around her back and squeezed her tight, pressing her fully against him. "I love you, Lindy."

She stiffened, but he seemed not to notice as he placed a kiss beneath her ear, then another against her jaw.

No. No. No. This wasn't supposed to happen. She might be allowed to love him, but he wasn't supposed to love her.

"Lindy?" He pulled back from her, his eyes turning from hazy to assessing. "What's wrong?"

"N-nothing."

His brows drew down. "Was I making you uncomfortable?"

"Uh, the kisses were nice." At least until he got to the *I love you* part.

"Then why are you so stiff? Why did you stop...?" It seemed to register then, the exact moment she'd stiffened.

"Seth, I'm sorry." She hadn't meant to hurt him. He was the last person in the world she'd ever want to hurt.

"Sorry for what? Marrying me? Yes, you've already told me." He picked her up and set her on the log with the same amount of care Jack might use when stringing up one of his rabbits. Brisk. Efficient. Emotionless. "Have you thought any more about the question I asked last week?"

A sudden coldness engulfed her. Because there was bite to the air, of course. It had nothing to do with Seth moving away from her and standing. "What question?"

"The one about whether you'd rather not have known your mother at all instead of having her and then losing her. Which do you pick?"

It was almost like watching ships collide in the harbor. She could see where the conversation was headed, what her answer would lead to, the wreckage it would cause, and yet she was helpless to stop it. "I'd want to know her, even if I lost her in the end."

He slung a hand on his hip. "Then you understand."

"I don't." She dug her fingernails into the soft bark of the log. "A person can't choose who their mother is, but they can choose their wife."

"Yes, and I made that choice. I don't regret it, even with you sitting there and telling me I can't love you."

"I never said you couldn't love me."

"But you thought it, and are still thinking it now, I bet."

She tore a piece of bark off the tree trunk and let it fall to the ground. Silence filled the air around them, but what was there to say? He deserved better than for her to sit here and lie, yet the truth wasn't going to make him happy.

"It's like you still have that blasted score sheet and tally up my every action against yours. How many times do I have to tell you? We're supposed to be overlooking each other's slights." He blew out a breath, full and free, so large she could only dream about holding that much air in her lungs at once. "God gave you to me for a reason, Lindy."

"For a reason?" She shot off the fallen log and threw up her hands. "What reason? I'm sick and I'll die and there's nothing you can do to stop it. God healed people in the Bible, but will he heal me of my lung condition? If you want a reason not to love me, there it is."

"Except I want to love you anyway, even if I end up losing you."

Then he must not have ever been forced to say goodbye to someone he loved. He couldn't know what it was like, otherwise he'd never open his heart up to all the hurt he seemed determined to suffer. "Why does God allow people to suffer like this? Why did he take my mother after years of struggling? My father in only a moment? Why did he take Hiram Cummings? Why is he slowly taking my life?"

Seth came toward her, stopping a few steps away but not reaching for her. "Why has this pregnancy sent Tressa Oakton to her deathbed when she's had three other pregnancies without any trouble? Why does a nine-year-old boy climbing a tree fall and break his neck? Why does a typhus epidemic spread through a town and kill a third of its population?" He shook his head, his face lined with the grief of a man that had seen too much death throughout his years. "I wish I had answers. Or even more than answers, I wish I had the ability to heal the way Christ did. One touch, one look, one word, and all the sickness and pain is gone."

He dug the toe of his shoe into the soft ground and surveyed the trees as though they could provide the answer they both sought so desperately. "I suppose, if nothing else, all the suffering on earth gives us reason to hope for heaven. No suffering there, no pain or sorrow. We just have to endure the earth part first."

"But if there's so much suffering you can't avoid, why invite more into your life? You don't have to love me, Seth. Numerous marriages survive without love."

He let out a small growl. "I can tell you that you're worth it, but I've already said that, haven't I? In a hundred different ways. The trouble is, you don't believe me. And until you do, we're at an impasse."

An impasse. It sounded like too small of a word, like a simple hurdle that could be jumped and overcome, when what they had was an insurmountable mountain between them.

Seth turned toward the trail as though ready to go, then paused and spun back around. He raised his hand toward her before fisting it and drawing it back in. "When Elijah first said I should propose to you, I asked him why God allowed things to happen the way they did. Why He let Ranulfson find us when five minutes later you would have been with Toby and he never would have known you were in my clinic."

"What did Elijah say?"

A smile curved his lips, but it wasn't the tender, lopsided one he usually showed her. "That the trying of our faith works patience. That he didn't have the answer as to why, except that sometimes God brings trials into our life to grow us, and we need to remember to honor God through our trials, even if His doings don't fully make sense."

"Well, His doings certainly don't make sense." At least they could agree on that.

He gave a scornful laugh. "They make more sense than yours."

Or maybe they couldn't agree after all.

"I might not know why God wanted you to be my wife, but it makes even less sense to say now that God has put us together, we're not allowed to love each other." He ran his hand over his hair in a jerky, frustrated gesture. "You're my wife. I'm supposed to love you the way Christ loved the church, even to the point that I lay down my life in place of yours."

She gritted her teeth and shook her head. "No laying down your life for mine. I'm not worth it."

He stared at her for a moment, his jaw working back and forth. When he finally opened his mouth, she expected words of assurance. Yes, she was worth sacrificing for; yes, he would love her no matter what; yes, he would happily pay for every last drop of medicine and every specialist he could find if doing so offered the slim hope she might be cured.

But all he said was, "And that brings us back to our impasse."

A chill slithered through her, and she wrapped her arms around herself to ward it off. She wasn't going to be disappointed he refused to argue. She wanted him to forget this foolish notion of loving her when she'd only bring him heartache in the end.

Didn't she?

He sighed and shook his head. "I'm going back to town. I need to stop by the mercantile to ask after a letter I'm expecting. Can you make sure my family gets home? I'd rather not leave them in the woods alone."

Her throat closed. There'd been times, many times, when she'd told him she needed to be left alone. Why did it hurt so badly when he asked the same of her?

"Before I go." He dug into his pocket and then held out a jar of white powder and unlooped the canteen from his shoulder. "In case you need your medicine."

The second she took them, he turned and headed off, his boots crunching against the bed of fallen leaves.

This was all happening so fast. He was praying they would grow to love each other, but growing took time. Like a whole summer. Or sometimes even years for things such as trees.

Whatever was happening between them was nothing like the slow growth of trees.

Chapter Twenty-Five

She was gone.

Seth looked at the note on the table once more, then stalked over to the stove to check the oatmeal. The water bubbled, but the soggy oats lay on the bottom of the pan, still not ready to eat. Not that he planned to eat anyway. As soon as this was ready to serve his mother and the others, he was heading out. He needed to find Lindy before she got too far ahead.

He glanced over his shoulder at the note again. It was startlingly simple. *Gone to the O'Byrnes for the day. Lindy.*

They hadn't said much to each other after their conversation on the hill yesterday, probably because there wasn't anything to say. He was falling in love with her, and she... well, she was as closed off as ever. She might have defended his doctoring, but evidently she wasn't excited to be his wife. She just didn't think he'd torture her under the guise of doctoring. Lovely.

He huffed as he stirred the thickening oatmeal. Maybe he'd read too much into the soft looks she'd been giving him this week, into her request to sleep by him two nights ago. Clearly she'd just been cold, and a fire would have sufficed as much as his body heat.

So that's precisely what he'd done last night, built her a fire. And it didn't hurt that he'd had a patient come knocking right before bed either. Lindy had been fast asleep by the time he'd finally retired, which he'd thought was a good thing.

He hadn't figured she'd rise early and leave before anyone else was awake. While he might be tempted to throttle the woman rather than hug her the next time they stood face to face, she was still his wife, he really was falling in love with her, and he didn't relish the thought of her lying on the hillside, gasping for breath and wishing she'd remembered her medicine.

A pounding sounded on the parlor door. He lifted the oatmeal off the stove and set it on the table, then headed into the other room and pulled open the door.

"Dr. Harrington," Victoria panted, her cheeks flushed and eyes wild. "You have to come. Now. It's the baby."

"Tressa's baby?" He reached for his medical bag, then paused. "Mac wanted the midwife from Central there, not me."

"She's been there since yesterday. Dr. Greely since the middle of the night."

Mac had called Dr. Greely before him? A sour fist of disappointment lodged in his stomach.

"Surely they don't need me as well." He couldn't quite keep the hardness from his voice.

"They do!" She grabbed his sleeve and tugged. "The baby won't come, and Dr. Greely has forceps, except they're not normal forceps. There's a hook at the one end and teeth. He says it's to… to… cut up the baby. That it needs to come out in pieces or Tressa will die." Tears filled Victoria's eyes. "You have to do something."

"What's going on?" Penelope's voice sounded behind him.

He looked over his shoulder as he picked up his bag. "I have a childbirth to attend. There's oatmeal on the table for breakfast."

"No." Tressa's groan echoed down the hall. "I won't let you."

"There's no other way." Dr. Greely's voice rose in answer, followed by a cough.

A cough in the birthing chamber? Was he trying to make Tressa sicker?

Seth stepped into the dim room, its curtains drawn tight against the sunlight. The scent of blood and sweat cloaked the bedroom, and beneath it, the more subtle, sour scent of death.

"We have to. Don't fret now." The aged midwife was positioned at the foot of the bed by Tressa's feet.

Dr. Greely stood across the room by the table that held a pitcher and basin, the cranioclast that Victoria had described in his hand. "There's always a chance for more babes. You should know that. You've already got three."

"No!" Tressa wailed, clamping her legs together. Her long hair lay matted against her pillow, sweat soaking her brow and the top of her nightgown. Lines of pain and weariness wreathed her face, and she struggled for each and every breath. "I want this one."

"I brought Dr. Harrington." Victoria entered the room, a load of fresh towels in her arms.

All eyes turned to him, then Tressa let out a wail that sounded akin to the noise a dying man would make. Her hands wrapped around her stomach, and she pressed her eyes closed.

The midwife's hands disappeared beneath Tressa's nightgown, then she frowned and shook her head. "It still won't come. The doctor's right. There's only one thing to be done when a babe gets stuck."

"Best let me over there so I can get to business." Dr. Greely stifled a yawn. "Been here too long already."

"I refuse it," Tressa panted.

Seth set down his medical bag and stepped to the bed, wrapping

Tressa's limp hand in his own. He was hardly an obstetrician, but he knew enough about birthing to understand that Dr. Greely and the midwife were right. Choices were very limited when a labor became obstructed.

"What does her husband say about using that?" He jutted his chin toward the cranioclast.

"The birthing chamber is no place for a man who's not a doctor," the midwife spat.

When decisions such as this had to be made, it seemed only right the husband have a say. Or perhaps more, that the husband be present to calm the wife.

"Does Mac know I'm here?" He looked to Victoria.

She gave a slow shake of her head. "Anytime Tressa moaned, he came upstairs and wanted inside. Elijah took him for a walk about an hour ago."

Perfect. He'd probably get kicked out of the lighthouse the second Mac arrived. "Get him."

"There's no reason." Dr. Greely took up the cranioclast as Victoria left the room. "I've been here since three o'clock this morning, and the situation hasn't changed. The child is breech and refuses to move into the birth canal." His words ended with a cough.

"I'm not letting you near her with the way you're hacking." The midwife scowled at him. "You shouldn't have even come. The birthing chamber needs to be clean."

Dr. Greely scowled right back at the woman. "It's just a little cough. Probably got it from his wife." He jabbed a finger at Seth.

Seth rolled his eyes. Of all the times to start arguing about Lindy. "You shouldn't be here, regardless of where you got the cough."

"Your wife has a cough?" The midwife eyed Seth suspiciously.

"It's due to asthma, not a contagion."

Tressa moaned again, but the woman kept her gaze on him,

running it slowly down him as though she could somehow sense whether he had an infection. "I haven't let Greely near her, not once. I've seen too many women die of puerperal fever over the years. All from doctors and their dirty hands."

"My hands aren't dirty!" Dr. Greely snapped.

"I wash all my instruments and my hands in antiseptic before treating patients." Seth dipped his head toward his medical bag at his feet, where the midwife would find two bottles of carbolic acid. "I find it reduces chances of infection."

"He's a quack, I tell ya," Dr. Greely muttered. "Doesn't know the first thing about medicine."

Tressa gave his hand a weak squeeze. "Make it stop, Dr. Harrington. Please make it stop."

"I already told you how to make it stop." Dr. Greely picked up his cranioclast.

"You've tried turning the babe?" Seth asked at the midwife.

The aged woman bit down on her lip. "It won't turn. There's not enough fluid. All she does is scream when I try."

Tressa was whimpering now, her eyes closed while lines of pain marred her face.

"This certainly isn't a part of doctoring I enjoy." Dr. Greely coughed again and rubbed his sagging jowls. "But you know what will happen if we don't take the baby. Better to take one life than two."

Tressa didn't even open her eyes to protest this time, but a moment later another contraction was upon her. Her hands moved to her belly while a low, keening wail escaped her mouth.

"Then you'd better give that instrument of yours to the other doctor." The midwife jutted her chin toward the cranioclast. "I'm still not letting you near her with that cough."

Seth swallowed. Could he bring himself to perform such a

253

procedure? He had a cranioclast at home in his supply room, but he'd never used it. Wasn't sure he could even now, considering what it would do to Tressa's baby.

"There's a third option," he said quietly. One that would spare the baby, but not necessarily the mother.

"No." Dr. Greely and the midwife said in unison.

"It's as I told her." The midwife glanced at Tressa. "She can have more babes, but a babe can't survive without its mother."

The midwife was right. He, a doctor who couldn't accurately diagnose a case of whooping cough, wasn't going to be able to save both Tressa and her child. Especially not with a procedure he'd only performed once before, and that posthumously.

"We should still wait for the father before we make any decisions." Seth gripped Tressa's hand tighter and looked over his shoulder at the door. Where was Mac? Hopefully Elijah hadn't taken him too far, because he wasn't sure he could keep Dr. Greely away much longer.

Tressa endured three more contractions as they waited, each one seemingly longer, each one seemingly sucking more life from her frail body. By the time the door finally opened and Mac ducked beneath the frame, Tressa was drifting in and out of consciousness, always coming around for the pain of the contractions, but slipping away as soon as they were finished.

"What's wrong? Victoria said there's trouble?" Mac headed straight for his wife, his hulking frame commanding the attention of everyone in the room.

Seth stepped out of the way so Mac could take his wife's hand, and Victoria slipped inside the room but stayed against the far wall near Dr. Greely.

"The child is breech and won't move into the birth canal. The only choice when this happens is to take the babe out in pieces." Dr.

Greely raised the cranioclast. "As unpleasant as the prospect may seem, this instrument will ensure the procedure is swift. Your wife should fully recover and be able to bear more children."

Mac's face drained of color. "No, I forbid it. And if Tressa were awake, I'm sure she would too."

"I've been here since yesterday." The midwife reached for a rag and mopped her brow. "It's either take the babe or lose your wife."

Mac looked down at Tressa's pale features. "Why isn't she awake? Why isn't she talking?" When he raised his eyes again, they didn't seek out the midwife or Dr. Greely, but Seth, though he was hardly the best person to answer Mac's question.

Seth cleared his throat. "A woman's labor isn't supposed to go on for this long, at least not the end part of it. When it does, she grows weak."

"And she'll die from it?"

"If nothing is done, yes."

Mac rested his hand on Tressa's stomach and shook his head. "I can feel the babe, so close, just right there. Can't we...? There has to be some way to save both of them."

Seth looked away from the towering brute of a man hunkered over his wife, and blinked against the heat gathering in his own eyes. "There's an operation sometimes done in hospitals."

"No!" Dr. Greely exclaimed. "I won't stand for it."

"What kind of operation?" Mac kept his gaze on his wife's face, her eyes closed with exhaustion and pain.

It was risky, yes, but he couldn't deny Mac the information, couldn't turn and walk out of the room without making sure Mac knew all of the choices available, as far-fetched as some of them were. "It's considered dangerous for mothers. So dangerous, in fact, that it's usually done only when a mother is assumed lost."

"You're saying... you're saying I have to choose between my child and Tressa?" Anguish laced Mac's voice, and he tightened his fist around his wife's hand.

"I didn't say that." Seth might be poor at doctoring, but he was even worse at attending deathbeds. How was he supposed to stand by and watch Tressa or her baby die without trying to aid them? "I've seen women survive, twice. But as I said, it's risky and usually done posthumously to save the child."

"He's insane." Dr. Greely jabbed a finger at Seth. "You let him do that, Mac Oakton, and your wife's life will be on your hands."

"You insisted that Lindy would lose her finger if Dr. Harrington refused to amputate. But she didn't." Victoria turned to Dr. Greely. "Besides, you shouldn't even be in here with that cough."

"You have a cough and you're attending my wife?" Mac turned toward the other doctor, his thick arms crossed over his chest.

Dr. Greely's face turned pale. "I—"

Tressa's eyes flew open, and she let out another wail, curling into a ball on her side and wrapping her arms around her stomach. "I can't..." She panted through the pain. "I-I... can't..."

"There, love, it will be okay." Mac bent over her and placed a kiss on her brow, then murmured a series of words so soft Seth couldn't make them out.

When the contraction passed, the other man straightened and looked at him. "What does this surgery involve?"

Seth moved to the other side of Mac and laid a hand on Tressa's belly. Mac was right. He could feel the life there, beating just on the other side of Tressa's taut skin and muscles. "We cut open her abdomen and remove both the babe and her uterus."

Mac's already pale face lost even more color. "You... you cut her open?"

"Yes. I'd make an incision right here." He drew a line down the center of Tressa's swollen abdomen.

"How will she survive if you cut her like that?" Mac clamped a hand to the back of his neck and bent his head.

He wouldn't think about the anguish in the other man's voice, not if he didn't want to break down himself. "I'll sew her back up. If infection doesn't set in, she'll heal, but as I said, there's a lot of risk. And there will be no future chance of having children."

Mac's eyes filled with moisture. "I don't want any more young'uns. She's been so sick with this babe, I'm scared to touch her ever again." Still keeping Tressa's hand clasped in his, he took a step closer to his wife's head and smoothed hair back from her face. "Tressa, love, can you hear Dr. Harrington? What do you think?"

She kept her eyes closed as she answered. "You can't let them kill my baby."

"You might not survive."

She shook her head slowly, weakly. "I'm not going to survive if this goes on either."

"I refuse to stay and be part of this." Dr. Greely tossed his cranioclast into his medical bag and stomped toward the door. "When she dies at your hand, Harrington, I just might have you drawn up on murder charges."

Mac looked at him as the door banged shut behind the other doctor. "Can he do that?"

"No." At least he didn't think so. "Your wife and the baby will die without medical intervention. If I attempt to intervene and things don't turn out, a court won't hold me at fault."

But if he failed, he'd hold himself at fault until the day he died.

Chapter Twenty-Six

"You can't keep working in Central." Lindy sat beside the pallet where Jenny lay in the cramped little cabin. After she'd greeted the children with hugs and kisses earlier, Jack had taken Alice and Toby with him to check his snares. There were some things little ears had no business hearing.

"Jack said you want to take the children back to Cornwall. What if I can come up with a way to pay for your passage across the Atlantic?" She'd yet to ask Seth for money, but she couldn't imagine him saying no. "Will you stop working then?"

Jenny wiped at her runny nose with a stained cloth that looked to be more rag than handkerchief. "I don't need your charity. Now leave me alone. I'm too sick to work tonight anyway."

"I'm not talking about just tonight. I'm talking about permanently." Lindy waited until the other woman met her eyes. "Jenny, you can't sell your body."

Jenny coughed into her handkerchief, and Lindy sat back, surveying her. She'd assumed Jenny had been in bed because she'd been working all night, but she truly did look terrible. Her face and neck were swollen, and her nose wouldn't stop running. The poor woman probably had a headache too.

"Do you have any tea?" Lindy rose and headed toward the stove. "Let me make you some."

Jenny's laugh was cold and brittle. "Where would I have gotten tea? I'm not one of them fancy girls with johns that bring her gifts."

"There are other ways to provide for yourself and your siblings. Even if you refuse my help for yourself, why not let me take the children to Eagle Harbor until their father returns? I can—"

"Stop meddling."

Lindy stilled and sucked in a breath. After all the sacrifices she'd made for the O'Byrnes, this was the response she got? Not *thank you*, just *stop meddling*. She opened the sack of food she'd brought and took out five carrots, then reached for the knife hanging on a peg. "Toby would be dead if not for my meddling."

"Maybe that's for the best," Jenny muttered. "Can't imagine what kind of life the boy will have."

Only someone that had never faced death could say such a thing.

Except Jenny had faced death, at least the death of her mother, which made her statement even more confusing.

"Toby doesn't have to live like this." Lindy slammed the blade into the carrots with a little too much force. "I can help. There's a whole town full of people down the hill that can help. And if you're too stubborn to accept, then at least let me take your siblings. They can stay in Eagle Harbor with me, or I know of another family that would take them for a time."

"Like the person you sent to help two days ago? Get out. I don't want help from a liar."

Lindy paused, knife poised over the carrots. "Someone came by your cabin?"

"Don't pretend like you don't know."

Except she didn't know. "Who was it? Did you get a name?"

"I told you to get out." Jenny muffled a cough with her handkerchief. "The deal was you'd keep us secret, and I'd let you keep coming back, but you didn't keep your end of the bargain, did you?"

Lindy brought the knife down on the carrots with a thwack. *Thwack. Thwack. Thwack.* What did it matter if an infant could eat the size of the carrots she was slicing for the soup? "I didn't tell anyone. Not even my husband knows where you live, though that's soon to change. He'll be accompanying me on my visits from now on."

"There won't be any more visits." Jenny rolled to face the wall. "We're moving."

"No." Panic ignited in her chest. They couldn't move. If all they could manage now was a cabin in the woods, what would their new home be? A cave? And if no one knew where they were or that they needed help, how would the children eat? "If you're that determined to move, why won't you take my money to go to Cornwall?"

"I don't owe you any answers. I said get out."

The woman was too ill to make her do much of anything, let alone leave, which was why she dumped the carrots into the pot and ladled water into it. There were two squirrels hanging outside the cabin door that would make for a nice soup. "Do you expect your father to return before winter? Surely he—"

"I said leave!" Jenny screamed, then coughed into her handkerchief. "Get out this second, and don't you come back, not ever."

Lindy set the knife down. Maybe it was time she started making her own threats. "I'll go home, but I'm coming back as soon as I get my husband. I've had enough. You need to see a doctor, and your brothers and sister need somewhere safe to stay—somewhere that has food, even if you refuse to admit it."

"I'll leave right now. Pack them up and take them before you come back."

Lindy crossed her arms, narrowing her eyes at the pale, too thin woman. There was no way she could move in her frail state, and even if she tried, the trail she and her siblings left through the woods would be easy to follow.

But staying longer right now was going to frustrate them both. She'd come back with help, like she should have done several weeks ago. "I'll go. But I'll return—"

"No!" Jenny pushed herself up on her elbows. "Don't you understand? You've ruined everything. I keep telling you I don't need your help, but you refuse to listen. Well, I'm telling you now. Leave and don't come back, you hear?"

Heat pricked the backs of her eyes. What had she ruined besides the starving bellies she'd filled with food? But did Jenny care? Maybe that was the bigger question, and it seemed she didn't.

Lindy headed toward the door without saying goodbye. Once outside, she looked around for the children, though it was too soon for them to be back. It was probably better she didn't warn them what she intended. Jenny couldn't take them anywhere when they were already gone.

Lindy started down the path, the blazing leaves around her doing little to lift her mood.

Why was Jenny so insistent on doing everything by herself? Couldn't she see the hardships she created for the children when she refused help?

Like the hardships I create for Seth when I refuse his help.

She gasped. Where had that thought come from? Surely her situation was different. She had reasons for keeping her distance from Seth. She was dying, after all.

Except she wasn't dying. She'd felt better this past week than she had since she was a girl. It wasn't that she never coughed, but his medicine helped when she took it, and those saunas seemed to aid her too.

Could God be healing her? She rubbed her forehead. No, it was dangerous to let her thoughts wander down that path. How many times had she thought her mother might be cured, only to fall ill again?

It was easier not to hope anymore.

Except for when she felt Seth's warmth beside her in bed, or he wrapped her in his arms and kissed her, or he looked at her and told her she was worth loving.

She swallowed the lump in her throat. At those times, the only thing she wanted to do was hope, regardless of how everything turned out in the end.

..*.*.*

"Is Lindy here?" Seth dropped his medical bag on the floor inside the door and slumped against the wall. His hands and feet felt as though they'd been weighted with copper ingots, his muscles ached, and his eyelids drooped.

God, please let her be here.

It was one in a long line of prayers he'd been uttering for the past six hours.

God, please keep my scalpel steady. God, please help me see where to make the next incision. God, please let that baby cry. God, please let Tressa wake from the chloroform. God, please keep infection from setting in.

It was too soon to know God's answer to the prayer about infection, but at the moment, Tressa had a small, yet healthy baby girl in her arms.

"Lindy went to visit friends for the day." Penelope looked up from where she sat with her embroidery on her lap. "There's a note on the kitchen table."

Seth squeezed his eyes shut for a moment and then forced them open. He should probably eat a bite or two of food before he headed out.

Provided he could walk to the kitchen without falling over.

"It's rather rude, if you ask me." Mother set her own embroidery aside. "Who goes calling without inviting their guests? We've been here a week, and I've hardly met anyone in this town."

"I doubt you'd want to go on this call." Seth unbuttoned his coat and hung it on the peg by the door. "She was visiting orphans, and it's a longer hike than the one you took yesterday."

"Orphans? I didn't realize there were…" Penny's embroidery frame clattered to the floor, and she pressed a hand to her mouth. "Seth, what happened?"

He glanced down at his shirt and grimaced at the bloodstains. He'd discarded the apron he'd worn during the surgery but had hoped his shirt could be cleaned.

A hope that now seemed overly optimistic, given Penelope's reaction.

The door to the kitchen opened, and Lindy stepped in. She must have come inside through the back door and headed into the parlor from the kitchen.

"Seth." A smile lit her face as she headed straight for him.

"Thank goodness." He took a step toward her. Perhaps he'd been foolish to worry, considering she'd made the trip to the O'Byrnes on her own before, but he'd not been able to help himself. "I was about to come looking for you. Penelope said you weren't back and—"

"Is that blood?" She froze mid-step, the smile on her lips dying as she took in his shirt.

"I've just returned from delivering Tressa Oakton's baby."

"Well, don't just stand there, go change!" Mother took out her fan and began whipping it furiously at her face. "Of all the improper things. You'd think I'd raised you in a barn."

"Is the baby well?" Penelope glanced worriedly at his shirt.

"She's smaller than normal, but otherwise healthy." The midwife had been surprised by the child's size, but she'd also said when the mother didn't have much fluid, the babes often came out small. She'd been even more surprised with the success of the surgery than with the baby's size though.

As had he.

He'd thought for sure his scalpel would slip, or that he'd accidently find something other than the uterus. That Tressa would never wake from the anesthesia, that the babe would already be dead. That something would go wrong and Dr. Greely would be proven right about his doctoring skills. But it had all gone beautifully.

"Why is there so much blood?" Lindy's face had gone stark white.

His wife likely had no idea the amount of blood involved in bringing a child into the world, and this birthing chamber hadn't been like most.

"I performed a surgery." He glanced down at his hands, stained yellow from being washed and washed again in carbolic acid. It still didn't seem real. Had he really saved Tressa and her child? Him? The man who'd been fired from the Marine Hospital Service? The man who'd been lucky to have one patient a day over the past week? A smile tugged at the corners of his mouth, and he couldn't help but give in until he felt the grin covering his face. "The baby would have died without it, and quite possibly Tressa."

"So they're both alive?" Lindy bit the side of her lip, the color still not returning to her face. "Even with all the blood?"

"What kind of surgery was it?" This from Penelope, who had picked up her embroidery from the floor, only to set it aside and listen.

"It's called a caesarian section. Sarah, the baby, was breech and couldn't come down the birth canal. I had to cut open Tressa's uterus and remove both that and the baby."

"You cut her open?" Lindy nearly screeched the words. "I can't… I just… can't…"

Her chin quivered, and she covered her hand with her mouth

before turning and dashing into the kitchen. The back door banged shut behind her a moment later.

"Considering your wife has been bled more times than most people get colds in their lifetime, I'd probably try hiding my bloody clothes from her in the future," Mother muttered.

Seth rubbed a hand over his face. He was a dunce. Even in his tired state, he should have realized blood would bother Lindy more than most.

"You did a caesarian section?" Penelope stood and came toward him. "On a live woman? My friend Florence had a boy born that way, but Flo…" The dimness in Penny's eyes told the rest of the story.

"It's not done often on living women, though it's becoming a little more popular in hospital maternity wards."

Retching sounded from the rear of the house.

"If you'll excuse me."

Seth darted into his bedroom, where he threw on a fresh shirt and pair of trousers before setting his old clothes aside to be burned. The retching noises had ceased by the time he headed outside, but Lindy was still hunkered in the dirt beside the house, her pins coming loose from her hair.

"I'm sorry." He kneeled beside her. "I should have been more thoughtful about the blood."

"You were so happy. You're covered in blood, and you're smiling while you talk about cutting open…" She groaned, her face turning pale once again. "I owe you an apology, and I need your help. But how… how can I…?"

"How can you what?" He reached out and took her hand, her skin hot and clammy. And what was she sorry about? How she'd responded yesterday when he'd told her he loved her? Or something else entirely? Surely she wasn't still sorry that she'd married him, was she?

"I'm not sure if there's enough time left today, so it will probably have to wait until tomorrow. I know I don't deserve it, but I was hoping—"

"Miss Lindy! Miss Lindy!"

Seth straightened and glanced around. A second later, Jack rounded the back corner of the office and skidded to a halt.

"Oh, good. You've already got the doctor." Jack seemed not to notice Lindy's hunched form and pale face as he bent to tug on her other hand. "You have to come quick. Jenny can't breathe."

"Jenny can't breathe?" Seth's heart began to pound as he dropped Lindy's hand and pushed to his feet. "Let me get my bag."

He dashed inside and headed straight for the parlor where he'd left it. By the time he returned, Toby and a little girl that looked to be between the two boys in age were beside Lindy, who was standing, though not all that steadily.

"Where is your sister?" he asked Jack.

"At the cabin. She was breathing hard when we got back from setting our traps." Jack turned from Seth to Lindy. "We called for you, but you were gone."

"I left early." Lindy rested a hand on his shoulder.

Seth's grip tightened around handle of his medical bag. "When you say your sister can't breathe, what do you mean? Is she struggling to breathe, not breathing at all?"

"Her face is all fat, and she sounds worse than Miss Lindy having a breathing attack." Jack gripped his sleeve. "Can you help her?"

He couldn't make any guarantees. "If her face is swollen, she might be having an allergic reaction. Did she eat anything unusual?"

Jack looked at Lindy. "Did you bring anything different today?"

"No, and your sister didn't want food anyway." Lindy guided Jack toward the kitchen door. "You children go inside and wait for us."

"You don't want us to come?" Jack worried his lip between his teeth.

"I'll show Dr. Harrington the way. Why don't you have some cheese and biscuits while you wait? I saw some sitting on the table. And there's a room where you can sleep if you get tired." Lindy led the children inside only to return a few minutes later, a lantern in hand, and a grim look on her face. "Jenny wasn't well when I visited earlier. I'd hoped you'd come with me tomorrow and then help me move the children to town."

"You were going to show me where the cabin was before Jack arrived?" It was a small gesture of trust, nearly insignificant considering all the other obstacles they needed to overcome. But here he was, like a dog racing toward any little table scrap she tossed his way.

Were all people this much of a mess while falling in love?

Perhaps, but he didn't have time for these kinds of questions, not when there was somebody who needed medical care waiting.

Chapter Twenty-Seven

"How much farther?"

"Maybe another quarter mile." Lindy glanced over her shoulder at Seth, hiking up the small path too narrow for them to walk side by side. "It's on the other side of the meadow."

She worried her skirt in her hands. Why had Jenny refused her help earlier? If she was sick enough to have trouble breathing, then the woman should have said so.

Not that she would have had a clue how to help without Seth. Maybe give Jenny some of the ipecac and atropine she'd carried with her.

"The other side of the meadow is too far for you to walk with how you're breathing." Seth's voice resonated up the path from behind her. "Let's sit."

"I want to get there first." She kept walking, half expecting Seth to argue about how she had to stop and take medicine this moment.

Instead he looked up the trail toward where evening sunlight bathed the meadow. "You'll rest as soon as we get there then."

"All right."

"I'm sorry about earlier." His voice came from behind her again. "About the blood. I'd not stopped to consider how much it would bother you."

"You shouldn't apologize. You saved Tressa and her baby. I'm the one that should be apologizing." She forged through the edge of the trees and into the meadow. Dusk was closing in, turning the autumn grass a vibrant orange. Any other time, and she'd stop to take in the burnished beauty of the evening, perhaps stare at the sky until the first stars of night twinkled down at her.

"No." His voice was firm as he came up to walk beside her. "You don't need to apologize because blood bothers you. It's understandable."

Was it? It didn't seem so. He'd saved two lives today. Surely that was more important than getting blood on his shirt.

"Will Tressa have a scar where you... where you...?" She clamped her jaw shut before it started to tremble.

"Any kind of surgical procedure leaves a scar."

Surgical procedure. He made it sound so crisp and formal. She glanced down at her arms, covered by the sleeves of her dress.

"No one will be able to see it, outside of Mac, that is."

"And you when you check to make sure there's no infection."

His gaze weighed heavily on her. "Yes."

Silence lingered between them as they crossed the meadow, the faint outline of the trail leading to the cabin growing visible through the trees.

"At least Tressa has a good reason for the scars," she finally spoke. "Unlike me."

Seth reached for her hand, gripping it tightly without slowing his pace. "Lindy..."

She squirmed. Must he always do that? Start to say something and then stop and look at her as though giving some kind of visual examination? Except this examination didn't seem all that medical in nature. Instead of his eyes sweeping down her and then coming back to narrow on the rise and fall of her chest, they lingered on her face.

Was he thinking of the kiss they shared yesterday on the trail? If he had time to kiss her tonight, would he do so now? Did he want to?

Of course not. Why would he when she'd told him not to love her yesterday?

He moved his gaze to the edge of the meadow as they approached the line of trees. "Is that the trail that leads to the cabin?"

She forced her eyes away from her husband and to the small break in the woods. "Yes."

"You don't mind if I walk ahead?" He may have asked it as a question, but his voice held no room for her to disagree. He dropped her hand and surged forward.

She hurried along behind him, rushing to keep up with his brisk pace as he headed into the shadow of the woods.

The cabin's sagging outline appeared a few minutes later. "This shack doesn't look fit for an animal." Seth looked at her over his shoulder as he approached the door. "Why didn't you tell me how they were living?"

Lindy cringed at the harshness in his voice. But then, she'd had a similar reaction when she'd first seen where the O'Byrnes were staying. "Jenny kept threatening to move without telling me where they went if I said anything."

"That should have warned you to get help sooner." He knocked on the door. "Miss O'Byrne? Hello? It's Dr. Harrington from Eagle Harbor. I'm the one who treated Toby. Your brother Jack asked if I would come examine you."

No answer. Lindy frowned. Was Jenny sleeping? Even with her fever and cough from earlier, she'd expected the woman to start screaming about being betrayed the moment she heard Seth's voice.

"Jenny?" Seth opened the door and disappeared into the dimness.

Lindy pushed the door farther open and stepped inside. "How

can I help? Do you need some...?" Her words faltered as she stared at Jenny's still form.

"No." She shook her head. Surely she was mistaken. Surely Jenny wasn't...

But Jenny lay on the pallet in the corner, as still as Ma had been after she'd passed. Jenny's rich brown eyes were open and glassy, her face and neck as swollen as they had been several hours ago.

Seth squatted beside Jenny, then looked over his shoulder. "Go wait outside." Once again, his voice was sharp and clipped, his movements brisk as he pulled back the quilt to examine Jenny's lifeless body.

"I'm so sorry," she gasped. "I should have brought you here earlier. I should have forced her to listen, never mind her threats. Oh, how could—"

"Lindy, sweetheart, it's not your fault. Now please go outside and wait for me."

But she couldn't move, not even a step. Like ice from the waves that formed atop the harbor rocks in winter, she was stuck, her eyes glued to Jenny's too-still form. "Why wouldn't she let me help?"

Seth lit the lantern they'd brought for walking back in the dark, then studied Jenny's hands. "Sometimes people can be too stubborn for their own good. You didn't want me to treat your finger, remember?"

"That was different." Jenny'd had no reason besides pride to refuse help. Whereas she'd had a good reason for not wanting a doctor to treat her finger.

Or rather, it had seemed good at the time, but had Victoria, Elijah, and Seth not been insistent on treatment, she might not have a pinky today.

"I still don't understand. She was young and healthy, far healthier than I. How could she die so quickly?"

Seth laid one of Jenny's hands gently atop her chest, then reached across her body for the other. "Only God can answer that."

Only God, the God who had given her asthma, but who hadn't let her die.

Here she was upset with God for letting her get sick so often, but He also spared her life each time. What if God was giving her a second chance? At life. At love. At everything. And she was refusing to take it?

Like Jenny refusing money to go to Cornwall. Refusing to come to Eagle Harbor and stay with either her and Seth or the Cummingses.

Was she being as stubborn about accepting Seth's care as Jenny had been in refusing hers? Her reasons to keep distant from Seth seemed good, but then, Jenny's decision to send her away a few hours ago probably seemed good to Jenny too.

Yesterday, she'd read the passage in Ephesians 5 that Seth had said commanded him to love her as Christ loved the church. So if God had arranged their marriage, then shouldn't they love each other as the Bible said?

Even if she didn't live much longer?

Except she had the answer to that too. Seth had already told her he wanted to love her for however long or short a time God gave them together.

And she'd refused to listen.

"I'm so sorry." She pressed her hand to her mouth.

Seth turned from where he was washing his hands in that yellow acid solution he always carried. "Lindy, this woman's death isn't your fault. Please don't blame yourself."

"No. Not for that. For not loving you."

He dropped the bottle of acid into his medical bag with a thunk.

"Or rather, not letting you love me. Or however you want to say it."

He stood and came toward her, taking her hand and leading her out of the cabin before turning to her in the dusky twilight. "Say that again?"

"I said I'm sorry for not letting you love me, for not loving you in return."

"What changed?" He spoke so softly she barely heard his voice over the rustle of the leaves above.

"I realized that I was being just as stubborn as Jenny. That even though I think I have good reasons to keep distant from you, I don't. Er… that is, my reasons probably aren't as good as I think they are, and… oh…" She twisted the fabric of her skirt in her hands. "I'm making a mess of this."

"No mess at all," he murmured. He was doing that examination thing again, when he watched her more keenly than a naturalist studying a bug he'd never seen before.

"Everything you said yesterday on the trail was right. I'm holding us back, and not even for a good reason. I'm just… scared. But that shouldn't matter, should it? Because I could lose my life at any time, or you could, or anyone could, and it might not have anything to do with a lung condition. Just look at Jenny. She never had trouble breathing until today." Lindy sucked a breath into her tight lungs and met her husband's gaze. "So as long as I have breath, even if it's weak and wheezy, I should focus on living the life God gives me, not mourning the day I'll die, whenever that will be."

Seth crushed her to his chest, his grip so tight that she nearly needed atropine to inhale. But her breaths didn't come out wheezy. If anything they felt free. Like the large weight strapped about her chest had broken and fallen to the ground.

He lowered his forehead until it touched hers. "I love you, Lindy. And I'm going to spend every day from here on proving it to you."

She sniffled and smiled as she dashed away a tear. "You don't have anything to prove. I already know you love me."

Raising up to her tiptoes, she tilted her head for a kiss, but he laid a yellow-stained finger over her mouth. "Not right now, sweetheart. As much as I want to kiss you, I can't."

She furrowed her brow. "Whyever not?"

The tenderness left his eyes, and his face turned grim, the lines of his skin further darkened by the deepening shadows. "Because Jenny didn't die from allergies, she died of diphtheria, and the disease spreads very easily."

~.~.~.~.~

Darkness had long fallen when Seth pounded on the door of the Spritzer's flimsy cabin. He'd spent the entire trek back to Eagle Harbor wondering if anyone in town beside Lindy and Jenny's siblings had been exposed to the diphtheria. Then it struck him. The Spritzers had a cough. Could they have been fighting diphtheria for the past week while Dr. Greely misdiagnosed them?

He knocked again, only to be greeted with silence. So he pounded harder and louder. Someone had to be home. Ruby Spritzer had so many children her house was never empty, though it was strangely quiet for a place with nine children, even for this time of night.

Finally the door cracked open, and Leroy poked his head out, the dark blonde curls of his hair nearly obscuring one of his eyes. "Doc Greely's supposed to be coming. Ma doesn't want your help."

Coughing sounded from deeper inside the house.

"I just came from finding a woman dead from diphtheria, and I know your family has been struggling with a cough. Is there any chance that's what you have?"

More coughing resonated while Leroy looked over his shoulder. "Ma, Dr. Harrington says there's a disease going around. I think we should let him in."

"No, I don't want him in here," Ruby Spritzer's voice echoed. "Doc Greely says it's consumption, and his wife's the reason …" Another fit of coughing drowned out her words.

Seth clenched his hand into a fist around the handle of his medical bag. Did they not understand how serious diphtheria could be?

Leroy turned back to him, his eyes shadowed. Standing in the light from Seth's lantern, his thin body might look like a fourteen-year-old's, but the bleakness in his eyes made him appear twenty years older. "Doc Greely says—"

"I heard." But if whoever was sick inside truly did have diphtheria, it could affect the whole town. "If it's a sudden onset of coughing and fever, accompanied by a sore throat and swollen neck glands, then it's not tuberculosis. Tuberculosis takes years to get severe, and at that point, it's accompanied by tremendous amounts of blood when coughing. Diphtheria will have occasional spotty mucous, but not nearly to the extent of tuberculosis. Does whoever's been sick have a gray coating on the back of their throat?"

The youth blanched, then swung the door open. "Ma, it ain't consumption like Doc Greely says. Dr. Harringotn's got the right of it, and he hasn't even seen Martin or Christopher."

"Dr. Harrington. I'm so glad you came." Ellie rushed toward him from the single bedroom at the back of the small cabin. "I've been telling Ma to get you for the past week, but she refused."

He headed across the room that seemed far too small for so many people to live in. In the corner, one of the children sat with a lantern reading to the cluster of younger ones. Probably the only time he'd seen them all so still and quiet. But most of the children weren't looking at the girl reading, they were looking at him.

Ruby appeared in the doorway to the bedroom, her graying hair gleaming silver in the lamplight and her hands folded tightly together at her waist. "We don't need no more sickness here. You best go."

Her shoulders were slumped with weariness, the lines of her face rough and haggard. Seth nearly shook his head. How did this woman raise so many children on her own with nothing more than the coin she got from taking in wash and odd jobs?

"I understand you don't want any more sickness or suffering, Ruby. But my wife has asthma. It's not contagious, and it won't get anyone sick. Diphtheria, however, is a communicable disease that spreads very easily through coughing. I need to look at whoever's sick, even it's just to confirm the diphtheria. If you want Dr. Greely to keep caring for you, he can, but at this point I need to know what kind of illness we're facing and whether it's a threat to the rest of the town."

A choking, gurgling cough emanated from the room.

Seth's heartbeat sped up. The choking sound didn't portend good things. "Please, Ruby, let me in."

"There's two of them." Ruby stepped to the side of the door, giving him room to pass. "Christopher don't look so bad, but Martin's neck is all swelled up, and he's having trouble breathing. I just sent for Dr. Greely again."

Indeed. He'd not been able to hear Martin's struggling breaths before he entered, but once inside, the raspy sounds filled the dimly-lit room. He headed for Martin on the bunkbed, his neck swollen like a bullfrog. A brief glance at the other side of the room revealed Christopher lying on another bunkbed against the far wall, but his neck wasn't very swollen, and his breathing sounded normal, even if he had an occasional cough.

Seth set his bag on the floor by the bed, then swabbed his hands with carbolic acid before examining the youth who was slightly younger than Leroy.

A cough wracked the boy's chest, and he stepped back lest any contaminated spittle land on him. Martin struggled to suck in the next breath, the edges of his lips turning blue. Seth picked up the boy's hands and glanced at the fingernails, which were also tinged with blue.

He turned back to Ruby, still standing in the doorway, where Ellie had joined her. "If your son has any chance of living past the next hour, I need to perform a tracheotomy. Now."

"Is he that bad off? You think... not even an hour?" Ruby pressed a hand to her mouth, tears glistening in her eyes. "What's... what's a tracheotomy?"

Seth bent and retrieved the chloroform from his bag. He nearly reached for his scalpel, but left it lest the sight make Ruby panic. "It involves sticking a small tube in Martin's throat to keep his airways open so he can breathe despite the swelling. Diphtheria causes an infection in the membrane that lines the throat and mouth. Sometimes the swelling gets so severe it can cut off the airways."

"Will you need to cut him?" This from Ellie, who stood hugging herself.

"It involves a small incision in the throat where I insert the tube, yes."

"Will Christopher need one too?" Ruby asked.

He glanced at the small boy across the room. "I don't know. Not everyone does. It depends on how severe the swelling gets. A tracheotomy won't necessarily help Martin fight off the diphtheria, it will just give him a chance to keep breathing."

"Otherwise he'll die?"

"He'll suffocate, yes." Which was likely what happened to Jenny O'Byrne. Had he been at her cabin earlier, a simple tracheotomy could have spared her life, at least for a few days. Though plenty of people with tracheotomies still ended up succumbing to diphtheria.

Martin sucked in another strangled gasp, followed by a cough, his lips growing an even darker shade of blue.

"There isn't time to debate any longer," he snapped. "Do you want the procedure done, or should I leave?" And leave he would. He wasn't about to stand here and watch a boy die when he had the ability to help.

"Yes, help my boy. Please," Ruby sputtered.

Seth didn't even glance her direction, just covered the boy's face with a chloroform-soaked rag, then reached for his scalpel.

The procedure only took a few minutes. He was vaguely aware of the door closing behind him and hushed voices in the other room as he made the incision and inserted the little tube that would keep Martin's airway open.

The boy's gasping instantly stopped, and the room filled with the gentle rise and fall of Martin's breath—and Seth's own more labored ones.

A cough shook the youth's chest, but the choking sound was gone, and the air Martin needed moved freely through the tracheotomy.

Did this make two lives he'd saved today? He hung his head. Tressa's surgery seemed like a lifetime ago, not twelve hours earlier. And he couldn't say that he'd saved Martin's life when the boy still might die, but at least he'd given the young man a chance.

"What do you mean Harrington's in there treating my patient?" an irate voice emanated from the other room.

Seth quickly bathed the tracheotomy site in carbolic acid, then swabbed his own hands and the scalpel before turning toward the doorway.

Dr. Greely barged inside, slamming the door against the wall with little thought for the resting patients. "What have you done?"

"Surely you know what a tracheotomy is. They've been used for centuries."

"He's my patient, and there was no need to…" A fit of coughing swallowed his words.

Coughing, like he'd had in the birthing chamber this morning. Seth took a step closer, then ran his eyes down the portly doctor. His jowls were already so large a person would miss the swelling in his throat if they didn't know what to look for.

He marched toward the man, but stopped far enough back so as not to get sprayed with spittle if he coughed again. "Who else in town has a cough?"

"Who doesn't? And it's all because of your wife. She's spreading..." A fresh round of coughing cut off his words.

Seth took another step back from him. "Cover your mouth before you get the entire town ill."

"I'm a doctor," the man wheezed. "It's not possible for me to make other people sick."

Seth reached out and touched the man's forehead. Burning up. "This isn't tuberculosis, it's diphtheria. You need to go home and stay there before it spreads any farther."

"It's too late to stop it from spreading," Ellie came into the room behind them. "Erik Ranulfson has a cough like Martin's, and Mrs. Kainer was complaining about a cough today while she was in the bakery."

"Surely it can't be as serious as all that," Ruby peered over her daughter's shoulder. "People get coughs often."

Seth shook his head. "It's what makes the disease easy to spread. The symptoms often don't even show up for the first few days, yet the disease can be passed to others during that time. When the symptoms do start, they stay mild for a few more days before becoming life threatening. I just came from burying a woman younger than Ellie. I assure you, Mrs. Spritzer, Martin has diphtheria. And if you don't want everyone in your family to catch it, you need to wash your hands with this after you touch Martin or Christopher. Every single time." Seth dabbed more carbolic acid on his hands, then he held out the bottle.

She took it and looked between him and Dr. Greely, who was slumped against the wall trying to stifle another cough. "I think it's time you leave, Dr. Greely. Dr. Harrington can see us through the rest of Martin and Christopher's illness."

A lump lodged in his throat. As much as he'd wanted his patients back, he hadn't intended for it to happen like this. "Actually, I need Leroy to help me get Dr. Greely to my clinic. The longer I watch him, the more I think he ought not be left to care for himself."

The trip to his clinic in the dark was grueling. He ended up shouldering most of the other doctor's weight himself while Leroy walked a few steps ahead with the lantern. He'd no sooner deposited Dr. Greely in a bed than he changed out of his contaminated clothes and darted off to the Ranulfsons'. Ellie had said Erik was sick, but even if it wasn't diphtheria, the head of the town council needed to know what Eagle Harbor was facing. There should be a meeting held first thing tomorrow and a discussion of the quarantine restrictions for those who fell ill. Hopefully the situation wouldn't grow bad enough to require a temporary hospital and people could recover in their homes, but if too many people got sick, the town wouldn't have a choice.

Bang. Bang. Bang. The sound of his fist meeting the wood of the Ranulfsons' door echoed through the otherwise silent night.

When no one came, he banged harder.

The door finally opened to reveal Mr. Ranulfson standing in his dressing gown, his forehead slick with sweat and his gaze bright with fever.

"Dr. Harrington." The man coughed into a handkerchief. "I was just about to send for you. I'm sick, and Dr. Greely said—"

"Dr. Greely was wrong. You have diphtheria, along with Dr. Greely himself, Martin and Christopher Spritzer, and a woman living in the woods named Jenny O'Byrne. She died earlier today."

It shouldn't be possible for the banker's face to grow any paler, but it did. "Diphtheria, you say? Betty and Erik are ill as well. Do you think we all have it?"

Seth scrubbed a hand over his face. They were going to need that quarantine hospital after all.

Chapter Twenty-Eight

Lindy narrowed her eyes and ran her gaze slowly around Seth's office. Had she found all the carbolic acid? What she had so far likely wouldn't last the week. He said he'd just gotten some shipped, so where was it?

Of course, finding it would be easier if he didn't have five rooms' worth of supplies crammed into a closet-sized space. She stepped to one of the shelves and moved aside several bottles of cough syrup, which she had to set on the table covered with his medical texts and papers, since there wasn't a spare inch to be found on the shelf.

Still no carbolic acid hiding behind the cough syrup. She sighed. The bottles she'd found would have to do for now. She reached for the bandages and gauze on one of the low shelves and filled the rest of her crate.

Leaving her lamp on the table, she cracked open the door and stepped into the darkened bedroom. The three O'Byrne children lay stretched out on the floor between where she stood and the door to the kitchen. Toby and Alice's little bodies curled up in blissful slumber, while Jack slept stretched out, his arms wide as though he could grab a knife and be on his feet within a moment's notice. She'd have told them to sleep against the far wall had she realized how many trips they'd need to make to and from the supply room after they'd gone to bed.

Seth's muted voice filtered through the log walls of the room as she picked her way over the sleeping children, the crate filling her arms. She then balanced the box against the wall and opened the door to the kitchen.

"The Spritzers, the Ranulfsons, and Greely are the only ones I know of for certain." Seth's commanding voice was clear now. "But come tomorrow morning, we need to knock on every door in town. Anyone with a cough and fever needs to be brought to the hospital so I can do a full examination. Families of ill patients who aren't sick themselves need to remain quarantined in their house for a week afterward."

"Do you think there'll be any trouble using your parent's old mansion for the hospital?"

Lindy didn't recognize the voice asking the question. One of the town council members, perhaps? She set the crate on the kitchen table and went back to shut the bedroom door before hefting the crate once more.

"It belongs to the bank now, not my family." Victoria spoke with nary a stutter.

Lindy pushed her way through the cracked door that opened into the parlor and stepped into a room filled with people. One would think it daytime rather than night with how brightly the room was lit. Either that, or that they were hosting a ball. There were probably enough people present to hold one too, except these people wore grim faces rather than happy smiles, and wrinkled, hastily thrown on clothes rather than fancy gowns and suits.

Everyone had gathered around Seth near the door to the large sickroom. Lindy looked around the side of the room where she stood alone. Where did he want the supplies that needed to be carried to the hospital stacked? By the door that led outside?

"If we run into trouble using the mansion," Seth answered, "I can buy it and convert it into a larger medical facility than my office here."

Lindy nearly dropped the box, causing several of the bottles to clatter together. Had Seth just said he'd buy the Donnelly mansion? She couldn't imagine living in such a grand house. Then again, it didn't sound like he'd be using it to live in.

"That is not what I meant when I told you to buy the mansion." Seth's mother sat at the back of the parlor, fanning herself vigorously, as though she could single-handedly create enough breeze to sweep away the epidemic that had crept into town.

Lindy set the crate down a few feet from the outside door, causing several of the bottles to clatter. Only then did she realize how utterly silent the room had grown. She turned to find everyone looking at Seth's mother. Surely they were taking in the fine fabric of her dress, the ornate ruby necklace she wore, and the numerous rings twinkling on her fingers.

Lindy scrunched the fabric of her skirt in her hands and then let it fall. At least she hadn't been the only one unaware of how wealthy Seth was.

"Turning it into a medical clinic sure seems a better use of the building." Seth's voice brought everyone's attention back to him.

"How do you plan to staff the hospital?" Elijah asked. "Victoria wants to help, but I'm not too keen on my wife ending up like Doc Greely or Martin Spritzer."

"We'll have each worker carry a bottle of carbolic acid, and wash their hands upon entering a sickroom and again upon leaving it. The sanitation protocol is being followed in some European hospitals, and when used properly, it greatly reduces the risk of contracting disease and infection."

Coughing sounded from the small sickroom, not overly loud, but everyone else was busy on the other side of the parlor. Lindy cracked the door open and stepped inside.

She'd not seen her former sickbed occupied before. The doctor's form filled it more than hers ever would, his round stomach protruding from beneath the quilt while his fleshy shoulders were nearly as wide as the mattress. He was still now, whatever coughing spell he'd had quickly come and gone, and he didn't appear to be awake. Should someone stay in here with him? It almost didn't seem right that he be left alone, not after what happened to Jenny.

She took a step closer and blinked. Seth's list of instructions continued on the other side of the wall, but she couldn't pull her gaze away from the little plastic tube sticking out of Dr. Greely's throat. She'd known Seth had done some sort of procedure to help the other doctor breathe when he'd returned from the Ranulfsons', but she hadn't asked any questions.

She raised a hand to her throat, covering the very spot where Dr. Greely had a little tube sticking out. Would the surgery save him, or would it only make things worse the way her bloodletting and co-irritation had? At least he was breathing evenly rather than gasping and coughing like he'd been when Seth dropped him off.

Firm hands landed on her shoulder, and she squeaked, then turned to find Seth standing behind her and the parlor beyond filled with muffled chatter.

"It had to be done or he would have suffocated by now." His voice was low and rough with fatigue. "Do you understand?"

She ran her fingertips over the skin on her throat again. "Was there no other way?"

"I don't approve of needless bloodletting, Lindy. But sometimes surgeries are the only way to save a person's life."

Like what he'd done with Tressa and little Sarah earlier in the day. "Will it leave a scar?"

"Yes, but if his body can fight off the infection, that tracheotomy will also leave him alive." He turned her to face him, then nudged her fingers aside and ran his own down the column of her throat, pausing just below her vocal cords. "The tube goes into the airway here and holds it open despite the internal swelling."

She swallowed beneath his touch. "I hope I don't get diphtheria. I can't tolerate the thought of being cut again, no matter the reason."

Seth's eyes, which had been glassy with sleep just a moment ago, turned instantly sharp. "You won't get it."

"You can't know that. Look at Jenny, there was no warning with her."

"Which is why I don't want you going anywhere near the hospital or the diphtheria patients. In fact, you're closer than you should be now." He tugged her away from the bed, never mind that she'd not been close.

"How will I help at the hospital if you don't want me near patients?"

He took the bottle of carbolic acid off the bedside table. "You're not going to the hospital. Now did you touch anything while you were in here?"

"What… What do you mean I'm not going?" She frowned up at him. Surely he couldn't be serious.

The grim set to his jaw told her otherwise.

He'd done so much to help her. It was only right she do all that she could to aid him through the epidemic. His eyes might be alert now, but his lids were weighted with fatigue, and his slumping shoulders and bent neck belied his weariness.

"Of course I'm going to the hospital. I want to help." It was the least she could do for him as his wife.

"Gathering supplies is helping."

"So is tending the sick."

"Your lung condition makes it even more likely your body won't be able to fight off the diphtheria, should you contract it." He took a handkerchief and swabbed her hands with the cool, yellow liquid. "You can stay here at the clinic with Jack and the younger ones until everyone's quarantine is over in a week, but at the first sign of a cough from any of you, you're going to the hospital. Let me get you a bottle of carbolic acid. I want you washing your hands constantly. Every time you touch something that one of the children has touched. Every time you come into contact with something or someone that might carry diphtheria."

"But what about—"

"Wash them anyway. It's not worth the risk."

She huffed out a breath. "You're not listening. I want—"

"No, Lindy. You'll still be helping, but by watching the children rather than nursing the sick."

She looked up into his eyes, hard and determined, and saw the heaviness of it all. The lives lost at Antietam, the life lost earlier today, the weight of trying to save people in a world where death reigned far more often than it should.

But wasn't that all the more reason to go with him? The burden was too great for him to bear alone. "What if I want to be with you?"

He clutched her yellow stained hands and drew them to his chest, where his heart beat a series of solid, unwavering thuds. "I won't risk it. I'm looking forward to a future with you. A bright, happy one."

She leaned her head against his chest. She wanted a future with him too, one far more fulfilling than she'd dared to imagine before. "You'll come home every night? You'll at least eat dinner and sleep by me?"

"No one working at the hospital will be leaving at night, sweetheart." He stroked a strand of hair behind her ear. "I can't risk spreading the disease around town that way."

It wasn't fair. She'd just told him she loved him. They needed time together, not apart. But then, she had only herself to blame. If

287

she would have opened her heart to Seth from the beginning, they'd have had nearly a month together already.

She pulled back to look into his eyes, though she still kept her hands on his chest. Tears welled up, which was ridiculous. She hadn't even been sure she loved him a week ago, so why did the thought of being separated now make her want to cry? "I'll write you letters every day."

He didn't smile as she'd expected. If anything, his eyelids drooped more. "Lindy, I'm afraid you don't realize how busy I'll be. I can't promise to write you in return."

"Don't worry about writing me back. Just know that I... I..." The words were still new on her tongue, but she wanted to say them, even more now than she had at the O'Byrnes' cabin earlier. "I love you. And I'll miss you."

"I'll miss you too, sweetheart. And I love you." His arms came around her, and he crushed her against him. "We'll have plenty of time to spend together after this epidemic is over, I promise."

"Stay well. You're all concerned about me getting sick, but what if you catch it? What if..." She clung to the solid warmth surrounding her. She'd feel this again, wouldn't she? Tonight wouldn't be the last time his arms wrapped around her.

"Shhh. We're trusting God for our future, remember? There was a reason he put us together." He cupped her cheek with his palm and stared down into her eyes.

He wanted to kiss her. She could feel it in the way the air grew still around them, in the way his breathing accelerated and he didn't take his eyes from her. She pressed up on her tiptoes and moved her arms around his neck—only to have him gently pull them off.

"Germs are easily transferred through saliva."

"But I want—"

"Me too." He bent to rest his forehead against hers. "It's going to have to wait."

The door opened. "Dr. Harrington, did you say... oh." Victoria paused in the doorway. "I'm sorry for interrupting."

"Come in." Lindy stepped away from her husband's warmth. "We're done talking."

And they were, because no matter how much she might want to be in Seth's arms, she couldn't stay there another moment knowing she'd need to say goodbye to him within the hour.

Chapter Twenty-Nine

Seth swabbed a bit more carbolic acid over the tracheotomy, then stepped back from the bed and ran his eyes over Leroy Spritzer. He'd been hoping Martin's older brother wouldn't get sick, but three more of the Spritzer children had landed themselves in the hospital over the past week, and Leroy had the most severe case.

Dear God, please save this boy.

He turned to the basin against the wall and washed his hands in the yellow liquid he'd long tired of seeing.

"Any special instructions for Leroy?" Victoria, who had assisted him during the surgery, set the bottle of chloroform on the shelf.

"No. You know the protocol from here. As soon as he awakens, move him to the main sickroom. He seems to be breathing well enough, but call me if there's any change for the worse."

"Do you think he'll...?" Victoria bit the side of her lip, then clutched her hands in front of her. "That is, I just can't imagine Ruby losing another child, especially not one old enough to help. Another year or two, and he'll be able to work."

Seth's shoulders slumped. "I wish I could make promises, but his case seems more severe than most."

They'd already lost three patients, and the hospital was currently filled with seventeen sick. Some of the first people to contract the disease, Martin and Christopher Spritzer and the Ranulfsons, would be returning home in two more days, though they'd still need to remain quarantined in their houses for a week. But Dr. Greely hadn't lived, and neither had two of the dockworkers that frequented The Pretty Penny with him. And he didn't think Jenkins—whom everyone still called sheriff—would last another night.

He scrubbed a hand over his face and blinked wearily. At least Tressa Oakton and her new baby showed no sign of the disease. If they'd contracted it from Dr. Greely, then their symptoms would have been present by now.

Victoria moved to the basin to wash her hands. "I'm sorry to have woken you, but I didn't want to wait lest Leroy—"

"No, you were right to get me. No need to risk suffocation." He glanced at Leroy once more, but the youth was breathing well now, the air moving cleanly through his tracheotomy tube.

"Go back to bed, Doctor. We can handle things from here."

Bed, at two o' clock in the afternoon, but he refused to feel guilty, not when he'd been up all night.

He left the room, closing the door behind him and then heading toward the stairs. Would the rush of patients ever slow? They were getting one or two a day, and the steady trickle showed no signs of stopping. Or perhaps the better question was how many people would be left after the diphtheria passed?

Seth rubbed his hands over his eyes as he made his way down the stairs. None of the O'Byrne children had contracted diphtheria from their sister. Their week of quarantine had ended yesterday, and Elijah reported all were healthy, including Lindy and Mother. But each time someone knocked on the door to the mansion, his heart gave a little lurch.

What if Lindy stood on the other side, coughing with diphtheria? God wouldn't give her to him for so short a time only to rip her away, would He?

His breathing hitched as he reached the bottom of the stairs. And what if God did take her?

"You look like you're lost." Elijah came up behind him. "I know the house is big, but I figured you'd be used to it by now."

Seth looked around. Somehow he was standing at the entrance to the hallway off the foyer, but he hadn't even started toward Edward Donnelly's former study, which had become his bedroom for the past eight days. "Why, Elijah?"

Elijah raised his bushy, caramel colored eyebrows. "Why do rich folk build houses so confusing you need a map to find where you're going?" The man shrugged. "Don't know. You're better off asking Victoria."

"No, why do things like this happen? In his Word, God claims to love us. He has the power to make all of this suffering go away. So why won't He?" Seth yawned and leaned against the wall. It was much easier to stay upright that way.

Elijah leaned beside him, his job as sheriff likely keeping him just as exhausted. "I asked that question a lot after Pa died. The truth is, I don't know why, but I do know I'm commanded to trust that God's ways are better than my ways." Elijah paused and ran his storm-colored gaze down Seth. "When we lose someone, or have a house full of sick people, it's easy to focus on our suffering. But our life isn't supposed to be about us or our feelings. It's supposed to be about bringing God glory. Just look at the story of Lazarus."

"Lazarus?" Seth muffled a yawn, trying to force his brain to concentrate. His concern so far had been about himself or others who were suffering, but had he ever stopped to consider there might be a purpose that was bigger than him or those he helped?

Elijah rubbed the back of his neck. "If ever there was an unneeded illness and death, that was it. Lazarus fell ill, and Mary and Martha sent for Christ, but what did Christ do? He only needed to speak the words from afar and Lazarus would have been well. But Christ didn't command it or even go see Lazarus. Instead he tarried three whole days, didn't even start for Mary and Martha's until he knew Lazarus had been buried. Why?"

Seth shook his head, this time unable to help the yawn that sneaked up on him. "I've never studied that story closely."

"Christ says in John chapter eleven that it's to bring God glory. I figure Mary and Martha went through a lot of tears and unneeded sorrow when Lazarus was dying. And Lazarus, well, you've seen enough dying people to know that death isn't all that comfortable. Was he in pain before he passed? Was he scared? But it wasn't about them, not in the end. God's power was highlighted more when Lazarus rose from the dead than it ever would have been had Christ healed Lazarus from afar." Elijah pushed himself off the wall and stood. "Reckon sometimes that's what's happening with us when we face trials we don't understand."

"Makes sense. Sometimes I suppose it's easier to focus on ourselves than God, and when we do that..." A yawn cut off his words, and he rubbed his bleary eyes. "...Then it's easy to start feeling sorry for ourselves."

The corner of Elijah's mouth twitched. "I'd be more apt to believe you mean what you're saying if you weren't ready to fall over. Normally I'd tell you to go read the story for yourself, but I think you best lie down before you end up a patient rather than the doctor."

"Thanks." He straightened and stepped away from the wall, then paused. "Wait. What are you doing in here? You're not sick, are you? The town needs a sheriff out there."

A slow blush crept up the back of Elijah's neck. "Come on now, Doc. You gotta let a man see his wife every once in a while."

Seth yawned again. He had a whole lecture prepared about contagions and safety precautions when dealing with epidemics.

If only he was awake enough to remember it.

Elijah smirked, then thumped him on the shoulder. "Go sleep. I'll be in and out before you can blink."

Sleep had never before sounded so appealing. He turned for the study.

"Seth! I mean Dr. Harrington." Penelope came bustling toward him. "We have a new patient, but I'm not sure it's diphtheria. It's a girl who's saying her ear hurts, and she doesn't have a cough."

If it was a girl with an earache, then the patient was probably Olivia Dowrick. No one else in town got ear infections the way she did. He started back into the foyer with Penelope. "Did you put her in a separate room? I don't want people in with the diphtheria patients unless we're certain they have the disease."

"Yes, yes. She's in the small salon off the foyer."

Small salon off the foyer. No one in Eagle Harbor would use those words for describing a room of the house, except maybe Victoria. Yet despite her primness and wealthy upbringing, Penelope had made an attentive assistant over the past eight days. Perhaps when she returned to Sharpsburg, she'd have a better understanding of life for those not born into privilege.

"Can you get my otoscope? I'll need it to examine her ear."

She gave a brief nod, spun on her heel, and bustled toward the pantry off the kitchen where they'd been storing the medical supplies.

Seth muffled a final yawn, then opened the door to the small room. Though Victoria's father's creditors were in the process of selling off the family's things, this room still contained some elaborate furnishings, the couch where Jessalyn and her eldest daughter sat being one of them.

Jessalyn rose the second he stepped inside, her eyes darting nervously toward him. "It's not diphtheria. I promise it's not. Just another one of her earaches."

Considering this was Olivia's eighth or ninth ear ache this year, "just another one" didn't begin to describe the problem going on in the girl's right ear, but he agreed she didn't have the feverish eyes and wheezing breaths of his diphtheria patients either.

"How's your hearing?" He squatted beside the couch where the blond girl of about ten sat.

She shook her head, a hand clutched over her ear, while her brow wrinkled in pain. "It's all clogged up again. I can't hear anything."

"Move your hand, love. Let me have a look."

Her bottom lip quivered. "Can you make it stop hurting this time?"

"Only with willow bark tea. But first I need to see if the infection is behind the eardrum so we can drain it."

The child lurched away from him, still covering her ear with her hand. "Not that! It hurts."

"Olivia." Jessalyn laid a hand on her daughter's shoulder. "It's the only way."

Actually, it wasn't the only way. He was starting to think the girl would need surgery, and not one he could perform himself. Did Chicago have a good otologist?

He stood, then glanced toward the door. Penny should have brought his otoscope by now. "Why don't you rest here for a minute? I need to get my otoscope to see inside your ear better."

Just then the door swung open, but it wasn't Penny. Instead Elijah clutched the knob, his face white.

Seth stilled, dread curling in his stomach. "Did we lose another patient? Was it Jenkins?"

Elijah gave a small shake of his head, his jaw trembling. "It's Isaac. He's sick."

~.~.~.~.~

295

Sweat beaded on Isaac's white face, while his lungs labored to suck in wheezy mouthfuls of air. He didn't have a tracheotomy like some of the other patients. Was that good? Bad?

Elijah slanted his eyes toward the door to his brother's room inside the hospital. He could probably go find the doc and ask. But then, Dr. Harrington just might make true on that promise to quarantine him for a week, and the town needed a sheriff, even a temporary one that only half knew what he was doing.

Isaac coughed, and Elijah turned back to the bed, twisting his hat in his hand. His brother couldn't die, not with so much left unresolved between them.

Unresolved, but not unsaid. If anything, they'd said too much to each other in the three years since their pa had died. How many times had Isaac told him he'd end up at the bottom of Lake Superior if he went on another rescue? He always promised he'd be fine, but each rescue did bring that possibility, no matter how often he practiced swimming in frigid, rough seas, or how many times he ran drills with his life-saving team.

And yet Isaac was the one lying near death. If Isaac lived, would he realize the irony of all his statements? His illness proved God truly was the One who gave and took life.

God, please let him live. I'm not ready for him to go. I want peace between us first, but not just that, I want more time with him too. Is it selfish to ask for time with my brother because I've squandered so much of what you've already given us?

"I'm not dead yet." Isaac rasped, his eyes fluttering open. "You don't have look at me like I'm already gone."

"You're awake." Elijah took a step nearer the bed, unable to dampen the hope unfurling through him. If his brother was awake and talking, that had to be good. "I'm the one who's supposed to be lying there, not you."

Isaac merely blinked at him.

"All those rescues I've gone out on. All those times I—what do you call it?—tempt God to take me home." He shook his head and blinked the moisture from his eyes. "You have to pull through, Isaac."

"Now you know how it feels to be the one waiting." Isaac's cough filled the room, his chest heaving while he gasped for breath.

Elijah sucked in a mouthful of air, something he rarely thought about doing, but now understood he took for granted. If only he could breathe for his brother, see that clean air got into Isaac's lungs. Maybe Isaac was right. Maybe it was harder on the one helplessly sitting and waiting than the one whose life was at risk. He reached for his brother's hand, but Isaac moved it away.

"Not getting you sick. You shouldn't be here."

"I had to come, just don't tell the doc. He'll quarantine me for a week."

Isaac started to chuckle, but it turned into another cough. "As though a quarantine would keep you inside. You're too stubborn by half."

No sense arguing the truth. "Promise me you'll get better. I can't stand the thought of you buried on the hill beside Pa."

Isaac shook his head, the movement weak and slow for one who usually moved with speed and strength. "Not making promises I can't keep."

Coldness swept through him, and this time he clutched his brother's hand before Isaac could pull it away. "I won't let you go that easily. You have to fight."

"Didn't say I wouldn't fight it, or that I planned to die…" Isaac's words drifted off and his eyelids closed, but then they fluttered open again and he sucked in a thin, reedy breath. "Just not going to make promises the way you do. About coming back, about living, when I can't say what will happen."

The comment pierced a place deep inside, a place he'd long ago learned not to dwell on. "I try my best to come back every single time. That's not a false promise."

Isaac sucked in a deep, rasping breath, then another before answering. "How's this for a promise then—if I live, I'll run for sheriff."

He laughed. "The election is only a week away."

"Long enough to know whether I'll live, even if I'm not well enough to vote."

His brother was serious. Isaac's eyes might be glassy and fevered, but Elijah could still read the truth in them. "Why the change?"

"Too much on you. I realized it when Victoria brought you dinner at the jail. Besides, I'm better suited for sheriff than you."

Elijah snorted. "Probably, doesn't take much."

"Nope."

He plopped down in the chair beside the bed. "So does this settle things between us? No more fighting?"

"Still can't stomach the thought of you on those rescues." Isaac's eyes closed again. "Doubt that'll ever change."

"Even though I save…"

Isaac held up his hand without bothering to open his eyes. "Not now. Not here. I know you save people. I just can't handle the idea of losing you that way."

His throat felt so gritty a quart of sand could have been poured down it. "I don't plan to stop going on rescues anytime soon."

"I don't plan to like it anytime soon."

Isaac's reedy breaths evened with sleep, and Elijah sat back in the chair. They didn't have a complete truce, but they had a start. Maybe they could disagree on this one thing but otherwise be friends. Maybe God would use this illness to show Isaac who truly held the power over life and death. Maybe they'd be able to sit down to Thanksgiving dinner this year without a word of argument. And Christmas too.

Maybe Isaac would help him build a little house on the property next spring, so Ma could have her own place and he and Victoria could have the big cabin to themselves. Maybe…

There were so many things he'd do with his brother if only Isaac were willing. But what was the point of sitting here and listing them all when he wasn't sure his brother would live?

Chapter Thirty

"I can go home tomorrow?"

Seth blinked and narrowed his gaze on Isaac, or tried to narrow his gaze, if his vision would stop blurring. He needed to lie down and rest. The past three and a half weeks of fighting this epidemic had exhausted him. Except with no new patients being admitted, he'd started getting a full night's sleep almost a week ago. So why was he this tired?

"Yes, you can go home tomorrow," he told Isaac. "But you'll still need to be quarantined for a week."

"A full week? Inside that little apartment?" Isaac sat on his bed, looking stronger and hardier than a person should after flirting with death the way he had. Did nothing slow the Cummings men down? "I'll go crazy. Did you hear I won the election for sheriff while I was stuck in here? I bet Elijah's hankering to hand me his badge."

"Yes, inside your apartment. We finally have a handle on this disease. I won't risk starting the epidemic all over again." His vision blurred once more.

He wasn't getting diphtheria, was he? No, he couldn't be. The epidemic was nearly over. Besides, he wasn't coughing, though his throat certainly felt sore. He reached for a handkerchief and blew his nose.

"Hey doc, did you hear me?"

Seth turned back to Isaac and blinked slowly. Hear him? "What was it you wanted?"

He stuffed the handkerchief back in his pocket then headed for the basin with carbolic acid. Had to wash his hands after blowing his nose—if he'd said it once, he'd said it a hundred times.

Except the washstand was moving. He blew out a breath and closed his eyes to steady himself. Maybe he needed to sit down instead of wash his hands. Or maybe he needed...

"Dr. Harrington, are you all right?"

He opened his eyes. Isaac's words echoed around him, as though he stood in the middle of a great, dark tunnel and Isaac was on the far end. It was beginning to look like he stood in a tunnel too, with the way blackness crept into his vision.

"Do you need help?" Isaac's words again, still echoing inside his head.

He opened his mouth to respond, then his world went dark.

⌐.⌐.⌐.⌐.⌐

"How much longer until we can go home?"

With her back to her mother-in-law, Lindy rolled her eyes and stirred the pot of soup on the stove. "You can go home now if you wish. Your quarantine has been over for several weeks." Had it really been almost a month since she'd seen Seth? Felt his arms around her? Told him she loved him to his face rather than with pen and paper?

Her mother-in-law had the right of it. When would they be able to go home... and Seth be able to see her?

She'd written him every day, always giving Elijah the letters to drop off at the hospital. But Seth had only sent two notes back, both filled with hasty apologies about how busy he was and warnings about staying inside and away from anyone who might be carrying diphtheria.

She reached into her pocket and fingered the folded edges of his most recent letter. She didn't need to open it to remember how it ended. *Know that I love you and eagerly await the day I can leave this place and be with you once more. Until then, stay strong and well. Love, Seth.*

"I'm not going home without Penelope," Seth's mother said from her place at the table, where she worked on yet another piece of embroidery.

How much could a woman embroider in a month before her fingers fell off?

"Can you imagine me traveling with her two children?"

Lindy stirred the soup again. It was difficult to imagine Seth's mother traveling with anyone at all. She was sure to gripe the entire way regardless of her traveling accommodations and companions.

"Then maybe you should pray the epidemic ends swiftly and with no further casualties—especially if you want to get home before winter." Her last words caused a tiny flicker of panic. The harbor was still open, but the waters were turning wild with the winds of late fall. Few ships sailed on Lake Superior during November.

Penelope and Mrs. Harrington wouldn't be stuck here all winter, would they? If that happened, Seth really would need to buy the Donnelly mansion, because she'd not be able to endure an entire winter of her mother-in-law's constant needling. But then, Penelope and her children might not be able to endure it either. Maybe they'd need to buy a house just for Mrs. Harrington.

The back door to the kitchen burst open, and in rushed Phillip Jr. on a gust of frigid wind, with Alice following closely behind.

"I won! I won! Miss Stella said I could have a cookie for winning." The boy raised his hands, a smile covering his rosy-cheeked face.

The nanny appeared in the doorway. "I said you could have an extra cookie after lunch when everyone else got one."

Alice stomped her foot on the floor. "I don't think he should get any cookies. He pushed me! Cheaters don't get to win. Jenny always said."

"Take this nonsense in the other room, children." Seth's mother's voice rang over the commotion. "I don't wish to be disturbed."

The door flung open again to reveal Jack with Toby and Emma.

"Phillip pushed Alice." Jack shut the door before more warmth from the fire escaped into the blustery outdoors. "I saw it. I don't think he should win."

"I want my cookie." Phillip stomped his foot.

Lindy set the ladle down and wiped her hands on her apron. "Just a minute, children. Maybe we can—"

"And I wanna push you back," Alice screeched, then charged for Phillip, who went crashing into the small hutch that held the dishes.

More crashing followed, this undoubtedly from the dishes that had been stacked inside.

Lindy rushed forward, along with Jack and the nanny, Stella.

"Alice, no." Lindy peeled the girl off Phillip. "Just because he pushed you doesn't mean it's right to push him in return."

"But he was mean." The girl's lip puckered, then she burst into tears. "I want Jenny. Where's Jenny?"

"Oh dear child." Lindy crushed the girl to her chest and held her. "Jenny's not coming back, honey. You'll have to make do with us until your father returns."

Jack's face darkened at the mention of his father.

Lindy sighed. In truth, she had no idea when their father would return, if he would even want his children, and if they would be safe living with a man who changed his surname as often as he changed his stockings.

"Come on, Alice. It'll be all right." Jack crouched beside them and rubbed Alice's back. "Living with Miss Lindy is nicer than living with Jenny anyway."

"I miss my daddy," Phillip wailed as Stella helped him up from where he'd fallen against the hutch. "I want my momma."

Lindy hugged Alice harder to her chest as she watched Phillip from over the girl's shoulder. These children faced so much sorrow, and all of them were in need of a father, even if Phillip and Emma had a mother. She'd tried to explain the epidemic time and again, but they didn't understand how busy Penelope was helping to take care of the diphtheria patients. Furthermore, she couldn't even promise Jack they could live with her after Seth returned. Who would care for the children when she got another lung infection? And the children certainly weren't quiet enough during the day to let patients rest. Besides, where would they sleep if the big sickroom was being used for patients?

"Lindy?" A male voice rang from the parlor.

She looked up, but before she could shift Alice into Jack's arms and stand, the door opened.

The grim set to Elijah's face caused her heart to hitch.

She scrambled to her feet. "What is it?"

Elijah's gray-eyed gaze flickered briefly over the disastrous kitchen before coming back to land on her. "It's your husband. You'd best pack a bag and come with me."

Seth? Her lungs tightened even as she opened her mouth to tell Elijah he had to be mistaken, that God wouldn't allow her husband to fall ill when he had so many people to treat.

But God's ways had never made much sense to her, and they made even less sense than usual as she scurried into the room she shared with her husband and began packing her things.

Chapter Thirty-One

"He n-needs a tracheotomy." Victoria laid a cool rag on Seth's brow. "He would have performed one on anyone else by now. But without Dr. Greely, there's no one to do it."

Lindy ran her eyes over her husband, his breaths labored and raspy. His breathing had only grown worse since she'd arrived several hours earlier, and though he'd opened his eyes and mumbled a few things, he'd seemed too feverish to understand what was happening.

Was this what she looked like when she was sick? If only she could cover her mouth with his and breathe air into him. But given the wheezy, whistling sound coming from him, the air would get stuck long before it reached his lungs.

"What are we going to do?" She took Seth's hand where it rested by his side and stroked his long, slim fingers. Fingers that had done so much good for others.

He tossed his head fitfully and coughed, except the cough ended with a sputtering, choking sound.

She turned to Victoria. "We have to do a tracheotomy somehow."

Victoria shook her head while she went about the room collecting soiled linens. "He n-never taught me. And while I'm happy to help with the patients, I'm not sure I could manage c-cutting into a person that way. Especially not someone's throat."

Lindy reached up and fingered the spot on her neck Seth had touched when they'd stood over Dr. Greely. Would her husband end up dying as the other doctor had?

Please God, no!

A soft knock sounded on the door, then Penelope stepped inside. "Is he any better?" The hope in her voice clashed with the worried lines on her face.

Lindy turned to look at Victoria. "Is he?"

Victoria shot Penelope a quelling look, then shook her head. "Patients don't turn for the better this swiftly. He'll g-get worse before he… or rather, if he… improves."

"What do you mean, if?" her voice cracked. "He has to get better."

Victoria merely swallowed and looked away, so she turned to Penelope, but the dark-headed beauty wouldn't meet her gaze either. "You said he needs a tracheotomy." She looked back at Victoria. "How long will he last without one?"

"I… I d-d-don't… that is, I'm n-not a d-doctor, so I c-c-c-c-can't…"

"We don't know." Penelope cut in. "He never let a patient get this bad before."

"But he said… when I saw Dr. Greely… he told me that the doctor would have died without…" She closed her eyes, unable to finish the sentence.

The memory of the last time she'd spoken to Seth rose in her mind, the very night they'd stood beside Dr. Greely's sickbed. What she wouldn't give to rest her head on his chest and hear the steady cadence of his breathing again, the continuous thumping of his heart. *I'm looking forward to a future with you. A bright, happy one.*

But there would be nothing bright or happy about their future if he died during the night.

"Where's his scalpel?" Lindy twisted her hands together and

glanced about the room, but found none of the supplies needed for a surgery. "The little tubes he uses for the tracheotomies?"

"Lindy." Victoria set her bundle of linens down and laid a hand on her shoulder. "You c-can't mean—"

"We have to at least try. What would you do if Elijah was lying here and there wasn't a doctor to help?"

"Have you seen one done?" Penelope's face hadn't eased with her pronouncement. If anything, the woman looked more worried than before.

"No, he told me about the procedure after he did it on Dr. Greely, but surely you two have seen it done enough. He said it wasn't hard."

Seth coughed again, or tried to, but the noise was silenced by another, far more worrisome, gurgling sound. His chest still heaved as though he were coughing, yet it sounded more like he was drowning.

"Well?" She nearly screeched. If only the sound would wake her husband and pull him from his stupor. Then maybe he could tell them how to do the tracheotomy. Except even if he was awake, she doubted he could talk, not when he could barely breathe. "Where are the supplies? If you two won't save my husband, then I'll try without you."

"You can't do it, not when you've never even seen the procedure." Victoria's worried eyes met hers.

"I'm not willing to let him die without trying." She closed her eyes against the sharp pricks of moisture threatening to overwhelm them.

"Maybe someone else in town knows how to do one?" Penelope suggested. "A retired nurse? Someone who served in the war?"

"Who do you think we should ask?" she snapped, then slanted s gaze at Penelope. "And even if there is someone, there's hardly time to go knocking on doors."

"I'll d-do it." Victoria took the soiled rag from Seth's brow and replaced it with a fresh one. "Lindy's right, there's no t-t-t-time to find someone else. And I'd never forgive myself if we didn't at least tr-try a tracheotomy, especially considering how many lives he's saved."

Lindy gripped Victoria's sleeve and met the other woman's hazel eyes. "Thank you."

"But you've never done one either, have you?" Penelope's gaze moved from Seth's pale face to Victoria and back again.

"No, b-but I've assisted for all he's d-done here."

Penelope shook her head. "I still don't like it. It's his throat, one wrong cut and—"

"One wrong cut will still be better than making no cuts at all." What was wrong with Penelope? She'd lost her own husband, surely she understood the gravity of the situation, that Seth would die if nobody tried to help.

"Fine." Penelope spun toward the door, her back straight. "I'll go get his scalpel and such, but don't blame me if the procedure turns sour."

Lindy wasn't sure whether it took an hour or a few seconds for Penelope to return with the supplies, all she knew was that her husband's breathing grew more ragged and spotty. The gurgling sound that had only been present when he coughed now saturated his every breath, and blue tinged the edges of his lips.

"I still don't think this is a good idea." Penelope piled the instruments on the table with the carbolic acid.

Lindy crossed her arms over her chest. "It's our only choice."

"Penelope, why don't you go check on the other patients? Lindy can assist me."

"Yes, that's precisely what I'll do." Penelope fled the room once more.

"Is she always like this?" Lindy turned to Victoria, who was washing her hands in carbolic acid.

"We've both offered to let her assist with tracheotomies before, but she's always refused. She's very eager to help when Dr. Harrington is around to notice, but that's about the extent of her helpfulness."

A sick feeling lodged in Lindy's stomach. Surely Penelope wasn't trying to get Seth to notice her, not when he was already married.

But if she'd been the one to get diphtheria rather than Seth...

Lindy pressed a hand to her chest, which was suddenly tight. At least Seth had strong lungs, a good chance of surviving—provided they could do the tracheotomy and get him breathing.

Victoria took a bottle and handkerchief from the supplies Penelope had brought, then moved toward the bed. "I'll start the chloroform, but you'll need to administer it during the surgery. If his breathing gets too slow, remove the handkerchief for a few minutes. If his eyelids start to flutter, then he needs more."

"Fluttering eyelids, more chloroform; slow breathing, less chloroform." Lindy picked up the tubing that would soon go into her husband's throat. "Does this need to be washed?"

"It all needs to be washed, starting with your hands."

Lindy did that first, then submerged the small tube into the yellow liquid. She picked up the scalpel next. The little blade was nothing like the knife the barber surgeon had used to bleed her in Chicago, yet it still seemed strange to hold such an instrument in her hands.

It can be used for good, not just for bad. She drew in a deep breath and stepped to the bed, where Seth had already succumbed to the effects of the chloroform. "Is this everything you need?"

"I think so." Victoria took the scalpel, then laid the tubing on a white handkerchief she'd spread near the side of the bed. "Here, let's switch positions. You stand by his head and watch his breathing."

She watched his breathing, yes, but she couldn't help looking as Victoria positioned the scalpel directly where Seth had shown her that night when they'd stood over Dr. Greely.

The skin gave beneath Victoria's blade.

Don't look at the blood. Don't look at the blood. Don't look at the blood.

Victoria pressed against his skin once more. Was the scalpel going deep enough? Too deep? Oh, there was so much he hadn't told her when he'd explained the surgery. All she'd wanted to know was whether the incision would leave a scar. Now she'd take a hundred scars on his neck—or hers—if it meant he would live.

Lindy glanced back at Seth's face, then bent her ear near his nose until she heard the gurgling rise and fall of his breaths. "I think you gave him the right amount of chloroform."

"I've had a little too much practice over the past month." Victoria pressed on the scalpel again, and a faint whistling sounded from Seth's throat.

"Is that good?"

Victoria gave her a small smile. "Yes, it's the sound his patients make at first."

"Did he cut more?" The slit didn't look big enough to fit the tube.

"Maybe two or three more incisions. He made a square, and then inserted the tube." Victoria's hand trembled slightly as she made another slit, and then another.

With each incision, Seth's breathing grew louder, the air whisking into and out of his lungs.

"I forgot I need the tweezers. They're on the table. Make sure you wash them first."

Lindy set the chloroform-soaked rag aside and darted to the table, where she quickly washed and dried the tweezers before returning them to Victoria.

The other woman took them and held the little flap of his skin up as she made the final incision.

They didn't even need the tube, not with the way he seemed to breathe fine on his own, but there must be some reason doctors used it, so she handed Victoria the small bit of piping anyway.

It took only a few seconds to insert. "Now we need to wash the area with carbolic acid. Will you soak one of the extra handkerchiefs and then bring it to me?"

Lindy took a step back. "Can you? I'm feeling... that is, I don't..." She pressed a hand to her stomach and fought back the urge to faint.

"Yes, yes, go wash your hands again, then sit. You look paler than your husband."

⌐.⌐.⌐.⌐.⌐

"You should get some sleep."

Lindy rubbed her eyes and blinked, then blinked again before Penelope's blurry image came into focus. "I'm not leaving him."

The other woman looked at the bed where Seth lay, his chest rising and falling evenly, though interrupted occasionally by a cough. She laid her hand against his cheek. "The fever's still raging."

"I'll get a cool cloth." Lindy scrambled up from her perch in the chair beside his bed, the chair she'd occupied ever since Victoria performed the tracheotomy. How many hours ago was that? Twelve? Fifteen? The sky outside was dark, the town quiet during the deepest part of night. Still, she couldn't leave her husband.

"How long until we'll know whether he... he...?" Unable to finish, she wrung the rag out in the basin of water and turned back toward the bed.

"Usually three days, but sometimes two."

"They stay unconscious all that time?" What she wouldn't give to look into Seth's calm green eyes again, hear the sound of his voice. She'd known she would miss him when he left to stay at the hospital at the beginning of the epidemic, but being with him now yet having him unresponsive was somehow worse than being completely separated.

Why had she been such a fool at the beginning of their marriage? Why hadn't she realized the gift God had given her in Seth right away and been grateful? Then they would have had more time, more memories... more of everything that mattered.

"He won't necessarily stay unconscious, but incoherent." Penelope settled a hand on his forehead again, as though there might already be some change in his temperature. "And even if he wakes, he won't be able to talk with the tracheotomy."

"He won't?" Lindy handed the rag to Penelope, while her gaze moved to her husband's throat. It was swollen and fleshy, but the little tube still stuck out of it, allowing air to flow freely.

"The incision is below the vocal cords." Penelope folded the rag and placed it on Seth's forehead. "A person can't form sounds without air passing through the voice box."

But she had so much to talk to him about. So much she'd never said before but should have.

She blinked. She wouldn't let tears fall, not in front of the woman who'd wanted to marry her husband—might still want to marry her husband if she caught the disease and succumbed. "Can I... can I have some privacy, please?"

Penelope gave her a look far different from the haughty one she'd received the first time they met.

But she didn't want Penelope's pity any more than she wanted her snub.

"There's nothing wrong with resting, Lindy. I lost my husband recently, and at the beginning, I tried—"

"Seth's not going to die." The words cut through the room, a sharp edge of glass in an otherwise silent house. Penelope stared at her for a moment, then dropped her hand.

Silence spun between them as they looked at each other. Lindy drew in a breath that felt far more labored than it should given her asthma wasn't bothering her.

Penelope sucked in her own breath before finally speaking, "Of course not. Do forgive me." Then the other woman ducked her head and hurried from the room.

Lindy stepped to the bed and took Seth's hand, limp and hot in hers. If he were awake, he'd tell her not to touch him lest she catch the disease. Yet she needed the contact, small as it was. "Don't die, Seth. Promise me you won't die."

He didn't move.

"I want a wedding." She sank down onto the bed beside him and sniffled. "After you're better, a real wedding. One at the church. I want a fancy dress too. And I want to walk down the aisle to you." She swallowed thickly. "Like a real bride."

She couldn't stop a tear from rolling down her cheek. "And I want a real wedding night." The tears reached up to choke her voice, but she managed the last few words. "I love you."

She wanted other things too. Children. A sewing machine. A future. A whole new life spread out in front of her that she'd never dreamed of having before.

But how could she have any of it without Seth? She didn't even want to try without him by her side, helping her, encouraging her, sharing each and every memory with her. She wanted him beside her for every lung infection and summer picnic. Every late night and early morning. Every snow storm and Indian summer. She wanted him for all of it.

Why would God do this to him? To her? Why, when she was so close to finally having happiness?

She closed her eyes against the onslaught of tears. Maybe Penelope was right. Maybe she needed sleep. She was too distraught to think, and sitting here crying by her husband's bedside wasn't going to help anything.

She rose and headed toward the basin filled with carbolic acid. After washing her hands, she let herself out the door and down the stairs toward the room Victoria had shown her earlier—Seth's room. That she'd sleep in without him.

Why, God? Why! No matter how many times she asked or what situation she asked about, God's answer was always silence and trials. More and more and more trials until they piled so high she couldn't see over them anymore.

She wiped the tears from her eyes and entered Seth's room, then dropped onto the bed and fought the hot well of tears building behind her eyes. A stack of envelopes sat on a table that had been pulled to the bedside. She reached for the one on the top of the stack, the one she'd sent Seth only yesterday.

A tear fell, staining the white paper with its solitary drop. She'd told Seth she loved him in this letter, and in the one before that. And the one before that, and the one before that. She'd told him every single day since the epidemic started. If he didn't survive, at least he'd die knowing he was loved.

But did he know how sorry she was for not loving him sooner? Not loving him better?

She set the envelope back onto the table before she ruined it with more tears, then shifted closer to see the piece of stationary lying beside the envelopes.

Dearest Lindy,

She picked up the paper and scooted back against the headboard to read.

I've discovered something over the past several weeks while working here. I know you're always asking God why. Why are you sick? Why did you lose both your parents? Why did your sister desert you for a life of ill-repute?

She sniffled. It was as though he'd known her thoughts before she had them tonight and had already written her a letter in response.

I must admit, I have my own instances of questioning God. Why do some of my patients get the same illness over and over? Why could Christ heal with a simple touch, yet I struggle for months to cure someone, only to have them die? Why is there so much pain and suffering in this world? Why didn't God give us the means to stop it?

I had a conversation with Elijah about a week ago, and he said something I've been studying and praying over ever since. What if our struggles and sorrow and trials aren't about us, but about God?

The story of Abraham demonstrates this. He didn't deal with sickness, but how long did he and Sarah wait for the son they'd been promised? Had Sarah conceived by normal means at a normal time, no one would have hailed the child as being a miraculous gift from God. Though the waiting caused much suffering for the family, God was glorified in the end, and that was the point. Not Abraham and Sarah's immediate happiness, but God's glory. Their story has been an encouragement and help to many through the centuries, and now they have the eternity of heaven to be happy.

Shouldn't that be the point of our lives, to bring glory to God, regardless of the situation? To allow those around us to see God in our actions?

Another example is Lazarus being raised from the dead. Christ could have healed him from afar as soon as his sisters sent word he was ill, yet Christ tarried three more days and only came to Bethany after he knew Lazarus was dead. Think of the pain Lazarus must have felt while he lay dying, the suffering Mary and Martha endured as they lost their brother. Christ could have spared them those hardships, but instead he chose the path that would bring the most glory to God, and others in the village of Bethany were reached in the process.

Job is the same way. He...

Seth's words stopped abruptly, likely because he'd been called away before finishing.

The letter trembled in her hand. Was he right? Lindy reached for the Bible that had been lying beside the letter. It was already open to John 11.

The passage was just as Seth described, the story of Lazarus falling ill and Jesus refusing to come, intentionally tarrying until he knew Lazarus had died.

All so that God would be glorified.

Was the same true of her life? Was she thinking too much of herself and too little of God? Was she forgetting that while God's plan for her might not be pleasant, He could use her to reach others? That no matter how hard her life on earth was, she would have rewards for her faithfulness in heaven one day?

She lay back against the pillow and let tears stream down her face.

Chapter Thirty-Two

"Lindy?"

She woke with a start, only to have her neck pulse with pain when she tried to raise it. Of course, if she'd been lying on the bed rather than on the desk, it probably wouldn't hurt so much.

She raised her head despite the ache, and something crinkled when she moved her cheek. Evidently she'd fallen asleep sometime between Job 36 and 37.

"Lindy?" Victoria came into the bedroom, then frowned at the empty bed.

"Over here." She yawned and stretched, then pressed a hand to her cheek, where the imprint of the Bible was stamped in her skin. "I fell asleep reading."

Again. But she wasn't going to explain to Victoria how many times over the past three days she'd come in here to sleep, only to end up reading the Bible and praying. She'd studied the first two passages Seth had given her in his letter and had made it most of the way through Job. She could see how God's importance rose above the lives of the people, and how those people all turned to God throughout their trials, regardless of the specific hardships they'd faced.

"Seth's fever broke about an hour ago," Victoria said. "I think he's starting to wake."

"Why didn't you tell me sooner?" Lindy jumped from her chair and raced for the door. If she'd spent time studying the Bible over the past three days, then she'd spent even more time sitting by his bed, a prayer constantly on her lips. She'd said as many prayers for her own heart as for his recovery. His letter was right. The main purpose of her life—or her suffering— shouldn't be her own contentment or pleasure, it should be to glorify God. The way Job had when his world had fallen apart, and Abraham when he was promised a son only to wander around in the desert for years.

And so she had sat by Seth's bed and held his hand and prayed, but not with the same desperation of that first night. She had peace now, a filling, satisfying type of peace that would give her the strength to go on regardless of what happened with Seth's diphtheria.

She rushed up the stairs and down the hallway to the room where Seth lay, then burst inside, her gaze instantly seeking her husband... who was looking back at her. His green eyes were cloudy but held none of the delirium of the fever that had been so prominent the few times he'd opened his eyes over the past few days.

She flew toward him. Could she give him a hug? A kiss on the cheek? Maybe tuck herself into bed beside him?

He held his hand up before she reached him, alarm replacing the cloudiness in his eyes.

"Don't touch him," Victoria said from behind her. "He'd throttle me if he came through this only to have you get sick."

Seth nodded slowly, the skin along his neck still puffy and swollen, but not stretched tight like it had been before.

"Seth." She took his hand before he could move it away and sat on the bed. He made a shooing motion, but she wasn't about to sit in the chair, not when he was finally awake. "Oh, Seth. I love you so much."

His chest rose and fell on a sigh, and a smile spread across his tired, swollen face. Then he reached up and fingered his tracheotomy.

She laughed. "Are you wondering who did that?"

He nodded slowly.

"It was Victoria. Can you believe it? I've never been more scared to watch anything in my life. But there was no one else to help, and if we wouldn't have…" Tears filled her eyes, but she wouldn't cry, not now, not when they had so much to be happy for. "How long until it can come out?"

"Probably another couple days." Victoria answered from where she stood by the washstand collecting the soiled rags they'd used during Seth's fever. "Dr. Harrington likes to be sure all chance of infection is gone first."

Seth squeezed her hand.

She sniffled and dashed a cresting tear from her eye. "I suppose it's childish of me to complain about not hearing your voice when I have so much to be thankful for."

He squeezed it again, while Victoria slipped from the room, her arms loaded with dirty linens.

"Oh, Seth, I missed you so much."

Another squeeze.

She sighed. This was going to get old rather quickly. And he wouldn't let her hug him or kiss him either, even though it was the only thing she wanted to do. "You probably didn't hear me while you were feverish, but I told you then, and I'll tell you now. I added some things to that list I have, the one of things I've wanted since I was a little girl? That's the one. And the first thing I want is a wedding. I know I already have a marriage, but I want a real wedding at the church, with a white dress and a big cake and even… even… a wedding night."

~.~.~.~.~

Seth nearly reached up and pulled his wife against him. Did she have to be sitting so close he could smell the soap on her hair? See the watery brightness of her eyes?

He wanted a wedding night too. And if she wanted a wedding, well, he could hardly blame her. Whatever she wanted, he'd give her that times ten. God was so good to them, and they had so very much to be thankful for.

It was almost as though she read his mind, because then she started talking about God, and how she'd found his letter and decided that she'd had things wrong. She needed to focus on glorifying God despite the trials that came, rather than eradicating all trials from her life. And didn't he think the same?

At some point Victoria had slipped from the room, but he couldn't precisely say when, because he'd been watching the smile that had claimed his wife's face as she spoke, listening to the calming, sweet sound of her voice.

And when, finally, Lindy's torrent of words stopped and she sat there looking at him as though she wanted their new wedding ceremony to be today, he reached up to his throat and did something he'd not allowed any of his patients with tracheotomies to do. He sucked in a lungful of air, then covered the little tube with his finger and pushed the air back out through his vocal cords, into his mouth and nose. "Lindy, I love you, and I thank God every day for giving you to me."

And he did. For better or for worse. In sickness and in health. As long as they both lived.

Chapter Thirty-Three

Two Weeks Later

"You look so pretty, Miss Lindy. I don't think you should ever take it off." Alice reached out and stroked a hand down the smooth skirt of Lindy's wedding dress. They stood together in the large sickroom where they were supposed to be packing Alice's things, but the girl kept getting distracted—and Lindy couldn't quite blame her.

"Never take it off?" She'd felt that way when she'd donned the gown this morning, but now that the wedding and meal were over, it was time to trade the dress for one of her worn shirtwaists and serviceable wool skirts. She reached up and fiddled with the collar, where her neck grew itchy beneath the tight fabric.

"Nope, never take it off." Alice gave her head an emphatic little nod, then fiddled with the lace overskirt Jessalyn had sewn on the gown. "I want one just like it when I get married."

The dress wasn't made of the finest silk—such fabric would have taken months to ship to Eagle Harbor—but the mercantile had a bolt of ivory muslin, and Jessalyn had some lace stored away in her shop. So over the past two weeks, while Seth recovered and went into quarantine, she and Jessalyn worked tirelessly to make her wedding dress. The end result was lovely, even with the plain fabric they'd been stuck using. Jessalyn had sewn a line of lace flounces along the buttons that trailed down the center of her bodice, and a partial lace overskirt covered three tiers of ruffles that cascaded to the floor. She'd never felt more beautiful than when she'd put the dress on this morning.

No, that wasn't quite true. When Seth had looked at her from the front of the church a few hours ago as she made her way down the aisle, that's when she'd felt the most beautiful.

A knock sounded on the door, followed by her husband's voice. "Lindy, are you finished? Elijah and Victoria just arrived."

"Almost." She turned to finish emptying the last drawer of the dresser, which contained two new pinafores for Alice.

"How long do we have to leave for, Miss Lindy?"

Lindy closed the carpetbag. "For a few weeks, at least."

The girl clutched her hand. "But that's too long!"

Lindy rubbed her brow. Seth had wanted some time alone after their wedding, so when Elijah and Victoria had offered to take the children for a few weeks, they'd accepted.

But how long until their father returned? Winter grew closer with each passing day, and as soon as the snow came, Eagle Harbor became almost unreachable. If the children stayed all the way until spring… well, would it be possible to give them up when their father did arrive?

"Miss Lindy, you're being awful quiet. Does that mean I don't have to go?"

Lindy knelt and met Alice's eyes. "You'll have fun at the Cummingses'. They live right on the water, and it's a beautiful house with big rocks that line the beach and even bigger trees in the yard. There's a loft you can sleep in, and when you climb to the top and look out over Lake Superior, you can almost see to Canada."

"Really?" Alice's eyes grew wide.

Another knock sounded, then the door opened and Victoria peeked her head inside. "Do you need...? Lindy, for shame! What are you doing kneeling on the floor in that dress?"

Her face grew warm as she stood. "Sorry. I hadn't thought about that when Alice asked her question."

"Are you r-ready to come to my house, Alice?" Victoria came around the bed where they stood and held out her hand to the child.

Alice pressed her slender body into Lindy's leg. "I don't want to leave."

"Oh, I'm sure you don't. Miss Lindy is awful n-nice to be around, isn't she?" Now it was Victoria's turn to get down on her knees, and though the woman wasn't wearing a wedding dress, her gown did look to be made of yellow silk that ought not be kneeled on.

"Does that mean I can stay?" Alice's voice quavered.

"You don't want to come to my house?" Victoria poked out her bottom lip, similar to the way Alice was sticking out hers. Given Victoria's and Alice's matching dark hair and hazel eyes, a stranger would probably guess them mother and daughter.

"What's taking so long?" Seth stuck his head into the room and frowned at her.

"I want to stay here," Alice blurted, her little jaw trembling.

Seth rounded the bed and came to stand beside them. "I'm afraid this is all my fault, Alice. Miss Lindy and I got married a while ago, but we've been so very busy, you see, and I've had hardly any time to practice being married to her."

Practice being married? Heat started in her chest and climbed into her face. Surely he wasn't talking about...?

"You haven't gotten any practice?" Alice's eyes grew round.

Seth nodded gravely. "Pretty serious, don't you think?"

The girl drew in a breath and nodded. "How long do you need to practice for?"

The heat on Lindy's face burned hotter. Surely Alice didn't know what she was asking.

Seth reached out and hugged her to his side. Hopefully he couldn't feel the additional warmth burning beneath her skin. "I don't know. How long do you think? Maybe five years."

"Five years?" Lindy swallowed. Surely her husband didn't think they'd need *that* much practice.

"That's too long!" Panic filled little Alice's face.

"Is it? Hmmm..." Seth drew his brow down and tapped his lips as though in serious thought. "What about five weeks instead of five years? That means you'd be at the Cummingses' for Thanksgiving, but back to our house by Christmas."

Yes, five weeks of... of... practice seemed plenty long to her too.

"Now w-w-wait a minute. What if I want Alice to stay with m-me for Christmas?" Victoria crossed her arms over her chest and gave Seth a look filled with mock sternness.

Alice blinked up at Seth. "If I come back here for Christmas, will you get me presents?"

"All kinds of presents, sweetie." He reached out to rest a hand on Alice's silky brown hair, and the smile that spread across his lips was filled with such warmth and genuineness that Lindy's nerves melted.

What had she done to deserve such a man? He had welcomed the O'Byrne children into their home a month ago, much as he'd welcomed her a month before that. It didn't matter that none of them had any money to their names or earthly possessions to speak of. He'd loved them as they were, similar to how God took those who trusted Him into His fold. No questions, no list of qualifications to meet, no chores or work to be done, only love.

"All right." Alice gave a decisive nod. "I'll go."

"That's good." Victoria bent and gripped Alice's hand. "B-because there's extra cake left over from the wedding, and I was thinking about eating some as soon as I got home. Would you like to eat some with me?"

The girl willingly left Seth's side. "Can I have a piece tomorrow too?"

Lindy smiled through the dampness filling her eyes.

"Hmmmm. We might need to hide some from your brothers and Mr. Elijah if there's going to be any left." Victoria turned, Alice's little hand still clasped in hers, and led the child into the parlor.

"Are you all right, sweetheart?" Seth touched her cheek, then smoothed a thumb over her wrinkled brow. "This isn't the look I wanted to see on your face today."

She sniffled. "It's nothing to do with you... or at least, not how you think." She wiped away the stray tear that slipped down her face. "They're good tears, I promise. Because I love you."

He raised his eyebrows. "I'd much prefer that your love for me didn't make you cry."

"Bye, Seth. Bye, Lindy," Elijah's voice boomed from the parlor. "We'll see you in five weeks."

"Jack and Toby! I need to say goodbye." She stepped away from Seth, but he only reached out and wrapped his arms around her once more, trapping her in his warmth again.

"Let them be. I said goodbye for both of us a few minutes ago, and you'll see them around town. They're only going two miles down the road."

The office door banged shut, almost as though Elijah could somehow hear her husband's words and rushed everyone outside before she could wriggle out of Seth's arms.

"Maybe we can go visit tomorrow, just to see how they're faring."

He grinned. "Probably not tomorrow, love. We need time to practice being married, remember?"

A fresh bout of heat burst onto her face. He'd been talking about what she'd thought earlier, hadn't he?

"What will Alice think if you show up there tomorrow, all done practicing?" He unwound his arms from about her and reached for her hand. "Now come, I have something to show you. Something to help with all that practicing."

Something to *show* her? To help with the…the… *practicing*? She stood rooted to the floor. When Seth had been delirious with fever, a wedding night had sounded like a good idea. Even when he'd been in quarantine and unable to kiss her, she'd wanted a wedding night. But now that it was here? And it wasn't even night yet. It was still afternoon. Surely Seth didn't intend to… to… to commence things so early in the day.

He gave her an odd look. His hand still holding hers, though he'd stopped tugging on it. "What's wrong? I just want to show you something."

"N-nothing."

"It's in here." He pulled her toward the small sickroom, where she'd slept for the past two nights since Seth had been out of quarantine. He'd been rather serious about waiting until after their ceremony today for their wedding night.

Oh, if only someone had explained the flock of hummingbirds that would be flying around her stomach now that the house was finally empty.

"Well?" He stopped just inside the door and looked at her. "What do you think?"

She pulled her gaze away from her husband to find a large, lumpy… something sitting at the foot of the far bed and covered with the bed's quilt. It certainly hadn't been there this morning when she'd left for the church.

"What is it?" And how was it supposed to help her practice being his wife?

He nudged her forward. "A wedding present for you. Go on and open it."

326

They were supposed to get each other wedding presents? She turned to him and drew in a breath. "Seth…"

"Sweetheart?" His gaze dipped to her lips and settled there, his head only a few inches from hers while the scent of his bergamot twined around her.

She drew a breath into her tight lungs and fiddled with the lace on her overskirt. All the times she'd wanted to kiss him while he'd been recovering, and here she didn't know what to do with herself.

Yes, they'd kissed at the church earlier, but the chaste peck on her lips wasn't going to keep her husband satisfied now that they were finally alone. What if she did something wrong? What if she wasn't good at kissing? What if this whole wedding night notion was a mistake?

"Stop working yourself up." He took an abrupt step away from her and tugged her over to the monstrosity in the corner that rose higher than her waist. Then he yanked the quilt off the lumpy object to reveal…

"A sewing machine." She looked at him. "You got this? For me?"

~.~.~.~.~

Seth watched his wife closely, but all she did was bite the side of her lip and blink dampness from her eyes. Drat, but he was making a mess of things. She was supposed to be excited, smiling, throwing her arms around him and thanking him until she was out of breath—preferably from kissing him, but he'd take talking at the moment. Or anything else besides a breathing attack.

Yet she stood there looking at the sewing machine, her breaths growing shorter and faster while her eyes grew moister. In another moment, he was going to need her atropine.

Hopefully this was just a breathing attack caused by… well, that was the problem. What would cause a breathing attack? Certainly not giving her a sewing machine. Could she be getting another lung infection?

God, please don't let her get sick, not now that we finally have some time together.

She reached out and touched the metal that had been painted a fancy black. "It's… it's…"

"It's what?" Surely her breathing wasn't severe enough to keep her from talking, even if he was putting off going for her atropine so he didn't have to leave her side. "You told me it was on your list of dreams, remember? Things you wanted one day? I believe it wasn't too far after the husband to hold you part."

"Thank you." Her voice sounded small and strained against the silence of the house.

"It's not new." He wrapped his arms around her waist from behind and settled his chin on her shoulder.

She sank back into his embrace with a sigh, her breathing suddenly calmer.

Curious. Could he have misread her earlier? What if her heightened breaths weren't due to a breathing attack, but to how close he'd come to kissing her before showing her the gift?

Or a case of wedding night nerves?

"There wasn't enough time to have one shipped from a manufacturer," he went on, feeling her relax a little more in his arms with each word he spoke. How odd. He hadn't even been touching her before, and yet she'd gotten nervous enough it affected her breathing?

But he'd been staring at her lips before, whereas now he simply held her. And that had been one of the things on her list. She'd never said she wanted a husband to provide for her or gift her things, but a husband to *hold* her. Though he planned on doing all three now that he finally had her to himself. "When you said something about wanting a sewing machine, I took out an ad in the Houghton paper. I figured if someone down there had a sewing machine in good condition they were looking to sell, I could get it here before winter. But if you'd rather have a new one, I can—"

She turned in his arms and pressed her hand to his lips, all signs of a breathing attack gone. "It's lovely, Seth. So lovely, in fact, that I simply don't know what to say. I… I didn't get you anything. I didn't realize I was supposed to, but maybe I can make you some trousers? I know it's not as fancy as what you got me, but I'm afraid I don't have much else to offer."

"I'd love a new pair of trousers." Never mind that he already had several pair too many. He'd wear the ones from Lindy straightaway after each new laundering. "And do you know what else I'd like?" He couldn't stop his gaze from dropping to her lips again. "It's something you could give me right now."

Her breathing hitched, and she sucked in a short, shallow breath. It must have been nerves earlier then. But instead of backing away from him and making an excuse about her breathing, she reached up on her toes and planted a kiss on his cheek. "Thank you, husband. I'll head to the mercantile first thing tomorrow and see what fabric they have."

"The fabric." He'd nearly forgotten. He stepped away from her and headed toward the wardrobe. And if he happened to notice that her breathing calmed when he put more space between them, well, who could blame a doctor for paying attention to such things?

"I should make Jack a couple pair while I'm at it."

"No need for that, either. I have Jessalyn making him three more pair already." He'd sent the town seamstress a rather large garment order while he'd been working at the hospital. "But you could certainly sew yourself a new dress. You'd look lovely in a rose color, or maybe in a green."

With all that flaxen blond hair and those soft hazel eyes, both pink and green would be perfect on her. He opened the door to the wardrobe he usually kept filled with blankets, rags, and towels and pulled out a bolt of shimmering rose fabric.

"Oh Seth," she gasped, coming forward and resting a hand on the smooth satin. "It's too much. I've no need of a dress made with this."

"Yes, you do, because your husband wants to see you in it." He swept his gaze down her in all her wedding finery. He'd thought she'd been lovely when they'd first met, and from a scientific perspective, he knew she hadn't changed overmuch in the three months they'd known each other. Such a thing was physically impossible.

So how was it she looked so much lovelier to him now? "Not that I'm complaining about how you look at the moment," he muttered. "I'm quite sure I've married the loveliest woman in America."

A blush spread across her cheeks, the pale pink hue only complimenting the ivory of her dress. "That's a kind sentiment, but I think you've forgotten how lovely Penelope is, and she's only been gone two days."

The smile dropped from his face. "Penny might be lovely to look at, but her heart needs a lot of work before she'll be as attractive on the inside as she is on the outside." Relief had washed through him as he'd stood on the town dock and waved goodbye to his mother and Penelope, who had of course decided to leave town before his and Lindy's ceremony. "Let's not bring her up, shall we?"

"Oh, sorry." She bit the side of her lip. "I suppose that's another thing I need to remember about being your wife. No bringing up former fiancées."

"Yes. And as for the next thing you need to know about being married to me..." He set the fabric back inside the wardrobe and walked toward her.

Her nostrils flared, and her breathing quickened as she backed up a step. "What's that?"

His gaze dipped to her lips. "My favorite pie is thimbleberry."

"Thimbleberry?" she squeaked.

"Made with a lattice top crust." He took another step forward, backing her against the sewing machine. "Not a regular one."

"All this to tell me you like thimbleberry pie?" Her breath fanned his chin when she spoke. "I thought you were going to..." She snapped her lips closed, and that lovely blush spread across her cheeks again.

"This is very important, Lindy," he whispered. "I take my pie seriously."

"Of course you do." Her breathing grew more labored, but he wasn't about to pull away again. "I'll see if I can find a jar of canned thimbleberries somewhere and bake you a pie."

"And now for the next thing," he rasped.

"The next...?"

He didn't let her finish. Instead he bent his neck and covered her mouth, cutting off her words and sinking into his wife's sweetness. Had they really only kissed three times since they'd been married? And two of those times had been so quick they barely counted. No matter, he fully intended to remedy the situation. His arms tightened on her back, and he pulled her against himself, his lips lingering over hers, probing, exploring, in no rush to end the kiss.

And she wasn't either, if the way her hands crept up into his hair was any indication, if the rapid beat of her heart against his gave him any hint. He could stay here all day, with his wife in his arms, holding and kissing the woman God had given him when he'd least expected it.

But he pulled back for a moment and caught his breath, which was nearly as labored as hers.

"Do we have to stop?" she whispered.

"Only so I can do this." He swept her into his arms and carried her out of the sickroom, his heart filling with an overwhelming sense of contentment. God truly was good, and though they might have trials ahead—due to Lindy's lungs, or him getting sick from his patients, or any number of other things he had yet to think up—he would never again doubt God's hand in all of it.

Epilogue

One Week Later

"What is this?" Lindy reached down and picked up the letter that had fallen to the floor of the kitchen, the unbroken seal on the back telling her it had never been opened.

Seth looked at the medical bag still in his hand, then blinked at the letter and scratched his head. "Oh, I'd forgotten about it."

"You forgot about another letter?" The last time he'd forgotten about a letter, his mother and a former fiancée had shown up on their doorstep.

She held the missive with one hand while she wriggled her arm out of her heavy winter coat—one Seth had ordered for her when she'd been sick and they'd married back in September.

Seth didn't bother to reach for the envelope. He dusted a bit of snow off his medical bag and set it on the kitchen table, then took off his own coat. "I had a patient to attend."

"Just how many letters have you forgotten over the years because you've been busy treating patients?" She hung her coat on the peg between the back door and cook stove.

He came up behind her and hung up his own coat. "Probably not enough of them."

Outside the snow was falling in a torrent of white flakes racing toward the ground. It looked to be the first good snow of the year, and it had only waited a week after their wedding to start. The snow had barely begun to fall when Seth had left to visit a patient, dropping her off to visit with the Cummingses and O'Byrnes on his way. But the snow had only increased its intensity throughout the afternoon. Now the curtain of white outside cut off any view of the rest of the town or harbor, almost as though they were alone in their own world.

Seth brushed a thumb over her cheek. "Your face is red from the cold. Maybe I should warm you up."

The coldness of her face turned hot. "I want to see what this letter says first." If he started warming her up, she'd forget about it almost as assuredly as he had. She flipped the missive over in her hand and traced her finger over the fancy insignia stamped in wax on the back. "It looks important."

"It's not." He headed back to the table and opened his bag, then spread some of the contents on the surface, likely seeing if any supplies needed to be refilled. "Just the Surgeon General telling me they won't hire me back to the Marine Hospital Service."

"What?"

"It's where I worked in Boston, at one of the Marine Hospital Service facilities." He didn't look up as he took more items from his bag.

"So why are they writing you?"

"I was trying to get my position back."

"Trying to get your…?" He wanted to move back to Boston? With her? Where she'd be surrounded by a bunch of doctors?

Tightness crept into her lungs, but she drew in a deep breath and fought against the constriction. Not all doctors were like Dr. Lathersop, as Seth had proven time and again. In fact, she doubted her husband would let her anywhere near a man like Dr. Lathersop, no matter whether they lived in Eagle Harbor or Boston or Sharpsburg or halfway around the world.

"I… I had no idea you wanted your old job back. Are they picky about who they hire?"

"Very."

If his mother had wanted him to work there, then it must be a rather prestigious place to hold a job. She swallowed. "I… I'm happy for you, Seth. I'm sure you'll be able to help a lot of people in Boston."

Certainly more than he helped in Eagle Harbor. The size of the city alone meant he'd see four times the patients he saw in Eagle Harbor.

"Come here." He moved around the table, his arms open in invitation as he came toward her.

But she stayed still, not declining her husband's embrace, but not heading into it either. "I'm allowed to be a little sad about leaving, aren't I? I grew up here. I'm sure I'll miss it."

He reached out and pulled her into his arms, giving her a hug so tight her lungs constricted. "When will you learn?" he whispered against her hair. "Holding you makes lots of worries disappear."

Warmth started in her chest and swirled outward, and the distraction almost worked. Almost. She struggled out of his arms before she forgot about the letter. "Oh, Seth, are you sure you want to move to Boston? This town needs you so much. If you leave now that Dr. Greely passed, there'll be no one to treat people when they fall ill."

The grin left Seth's face. "I know, but when Dr. Greely was here and everyone was upset about what happened with you the night I treated Toby, well… I just wanted to doctor somewhere that people appreciated me. Somewhere I felt I could actually help."

Now it was her turn to open her arms, to tug him against her. "You do help people. Every day. Your clinic here might not be as fancy as the hospital in Boston, but you're needed far more. Can you imagine what would have happened had you been in Boston when the diphtheria hit? The entire town probably would have died."

"That's when I got the letter, actually, during the epidemic. I really was too busy treating patients to read it, but by then it didn't matter what the letter said. I'd married you, and something told me you'd not care to live in another city or be surrounded by doctors curious about your lung ailment. And when I delivered Tressa's baby... well, I knew I couldn't leave then. Had anyone else been in that bedroom, the babe would have died, and possibly Tressa too. I decided then and there I didn't care if I only treated one patient a year. I couldn't walk away from Eagle Harbor, because I never knew when the Lord might use me to heal someone."

She blinked away the tears in her eyes and squeezed her husband tighter. "I don't deserve you, you know."

"Deserving or not, you're stuck with me anyway, Mrs. Harrington." He dropped a kiss on her lips. "And I know exactly what I intend to do with you."

He swooped her up in his arms, and she screeched in protest.

"I'm not ill. I can walk."

"Maybe I like the feel of you in my arms."

"I can hardly read the letter while you're lugging me about." She ripped open the sealed envelope and glanced at it. But she didn't find any sentences about refusing to hire Seth. "It says something about a new Surgeon General and wanting you to come to Washington. They like a splint you sent them, or something like that."

"It does?" He paused for a moment, stopping in the doorway between the kitchen and their room, then shook his head. "Doesn't matter. I'm staying in Eagle Harbor."

"You don't even want to read it? Surely this Surgeon General man expects some kind of response."

Seth set her on the bed and leaned in until their foreheads touched. "I have everything I want right here, sweetheart."

He bent to kiss her, and this time she dropped the letter and wound her arms around his neck, because she had everything that she wanted right there too. In fact, she had more than she'd wanted, or dreamed about, or ever imagined putting on her "One Day" list. It all started with having the faithfulness and love of her God, and then it moved to having the faithfulness and love of a wonderful man. And though she might not know what lay in store for them over the coming years, she was never again going to hide from the future. Oh no, she was going to entrust that to the Fulfiller of Dreams, and spend every possible moment savoring the love of her husband, and loving him in return.

⌐.⌐.⌐.⌐.⌐

Want to read more Eagle Harbor novels?
Don't miss Thomas and Jessalyn Dowrick's story in
Love's Winter Hope.
Keep reading for a sneak peek on the next page...

Love's Winter Hope
Chapter One

Eagle Harbor, Michigan; November 1883

"Look out!" Thomas Dowrick's shout echoed over the angry noise of the waves. He headed toward the gunwale, moving as quickly as he could over the water-slickened deck toward the young sailor caught against the railing.

"Help!" Young Ronnie called from where he clutched the railing.

Snow drove down from the heavens with the force of buckshot, stinging Thomas's face if he dared look up at the sky. The frigid waters of Lake Superior sloshed across the deck, soaking the bottom of his trousers as he hurried past where the captain and sailors huddled, readying the dinghy that would carry them away from the rocks that had wrecked their ketch.

One of the sailors looked up from securing a rope to the small boat. "Do you need me?"

"I think I can get him on my own." Never mind that he was a miner by trade, not a sailor, and that it had been five years since he'd last been on a ship. The captain needed every spare hand to prepare the dinghy.

"What's wrong?" Thomas neared the brown-headed boy that

seemed far too young to have a job at all, let alone be a sailor.

"I'm caught." Ronnie called over the wind lashing across the lake.

Indeed he was. The cabin boy was wedged between the gunwale and a crate that had broken lose from its chains when the ship hit the rocks.

"Let's see if we can move this crate." Thomas pulled at the wooden box trapping the boy, but pain ricocheted up his shoulder. The crate wasn't overly big, but whatever it held weighed a great deal.

"Watch out. There's another wave."

Ronnie's warning came an instant too late. A vicious wave doused him from behind, splattering its icy spray against his back. Then the ship swayed, and his foot slid out from beneath him, the deck sloping so steeply he careened into the gunwale.

"Don't go overboard." Panic laced Ronnie's voice.

"I don't plan on it." Thomas clung to the top of the railing with both arms, his feet fighting for purchase against the slippery, slanting deck. Then he glanced down into the water below.

Mistake. The sight of craggy gray rocks and white, churning waves greeted him. He clung tighter to the railing, but the narrow strip of wood suddenly seemed too flimsy to hold a man of his height and weight.

He should've taken the train and rented a horse rather than boarding the mail ship this morning in Houghton. It might have meant three more days of traveling, but he would have at least been alive—even if his wife and daughters were still missing.

You can't let me die, God, not here, not now. I at least need to find them first, at least need to know they'll be safe without me.

"Can someone else help us?" Ronnie called to the sailors handling the dinghy.

"I'm all right. I just need to…" Thomas inched his foot all the way against the gunwale and put a bit of weight on it. Then he did the same with his second foot before standing and releasing the railing. "There. Now let's move this crate again. As soon as the weight shifts, you slide out from it, understand?"

The boy nodded, his face white.

"One, two, three." Thomas braced his feet against the gunwale and shoved. Pain shot up his arm like lightning. He gritted his teeth and put the full weight of his body into the crate. It moved about a half foot, just enough for Ronnie to scoot out from beneath the box.

A loud crack sounded above the roar of the storm—the unmistakable sound of splintering wood. Thomas clutched the railing and looked up. Were the waves breaking the ship apart already?

Shouts and curses rang over the howling wind, then one of the sailors hastened over to them.

"The waves dashed the dinghy into the rocks." Even though they stood face to face, the sailor still had to shout to be heard over the crashing waves and raging wind. "There's a lifesaving team at this port though. We'll just have to jump rather than take the dinghy to meet them."

A life-saving team? Thomas blinked away a fleck of snow clinging to his lashes. "What in tarnation is that?"

"They've coming to rescue us." The sailor gave him a thump on the shoulder. "Let's go."

"Can you walk?" Thomas settled his hand on Ronnie's shoulder.

"I-I think so," the boy stammered. "My leg got stuck when the crate slid into it, but I don't think its broke."

"I'll help you." The sailor swooped Ronnie up in his arms.

"I can help too."

The sailor looked over at Thomas. "Save your landlubber legs for walking yourself across the deck."

Thomas took a step across the deck with the sailor, but the slope was so steep and the wood so slick he nearly slid back down to the gunwale.

"Come on. We don't got all day. Least not if you want to be off this ship before it goes down."

"Coming." Thomas inched his way farther up the deck. White snow, gray sky, and churning, white-capped seas, surrounded the boat. A little town sat shrouded in shadows across the harbor. It seemed so close, and yet so very far. Beside it, the Eagle Harbor lighthouse swathed a path of illumination across the storm, but the beam was weakened by the snow, probably only visible for half its normal distance.

He reached the side of the ship and leaned over to glimpse a rowboat filled with people floating in a patch of water that wasn't churning as much as the rest of the lake. Something hit the deck beside him with a thud.

The sailor next to him picked it up and held out a ring that looked to be made of cork. "Put this on," he shouted over the storm. "It will make you float."

"Don't you need it?"

The sailor shrugged, then pointed to one of the men that had just jumped into the water. Sure enough he was floating over the swelling waves, the cork ring keeping his shoulders and head above the water. "I'll find Johnson once I get in the water. We can share."

"What about Ronnie?"

The sailor who'd carried the cabin boy across the deck was already slipping another one of the cork rings over Ronnie's chest. "We'll share." The man looked at Ronnie. "You ready?"

The boy gave a nod, and the two of them tumbled over the side of the ketch together, leaving him completely alone on the wrecked ship. Thomas clutched the large ring and slipped it over his head, only to have it get stuck around his wide shoulders. He forced the ring down anyway, never mind how tightly it squeezed his chest.

A foaming wave slammed into the wood and rocks below, and

Thomas swallowed. Give him a pickax, and he'd burrow into the dankest, darkest, narrowest tunnel and splinter rock until he found precious metals. Give him a mining town ravished by fire, and he'd exchange that pickax for a hammer and build half a dozen boardinghouses for the miners to stay in, then a hotel from his profits from the boardinghouses. But put him on the sea, and he was useless. He'd spent his childhood days in Cornwall hauling rocks out of mines, not fishing off the coast.

Ronnie and the sailor helping the boy surfaced in the water and swam toward the small boat.

Maybe if he timed his jump to miss one of the large waves, he'd have a chance of reaching the rescue boat. He had to try jumping. Either that or give up all hope of finding his missing wife and daughters.

Just the thought of Jessalyn, of her long, blond hair and vibrant blue eyes and hopeful smile, caused guilt to rise in his chest, so thick and cloying it nearly choked him.

On the little vessel, a form stepped apart from the others huddled together. It almost looked like he was preparing to…

"No!" Thomas shouted.

But the man jumped anyway, diving off the side of the boat and disappearing beneath the water. Was the man trying to swim to him? He'd never forgive himself if the swimmer drowned.

Clutching the ring about him, he balanced on the railing, drew in a breath of stinging, frigid air… and jumped.

Chapter Two

Jessalyn Dowrick bent her head over the sketch of the bridal dress for the Hanover wedding and rubbed her bleary eyes. Should she use four-inch lace around the sleeves, or three? And what about adding lace to the collar? The sketch she'd been sent from Chicago didn't have any, but unless styles were changing, she—

"Ma." A slender hand settled itself atop the dress pattern. "Can we go to the doctor?"

Jessalyn drew her head up and blinked at her oldest daughter, who was tilting her head to the side and pressing a rag to her right ear.

"Oh, honey. Another one?" She set down her pencil and held out her arms.

"It hurts." Tears glistened in Olivia's eyes as she climbed onto her lap. "I don't know why I keep getting them."

"Sometimes earaches just happen."

"Then how come they don't happen to Claire and Megan?" Olivia rested her sore ear on Jessalyn's shoulder. "Or you?"

Jessalyn sighed, her chest rising and falling beneath the weight of Olivia's nine-year-old body. "I don't know."

And it was hardly fair to say they "just happened." They'd been "just happening" a lot over the past two years, almost to the point that her daughter had a constant ear infection.

Jessalyn glanced out the large display windows facing North Street to find the snow coming thicker and faster. The tiny pellets of white weren't obscuring the tavern on the other side of the road yet. But it wouldn't be long given the dark gray clouds and whipping wind. It might only be November, but the first storm of the season was here, and winter in Copper Country was harsh. By tomorrow morning the dirt road and dry autumn grass would be covered in snow, and they'd stay burried for the next six months.

"Let me see if we have any willow bark tea in the kitchen. Perhaps that will suffice until the storm stops. We can visit Dr. Harrington tomorrow." Provided the storm didn't keep up for two or three days.

"We're out. I checked."

"Drat." Though she shouldn't be surprised. Olivia's last infection had only faded a week ago, and she'd not replenished the usual supplies and medicine yet.

Olivia bit her lip and glanced at the sketch Jessalyn had been working on. "Will you be able to get your work done if we visit the doctor?"

"Of course." She'd just be up past midnight doing it. She patted Olivia's hip. "Get your coat and boots on while I fetch Claire and Megan. Maybe we can make it back before the snow gets too deep."

Ten minutes later she pulled open the door to her shop and herded her three girls out into the storm. The frigid wind nearly sucked the breath from her lungs, but she bent her head against it, gripped five-year-old Megan's hand, and started down the road. "Stick close, girls."

"The cold makes my ear hurt," Olivia whined.

"I know, honey. I'm so sorry."

"Jessalyn? Is that you?"

She looked up to find Isaac Cummings, the newly-elected town sheriff, crossing the street toward them.

"What are you doing out in this?" His breath puffed cold little clouds into the air as he took the hand of her middle daughter, Claire, and started walking.

"I should ask you the same question." She closed her eyes against a particularly harsh gust of wind, then looked over her shoulder to make sure Olivia was still following.

"Just came from The Rusty Wagon." Isaac jutted his chin toward the bar they'd already passed, the one that sat opposite her seamstress's shop. "Wanted to make sure things were staying calm inside."

She nodded, though he probably couldn't see it with the way his head was bent against the wind. The sailors, loggers, and miners that filled Eagle Harbor never needed much excuse to visit the bar, or the brothel farther down the road, for that matter. Rainstorms and snowstorms actually gave them an excuse, though. But she hadn't considered Isaac would have to work in storms such as this. Would the jail be full by the end of the night?

"You still haven't told me why you're out here," he called to her. "Or where we're going."

She trudged through a snowdrift that rose overtop her boots. "Olivia has another earache, and I was out of willow bark tea, so—"

He looked over his shoulder and scowled at her. "You should have waited a few more minutes. I was headed to your place to make sure you had enough firewood to get through the storm."

He was? Though she shouldn't be surprised. Isaac Cummings helped her whenever he could. And since they were neighbors, with him living in the apartment above the telegraph office that sat next to her shop, those situations arose more often than a person might guess.

"I could have gotten Dr. Harrington, and then you wouldn't need to bring your girls out in this. The doc would have paid a house call." Isaac turned down Front Street and headed south along the harbor, toward Dr. Harrington's office on the far side of town.

"We've survived worse, but thank you."

"Ma, you're going too fast."

She turned to find Olivia struggling through a drift the wind had blown across the road, a mitten-covered hand still pressed to her ear.

"Here. You take Claire." Isaac thrust Claire's hand into hers and tromped back toward Olivia, then swooped her into his arms. The low sound of his voice rumbled through the storm as he spoke to her oldest daughter, but she couldn't make out his words.

Her heart lurched at the sight. What would it be like to... but no. She'd not let her thoughts wander in that direction. What would it be like if Thomas had never left, if he were the one carrying Olivia now and not a neighbor with an overly vigilant sense of duty?

That was the better question, but she didn't know the answer, nor did she care. She'd stopped asking herself what things would be like if Thomas had stayed years ago. There was no sense in letting her brain wander into the land of "what if," only in taking stock of the resources she had and making do. Which meant a trip to Dr. Harrington's at the moment, snowstorm or not.

Numbness was creeping into her nose and cheeks by the time they reached Dr. Harrington's sprawling log cabin. She guided her children up the steps while Isaac pulled open the door to let them pass, all while keeping Olivia tucked against his chest.

Warmth enveloped her the instant she stepped inside the parlor...that was filled with people despite the storm?

"Take your things off and hang them on the pegs." She tugged at Megan's hat and surveyed the men. Most were strangers, with Ian Fletcher and Emmet Stone being the only familiar faces.

"Was there a shipwreck?" Isaac's voice was rough and dark.

The bearded man nearest them nodded his head. "Afraid so."

"Is Elijah all right?"

"Elijah?" The man gave Isaac a blank stare.

"He's fine," Ian Fletcher, one of Elijah's lifesavers, called from across the room. "Took a little swim, but Doc Harrington has him warming up. He's in the sickroom while the doc looks at the passenger he rescued."

Isaac kept his jaw hard, his face resolute, but she caught the flicker of relief in his eyes. The entire town knew Elijah Cummings went out on volunteer rescues, just as assuredly as the entire town knew his brother Isaac opposed the idea. What must it feel like to be Isaac? Stuck waiting while a loved one risked his life to save others?

"Will Dr. Harington be very long?" Olivia huddled against Isaac's chest.

Isaac looked down, seeming to realize he still held Olivia, then carried her to the sofa and set her down, never mind Olivia's boots getting snow on the couch.

"Something wrong, sweetheart?" A weathered sailor crouched down beside her, concern in his eyes.

Jessalyn bent to undo Megan's buttons, then hung her daughter's things on the peg before scurrying over to Olivia.

"My ear hurts." An icy little tear slipped down Olivia's cheek.

"I'm sure it won't be much longer." Jessalyn laid a hand on Olivia's brow. Though the girl had just spent a quarter hour outside, her skin was turning warm with the fever that often accompanied her earaches.

"I'll get the doc's wife." The sailor straightened. "See if she can help with anything."

"Thank you." Jessalyn bent to work at the laces on Olivia's boots. She couldn't complain about Isaac laying her daughter down, but surely Dr. Harrington and his wife Lindy didn't want snow ruining their sofa.

She'd just set the boots on the floor when Lindy swept into the room, her flaxen blond hair glistening in the lamplight. She headed straight for them and gave Olivia a side hug. "Don't tell me you have another earache, Olivia? I'm so sorry."

"Do you have some willow bark tea while we wait?" Jessalyn unbuttoned her own coat.

"Of course. Though it shouldn't be much longer before Seth's done with his patient." Lindy gave Olivia another squeeze before scurrying into the kitchen in a flurry of swishing petticoats.

"Here, let's unbutton your coat, even if you don't want to take it off." Jessalyn began at the bottom of the coat while Olivia started at the top. A quick sweep around the room told her Megan and Claire had headed straight for the toy box in the corner—bless Dr. Harrington for thinking of children and keeping toys in his parlor. Isaac paced over by the door to the sickroom, his face as dark and brooding as the storm clouds outside. The other men were milling about, some drinking coffee and eating cookies, some sitting in the chairs placed around the parlor.

"I said I don't need any more treatment." A voice rose from behind the door of the large sickroom, loud enough to drown out the chatter in the parlor. "I'm perfectly fine, or I will be…" The door flung open and a large man stood in the frame. "As soon as I find my…"

The man stared at her.

Jessalyn sucked in a quick breath, but just as suddenly, her lungs forgot to work, trapping the air inside her.

"Jessalyn," he said.

Or maybe he didn't say it. Maybe he whispered it, or mouthed it, or thought it.

But she felt the impact of her name on his lips through every inch of her body.

"Thomas." Her heart hammered against her chest. He was back. Her husband. The man who had once shared her life. Hope welled inside her. How many times had she dreamed of this day, ran it over and over in her mind until her body ached with the loss of not having him beside her? How many times had she imagined what she'd say when he finally returned, each and every word of it?

He took a step toward her, his body so large and familiar she nearly went to meet him, nearly wrapped her arms around his chest and settled her head on his shoulder. How long since she'd felt the strength of her husband's arms as they held her?

How long? She stiffened. Five years, five months, and eleven days. She'd thought him dead, but he was certainly alive and well.

Which meant he'd knowingly abandoned her and their daughters.

And if it had taken him that long to come back, then she could stand on the other side of the room for five minutes without going to him. She could force herself to forget about the way his arms would feel wrapped around her and his heart would sound beneath her ear. She'd already forced herself to forget a great many things about him. Two more shouldn't be any trouble.

Except her husband hadn't been anywhere close all those other times. It was a lot harder to ignore a person when they stood in the same room.

"What…" She forced her tongue to move, forced her dry mouth to form words. "What are you doing here?"

"Do you need to ask? I came for you, Jess." His gaze slid past her to Olivia on the couch. "For my daughters." He came toward her, his heavy footfalls causing the floor to tremble. Whatever he'd been doing the past five years hadn't turned him soft or weak. She didn't need him to roll up his shirtsleeves to know that corded muscles still rested under the fabric. If anything, her miner husband seemed larger and stronger than she remembered.

She swallowed, and the dryness in her throat made the simple action painful. If he wasn't hurt or injured, then why had he stayed away so long? And why had he decided to come back now? The time for that had been in the months after he'd left, when she hadn't known what to do with herself, when she would have starved if not for the generosity of folks like Elijah and Isaac Cummings.

"Aw, shucks. I'm sorry, Jessalyn." Elijah came up beside her, his cheeks ruddy and wind-chapped. "I was going to bring Thomas by your shop when we left, that way half the town wouldn't... well..." He scratched the back of his neck. "Know he was back before you did."

The entire town. She glanced around to find every person in the room staring at them, save Claire and Megan, who were playing with a doll and swing in the corner. Even Lindy had returned from the kitchen and stood with a steaming mug in her hand.

If only she could close her eyes and melt into the floor. Why here? Why now that she finally had a way of providing for herself and her daughters on her own? There was a time when she would have thrown herself at him and wept at his return, no matter how callous he'd been when he'd left them. But those days had come and gone like a late spring snow.

"Mama, my ear." The small voice behind her shattered the stillness of the room.

Dr. Harrington stepped around a cluster of sailors and crouched down by the sofa. "Is it bothering you again? Why don't you come to the small sickroom with me and I'll take a look? Maybe we can let your parents go into the big sickroom to talk."

"Parents?" Olivia asked. "I don't have a pa, just a ma."

Thomas made a low, strangled sound in his throat.

Jessalyn wasn't sure what to call the look he'd given her when he'd first seen her earlier. Surprise, perhaps. Or hope. But there was no hope in his face now.

"Unless…?" The weight of Olivia's gaze bored into her before it shifted to Thomas. "Unless you're my pa?"

"No," Jessalyn whispered.

A storm gathered in his eyes, and the small muscle at the side of his jaw pulsed.

It only made her own jaw harden in response, her own muscles tense. "A real pa doesn't walk away from you for five years, especially not without sending letters."

"I sent a letter every week." Thomas crossed his arms over his impossibly broad chest.

She shook her head. "I only got two letters from you, both while you were traveling to California. The last letter was about around the time I learned I was expecting Megan."

Thomas's gaze traveled across the room to the youngest of their three daughters. "She's mine?"

"How dare you." She took a step forward, bringing her toe-to-toe with her vagrant of a husband, and raised her hand.

Before she could let it fly toward his face, someone caught her arm.

Not Thomas. He was looking at her with a calm complacency, something he'd certainly never had during their arguments before he'd left. He'd been prepared for her to hit him and hadn't intended to stop it. A sickening sensation twined through her stomach.

"Jess." Isaac's voice was low, his mouth near enough her ear he wouldn't be overheard. "How about you move this conversation to the sickroom, like Dr. Harrington suggested?"

She drew in a shaky breath and looked at Isaac, his face sincere, his hazel gaze filled with concern. Tears burned her eyes. But when she looked back to Thomas, something else burned entirely.

"I don't want to talk to him." Her voice was sickeningly soft, perilously close to breaking. How was it that she could look at

Thomas and banish all thought of tears, but the second she turned to Isaac, she wanted nothing more than to go home, crawl into her bed, curl up, and cry until morning?

Because Isaac chopped her firewood, escorted her through snow storms, and helped wrestle giant sewing machines through small shop doors. Because Isaac took the children to the beach in the summer so she could squeeze in a few hours of work, and invited her to Thanksgiving dinner with his family. Because though Isaac Cummings was only her neighbor, he gave her more support in half a day than the man she'd once called husband had given her in the entire decade they'd been married.

"Well, I want to talk to you," Thomas said, his voice calm and controlled, not shouting, not drenched with fury like hers would be if she spoke. "I thought you were in Chicago. I told you to go back there, remember? It was one of the last conversations we had."

She pressed her eyes shut as the memories filled her mind. Not one of the last, the absolute last. Though calling it a conversation was rather charitable on Thomas's part. They'd argued about money, of course, the same thing they always argued about. Thomas had lost most of their savings investing in a copper mine that played out early and didn't yield dividends. He wanted to take the last little bit they'd saved and use it to go to California where there was gold. She'd said no, that they needed to save more first, that they couldn't afford to take four people across the country, even if Thomas could find better work there.

And she'd probably said a thing or two about him not being responsible enough to decide what to do with their savings anymore, since they'd lost so much on his copper mining investment.

She could still recall his hard jaw, the angry note in his voice as he told her he was taking the little money they had left and leaving in the morning, but if she didn't want to go with him, he wouldn't force her. She could go to Chicago and stay with her cousin while he got settled, and he'd send for her later.

She'd thought they'd been empty threats. The last thing she expected was to get up in the morning and find him already gone.

A lump rose in her throat. She couldn't deal with this, not now, not with a room full of people. Not when she'd been completely unprepared to face the man who had been all but dead to her for five years. She met Thomas's eyes and forced a calm to her voice despite the shaking that had taken over her hands and jaw. "I don't know what brought you back to Eagle Harbor, but I hope you conclude your business here quickly and leave me out of it. Now if you'll excuse me, my daughter needs to see the doctor."

She turned her back to Thomas and found Dr. Harrington looking into Olivia's ear with his otoscope. "Do you mind carrying her into the sickroom for me?"

"Certainly. Can you take this?" He handed her the instrument that allowed him to see deep inside her daughter's ears, then stood and hefted Olivia into his arms before heading across the parlor. She rushed behind him, head down to avoid the questioning gazes of everyone else, but Thomas's unmistakable footfalls resonated behind her.

When she reached the door, she paused and turned back. "I'm afraid you don't understand. You're not the one who's cared for Olivia for the past five years, so you're not welcome inside."

She swept into the room and closed the door, or would have—if his arm didn't catch the door before it latched. He pushed back on the wood, forcing it open in a match of strength she had no hope of winning. But rather than come inside and settle himself on one of the chairs, he stopped in the doorway, his burly form so tall he had to duck his head.

"You can go into the room, that's fine. I'll wait out here and visit with Megan and Claire until you're ready to talk. You can leave the doctor's office, that's fine too. I don't mind following you, or talking in a blizzard, or doing any other number of things to get you talk to me. But how quickly I finish my business in Eagle Harbor depends on you, Jess." His gaze swept quickly down her, but not in a way that had anything to do with romantic feelings. He may as well have been a clerk taking inventory: blond hair—check; teeth—check; four limbs—check. "Because you and our daughters are the reason I came back, and I'm not leaving town again without you."

He'd come back for her? This man who'd abandoned her and their daughters, leaving them with only the money she kept stashed in the jar in the kitchen? He'd have an easier time of swimming across Lake Superior to Canada in this snowstorm than winning her back.

"I don't intend to go anywhere with you. Not now, and not ever. I'm happy here." Except that wasn't quite true since she was planning to relocate her dress shop to Chicago next summer. But she was happy enough in Eagle Harbor for the winter, and she was certainly happier by herself then she ever would be with Thomas. "I wish you well with your life, wherever you live, and whatever it is you're doing. Goodbye."

She swung the door shut again, though she knew he'd stop it from latching once more, but what else could she do? How else could she convince him that the door was shut on their past, even if he refused to let the physical door between them close?

Sure enough, the door bounced off the tips of his shoes and sprang open, leaving him to stand there and cross his arms. "It's been five years. You can't tell me you don't have questions, something you want to say to me." He dipped his head toward her, his voice turning softer. "That you haven't thought up what you would say to me a hundred different times and a hundred different ways."

Then he didn't know her quite as well as he thought. "Possibly,

Thomas. Right after you left. Maybe even a year after you were gone. But not anymore. Now please leave me alone, my daughter's sick, and she needs me right now, whereas you haven't needed me for five years."

"I'm not leaving you alone until we talk." He gripped the top of the door, one hand on the door and the other on the trim lining the doorway. "I don't care where, but there are things we need settled between us. Today."

He was still as demanding as always. Still insistent on getting his way. She may have changed while he was gone, but he hadn't seemed to change at all. Oh, sure, he'd ask politely for what he wanted at first, toss her a smile and wink and try charming her into it. And if she refused, well, then the demands would start.

"I said no."

"Ma," a small voice sounded from the bed.

She glanced at Olivia, who was lying down watching them with large, moist eyes and a trembling jaw. She was nearly oblivious to Dr. Harrington using a candle with his otoscope to see inside her ear.

Jessalyn's heart lurched. Claire was too young to remember Thomas, and Megan hadn't even been born when he'd left. But Olivia had been four. Was that old enough to have memories of her father?

Yes, if the way she watched Thomas was any indication.

She turned back to Thomas, and the determination in his eyes and stubborn set to his jaw only tightened the vice around her heart. If she didn't listen to him now, he'd make good on his promise to follow her home. At least here they could talk behind closed doors, without Olivia hearing more than she already had.

"Fine, we can go into the other room." The words tasted bitter on her tongue, yet maybe if they talked, he'd see there wasn't any hope of restoring their relationship, and he'd leave her alone—for the rest of her life this time. "But I have one condition. After you've said your piece, I want you to leave town, and I don't ever want to hear from you again."

~.~.~.~.~

She expected him to leave town after only one conversation? Thomas wasn't about to agree, but he wasn't going to stand in the middle of the doctor's office and argue over it either, not when it had taken him a half hour to convince her he was worthy of a conversation.

"Let's go." She stomped ahead of him and crossed the crowded parlor, her back stiff and shoulders set, heading toward the room full of bunk beds where the doctor had examined him earlier.

He glanced at his daughter lying still while the doctor looked at her ear with an odd contraption that attached to a candle. Maybe he'd been too demanding by saying they needed to talk right away. Didn't Jessalyn want to wait until the doc had finished his examination?

But she'd already entered the sickroom and closed the door behind her all but a crack. He looked back at Olivia one more time, her angel blond hair spread against the pillows the doc had piled behind her. She was big now, much bigger than he'd imagined. Somehow in his mind she'd stayed four years old the entire time he'd been gone, and Claire had always been a baby.

He'd come back and visit with Olivia after he talked with Jessalyn, maybe even pull the doctor aside and ask for a report. And then he'd visit with Claire and Megan. He'd already missed Claire's first steps and Megan's birth and Olivia's first day of school. So much of their lives gone without him being a part of it. How did he begin to catch up? An ache started in his chest, almost as painful as the one in his shoulder. Except the one in his shoulder had a medical explanation.

Jessalyn peeked her head out the door. "Are you coming?"

"Yes." It'd be mighty hard to father his girls if their mother didn't want to take him back.

He headed toward Jessalyn, stopping to grab the soggy letter he'd left drying by the wood stove before he entered the room and closed the door.

She stood by the window, peering out into the storm that would soon be covered by the gathering dark. How often had he seen her do that very thing before? Summer, autumn, winter, spring, the curtain drawn aside and her face peeking out the window to watch the weather.

She looked so very much the same to him. Did he look the same to her after all these years? Her elegant green dress wasn't made of silk or satin or any other fine fabric, and yet she looked as stylish and put together as one of the women living on Prairie Street in Chicago. A ribbon cinched tightly about her narrow waist, an extra splash of lace around her collar and sleeves, the row of double buttons that started at her neck and went clear down to the ribbon. She'd always been able to take a nickle and somehow make the coin go as far as ten dollars.

Her hair was done up in an elegant twist at the back of her head too, yet another thing that hadn't changed. No simple bun or sloppy knot for Jessalyn, no. Somehow she'd learned to do her own hair as masterfully as any lady's maid in Chicago.

She turned from the window and crossed the room to him, her gaze sweeping down him once before she sighed and rubbed her temple. "All right, you have me alone. What is it you have to say?"

That I want you back, that I want to be a husband to you, and a father to our daughters.

If only she was ready to hear it.

~.~.~.~.~

When Jessalyn Dowrick's husband left her and their three daughters to head west five years earlier, she had no choice but to pick up the pieces of her broken life and continue without him, eventually supporting herself as Eagle Harbor's seamstress, and secretly hoping her husband would return. But days soon slipped into months, and months into years, all without word of Thomas or a cent of the money he'd promised to send.

While working day and night to build a new life that his wife would be proud of, Thomas wrote Jessalyn every week, asking her to come to South Dakota. But she never arrived. In fact, she never answered a single one of his letters. When he returns to Eagle Harbor in search of answers, he finds a woman who thought him dead . . . and regrets he didn't come after her sooner.

As winter closes in and storms trap Thomas in town until the harbor opens in the spring, will he be able to convince his wife he's worth a second chance?

Order your copy of* Love's Winter Hope *today.

Thank You

Thank you for reading *Love's Eternal Breath*. I sincerely hope you enjoyed Seth and Lindy's story. The next full length novel in the Eagle Harbor Series is Thomas and Jessalyn story, *Love's Winter Hope*. Click here to purchase.

Want to be notified when the next Eagle Harbor Novel is releasing? Sign up for my author newsletter. Subscribers also get a free copy of *Love's Violet Sunrise*, a prequel novella to the Eagle Harbor Series. Sign Up Here.

Be sure to add naomi@naomirawlings.com to your safe email list so that the emails go through. I keep all subscriber information confidential.

Also, if you enjoyed reading *Love's Eternal Breath*, please take a moment to tell others about the novel. You can do this by posting an honest review on Amazon or GoodReads. Please note that to leave a review on Amazon, you need to go directly to Amazon's website. Your e-reader may ask you to rank stars at the end of this novel. The star ranking that you give does not show up on Amazon as a review. I read every one of my reviews, and reviews help readers like yourself decide whether to purchase a novel. You could also consider mentioning *Love's Eternal Breath* to your friends on Facebook, Twitter, or Pinterest.

Author's Note

Thanks for sharing Lindy and Seth's story with me. I'm very excited about this novel, and part of the reason, dear readers, is you. You were the inspiration for this story. Over the years I've been writing, I've found many of the readers who take time to write me are sick, suffering, or dealing with some type of chronic pain.

While I can't offer you hope that your suffering and difficulties will disappear on earth, I can remind you of the hope heaven offers. Also, I wanted to write a character who was less than perfect. Someone who woke up in the morning sometimes and struggled with pain and suffering. Someone who wouldn't necessarily have years of a perfect marriage to look forward to at the end of the novel, but who found hope anyway.

And that, my friends, is the purpose of this novel and the reason I'm so excited to see it published. God's Word offers more comfort than anything I write ever could, and I encourage you to find your strength first and foremost in the Bible. However, I hope that this story will be an encouragement to you anyway. I hope that after reading a novel about a fictional person, you can carry a reminder with you in your own everyday life. All the joy of life doesn't need to disappear when suffering comes. There is still joy you can seek, and still a role for you in this world for as long as God chooses to keep you here.

Now for another small detail of the novel, I started writing Tressa's pregnancy when I was miserably pregnant myself, so I gave Tressa a lot of my own symptoms. After all, if I was experiencing lightheadedness and weakness to the point I had trouble standing, surely I could have a pregnant character in one of my novels suffer those very things.

Except I was far sicker than I realized, and so was my baby. I ended up hospitalized for the last six weeks of my pregnancy, and when my daughter was born at 36 weeks, she was 3'11, just over half the size she should have been for a baby her age. Only after my daughter was born did we learn that she had a very unhealthy placenta and umbilical cord, and so she didn't get the nutrients she needed while she was inside me. In truth, Tressa Oakton's baby if a hundred and thirty years ago suffered from the same problems that my own daughter had, Tressa's baby probably would have died. I couldn't quite force myself to give Tressa a stillborn baby in the story, but please understand that little Sarah's survival in 1883 would be a miracle of miracles, medically speaking. My personal experiences as well as telling Tressa's story make me so very thankful for the medical care we have today, especially when it comes to prenatal and neonatal care.

I hope you're enjoying the Eagle Harbor Series. It's been my favorite series of novels to write, though I admit to being a little biased since I live in a little town on Lake Superior myself, only a couple hours from the real-life Eagle Harbor. I look forward to writing many more books in this series. Jessalyn Dowrick and her long-lost husband, Thomas, are next in *Love's Winter Hope* releasing in the spring of 2017.

Other Novels by Naomi Rawlings

Eagle Harbor Series

Book 1—*Love's Unfading Light* (Mac and Tressa)

Book 2—*Love's Every Whisper* (Elijah and Victoria)

Book 3—*Love's Sure Dawn* (Gilbert and Rebekah)

Book 4—*Love's Eternal Breath* (Seth and Lindy)

Book 5—Love's Winter Hope (Thomas and Jessalyn)

Book 6—*Love's Bright Tomorrow* (Isaac and Aileen)

Short Story—*Love's Beginning*

Prequel Novella—*Love's Violet Sunrise* (Hiram and Mabel)

Belanger Family Saga

Book 1—*Sanctuary for a Lady*

Book 2—*The Soldier's Secrets*

Book 3—*Falling for the Enemy*

Stand Alone Novels

The Wyoming Heir

Acknowledgments

Thank you first and foremost to my Lord and Savior, Jesus Christ, for giving me both the ability and opportunity to write novels for His glory.

As with any novel, the author might come up with a story idea and sit at her computer to type the initial words, but it takes an army of people to bring you the book you have today. I'd especially like to thank Melissa Jagears, both my critique partner and editor for *Love's Eternal Breath*. I'd also like to thank my family for working with my writing schedule and giving me a chance to do two things I love: be a mommy and a writer. Also thank you to Roseanna White and Lynnette Bonner for assisting with the editing and providing early feedback. And finally, a special thanks to my former agent Natasha Kern for encouraging me to keep working on the Eagle Harbor Series.

About the Author

Naomi Rawlings is the author of seven historical Christian novels, including the Amazon bestselling Eagle Harbor Series. While she'd love to claim she spends her days huddled in front of her computer vigorously typing, in reality she spends her time homeschooling, cleaning, picking up, and pretending like her house isn't in a constant state of chaos. She lives with her husband and three children in Michigan's rugged Upper Peninsula, along the southern shore of Lake Superior where they get 200 inches of snow every year, and where people still grow their own vegetables and cut down their own firewood—just like in the historical novels she writes.

For more information about Naomi, please her at www.naomirawlings.com or find her on Facebook at www.facebook.com/author.naomirawlings. If you'd like a free Eagle Harbor novella (Mabel and Hiram's story), sign up for her author newsletter.